RAPTOR LANDS

The Story of the Harrowing Return of the Dinosaurs

JEFF OTIS

First paperback edition March 2024

Book Cover design by Mihai Costea

Illustrations by Jeff Otis

ISBN: 979-8-218-33307-2 (paperback)

Published by JSOArts Publishing LLC

www.jeffotisauthor.com

"Do Not Go Gentle Into That Good Night" (three-line excerpt) by Dylan Thomas, from THE POEMS OF DYLAN THOMAS, copyright ©1952 by Dylan Thomas. Reprinted by permission of New Directions Publishing Corp.

This book is dedicated to Ida, Gina, Tommy,
and paleontologist Jack Horner

Table of Contents

Chapter 1 Touching the Past..1
Chapter 2 Innocent Beginnings...3
Chapter 3 Digital Evolution..15
Chapter 4 Warning Signs..23
Chapter 5 Unintended Consequences...29
Chapter 6 Never Turn Your Back...39
Chapter 7 Walking Koko..47
Chapter 8 Arthur...51
Chapter 9 Fire...52
Chapter 10 Corruption...62
Chapter 11 Cantor as Mom...65
Chapter 12 An Unholy Bond...69
Chapter 13 Exponential Growth...71
Chapter 14 Five Big Ones...78
Chapter 15 Cain...83
Chapter 16 Through Another's Eyes...88
Chapter 17 Cosmic Pawn..98
Chapter 18 Hurting Kumiko..102
Chapter 19 Checkmate...114
Chapter 20 Raptor Ranch..118
Chapter 21 Mating..131
Chapter 22 Maryann Escapes...142
Chapter 23 Raptor Lands...150
Chapter 24 The Benefactor...158
Chapter 25 George Looks for a Job..163
Chapter 26 Muli..165
Chapter 27 Temptations of George...178
Chapter 28 No Electric Fences...182
Chapter 29 Luna's Painting...185
Chapter 30 Tiny Tim..187
Chapter 31 Where Angels Fear to Tread..194
Chapter 32 Worst Case..203

Chapter 33 Your Soul is in Danger..205
Chapter 34 Thin Ice Under Tusker..214
Chapter 35 Commercialism..218
Chapter 36 Saxton's Belligerence..232
Chapter 37 Informer?..237
Chapter 38 Leon..239
Chapter 39 Moles and Magpies...242
Chapter 40 Passion to Ride...244
Chapter 41 Maryann Hunts..250
Chapter 42 The Moth to the Flame..262
Chapter 43 The Dexters..267
Chapter 44 Cantor's Great Ride..272
Chapter 45 Remus Falls..280
Chapter 46 Time to Terminate?..304
Chapter 47 Talk of Tours..305
Chapter 48 The Secret in Dex..307
Chapter 49 Kumiko's Pain...313
Chapter 50 Confrontation..314
Chapter 51 George's Redemption..321
Chapter 52 Mako in Chains..325
Chapter 53 My Life for Wine...330
Chapter 54 Fools Rush In..333
Chapter 55 Judgement in Rome..339
Chapter 56 The Agony in the Gondola....................................341
Chapter 57 Dinner..349
Chapter 58 A Russian..353
Chapter 59 Lingering Effects...354
Chapter 60 Where is Huey?...356
Chapter 61 Kumiko Declines..364
Chapter 62 A Long Journey Toward the End.............................368
Chapter 63 How Can This Be?..371
Chapter 64 Death...374
Chapter 65 Aftermath..386
Informal Responses from Facebook Users................................397
A Word from the Author..399
Acknowledgments...401
About the Author...403

Chapter 1

Touching the Past

"That's one magnificent hand," Doctor Cantor Hoffman commented, pushing his brown hair out of his eyes. He marveled at the fossil from the 2027 dig in Utah.

Alex, a grad student at the Berkeley paleontology lab, carefully removed the rock from around the dark fossil with a small grinder. The semi-circular table held several other specimens at various stages of completion.

"It's bigger than anything I've seen from a *Utahraptor*," Cantor said. "I think the animal must have been at least 1100 pounds."

"And deadly as hell," Alex said, brushing off some of the dust his grinder made.

"Yeah. Quick and powerful. There isn't a predator on earth today that could stand up to this. How long before the foot is ready, Alex?"

"Another month I figure."

"Sweet."

Alex held up the partially prepared fossil foot. "As you can see, I've already freed the foot's sickle claw. It's one for the record books, 9.4 inches long."

"Seeing that must have made some dinosaurs very uncomfortable," Cantor replied, shaking his head.

"How are you going to feel when you get to see the real deal?" Alex asked, tapping a finger on the claw's sharp tip.

"Thrilled! But only if Kumiko can pull it off."

Chapter 2

Innocent Beginnings

In 2029, an oddity was born of an idea. In 2030, humans reverse-engineered the oddity further, gradually bringing back a life form from the distant past. In 2031, its arms unfolded.

* * *

Doctor Kumiko Chen sat in her U.C. Berkeley office, scanning student test grades. She wished the grades had been a little higher.

Her face flushed as she glanced at the two letters on her desk. When she heard the sound of her husband's squeaky shoes, her mood lightened.

"Hey, sweetheart," Cantor said, grinning as he strolled into her office, then draped himself over one of her leather chairs. Despite winter coming, he wore a blue T-shirt with an orange silhouette of a *Tyrannosaurus*. The pockets of his brown cargo pants bulged with papers, pens, and a crunchy oat bar.

She shook her head at the coffee stain on his shirt.

Running his finger along the shiny wooden surface of her desk, he said, "How do you find time to keep your desk so well organized?"

"How is it you don't?" she replied, wondering when he'd last even seen the surface of his desk.

She noticed him looking at the tall wooden bookshelf behind her, filled with genetics papers, journals, and books. Then he picked up the framed photo of her, himself, and their son, George, at a fossil dig in Utah. She remembered how new it was to her and young George, being among the first humans to recover and admire the remains of a creature entombed for millions of years.

"Well, we're making progress," she said as she hit a key on her keyboard, sending the student grades into cyberspace. Pushing against the arms of her chair, she stood up, grabbed one of the letters, and walked around her desk. "Look at this letter I found in my mailbox."

She watched his expression as he read.

"Why can't people understand we aren't interested in selling the dinos?" he said with a grimace.

"This is becoming a problem," Kumiko replied. "This is the second letter I've received from this individual. They even hint at legal action!" She held her hands out, shaking her head, allowing some strands of straight black hair to escape from behind her ears. "They're claiming we can't possibly provide a proper habitat for the animals."

"That's twisted," he said. "I'm no expert about the law, but wealthy jerks like this can take us or the university to court. They can drag this out for years."

Kumiko took the letter and tossed it in the trash. "Habitat indeed! I'm betting the habitat they'd prefer is a circus." She picked up the other letter from her desk. "Here, look at this."

Cantor opened the envelope and read: *Your Frankensteins shouldn't exist. You don't belong in America. Go back to China. You are playing God. Stop what you are doing now! There are consequences!*

"That pisses me off," he said, crumpling the paper in his hand.

"Me too. It's frightening."

"What an ignoramus."

"Cantor, he's threatening us!" *My given name isn't even Chinese! Nor was my mother!*

"Have you notified campus security?"

"Yes. What can they do? This will just go into a folder with the other twisted letters."

Without a word, Cantor took the first letter out of the trash and uncrumpled the second. Then he held her hand and looked into her dark eyes. "I'm sorry, Kumiko."

She shook it off and held her head higher. "Before we look at the C4s, I've got something more uplifting. Look at this C5 diagram." The computer displayed the expected appearance of the next iteration of proto-dinosaurs.

"Beautiful," Cantor said. "Those arms look just like a *Utahraptor's*. Wow. How soon?"

"Not for at least a year." Kumiko knew her husband dreamt of coming face to face with a real dinosaur. It was this boyish part of him that attracted her. He lacked all pretensions.

"Finally, we're going to understand dinosaur behavior," he said, rubbing his hands together.

"Not so fast, Cantor. It's going to take many iterations. The C5s will only be halfway to being real dinosaurs."

"Yeah, I know. When will we have the real deal?"

"I don't know," she said. "I'm puzzled by the C4s. When we created them, the only genetic changes we made involved improvements in the hands, tails, and arms."

"So, what puzzles you?"

"Their bodies are bigger. They're growing faster than their C3 mother did," she said, hands on her hips.

"I'm not worried," he said. "It shouldn't affect my research on their behavior. Things happen. It's a significant achievement."

Kumiko shook her head and sighed. "Let's go look at the C4s in the lab. They're vaccinated and out of quarantine. You're going to love them."

Cantor rose from his chair and followed her down the hall, past offices, and inquiring students.

In the lab, two Golden Eagles studied him from their large cages near the windows. Several grad students looked up, smiled, and returned to their work. He sauntered over to the two-foot by three-foot wire cage sitting on a metal table where a mother from the previous iteration tolerated her playful children. Several tanned-colored chicks with green eyes snapped at one another or squabbled by grasping their opponent with arms and hands while using their tails to keep balance.

The chicks checked each other out and the surrounding humans, pecking at anything they found at the bottom of the cage. If someone made a sudden move or a loud sound, they ran to their mother.

It was a little warmer in the lab than other parts of the building. All for the good of the chicks. The smell of birds, straw, and cleansers hung in the air.

"These animals look nothing like chickens now, Kumiko. They're amazing. The hands are there and the tails aren't so wobbly. You're so good."

"Don't forget how good Arthur's computer simulations are. It's like solving a genetic puzzle," she said, smiling and pushing her bangs off her brow.

He continued to study the chicks. "I see the flight muscles are smaller. No need for them now. The feathers are nice." He stuck his finger into the cage. "Ow! Damn, the little guy bit me!" he said, holding up his damaged index finger for Kumiko to see. An arc of little red beads appeared where each tooth had penetrated his skin.

"I'll get you a bandage," Kumiko said, examining the small cut. "I'm not sure who in the family is more injury-prone, you or George. We'd better put some antibiotic on it just to be safe." She pulled a tube from her lab coat pocket.

"You carry this stuff around with you?" he said, trying not to look at his finger.

"I figured someone would get bitten eventually," she said, also retrieving a small box of bandages.

"I'm the first human to be bitten by a dinosaur!"

"Be glad it's a baby."

"It's like being a time traveler!" Cantor said softly. He took Kumiko's hand and raised it to his lips.

"Cantor, not in the lab!" Kumiko whispered, noticing the smile on a grad student's face. But she didn't pull her hand away.

He smiled as he picked up a chick from the backside, avoiding the little snapping jaw, and examined the three fingers on each hand. They were clawless and pointed in odd directions. "Definitely incomplete. We have a lot of work to do before those fingers can bend properly. Nevertheless, I don't think any roosters are going to want to tangle with this guy when he matures." He gently placed the wiggling chick back in the cage.

"Nor paleontologists. How's your finger?" Kumiko asked.

"No worries," Cantor replied.

Kumiko knew when it came to blood, his stomach often went into boa mode and squeezed itself, pushing out whatever he'd last eaten.

The latest high-tech equipment surrounded the chicks. Usually, one to three graduate students worked the machines, fed the animals, or took notes.

She watched as Cantor gazed at all the glinting hardware. Paleontologists, like himself, rarely used most of these things. There were gene-splicing machines, cell analysis machines, DNA sequencing machines, and more. All with flashing lights in green, red, and yellow. "I'll never understand how these contraptions work."

"No problem, I do. You know, we have a lot more work ahead of us," Kumiko said. "The genes that control diet are so complicated, I'm thinking it'll take at least one more iteration before I can change these dino-chickens into pure carnivores." She turned and looked at him. "I still wonder if we shouldn't try to reproduce a plant eater instead. I think you'd relate to them better."

"Good vegetarian joke. Thanks a lot. As for vegetarian dinos, it ain't going to happen. Even the chicken's ancestors loved their steak. Deep down inside – really deep – chickens are yearning to be predators."

"Oh? Did you take a poll of all the local chickens?"

"As a matter of fact, I did. They all want to rebel against the junk the farmers feed them and yearn to be masters of their domain," Cantor said, trying to pick up another chick. "Anyway, all birds came from meat-eaters similar to *velociraptors,* as far as we know." Gradually, his hand approached another chick.

"I'm aware," Kumiko said. "Honey, you're going to get bitten again. Please put on some gloves."

Cantor continued, "So, when do you think you'll be able to start work with the eagles? Are you up for that?"

"I love a challenge," she said, toying with her dragon necklace. "Since they're already genetically programmed to eat meat, it might be easier to devolve them into dinosaurs. I'm still waiting for Arthur's recommendations."

He began doing a two-step with her, holding her close, then twirling her in a circle. "I don't know how many more iterations we'll need, but we're going to make a real dinosaur. You are the only one that can do it," he whispered in her ear.

The grad students stood and clapped, which only encouraged Cantor.

* * *

Kumiko loved to enhance her class lessons with real examples of creatures or vivid visual aids. The next morning, Kumiko discussed her research with her sophomore genetics class. She didn't adhere to university norms and wore a yellow blouse and a flowered orange dress. Using a laser pointer, she discussed the images on the large wall screen. The classroom lights were off and the blinds closed.

"Today, I have a surprise for you. But first, let me lay some groundwork. Scientists have long known that the body structures of ancient ancestors often appear and then disappear during the development of the embryos." She clicked the remote in her other hand and a new photo appeared.

"For example, whale embryos have tiny buds for hind limbs, all of which disappear as the embryo develops further, and the associated genes are turned off. Well, scientists like myself are turning them back on," she said, her eyes sparkling.

Kumiko handed out a sheet of paper titled *Devolution* as students stopped writing and socialized with one another.

"Everyone got a copy?" She waited for the chatter to fade away. "You can follow the outline as I cover the next topic. Today I want to talk about my own research. I call it Devolution, basically running evolution backward starting with an existing organism, in this case, a bird. It's like reversing evolutionary time.

"Because of the publicity around my research, you may know I work with a scientist named Arthur Saxton, at Los Alamos, New Mexico. We are turning chickens and eagles into dinosaurs." The slide showed a cartoon mother chicken chasing a dinosaur youngster, three times her size, out of her kitchen.

"Los Alamos provides the quantum computer simulations of genes that work out their hypothetical expressions. I apply the results in the lab by altering the genes in the previous iterations to produce a new animal closer to a dinosaur. The latest iteration is called C4. Please turn on the lights." A student flipped the switch on the wall.

"And here is a C4." Kumiko put on a set of leather gloves and put the cage on her desk. When she took off the cage's cloth covering, the room erupted with 'oohs' and 'ahhs'. Carefully, she pulled the young eleven-inch-long C4 out of the cage and held it in her extended arms.

"As you can see, it's a bird-like animal, but with teeth and hands. What makes this guy different from my previous version, the C3s, is he has the neural 'knowledge' to use them. He will chase mice and anything else that moves, including my husband's finger."

The students laughed as they strained to get a better view.

"And the tail doesn't just stick out and wobble. It is now used expertly for balance while running."

Many hands were in the air.

* * *

Later that day, Cantor and Kumiko attended a meeting with members of the Board of Supervisors as well as city and federal representatives. The board members insisted they could not allow any of the animals to be housed near Cantor's home, despite its semi-rural designation.

"We don't allow lions, or hippos, or elephants to be kept in residential areas as pets. We certainly don't allow these things you say are proto-dinosaurs," a city councilman said, as if that settled the issue.

A federal lawyer responded, "Sir, can you show the city ordinance that says people cannot own dinosaurs?"

"Don't be ridiculous."

"Look, Berkeley's facilities are strained as it is," Cantor said. "The pens I'm proposing will be sturdy and subject to your inspection. We don't exactly live in a residential neighborhood; my nearest neighbor is a half mile away."

"It doesn't matter," the city councilor said.

"It does matter," the federal lawyer added. "These animals, even in their current incomplete state, are a national treasure. Dr. Hoffman and Dr. Chen are qualified to give them the best care, albeit only temporarily. Someone will find a better habitat, eventually. Is that correct, doctors?"

"Yes," Cantor and Kumiko said together.

"Given their value, it would be advisable for no one, other than those directly involved, to know of the whereabouts of the animals. They are priceless," the lawyer said.

The councilman objected. "They belong in zoos."

"We must resolve this issue soon," the president of U. C. Berkeley reminded them. "No one is better equipped to study these wonderful creatures than the professors here. There are no other facilities where they can do their studies of dinosaur behavior. It is too important in the minds of the public for red tape and ordinances to stand in the way of this research."

* * *

Finally, approval for the construction of dinosaur pens near Cantor's house was granted. The pens would be built ten feet outside his backyard wall.

"I think we can learn a lot if the animals roamed freely in an enclosed setting," Cantor told Kumiko in his office later that week. He had his feet up and a coffee mug in his hand. Outside, the rain pelted the window and students ran to their classes. It made him glad his next class was over an hour away.

"I suspect you are talking about your backyard," Alexander Petrov added with a grin, his Russian accent apparent. His friends and colleagues knew him as Alex. For his doctorate, he'd switched from the study of fossils to the new field of experimental and behavioral paleontology under Cantor. Alex was almost a foot taller than his mentor, with gray eyes and a perpetual five o'clock shadow.

"Every paleontologist on Earth would give their big toe to watch dinosaurs in the flesh," Cantor said, looking at Kumiko eagerly.

"Our knowledge of dino behavior will grow exponentially," Alex said, rubbing the stubble on his chin.

"Are you suggesting you'll let them out of the pens?" Kumiko asked. She sat with her legs crossed, one hand cupped under her chin. "I don't think the administration agreed to that. And what will you do about cats and hawks?"

"Our backyard will be fine. Once the animals have grown a little larger, no cat will want to fight a 'chicken' that can fight back," Cantor said with a grin.

Kumiko replied, "Don't get too cocky, sweetheart."

"They'll remain in their pens at night. For predatory birds, we'll use ultrasound devices to keep them away," Cantor added. "Once the proto-dinosaurs are as large as a cat, we'll reassess whether we can continue studying their behavior in the backyard."

"But we will need to be very circumspect," Kumiko continued. "Have you thought about how you'd deal with an escapee?"

"From the pens? We'll have to make sure that doesn't happen. Don't forget, if they got out of a cage, they won't be able to get out of the building," Cantor continued.

"I'm talking about the backyard," Kumiko said, shaking her head.

"It's a good thing your nearest neighbor lives so far away," Alex added.

"Yeah, I like it that way," Cantor said, taking a gulp of coffee.

"I'm more worried about humans. They're a bigger threat to the animals than the animals are to them," Alex continued.

"Not for long," Cantor said enthusiastically.

"Cantor, bigger isn't better," Kumiko said, sounding frustrated. "I know I haven't asked Arthur to model genes that increased the C4's size."

"How big will they get?" Alex asked.

Cantor answered, "Based on my calculation, they'll get to be the size of a goose. Size also depends on how long they live since they grow even in adulthood."

"That's manageable," Alex said. "I don't think you want later iterations to get large. But it's fun to imagine if Kumiko produced something truly huge."

"It would be amazing, but we'd be run out of town," Cantor responded, lost in thought.

* * *

That day ended with a beautiful evening. Cantor and Kumiko, both in short cargo pants, sat on the patio of their house on the other side of the hills, east of Berkeley. Alex joined them.

The last of the sun's rays lit the underside of the clouds, and the breeze was just enough to lessen the humidity. The three scientists sat sipping their wine, talking about their research. Light from the dining room lit the base of the magnolia, making its leaves look like clumpy waterfalls of green emerging toward the house from the darkness.

"I need to redesign the bones of the wrist for more functional hands," Kumiko said. "It's going to take some serious computer power to solve this puzzle. I'm so ready."

"I can upload the wrist bone measurements from the fossil raptor discovery at Gaston, Utah, a couple of years ago," Alex offered.

Kumiko shifted in her chair. "Thanks, Alex. This week, I'm going to dissect two of the C4s, a male and a female, to get a better understanding of their inner organs."

Cantor sat up. "Is that necessary? Can't you get all the data you need from blood samples and MRI scans?"

"I get a tremendous amount of data in that way. But dissection is the only way to get a lot of other important data. I hate that I need to do this, but I don't know any other way." She held out her hands, palms up.

"What kind of data?"

"Things at the cell and molecular level. Pathologies. I need neural samples, liver samples, kidney samples, and brain samples. Data I can't get any other way."

Cantor looked at his glass, shaking his head. "You can take samples using biopsy tools without even making an incision."

"I know this is difficult, Cantor. But this is how we can provide the next generations with properly functioning organs. Proper digestion. Proper…"

"Would you do this on a Bengal Tiger? There are 915 of them left in the wild that we know of. That's more than all the C4s and earlier iterations put together."

"Cantor, we both know how science works. It's facts I'm after. I don't hear you suggesting that labs shouldn't use mice for drug development."

Alex stepped in. "OK now. Let's take a breather from this. Everyone here understands how precious the C4s are."

* * *

Later, as Kumiko was preparing for bed and brushing her teeth, Cantor walked into the bathroom to do the same. He noticed how she avoided getting bubbles of toothpaste on her chin. He'd never mastered the technique.

"George is in bed," Cantor said, referring to their young son. "I'm sorry for the dustup earlier," he mumbled with the brush in his mouth, looking at her in the mirror. "I know you're only doing what has to be done. Does it make you uncomfortable?"

"Yes, it does. I'm not a cold, unfeeling person. It hurts when you imply otherwise."

"I know you aren't that way," Cantor said and stopped brushing. "You know how I am."

"Yes, I know. But if you're going to study life, you have to deal with death. I could hand off the tough stuff to a grad student, but that seems unfair and cowardly," she said, shaking her head.

"I guess I'm a contradiction," she added. "I want to advance our program, but part of me dislikes what I have to do. That part of me I have to compartmentalize. I stuff it into a dark room somewhere in my head and try not to shine a light on it."

"Yeah," Cantor said, replacing his toothbrush. "After I've dug up a fossil, I don't have to deal with those issues."

Kumiko nodded and continued brushing.

"Ever since a deranged neighbor shot my dog, Quincy, I've never been the same," he added, wiping his mouth with the hand towel. "Blood freaks me out, and I don't think I could kill anything. Or ever eat meat again."

"I know. But I'm not you."

When they got into bed, he sensed she was still upset. She wished him a good night and turned on her side. He put his hand on her back and gently ran his fingers up and down until her breathing softened.

Chapter 3

Digital Evolution

"Eagles come in all shapes and sizes, but you will recognize them chiefly by their attitudes."
— E. F. Schumacher

In early 2031, Kumiko and Arthur Saxton collaborated to create an animal called an E4, similar to a C4 but derived from eagles instead of chickens. Unlike the green eyes of the C4s, the E4 proto-dinosaurs had striking orange eyes.

Soon afterward, Kumiko began using Arthur Saxton's computer simulations to alter the C4 and E4 genes in stem cells stored in the lab. The result would be the C5s and E5s.

In the meantime, using grant funds, the pens were completed next to Cantor's backyard wall. A tall wooden structure, three times longer than the house, surrounded the pens.

* * *

Cantor and Kumiko designed and successfully hatched the fifth iteration in late 2031. Both the C5s and E5s were flightless and could grasp with their arms and improved fingers.

"You're right, Kumiko. We have some meat eaters here," Cantor said, watching as the chicks gobbled up their breakfast of mice in the lab. "I don't like to watch them eat, though."

"I'm pleased with the C5s in that regard. It wasn't easy changing their digestive tract to handle meat, like the E5s."

"The E5s have even brighter orange eyes," Cantor noted. "I don't think I've ever seen such an intense orange in an animal's eye."

"Their eyes are very unusual," she replied. "The genes for eye color shouldn't have been affected when the ancient genes were activated."

Her lab smelled like poop. Meat eater poop.

"Hello, little raptorling," he said to the closest chick. "My, what big claws you have." Unlike earlier iterations, both the C5s and the E5s had a sickle-shaped claw on the inside toe. Proportionally, it wasn't as big as the fossil claws he'd seen, but it could do serious damage.

"They look more like little *velociraptors* now," he said. "I still think we should have tried to make tiny Tyrannosaurs. As long as they stayed small, they wouldn't be hard to handle."

Kumiko knew the grant for their research had specified raptors, not Tyrannosaurs. "It was raptors or nothing."

Cantor nodded. "I've got to admit, I'm having a hard time looking at the sickle claws without flinching." He grimaced, putting one hand on his stomach.

* * *

Cantor studied the C5s and E5s in their cages in Kumiko's lab and learned several things. First, they cleaned their feathers like a cat, although their tongues didn't have the bristles cats had. Second, like dogs, they liked to chew on pieces of wood or bones. Third, they grew even more rapidly than chickens or eagles.

The C5s and E5s were larger than their predecessors and, after a few months, had to be caged separately from the earlier generations. Cantor took several of the C5s home to study and the rest stayed at the University where Kumiko could monitor their health and perform tests. While they were small, he'd let them run freely in the backyard until evening, when he'd return them to the pens. Because of their aggressiveness, the E5s always stayed in the pens, even when they were small.

"It's entertaining watching them play," Cantor said to Kumiko as they stood in the backyard watching the C5s romp.

"You want something to chew?" Kumiko asked a chick that stood by her chair, looking at her expectantly. She handed it a small chew toy. "By the way, Arthur is flying in from Los Alamos tomorrow to observe the animals that are still at the university."

* * *

The next day, Arthur let his new Peregrine aircar fly itself from Los Alamos to see Kumiko in Berkeley. Upon arrival, he verbally instructed the aircar to land at the small Berkeley Airpark using the pathway approved by the San Francisco Air Authority. The chain-link fence that surrounded the landing area didn't prevent the wash of the propellers from buffeting a couple of students walking nearby. *Ha*, he thought, *I love stirring things up.* He noticed Kumiko near the gate, trying to hold down her long purple dress. She had nice legs. He held his wrist phone up and snapped a picture.

On the ground, Arthur instructed the orange Peregrine to start standard post-landing procedures after its vertical landing. The whirring rotors slowed, and he stepped out onto the new tarmac once the cockpit opened. Only one other aircar sat in the landing zone. *Mine's better*, he thought.

"Welcome to Berkeley, Arthur. Did you have a pleasant flight?" Kumiko inquired.

"Sure. I even treated myself to a bag of peanuts. Check out my flying car. Snazzy right? Auto-pilot the whole way. I'm surprised you don't have more aircars in the park."

"Professors can't afford aircars," Kumiko said.

The two scientists walked to the west side of the Berkeley campus, where the animals were kept.

"I keep some of the C5s and E5s and previous iterations in this building, affectionately called Animal House by the students and faculty," she said as they walked through the large, open doors.

Cages filled with animals lined one wall. A humid mixture of straw, proto-dinosaurs, dirty water, and red meat assaulted Arthur's nostrils, and he scrunched up his nose. In the metal rafters, sparrows flew in and out, chirping and ignoring their cousins in the cages below. Next to Animal House sat a half-acre of open space, surrounded by a sturdy fence. It allowed the animals a more natural setting and a chance to stretch their legs.

"Passageways between cages and the outdoor fenced area allow easy passage between the two," Kumiko said. "Our animal cages take up over half of the building. We keep the temperature on the warm side for the sake of the animals."

"No problem."

"The concrete floors make maintenance and cleaning easier. Each evening, we wash the bottoms of the cages with a hose. We put the meat in a trough for the C5s and there isn't a lot of squabbling. But we separate the E5s at dinner time."

"Why?" he said.

"In the presence of meat, the E5s tend to fight."

"Wonderful!"

Kumiko looked at Arthur with furrowed brows.

Chirps and barks filled the air as they got closer to the cages.

"These guys seem to be pack-oriented," Arthur said, running his hands down his shirt as if they were dirty.

"I agree. As you can see, even at this young age, the C5s are already significantly bigger than a chicken would be around the same age. Even more so for the E5s."

Arthur looked at them for a brief time. "Do you mind if I take a few pictures?"

"Of course not, Arthur. Please take all the pictures you like."

The C5s watched him intently, opening and closing their clawed fingers as their necks weaved back and forth and their heads tilted, almost like dogs when surprised by something new.

But the E5s stared unwaveringly at Arthur and seemed to stalk him, slowly closing in on his face when he knelt to see them. They walked parallel to the cage as if they weren't interested in him and then in a flash, leaped against it, trying to bite and claw him while hissing and growling ferociously.

"I may need to euthanize that one, I'm afraid," she said as they came to a bandaged E5 in a cage by itself. It had chewed off half of its tail.

"What a shame, Kumiko. Why did he do that?"

"His attack instinct never seems to shut off. See how he's biting the bars? Don't get too close."

As Arthur bent closer, the creature tried to hook him with the claws of one three-fingered hand as frantic groans gurgled in its throat.

"Oh, dear," Kumiko whispered. As they walked to the next cage, she glanced back. The E5 was swallowing something. Blood dripped from its hand where a finger once grew.

"Excuse me," she said, walking rapidly toward a grad student. "Please put him down, now," she whispered. Then she rejoined Arthur without speaking.

They continued walking. "I'm impressed by their hands, not to mention their teeth," he said. "They certainly aren't shy. What I need to do is confirm that my programs gave you the guidance you needed. In other words, did the quantum computer and my software pass the test?"

Grimly she said, "The programs worked, Arthur. The computer was accurate in predicting how certain dormant genes would behave if we re-activated them. As you can see, the animals are looking more and more like dinosaurs." She let out a sigh. "The only thing we didn't expect was the increase in size. That and the E5's aggressiveness."

"Well, think of it like this," Arthurs said. "If you look at ancient Egyptians, not the upper nobility, but the less affluent people, they were smaller than us. Same for early humans, same for ancient Romans."

"OK. What does that have to do with our dinosaurs?"

"Well, my dear, it is a matter of processing food and getting enough of it. Getting enough vitamins, proteins, fiber."

"Well, we feed our animals very well."

"Yes, but you've changed many aspects of their digestive systems. The dinos haven't been efficiently processing the food you give them. But it is getting better."

"OK."

"As you upgrade their digestive systems to be more efficient, you are going to get bigger animals. You see?"

Kumiko pondered this.

Arthur snapped a few pictures of the E5s. "Sometimes bigger is better." He grinned, winked at her, and briefly placed his hand on her back.

"Why don't we head to my office and I'll give you all the details? You can meet my husband, Cantor."

* * *

Cantor was surprised Arthur hadn't accepted an invitation to spend the night and have dinner with them on Saturday.

It was his turn to be the chef. He stirred the vegetable soup before frying some pork chops separately for Kumiko and George, the family meat-eaters. The surgical gloves allowed him to avoid touching the meat.

He'd met Arthur the day before in Kumiko's office and didn't quite know what to think of him. Arthur had nervous eyes and a tendency to punctuate other people's words with a puff of air through his nose. His white skin suggested the outdoors wasn't where he spent his leisure time.

After dinner, Cantor went to feed the raptors in the pens. Normally, he'd pull the meat from the refrigerator near the cages and put it into a small wheelbarrow. Unfortunately, the wheel was flat, so he made several trips while holding the meat in his hands. He had trouble opening the cage's gate and dropped some meat on the floor. A C5 named Koko ran between his legs and through the building's outer door.

Cantor tried to follow Koko, but the little dinosaur was too fast and soon was out of sight.

Koko trotted to a rocky area and climbed the boulders, scanning the area.

She hopped to the ground, holding out her feathered arms for balance, and ran through the empty fields until she came to a residential fence, which she scaled without too much trouble. There wasn't much to see, so after checking out the contents of the cat bowl, she climbed a plum tree. From there, an easy hop landed her on the next-door neighbor's fence. Koko was fearless, and the blond Labrador in the yard didn't prevent her from climbing down to investigate.

The first thing Koko smelled after entering the yard was the Lab's dog food. The dog ran up to her and then stood at attention, studying this strange new invader, unsure what to do. She sniffed the newcomer's scent and watched for signs of aggression or signals showing fear or submission. She found neither, just a calm, confident Koko. Finally, the lab drew closer and let out a little woof. When the creature headed toward her bowl, took a bite, and gulped it down, the Lab didn't challenge her. Instead, she chose to play.

The Lab lowered her front legs and gave a little whoop, then ran away, only to return and repeat the process over again. After a couple of rounds of this, Koko caught on and chased the lab across the yard. When the Lab turned, Koko let herself be chased. This continued for several minutes until both tired and rested. Now, the C5 climbed a tree but the Lab couldn't follow. Noticing this, Koko climbed back down, turned around, and climbed the tree again. Still, the Lab didn't follow. After watching the Lab curiously from a branch, the raptorling moved on to the next yard.

By morning, Koko was sound asleep in Cantor's backyard magnolia, resting from her great adventure. In addition to making a friend with the Lab, she taught a poodle a lesson in manners, and convinced a little girl, who should have been in bed, that an elf passed under a nearby street lamp.

Kumiko led her back to her pen. A little bacon helped as well.

Chapter 4

Warning Signs

As 2032 turned to 2033, Cantor recognized that the "5s" were exhibiting fascinating behaviors not found in the earlier iterations. They would leap or strut past each other to impress. Initially, there were only two E5s kept in separate cages from the C5s in the pens near the house. The rest were in Kumiko's lab. Then the earthquake happened.

As earthquakes go in the San Francisco area, this was not uncommonly large, but it did some damage, especially around Berkeley. Kumiko's lab suffered broken pipes, cracked walls, and flooding. Luckily, no animals were hurt, but they needed to be removed until the repairs were complete.

Unfortunately, Animal House wasn't available. Several months before the quake, the old building was demolished to make way for a larger structure.

So, Cantor brought the remaining raptors home, mostly E5s.

He estimated that, when mature, the E5s and C5s would be the size of a swan, over half again as big as their predecessors. When he thought of the C5s, he thought of laid-back *velociraptors*. When thinking of the E5s, he thought of *velociraptors* on speed and full of testosterone.

The E5s were vicious and violent around strangers or anyone who challenged them by staring. Cantor would go in their cages, sure that his familiarity and size made him safe.

* * *

George, now ten, was a slender youngster with straight black hair and his mother's dark brown eyes. When he was born, Cantor wanted to name him after his namesake, the great mathematician Georg Cantor, but Kumiko insisted the English spelling, George, be used.

George's dresser was a zoo. In a terrarium, rested Smaug the lizard, in another terrarium sat the tarantula, Minky, and nearby, his hamster Cantide busied himself running on his metal wheel. Looking down from the bookshelf, a plastic *T. rex* lorded over the others. And, wherever there was human activity, the family's ever-curious beagle, Lily, was found wagging her tail.

Sometimes, Kumiko found George sketching the animals next to their cage. She collected his drawings and helped him hang some of them in his room.

"Those are lovely, George. I like the one where you're riding that dinosaur."

"Thanks, Mom. What about the dragon?" He pointed to another drawing he'd hung over his bed. "I did that one for you."

"You are so talented. That is definitely a Chinese dragon. I love it!"

Drawing was a solitary activity. It hurt Kumiko to see George always by himself.

George had trouble making friends. Cantor and Kumiko knew his medical condition played a role.

George took unnecessary chances. Both parents remembered sitting in the doctor's office at the Mayo Clinic, hearing the diagnosis.

"It's a form of OCD: Obsessive-Compulsive Disorder," the doctor said. "George is obsessed with dangerous things. He has to prove to himself that the danger is real, that he can survive it. I'm also seeing neurodivergent signs in his brain. It is important he take the medications I'm prescribing."

"I've never heard of this type of OCD," Kumiko said, looking at Cantor.

"It's very rare," the doctor replied. "Moth Syndrome is the name for his condition. He'll always be drawn to the fire."

* * *

It was what should have been a typical evening: a quiet household and all soundly asleep in their beds. Kumiko switched on the bedside lamp when she heard a muffled sound at the bedroom door. She opened it and found George standing in the hallway.

"Is that you, George? What's happened to you?" she cried.

Cantor leaped out of bed.

"My face hurts," George whined. It sounded more like, "Maa fwath hurf." His eyes looked like little buttons on a fat-faced doll with red, swollen lips. He had two tiny puncture marks near one corner of his mouth. Lily had her front paws on his legs, clearly agitated.

"What the heck!?" Cantor said as he got his bearings. His eyes widened when he saw his son.

Kumiko rushed to the boy, trying to calm him. "He's having an allergic reaction to something. I think something bit him!"

Cantor put his pants on. "I'll take him to the emergency room. Don't worry, son, you're going to be all right."

Several minutes later, the three of them were in the car with Cantor at the wheel. "Do you know what bit you, George?" he asked.

"Ahh thin da bwak pider."

"Don't worry, George," Kumiko said, "You can tell us after you get treated."

George was given antivenom in the emergency room and after a couple of hours, he could speak intelligently. Cantor looked at his watch. It was past three in the morning when they returned to the car. "Tell us again what you told the doctor."

"I think a black widow spider bit me."

"George, remember that talk we had about spiders?" Cantor continued, trying not to sound alarmed. "Did you pick it up?"

"I held it in bed."

"You held it!? In bed!?" Kumiko exclaimed, turning to look at him from the front seat.

"Yeah. I guess I fell asleep on it."

Kumiko shivered. "Is it still in your bed?"

"I don't know where it is."

"I know you know spiders can be dangerous, honey," Kumiko said, eyeing the two punctures on his cheek. "I want you to try your best not to pick up spiders, OK?"

"I'll try. I know they're dangerous." Then, sheepishly, he mumbled, "I needed to pick it up, though."

Cantor looked at Kumiko.

When the family returned home, the search began. There it was, barely alive in his bed, its red hourglass clear on its black belly.

* * *

While his parents were at work, George sometimes entered the pens with the young C5s, using the key he'd found in Cantor's study. The raptorlings allowed him to scratch behind their heads if he was calm and gentle.

The E5s were a different matter. He played a game with the E5s by sticking his finger between the bars and pulling it out just as the animal lunged. It wasn't teasing; it was testing both the E5s and himself. George had to verify that something was dangerous, and he'd do it repeatedly, to be sure. By testing something concrete, he could challenge the invisible life-ending cloud that suffocated his mind.

One day, George invited Sherri, another ten-year-old from school, to hang out. She lived about a mile away. Kumiko took the day off and provided the kids with a good lunch. Afterward, she let the kids know she was going to the grocery store and would return soon.

George led Sherri into his room to see his personal zoo. He was thankful he'd followed his mom's request and put his clean underwear in a drawer, and his dirties in the hamper. Pointing to his lizard, he said, "This is Smaug. He's a bearded dragon. I put some coins in his terrarium because dragons like treasure."

"He seems curious. He looks at me with his head sort of sideways," she said, looking at him from under her blond bangs.

"Yeah. I think he still hasn't figured humans out."

"And here is Cantide. He likes to keep busy," George said, looking at the hamster running on his wheel.

"I've never heard that name before."

"I called him that because he's always running. He can run, but he can't hide." George looked hopefully at Sherri to see if she got the joke. She rolled her eyes.

"That's funny, George."

"I used to have a tarantula named Minky, but I had to give her away. Hey, would you like to see the dinos in the pens?"

"Yes!"

"Um, don't tell anyone, OK?" George said, feeling guilty about taking his dad's keys. They walked to the wooden building, where they could hear growls and barks from within.

"They look so... so like dinosaurs!" she exclaimed when they stood before the cage.

"I have individual names for them," he said. "Look, there's Nosey. He sticks his nose into other dinos' business. And there is Georgia, Ursula, and Byron. Byron is always preening his feathers."

The pens smelled of hay and some poop. She looked at the E5s. "Those ones have orange eyes. They seem different." The goose-sized predators followed her every move.

"Yeah. They're mean. I wish I didn't have to touch them."

"Why do you have to touch them?"

"Oh, ah... I don't have to do that. I didn't mean to say that. "

When Kumiko drove up the driveway, George slipped into Cantor's study and placed the keys in the desk drawer, exactly as he'd found them.

* * *

That evening, after Sherri's parents picked her up and Cantor returned from the university, he asked George how his day with Sherri went.

"We had fun. We talked about dinosaurs. I think you should give the C5s a name, like Elvins, or Dorians, or maybe Whippersnappers?"

"That's an interesting idea, George. What do you think, hon?" Cantor said, turning to Kumiko, who was reading from her laptop.

"Sounds like fun," she said with a smile for both of them.

"What would you call the E5s?" Cantor asked as he headed to the kitchen.

"They're so weird. I think you should call them Touch-me-nots."

"That's an interesting name," Cantor said, opening a cabinet.

"Yeah. It reminds me to stay away from them."

Kumiko looked up from her laptop and studied her son for a long time. "When you're in the pens with Dad or Alex, please don't go near the E5s, OK?"

George nodded and seemed to have something on his mind. "Mom, I ah…"

"Yes?" she responded. By now, Cantor was watching from the kitchen.

"What, son?" Cantor asked.

"Oh, nothing. I'm going to go read now."

Chapter 5

Unintended Consequences

"Pandora left us a box in her will."
– Cantor Hoffman

Months passed and the research continued. The lab was repaired, although the new Animal House wasn't completed until late 2034. Several E5s and C5s were returned to Kumiko's lab from the home pens.

One of Kumiko's graduate students named Tamara was in the lab working with an E5 named Wart, so named because of the unusual bumps on the back of his hands. The student's research attempted to answer whether the raptors could recognize themselves in a mirror in the manner of elephants or chimpanzees. After donning leather gloves, she opened Wart's cage, intending to slip a mirror inside. Unexpectedly, Wart charged the cage door, causing the mirror to fall and shatter. Tamara fell backward, taken by surprise.

Wart leaped onto the student, then jumped to the floor and vanished out the lab door.

* * *

Tamara sprinted after the small dinosaur, but Wart was too fast. She yelled for help. The dinosaur stopped at a door up ahead but ran away when a man opened it. Together, Tamara and the man followed the dinosaur. Wart scampered up the stairs at the end of the hall. Then they heard a scream.

* * *

Wart slipped on the floor but quickly recovered. He looked down a long, bright cave with more openings like the one he'd just run through. The lumbering flat face was running behind him, barking in an annoying way. Wart didn't like the flat face. It was always staring at him.

The urge to bite something was strong. How wonderfully powerful his legs felt. He could do anything. Using his long tail as a counterweight, he could turn sharply. The flat face couldn't do that. There were weird openings to the sky above him, each one showing the sun. Wart wanted to see the sun.

He passed Ir closed wooden slab attached to the cave wall. With his claws, he scratched at the straight sides. He'd seen flat faces open the things. But it didn't open for him. He could hear and smell them on the other side. The flat face who had freed him was getting closer. Now the wooden structure opened and a head peered out. Flat faces were loud. They made Wart angry.

He turned and easily outran them. Now he came to the end of the white cave. Strange ledges rose before him. The feel of his legs easily bounding over the rising ledges emboldened him. At the top of them, another flat face stood. Wart wanted to taste it. Bite it.

The flat face made a sound he recognized. Scream, scream. Finally, a sound he liked.

* * *

Security evacuated the building until Wart was tranquilized and captured.

The department head, Doctor Swanson, asked Kumiko to report to his office.

"Can you meet me in Swanson's office?" she texted Cantor, but he didn't answer. He was in class.

"Doctor Chen," Swanson said from his black leather chair. "I have to think there's some negligence here. This animal injured a student and traumatized others. Here is my decision. You can no longer keep animals more than three months old in your lab and you can put no more than four in Animal House. If they can escape your lab, they can escape Animal House as well. This is the way it has to be."

Kumiko returned to her office, shut the door, and sat at her desk, head in hand.

As soon as Cantor finished lecturing, he saw her message and rushed to her office. "Are you OK?"

She sat gazing at nothing, twirling a pen nervously.

He leaned over and hugged her. "What happened?"

"There was an accident with an E5," she said and explained everything.

"That poor student," he said. "We need to meet with her. See if there is anything we can do."

"I suspect we'll also need to meet with the press."

"Jeez. Well, don't worry about the dinos," he said. "We'll put separators in the pens at home so they can hold more animals."

"You'll have to. When they get crowded, they begin eating each other."

"I know. What a mess."

"I'm so ashamed," she said. "First thing, I'll ask Swanson for the student's number."

"It wasn't your fault, sweetheart," he said, hugging her again.

* * *

After the fiasco with Wart, Kumiko felt her colleagues would always think of her as that reckless lady whose animals were a danger to everyone. She picked up all the injured student's out-of-pocket medical expenses. The young lady was sweet and forgiving, and Kumiko occasionally met her for lunch.

She shook off the incident, determined to complete her work. She was appalled at the idea that maybe she should stop. She just needed to try harder to make sure nobody could be injured. Failure was not an option. Mentally and emotionally, she couldn't deal with failure. This trait was hammered into her from childhood.

Kumiko, with Arthur's help, developed new iterations of the dinosaurs in 2035. Each iteration corrected the problems with the previous iteration and resulted in more accurate dinosaurs.

After the E6s and C6s came the '7s'.

"These 7s truly seem like dinosaurs – not just in appearance, but probably in behavior," Kumiko said to Cantor in her lab, surrounded by machines that manipulated genes.

"Yeah, it's fantastic," Cantor replied, looking at the six-week-old chicks, already bigger than an adult chicken. "And the C7s don't regurgitate the meat or develop digestion problems."

"They use their teeth to tear pieces of meat apart, which they swallow whole. They won't even look at grains now," she added. "No surprise, they're going to be bigger than the C6s."

"Crazy. I want to bring a few of them home for study," Cantor said.

The C7's eyes were large for their body size and took on a green color with small yellow patches. Sometimes, when they felt threatened, they would hiss or make a growling sound, followed by sharp barks while they opened their hands toward the offender.

When feeling threatened, the C7s could be aggressive. But the E7s were much more dangerous. Unlike most animals, the E7s didn't always communicate their mood. There were no warnings.

Four of the E5s and two of the C5s had died of disease or infection, increasing the available pen space for the C7s.

* * *

George loved the way the new C7s reacted to his mom when they were little.

"Why do they want to be around you so much?" he asked her when the C7 chicks first arrived at home.

"I'm their mommy."

"Can I be their daddy?"

"Not in their minds. Birds, and our little dinos as well, imprint on the first living thing that moves and touches them after hatching."

"What's imprinting?" he asked.

"When a chick imprints on its mother, it forms a deep bond with her for life. You see?"

"Is that why they seem to follow you everywhere?"

"Exactly. I'm often the first thing the chicks see after hatching."

When Cantor was home studying the young dinosaurs, they ignored him, unless he had food or acted vulnerable. They focused on what was in his hand. He was just the odd critter that went with it.

If the baby dinosaurs were in the backyard when Kumiko came home, at first sight of her, they piled up at the edge of the sliding glass door, trying to push their way to "Mom". And when she stepped into the backyard, they followed her everywhere, like ducklings, filling the air with their chirps.

George laughed when he saw this one day. He began following her, saying, "I'm here, Mommy. I'm here. You can look at me now because I'm here. Did you hear? I just want to let you know I'm here. OK? Look over here. That's me."

Kumiko couldn't help but laugh. Later, when she was indoors near the sliding glass door, she looked out and George was squatting with the younger dinosaurs, thumping and mushing his face against the glass, his arms bent on each side of him, mouthing the words, "Look, Mommy, I'm here."

* * *

Months later, when the dinosaurs had grown significantly, Sherri came for a visit with George. Tommy, a paid college student who helped with the raptors now that Alex had finished his doctorate, was preparing to feed the animals while George and Sherri watched. Both kids were taller now and more mature. In another year, they would be teenagers.

"We have to place the beef mixture in different bowls for the more aggressive E7s otherwise, they fight," he said as Tommy slid the bowl through the spring-loaded feeding panel at the bottom of an inner "E" gate.

He preferred not to carry their meat inside the cage like he did for the C7s. But when it was time to clean the cage, he still entered both cages, sure that the young animals were fed well. He was big enough to discourage even the E7s from getting any ideas. Perhaps, in a few more months, things would be different.

"Those are big," Sherri said, pointing to the already goose-sized and still-growing E7s.

One large male, named Spartacus, hissed at a female too interested in his bowl, swiping her with his hand. His claws left three jagged, seeping red lines across her downy feathers. The damage wasn't great, but it startled both kids.

Sherri looked at the male. "That's not nice!" she exclaimed and wagged her finger. Spartacus stared back and started walking toward her. Not in the awkward way of a goose, but with sure, stealthy footing. His orange eyes locked onto hers. He let out a warbling sound and stretched out his hands as he slowly approached, his talons pointing directly at her.

"George, he's hunting me," she said nervously as she stared into the creature's unwavering tiger eyes. Spartacus bared his fangs.

"Spartacus, back off!" George shouted. He knew the outstretched hands were a bad sign. So were the bared teeth. "We have nothing to worry about. He can't get out." Normally, Sherri was very spunky, but not now.

"Oh, my God. If he does, he'll kill me."

In a flash, Spartacus threw himself against the bars, claws reaching toward her. His screams hurt George's ears.

He waved his hands, trying to get Spartacus' attention. "No, Spartacus! Look away, Sherri. Don't look at his eyes!"

When George stood between her and Spartacus, facing her, she came out of her trance.

"I'm so sorry, Sherri. I should have told you not to look directly at him. You didn't realize you were challenging him."

"I don't feel good," she said.

"Please don't worry, Sherri. Please. He won't get out."

"I'm going in the house," she said and backed towards the outer door. Tommy looked up from his work as she passed. "Her first visit with Spartacus?"

George followed her. "Yeah."

Spartacus stood staring with the red feathers along the rear of his head rising as his large hands opened and closed. Even after the kids were out of the enclosure, the leering eyes stayed locked on the outer door.

"Are you OK?" George asked. "I'm sorry. That was a little weird."

"That was more than weird, George," she said with a tremor in her voice. "I don't think Spartacus likes me. The way he stared at me while he opened his hands and claws really bothered me. I'm afraid of him."

"Please try not to be afraid, Sherri. He may have sensed your fear, and that's why he acted so strange."

"That thing gives me chills," she said. "It wasn't his size. It was his attitude. And his eyes. How can those orange eyes not bother you? They're so intense. Like some kind of awful hypnotic stare. I think I should go home now." She called her parents.

Spartacus continued to stare, flexing his black-scaled fingers, clicking the claws together, and making a low growl. His eyes, contrasting with his scaly head, were eerily bright and menacing.

After Sherri had left, George returned to the pens and studied the raptor for a long time. He fought the urge to hold his hand against the bars of the cage.

* * *

George was quiet throughout dinner and ate little. He hadn't mentioned the incident with Spartacus. But later, he confronted his dad in the living room.

"Dad, why can't you make something gentle, something that helps us, something that won't bite if we try to pet it?"

"George, you know you can't pet the larger ones. That's why we keep them locked up," Cantor said, putting down his book. "Did something happen today?"

"Tommy let Sherri and I watch as he fed the raptors. Spartacus was stalking Sherri. There was something in his eyes and how he moved that scared her."

"You didn't try to stick your fingers through the bars, did you?"

"No."

Cantor thought about what George was saying. Normally, George spent as much time as he could watching the animals when Cantor or Tommy unlocked the door. He realized George was obsessed with them. Perhaps in an unhealthy way.

"I'm sorry, son. I'm going to tell Tommy not to allow visitors in the pen area." Now the problem wasn't the animals getting out, but someone getting in. They were a lure to George's OCD.

"I like most of them," George admitted, "but after today, Sherri doesn't. Why make carnivores with teeth and big claws on their fingers in the first place?"

"Let me try to explain. Birds are related to dinosaur predators – certain meat-eaters. But there aren't any descendants of plant-eating dinosaurs like the huge four-legged ones with long necks. So, they're lost forever."

George looked as though he'd tuned his dad out.

Kumiko entered the room. She'd heard the conversation from the kitchen.

"Was Sherri mad at you, honey?" she asked.

"I don't think so." He shuffled his feet and looked away.

"Cantor, maybe the E7s are getting too big and dangerous," Kumiko said.

"Mom," George said, "since you're designing these dinosaurs, can't you design them to be friendly to people? To be gentle?"

"Like a cat or dog? I could, but your dad and I are scientists, honey."

Cantor chimed in, "We're studying an animal that wasn't evolved to like people. There were no people. We want to know what the real thing was like."

"Yeah, I know. I just don't want my friend to get scared," George said and headed back to his room.

Kumiko looked at Cantor. "I'm worried."

Cantor sighed and looked back. "You're right. Maybe we shouldn't keep the 6s and 7s here once they reach a certain size. I've been thinking about it. I expect in another six months we'll have to convince the university to take them."

"George doesn't have company over very often," Kumiko said. "This was a big FAIL for him. It makes me sad."

Chapter 6

Never Turn Your Back

After George and Sherri's experience, Cantor kept the drawer with the keys to the pens locked for everyone's safety.

He spent the next week negotiating with the Berkeley administration about Animal House. The limit of four dinosaurs was arbitrary. Since most of Cantor's time was at Berkeley, he argued it was essential for his research that the larger raptors be housed there as well. Finally, the administration relented. In six months, once the space was prepared at Animal House, the bigger dinosaurs would be transferred to Berkeley. What Cantor didn't know was the administration decided to allow the public into animal house for a fee. The money would be used to shore up the struggling humanities departments.

* * *

On the following Saturday, Kumiko had spent the morning with a sick C7 at Berkeley and was now on her way home. At the same time, George went on a short hike, leaving the place to Cantor.

Pleased that a solution to the E7 problem was at hand, Cantor entered the E7 cage to sweep and remove the empty food bowls for cleaning. Tommy didn't work weekends, so he had the raptors to himself.

Cantor had always felt confident that his relative size and the fact that he fed them in Tommy's absence would avoid any aggression. He compared himself to a dog owner whose dogs believed he was the alpha male. The raptors knew him, whereas they hadn't known Sherri.

He was surprised when he needed to use the broom to keep the aggressive E7s at bay.

Spartacus and two other E7s surrounded him, barking and hissing. He shooed away the one in front using the broom's bristles. "Get back.

You guys know better," he said sternly, as if he were talking to a class of sixth graders.

Like wolves, the dinosaurs worked as a team. He'd never seen this behavior before. No matter which way he turned, there were two E7s behind him, each as powerful as a badger and almost as heavy.

He was glad that he wore heavy construction boots and jeans. Maybe he'd underestimated the predatory instinct in the E7s.

In a flash, Spartacus clawed into the back of his right leg, causing searing pain. Growling and grunting, the raptor inched higher in spurts, like an enraged cat, biting and clawing.

Cantor, wincing with each bite. *Damn, that hurt!*

"Spartacus! Off! And you—back off!" he shouted, pushing another male with the broom. "Back off, dammit!" *I need to get out of here!*

"George, come out here please!" he yelled, hoping George had returned and trying not to sound panicked. The E7s responded to his distress by attacking with renewed vigor.

A second dinosaur latched onto his other leg from behind. Cantor could feel the blood seeping into his pants. The raptor climbed up his leg using its sickle claw and hand talons, growling and screeching. *Oh, man! This is bad.*

Things were happening too fast. Blood flowed from his legs, staining the ground. He felt light-headed.

"George, help me!" Cantor shouted, suddenly realizing he was alone. Everything around him seemed to pulse along with his pounding heart.

He felt for his phone in his back pocket but instinctually pulled his hand away as relentless teeth bit through the glove into his fingers. Spartacus grabbed the phone, bit it, and threw it to the floor.

Cantor realized sitting on the two dinosaurs wasn't an option. *Keep upright! Keep your neck as high as possible.* A third animal prepared to jump him in the front. A sharp jab from the broom sent it backward.

He pushed each gnashing head against his legs and waddled toward the gate. Sharp pains seared his legs as the writhing creatures pushed and pulled at his flesh, cutting through the layers of fabric and skin. Scraping the dinosaurs against the bars just enraged them more. Adrenaline sent his mind into overdrive.

Desperately opening the gate and holding down the angry raptors, he shuffled out of the enclosure and into the glaring daylight. He moved erratically toward his front lawn. *Just twenty feet more.* Awkward, painful steps. At last, he pushed the house door open, stumbled inside, and slammed it shut. *What now?*

More slashing and biting. He cried out as Spartacus bit into his glove again. All his attempts to push the dinosaurs to the floor failed.

Lily bolted into the foyer, barking and baring her teeth.

Cantor staggered down the hall to the bedroom and grabbed two pillows off the bed. As he frantically pushed a pillow against each animal, Lily bit at their tails. The two raptors growled and tore into the pillows, shaking their heads back and forth, but were unable to do further injury to his hands. Lily's barks merged with his groans and the growls of the raptors, creating a hellish cacophony.

One attacker let go and ran out of the room, hissing after Lily bit its leg. Lily followed.

"No, Lily!"

Growls and shrieks came from the hall. Lily limped back to the bedroom, her face and belly bleeding. She was seriously injured.

Spartacus held on—his growls muffled by the pillow. *DAMN, THAT HURTS!*

Cantor felt dizzy and his stomach was sick. Time was running out.

Then he remembered the bear spray he kept for protection against intruders in the drawer of his nightstand.

Grabbing the canister, he sprayed the repellant into Spartacus' ferocious eyes. The dinosaur screeched and ran into the closet, but soon reversed course, realizing the trap. Cantor was already at the door and caught Spartacus mid-leap with his boot as the creature frantically tried to escape. Slamming the door, Cantor listened for the sound of tearing wood. Instead, he heard Spartacus rip into Kumiko's boxes of shoes.

Limping into the hallway, he found the other E7 in the bathroom.

The raptor was on the sink, scratching and biting at its image in the mirror. It turned and glared at Cantor in the doorway. With a screech, it leaped to the floor and ran toward him.

Cantor threw the door shut as the raptor hit it with a thunk.

He lowered himself to the floor, gasping. His heart pounded in his head. *Lily! Check on Lily!*

He crawled on all fours to the bedroom. "Hey, Lily. Come on girl." She was under the bed and wouldn't come out. He grimaced as he bent to look at her. Her nose and belly had been slashed.

Cantor groaned as he got to his feet and slowly peeled his ripped pants off. *Damn those little bastards.* The sight made him lightheaded and sick. *Come on Cantor, don't look. Don't think about the blood.* He realized how lucky he was. One sliced tendon and he'd have fallen.

Limping to his dresser, he pulled out some undershirts to staunch the bleeding, then headed into the living room, looking away from the blood on the carpet. He couldn't ignore the hot liquid flowing from his hand anymore. Now, his stomach cramped up.

He made it to the kitchen sink and vomited. Wiping his mouth, he walked with stiff legs back to the living room. His wounds stung, and he felt cold.

Five minutes later, George walked in the front door and gaped at the disaster. His wide eyes watched his dad as he stood undressed in the kitchen, wiping his legs with an undershirt as snarls and growls came from other parts of the house.

"Dad! You're bleeding!" George ran to Cantor's side.

"I'm fine," Cantor said. "Help me tighten these shirts around the wounds."

Another crash in the bathroom.

"Give me your phone, son."

George handed it over. "Is there a dinosaur in the house?"

"Don't open my closet or the hall bathroom." He phoned Kumiko. She should be on her way home now. *Stay calm.*

"We have a problem," he said, trying to suppress his ragged breathing.

"What's happening?" she asked.

"Some E7s cut me up." He tried to sound in control, but his shaking voice gave him away.

"What! How serious?"

"Just some cuts. We can treat them later."

"Are you telling me the truth?" she asked, her voice fearful and rising.

"Don't worry, George is here with me." Cantor's body felt as though it was on fire.

Something crashed to the floor in the bathroom.

"What was that?" she asked shrilly.

"Lily is injured. Um, I've subdued the two culprits," he answered in gulps. George ran to the bedroom.

"Lily too!? Oh my God! I'm turning off the freeway now. Put George on."

"He's gone to check on Lily."

"Is he OK?" Her voice was choppy. Cantor could tell she was scared.

"Yes. Hold on," he said, wobbling toward the bedroom. George was holding Lily and crying. Cantor handed him the phone. "It's Mom."

"Hi Mom," George sobbed. "Dad and Lily are bleeding…"

"Tell me the truth. How badly?"

"There's blood everywhere, Mom!"

Cantor realized it might be hard as hell to get the dinosaurs back in their cage. Although they were imprinted on Kumiko, making her the ideal one to handle them, it was humiliating. He was determined to take care of the mess himself.

Cantor heard something being shredded in the bedroom closet. His mind was fuzzy as he wrapped Lily's belly with an undershirt to staunch the bleeding. At the sight, his stomach seized up again. Stumbling toward the kitchen, he continued to lose blood. George followed him.

"George, I want you to go into your room and close the door. I'm going to put a couple of dinos back in their cages."

"But you're hurt!" George said, his eyes wide. "I'll call 911!"

"I don't want to do that."

"Why not?"

"It's a long story. It'll embarrass me."

"But, Dad!"

"We have a lot of critics, son."

"Well, I'm going to help you put the dinos back!"

"I can't risk you getting hurt, son."

"No way!"

Cantor sighed and looked hard at George, who didn't waver. "OK, here's what we're going to do. Grab some blankets and gloves."

George ran to the garage and when he returned, Cantor was leaning on the kitchen counter with his head down. "Give me a second."

* * *

When Kumiko arrived, she gasped at the carnage. Blood was on the floor, the walls, the carpet, down the hall. She found Cantor and George holding blankets, standing outside the hall bathroom.

"Oh, no!" she cried, looking at his hand and legs. "We're going to the hospital now!"

"I'm not that bad, honey. It just looks bad."

"Cantor! Let's go!" she said, her eyes wide.

"We managed to get Spartacus back in his cage," Cantor replied, shaking his head. "Now we've got one more to go."

"No, dammit!" Kumiko roared. "You will do no such thing!" She glared at Cantor, then George.

"It's OK, Mom. We can do it."

A growl emerged from under the door. "I'm calling animal control!" she cried, pulling out her phone.

"Wait," Cantor urged. "I don't want this to get out. Please!"

"Look at you! You can hardly walk!"

"I'm up to this!" Cantor insisted.

Kumiko stomped away, then came back. "George, go to your room and close the door."

"Mom! I can do this!"

"Please, honey. I need you to do what I ask."

George stood his ground. "I'm sorry, Mom. I need to help."

"Ahhh!" she said and banged her fist against the wall, causing the dinosaur to screech and tear at the door.

"I think we need to act now!" Cantor said loudly. "That door isn't all that thick."

Kumiko crossed her arms and looked at the ceiling, lips taut. Finally, she exhaled and asked George for another blanket. "We do this together."

When George returned with a blanket off his bed, she said, "I'm going to put the blanket around the animal, but you've got to open the door quickly, Cantor. George, you follow me in only if I'm on top of it, holding it down. You'll put your blanket over mine and all three of us will push the blankets under its feet. Understand?"

"Well… I think I should go in first because…" Cantor began, but the fire in Kumiko's eyes shut him up. "Right."

The plan succeeded, although the raptor went nuclear rather that calming down once covered. The bathroom curtain was shredded, along with the rug. Shampoo and lotion covered the floor next to chewed plastic bottles and splinters of wood.

Cantor put his arm around George once the gate to the cage was locked. "Thank you, son. I appreciate your help. Now, let's get Lily to the hospital."

"I'm taking you to the hospital first, Cantor." Kumiko insisted.

"No, no, first we get help for Lily."

They argued and Cantor won.

* * *

Cantor, Kumiko, and George had a family meeting after Cantor returned with twenty-three stitches as well as Steri-Strips on his legs. Two of his fingers had been bitten to the bone. Lily stayed overnight at the Vet hospital. She too was full of stitches, but luckily, her intestines hadn't been punctured.

Now that Cantor was sewn up and safe, Kumiko was angry. "Do you realize the danger you put George in? And poor Lily? You should never have been in that cage!"

That stung him. "I know. This is all my fault. Until we transfer all the larger dinosaurs to Animal House, no one should enter the cages, including me," Cantor said, sitting in the living room recliner with his legs raised, avoiding her eyes. *I'm such an idiot!*

There was a nasty surprise for Kumiko in the closet. Spartacus had shredded some of her best dresses and ripped apart her walking shoes. An unusual odor clung to the carpet, where he apparently had marked his territory.

Cantor took a week off from work to give his wounds time to heal and cursed himself when he thought of how his complacency and false confidence led to Lily's injuries and his family's distress.

* * *

Kumiko was plagued with guilt over Cantor's injuries. *My fault. Why can't I keep these things from happening?* After all, she created or altered the genes in the raptors based on Arthur's computer simulations. Sometimes she would hug Cantor tightly, grateful he was there.

As she reviewed her lab notes, she couldn't find any errors. Slowly, her shame began to lift. In its place was a greater suspicion of Arthur's input. She wasn't completely onboard with the idea that improvements in the dinosaur's digestive system explained their increasing size. It certainly didn't explain the growing ferocity of the E7s. But she abhorred colleagues that pointed fingers at others. Her upbringing in Taiwan had drilled into her the necessity of taking responsibility for her actions. Because she had undertaken the dinosaur project, it was her responsibility, even if there was an error on Arthur's side. Honor dictated it was the CEO or the commanding general that took the heat.

Chapter 7

Walking Koko

Two weeks passed and George watched his dad head for the kitchen with his empty coffee mug. "We could play tic-tac-toe on your legs, Dad."

"Sure, George. Just what I need." The bandages were off now and Cantor's legs looked like a cutting board. George was still adjusting to his dad's jigsaw appearance. Two slashes below Cantor's right short pant leg formed a crescent moon.

"We could play under the moon," George continued.

"Funny, George."

"When you get undressed, you moon your moon."

Returning with his good hand holding a full cup, Cantor replied, "Ah yes. I remember adolescent humor. It once served me well." He eased himself slowly into the recliner with a sigh. "Sitting is such a luxury. I've missed it."

"It's a good thing you're married. If a girl saw you in your short pants, they'd think you were a nice man. But when you turn around, they'd run away."

"They wouldn't run away. They'd feel sorry for me."

"They'd think you were a knife fighter that lost a fight."

"You're a funny fellow," Cantor replied.

* * *

Later, during lunch at the dining room table, George finished his tuna sandwich and asked Cantor if he'd let him work with Spartacus. "I think I can reach him. Make him safe."

"No. You'd end up looking like me."

"Don't even think about it," Kumiko chimed in.

"Well, if I was kept in a cage by people, I'd get mad, too. That's the problem. If someone worked with him, it would be different. I could fix him."

"Nope," Kumiko said, emphasizing the "p".

"OK, not Spartacus. But maybe a C7 like Cronkite? Can't we put him on a leash in our backyard? We could trim his claws."

"George, maybe someday we can let an animal like Cronkite have his own place to run and do his thing. But we can't right now," Cantor said, taking a bite of his vegetarian delight – tofu salad.

"George, remember why we're moving the animals back to the university?" Kumiko reminded him.

"That's why I want to understand him. Maybe a little affection would change him. Maybe he could learn to trust me."

"Are we talking about Spartacus or Cronkite?" Cantor asked, sitting back and studying his son.

"Remember the black widow?" Kumiko added. "Remember how we talked about how you can break bad thoughts?"

"Yeah. But I'm talking about good thoughts."

"Why the big ones?" Cantor asked. "Why not a smaller friendlier one like that C5, Koko, or Kai?"

"Cantor! Please!" Kumiko said emphatically, shaking her head, giving him the stink eye.

"Yes! We could trim her toes and claws," George exclaimed excitedly.

"I suppose we could put a muzzle on her," Cantor mused out loud.

Both guys looked at Kumiko. She looked angry. Or fearful. Or both. "Cantor, you're the adult in the room. Please act like it." She picked up her dish and marched to the kitchen without another word.

* * *

A week later, Cantor examined his handy work. A dog's muzzle nicely covered Koko's snout, although she kept picking at it. Her sickle claws were shortened and rounded. It had taken several hours to file down the talons on her hands.

"Please come with us," he said to Kumiko that morning when she joined him in the garage. Koko trotted up to her, giving her a sniff.

"Nope."

"George can't wait. It'll be fun."

"I can't believe you are doing this."

"Please? I want you with me."

"This is crazy, Cantor."

"This will be fun for Koko, too."

"What if a dog attacks her?"

"I'll bite it for her."

"You're an idiot," she said, but a small smile suggested she was beginning to give in to the idea.

* * *

Cantor released Koko from her pen, securing her with a leash. She had the curiosity of a cat and the persistence of a dog. She pulled Cantor to a clump of rocks where she hopped to the top and surveyed her world. A chittering sound filled her throat the whole time. George laughed contagiously, and soon even Kumiko laughed. For a while, she tried to keep George from getting too near the twenty-pound Koko, but to everyone's surprise, Koko came to him. She jumped several times, reaching chest height and then ran ahead of Cantor.

"I guess when you haven't seen the world for 125 million years, you make up for lost time," Cantor said, running behind the little dinosaur.

Koko stuck her nose into every hole and bush. Occasionally, she'd flap her arms as though they were still wings. Pecking at the ground was another vestige of her chicken ancestry.

Kumiko was concerned when Koko ran back to Cantor and grabbed his leg.

"It's OK, she isn't hurting me," he said. "I think she's trying to get me to hurry."

Occasionally Koko would claw at her muzzle, then give up and continue her pursuit of the scents, colors, textures and all that the sweet sun laid before her. At one point, she raised her eyes to the sky and called out a long, melodious sound.

"I think she's calling for her own kind," Cantor said.

"Or just singing with joy," Kumiko said, smiling.

George showed Koko every bug he could find. Sometimes she'd place her hand on his, pulling the bug in for a closer examination. When he put a bug in her hands, it was apparent that her hand control wasn't especially good and often the bug would escape.

"Here you go, George," Cantor said, handing his son the leash. As he watched the human and the dinosaur stumbling after a lizard, he took Kumiko's hand.

Chapter 8

Arthur

Three days after the incident with Spartacus and Sherri, Arthur Saxton, in his Los Alamos office, sneered when he saw Peter Crawford's name on his phone screen. He saved his computer code and braced himself. *Damn bureaucrats!*

"I received an email from Doctor Chen," Crawford said. "She tells me the animals that grow from embryos implanted with genes designed by your computer are larger than expected. She said this is unsatisfactory. What do you have to say, Arthur?"

"I like working with Kumiko," Arthur said. "She's a talented scientist. But even she hasn't always been able to produce the genes specified by my programs accurately. That's my opinion."

"I want you to double-check your code. Also, rerun your simulations, so we are sure the results don't contain quantum errors."

Arther closed his eyes and rubbed his forehead. "I've already rerun the simulations, Peter. But I'll do what you ask. I'll also update the security on my files."

"You think someone is tampering with your code?"

"Not likely, but better safe than sorry."

"Thanks, Arthur," Crawford said and ended the call.

Arthur tossed his pen across the room. "Bitch!"

Chapter 9

Fire

After a few weeks and several more walks with Koko, Cantor was back to his old self; his injuries had healed nicely.

As his student, Tommy, arrived to clean the cages, he found graffiti painted on the outer wall of the pen building. He immediately phoned Cantor at the university.

"Damn. What does it say?"

"Diabolus operarius," Tommy answered, speaking the unfamiliar words slowly.

"Sounds like Latin," Cantor replied. "I think the first word means devil. Hold on, let me get a translation for the second word." While Tommy waited, he checked his phone. "The graffiti means 'devil worker'. Do you see anybody around?"

"Nope, I don't see anyone," Tommy answered.

"OK. If you feel unsafe, I want you to leave immediately."

"I'm not worried. I'll finish up and head back in a couple of hours. I'll let you know if I find anything else."

Cantor stuffed his phone in his back pocket and looked out his office window, deep in thought. Kumiko had received several more threatening letters over the last year. *This has to stop!*

When he got home, he checked the videos from the camera attached to the building. A figure in a hoody could be seen approaching and painting on the wall.

* * *

It didn't stop. Three days later, while Kumiko was reading poetry in bed and Cantor had just fallen asleep, he was awakened by a boom. He sat up as Kumiko ran through the bedroom door toward George's room. Cantor stumbled after her and saw that George was awake in bed. Despite the loud music in his earbuds, he'd also heard the boom and already had his feet on the floor.

Bolting out the front door, Cantor saw orange lights flickering on the grass and rocks beside the lawn before rounding the house and running the forty feet to the pens. He hardly felt the pain as stones gouged his bare feet. The wooden building was burning. Great flames crackled, shooting out swirling sparks that fled into the night. Inside, he heard the roars of the raptors. *Oh my God. No!*

Kumiko and George emerged into the orange light as Cantor ran past them toward the house again. Jumping over the water hose, which was too short to be any good, he rushed inside the house and grabbed the keys to the pens from his desk and dashed outside again. His legs couldn't move fast enough. The roars of the animals were becoming fewer, replaced by the roars of the fire.

Cantor fumbled with the building's lock as the smoke burned his eyes. The fire was getting closer. At last, he opened the door, but a cloud of hot, thick smoke rolled out of the building and pushed him back.

He bent over, coughing and hacking. "Are you OK!?" Kumiko cried with her hand on his back.

Cantor nodded, yes. There was still time, but the fire was spreading rapidly. She called 911.

Kumiko and George ran to the house and returned with a bucket of water and the kitchen fire extinguisher. George tossed the water and Kumiko emptied the extinguisher on the burning wall. By now, the fire was too big.

Cantor tore off his T-shirt and wrapped it around his nose and mouth. After inhaling deeply, he thrust himself into the doorway, groping for the larger fire extinguisher kept inside. He grabbed it. It was hot to the touch. Kumiko shouted after him, "No, Cantor! Get out of there!"

Squinting his eyes, he ran a short distance along the cages and sprayed the fire retardant into the creeping flames until the smoke drove him out of the building.

Again, despite his watering eyes, he entered, keys in hand, breaking away from Kumiko's grasp. The first cage's lock clicked, and he swung the gate open. Koko and her brother, Kai, moved toward the sound of his shouts in confusion, but no other C5s stirred. The two raptors ran outside after he pushed them toward the outer door.

Now dizzy, his mind screamed for him to keep moving. He crawled to the outer door and fell out, gasping for air. George and Kumiko pulled him further from the smoke.

"Give me the keys, Dad!"

"No. Get more water!" Cantor cried as he circled back toward the relentless fire. Kumiko put her arm around him.

"You can't go back there!" she shouted, clinging to him.

In a flash, George grabbed the keys from his dad and ran to the belching door.

"No, George!" both parents screamed. It was too late. George plowed through the door on his hands and knees.

Kumiko tried to follow, but Cantor pulled her back and crawled through the door after his son. The flames were moving along the building with frightening speed. *Please. Please.* "George, come out!" he croaked, crawling into the hellish smoke and heat. At last, he bumped into George on all fours, who was carrying a C7 on his back and coughing loudly. Cantor pulled him as far as the door where Kumiko grabbed his arms and dragged the boy and the unconscious dinosaur onto the ground. Cantor rolled on his back, gasping. Through the blur in his eyes, he saw George laying on his side, coughing.

Kumiko gave them both what little water was left in the bucket. George's hair was singed and the palms of his hands were burnt from the hot metal of the cage. He sat up and looked at Cantor, then the raptor.

"It's Moxi!" George cried in a raspy voice, looking at the young dinosaur's body lying still on the ground.

Kumiko knelt and placed her ear on the feathered chest. "I hear a weak beat! Cantor, can you get some more water? Oh, poor Moxi."

As Cantor stumbled to the lawn, George put his hand next to Moxi's nostrils. She wasn't breathing. "Mom! Help her!"

Kumiko placed her mouth over Moxi's and pushed life-giving oxygen into her lungs until Cantor returned with a pitcher of water. Gradually, Moxi began to respond, and her scaly head rose with swollen eyes. George hugged her, and both parents hugged him as he sobbed.

Moxi accepted a small drizzle of water poured slowly down her throat. The tips of her arm feathers were blackened. Cantor looked at Kumiko when George dipped his blistered hands into the buckets. Anger and fear surged through him.

"Help me!" Cantor cried as he leaned on Moxi to keep her from standing. "Kumiko, open the garage and drive both vehicles out! George, get the duct tape from the garage shelves!"

George returned just as Moxi panicked and bit Cantor's arm as he held her down. "Quick son, tape her legs," Cantor said, crying out as her sickle claw sliced into his bare leg.

George wrapped Moxi's ankles together, managing to avoid the big claws. She was getting stronger and more alert. With his knee gently on her neck, he taped her jaws shut, careful to leave the nostrils exposed. Her wrists were next, but the clenching talons made it difficult.

Cantor heard the second car screech to a stop in the driveway. In seconds, Kumiko was back. She held Moxi's thrashing head down while George finished applying more tape to her arms.

Cantor lifted the heavy dinosaur in his arms. Kumiko turned and rushed to the house after seeing the blood on Cantor's body. He laid Moxi on the garage floor.

"Now what?" George asked as Kumiko hurried back with bandages and rubbing alcohol.

"Let's close the garage door for starters," Cantor said, accepting an alcohol-drenched cloth from Kumiko.

* * *

Kumiko sat in a chair between George and Cantor's beds in the emergency room. A nurse practitioner stitched Cantor's leg wound where Moxi had slashed him. "Weren't you here last month?" the NP asked him.

"What can I say? I love this place," Cantor said with a grimace.

George's hands had second-degree burns, and he needed a shot of a strong painkiller on top of a tetanus shot.

The fire department put out the fire, which had begun to spread to the vegetation surrounding the pens. The only survivors were Moxi, Koko, and Kai. The latter two had gone rogue.

For the first time, the tragedy sank in. Kumiko sat in the hospital chair exhausted, shaking her head.

"There are some very disturbed people out there," Cantor growled as more local antibiotic was spread over his swollen arm. "I think people are more dangerous than the dinosaurs."

"Those poor animals suffered terribly tonight," Kumiko lamented. Her face was covered in soot and dried rivulets where tears had coursed. "If we didn't have the few C7s at Berkeley and Moxi, we would have lost years of work."

"Yeah. We have a few E7s there as well," Cantor said. "I'm pretty angry right now."

"Even Spartacus didn't deserve to die like that," George added. "I couldn't forgive myself if I hadn't tried…" His voice cracked. "…to save them."

Everyone was quiet.

Then Cantor said, "George, I appreciate all you did tonight. You were very brave, but you risked your life. Please don't ever do that again."

"Losing you would hurt infinitely more than losing the dinosaurs," Kumiko added, shaking her head as she looked at the gauze bandages on his hands.

George gazed at her blankly.

"George, please promise us," Cantor said.

"OK. I did what I had to do, though," he said with half-closed eyes.

"Are you OK, George?" Kumiko asked.

"Don't know."

"I think his painkiller has kicked in," Cantor said.

Kumiko rubbed her red eyes. "Are we bad parents?"

"No. Don't think that, Kumiko. I know how much you worry about George. We both do."

"That doesn't make us good parents."

Cantor looked at her. "I know. All we can do is try our best, right?"

"My mom was always home," she said. "When I woke up, she was there. She'd make breakfast. After school, she'd be there cooking our dinner."

"Those days are gone for most of us. I can't see either of us being anything but professionals."

Kumiko pursed her lips and said, "We'll have to search for Koko and Kai tomorrow. They could be miles away by now."

"Moxi is going to be a handful. I think we'll need to tranquilize her to get her back in a cage," Cantor sighed as the nurse finished the last suture. She was still in the garage. He looked at the bloody gauze on his legs and gagged, gripping his stomach.

* * *

Koko and Kai showed up the next morning. Unfortunately, they were only around long enough for Kumiko to chase them into a grassy field. With their heads bobbing up and down above the tall grass, they moved too quickly for her. They climbed a laurel tree with surprising ease, but before she could catch up, the raptors slid to the ground and the race was on again.

"You are being bad!" she cried, giving up. "Come home!"

Toward the end of the day, Kumiko spied the two lithe creatures hot on the trail of some poor mammal.

The next morning, Kumiko made a fire near the ruins of the pens from unburnt wood and, with Cantor's help, placed some rocks around it, narrow enough to set a frying pan on. Then she began making bacon, periodically picking up the pan to keep it from cooking too quickly. Within ten minutes, she and Cantor heard a high-pitched *chira-chira-who chira-chira-who* from the surrounding brush. Holding some bacon with metal tongs, she walked toward the sound.

"Oh, so now you want to visit Mom," she said when the two stepped from behind a bush, nostrils sampling the air. "Never mind how much worry you've caused me."

She walked toward their newly cleaned cage, surrounded by blackened wood. The escapees paused when she opened the cage door and watched as she laid the bacon in a bowl inside. Like hawks scanning for prey, their heads moved from side to side, assessing the situation as Kumiko stepped out of the cage.

"Go in, you naughty dinosaurs," Kumiko said, pointing at the bowl.

Koko trotted back to where Cantor had more bacon cooling in the pan, squawking when Cantor raised the pan above her jumping body. After several futile leaps and plaintive squawks, Koko noticed Kai had entered the cage and was wolfing down the contents of the bowl. With amazing speed, she raced into the cage and bit her brother's tail. As Kumiko closed the cage door, Koko let out a wailing sound, looking at her, then Kai, then back at her.

"Bring some bacon, Cantor, before Koko and I start crying."

* * *

Now was the time for healing: George's hands, Cantor's injuries, Kumiko's shock, and the pain they all felt in their hearts.

Cantor's confidence in the future waned for a time. Before the video camera had been destroyed in the fire, it recorded the hooded figure again that night. He watched people more closely. When two evangelicals rang his doorbell, Cantor angrily asked them to leave him and his family alone. They appeared shocked and unprepared for his outburst.

On another occasion, a boyish representative from Solar Satisfaction ignored the No Soliciting sign on the screen door and tried to interest Cantor in conversation.

"Do you see that sign?" Cantor said. "No soliciting."

"I'm sorry, sir. I guess I missed it."

"It's written in plain English."

"My apologies. I'll be quick."

"Perhaps I should have a sign written in Latin. Do you read Latin?"

"What? No. No, sir. I'm afraid I don't."

"What do you want?"

"Um, well, I'm glad you asked. I…"

"No!"

"Um. Perhaps I could speak to you about developments in solar…"

"Just like the no soliciting sign, the panels on my roof are plain to see."

"I… Yes, you're right. If I may, Solar Satisfaction has some hot new deals on upgrades and…"

"I'll bet. Real hot. Like to play with matches by any chance?"

"I don't believe so." The young man looked confused.

Cantor sighed and looked at his feet. "I'm sorry. Caught me on a bad day."

"I'll be happy to come back at a better time."

"No!" Cantor said and began to shut the door.

"I'm so sorry, sir," the young man said with wet eyes. "I don't mean to bother people. I'm trying to pay for my tuition. I'll go now."

Cantor looked at the kid as if for the first time. "See this on my arm? See the scars on my legs? I've had a bad month."

"Dang, mister."

Cantor pulled out his phone. "What is your username on Venmo?"

"Um… That's not…"

"Username please," Cantor repeated. With the required information, Cantor transferred money to cover some of the kid's school supplies.

"Have a good day, son."

"Yes, sir. Um, thank you, sir."

A week passed without an improvement in Cantor's mood. He cursed whenever he watched another video of domestic terrorism or an actor's testimony that slime from Hawaiian snails cured arthritis and an upset stomach. But eventually, Cantor's wounds, along with his spirits, healed, and he returned to his old self.

* * *

With Moxie, plus the C7s and E7s at the university, Kumiko and Arthur eventually continued their work. In late 2035, the research "birds" were pure dinosaurs on the outside in just about every way, although work on the inner organs still remained incomplete. Called the 8s, they were bigger than the 7s in size.

Cantor distinguished the two varieties of this iteration and it became customary in academic circles to refer to the devolved chickens as C-raptors, and the devolved eagles as E-raptors.

"They're magnificent," Cantor said, admiring the caged C8s in Kumiko's lab. Moxi was attentive to each chick. "I've estimated that the C-raptors and E-raptors will grow to the same size, over four feet tall at the hips and eight feet long."

"Why am I not surprised?" Kumiko said, sounding resigned.

"Except for the largest bears and cats, these will be the biggest predators on land anywhere."

The chicks now hatched within the enclosure with the mother. This prevented them from imprinting on humans. As a result, none of the 8s considered Kumiko their mother.

All the dinosaurs were kept in Animal House except when Kumiko needed them in the lab. Behavioral differences between the C-raptors and the E-raptors became more apparent in the latest generation, especially as they grew larger. The E-raptor juveniles fought with other E-raptors in their cage and would exhibit more extreme stalking behaviors with their captors. The E-raptor males were especially dangerous.

Cantor's vision of a large fenced range for the dinosaurs, where they could run and hunt, was stronger than ever.

Chapter 10

Corruption

A year earlier, in 2034, Arthur, at Los Alamos, received an unwelcome call. He was developing a new section of code for the latest quantum computer being used to guide Kumiko's genetic manipulations. "Dammit," he said, as his train of thought shattered against the unyielding chiming of his wrist phone. When he understood who was calling, his demeanor changed.

"Let's meet," was all the heavily accented Russian voice said.

"No problem. I'll meet you for lunch in Santa Fe, our usual place." Arthur tapped the screen and his wrist phone disconnected.

What does he want? Maybe he has something for me. With his concentration broken, he saved the code for another day. He decided to travel by ground car. Although it was much more fun to fly in the Peregrine, it meant having to log his flight with Santa Fe and Los Alamos. Better to remain less noticeable and take his Tesla with its dark windows.

He ignored the rugged cliffs and mountains as he neared the Española Valley. His mind was full of thoughts about money and resentment. *Someone with my talent shouldn't be asked to do this or that. If anyone should be making requests, it's me.*

In Santa Fe, he could get a great New Mexican meal at Tia Sophia's. After the car parked itself, he walked a couple of blocks to the restaurant. He knew to never make it obvious where you were. The sun heated his head and made his eyes squint. He hated the sun. It reminded him of the time his dad had locked him out of the parked car in 105-degree heat for three hours while he napped behind the wheel.

Arthur saw Yuri sitting at a table with a cup of coffee, motioning him over. The window silhouetted the big man, hiding his features.

"How're things, Saxton?" Yuri asked in a quiet but deep voice once Arthur was seated. Arthur winced at being addressed by his last name. He preferred Doctor Saxton.

"Good. I assume you received my last correspondence," he answered.

"Yes. It was very helpful. Next time, you'll leave your correspondence under the first bench in Valdez Park in Española. We don't want to get sloppy."

"Of course. I'm a very meticulous man," Arthur said, checking his nails.

"My boss wants you to get more specific about the quantum chips."

Arthur began to speak, but stopped when Yuri tapped his hand. A server stepped up and topped off Yuri's coffee. "Would you like to see the menu?" she asked Arthur.

"Just water, thanks," he said with a frown. After the server left, he continued, "You've got to understand, Yuri. I'm a writer of intelligent software. I didn't design the computer chips." He noticed Yuri's eyes harden.

"Surely there are others at Los Alamos that know more about chip architecture," Yuri said. "Time to get a little more social, Saxton."

"All right, all right, I'll see what I can do," Arthur replied, sounding bored. "I can tell you a lot more about the dinosaurs."

Yuri leaned back in his chair with a smirk. "We can read publications as well as you. We want you to include more gene designs to make the dinos bigger in your computer simulations for Doctor Chen. The boss wants big and aggressive animals."

"I've already been doing that. The eagle-derived animals are big and mean as hell," Arthur said.

Yuri leaned forward, pushing his coffee aside. "It's not enough. Not only does the boss want giants, but he also wants to see extreme fierceness. Animals that shock us with their cruelty."

"Cruelty? I'm not sure there is a gene for that. What kind of person wants animals to be cruel?"

There was an uncomfortable pause. "I assume you aren't criticizing your benefactor. That would be foolish," Yuri said, as his steel-blue eyes bored into Arthur's. "Some people admire deadly and powerful animals. For a wealthy individual, it can be a status thing. 'Hey, I hear you have a real dinosaur in the basement. One that's big and deadly. Can I see it?' Those are the animals that bring a hefty price. Anyway, no more questions. Be happy with what you're paid. Speaking of which, I'll transfer some cryptocurrency to your account after our meeting."

Arthur grimaced. He loved the money, but when Yuri paid him, it was Yuri who was in control. *I'm not some clever monkey getting his reward for a brilliant performance!*

"And Saxton, try not to be so obvious when you spend it. Buying that Peregrine aircar wasn't smart."

"Listen, aircars are going to be ubiquitous within five years. Anyway, with my hard work, I deserve it. I don't think you appreciate genius."

"Your benefactor is concerned, Saxton. He is not someone to be trifled with. Play it smart."

Chapter 11

Cantor as Mom

2036 was the year Kumiko introduced the 9s to the world. Her relationship with Arthur became more strained. He hinted that she needed to improve how she organized the controller genes in charge of turning on and off other genes at critical times. Occasionally, Cantor brought a C9 youngster home for observations, but never an E9.

She and Cantor continued to receive threatening letters, which they reported to the police. No one came forward to claim responsibility for the destruction of the pens.

* * *

Life didn't get any easier for George. In that same year, he turned fourteen and took Sherri to a dance. His parents hoped they would continue to date, but it didn't happen.

George missed taking Koko for walks. After the destruction of the pens, she and her brother, Kai, lived at Animal House, where George visited them often. As Cantor and Kumiko's son, he was allowed in free of charge. During one winter visit, an E8 in a nearby cage got a claw into the palm of his proffered hand. He reluctantly told his parents that he'd fallen on a piece of wood with a screw sticking out of it.

George tried climbing the tallest tree at school. He survived, but Mom and Dad had to meet with the principal. When he was caught during a weekend trying to climb the university's South Hall, his doctor upped the dosage of his medications.

2037 was the year a stray dog bit George despite his friendly overtures. Because the dog wasn't seen again and couldn't be tested for rabies, George needed to have the shots. This was also the year he landed a belly flop off a high dive for the first time. His behavior sometimes went to extremes. He was punched in the face when he dared himself to tell a bully that he didn't deserve his girlfriend – a girl George didn't even know.

For George, adolescence was a struggle.

* * *

2038 was special. It was the year Kumiko completed the last iteration of the dinosaurs.

Whoa, there's one hatching now, Cantor observed while substituting for Kumiko in her Lab. She was back home with a nasty cold. The grad student in attendance had just left for lunch. *I can do this*, he thought.

A C10 chick had begun poking a hole in the egg. It would be designated C10-3 since it was the third chick to hatch. He'd never watched the process, and he began taking notes. To study it more closely, he took the egg to a table covered with soft carpet.

Cantor spoke into his wrist phone.

"Time 11:42 a.m.: C10-3 has broken part of its shell. It's using a sickle claw to pierce the shell. Making a squawking sound.

Time 11:52 a.m.: C10-3 resting inside the egg. Hole in shell 1.2 centimeters. More squawking now.

Time 12:02 p.m.: C10-3 has enlarged hole to 2.5 cm.

Time 12:16 p.m.: C10-3 head has emerged.

Time 12:24 p.m.: C10-3 chick free of egg. Not moving much. Sickle claw on the inside of each foot – larger than expected.

Time 12:26 p.m.: C10-3 trying to stand.

Time 12:29 p.m.: C10-3 walking toward me. Green eyes are open. Making a cooing sound.

Cantor used his finger to nudge the chick and stimulate it. He touched its wet downy body, then its snout. *There you go. You aren't alone, don't worry, you'll be well taken care of.*

Time 12:38 p.m.: C10-3 cooing sound continues. Dried with a towel. Used my hand to stimulate it.

I really should stop. Let the mom take over. But this is too awesome.

Time 12:45 p.m.: C10-3 doesn't struggle when picked up. Chick likes to be held. Actually, tasted my hand with its tongue. Smelling my arm then looked at my face.

The grad student returned. "Whoa. Doctor Chen wouldn't be happy if she knew you were picking up newborns."

"Right. You're right. I shouldn't have done that. I'll mention it to her tonight," Cantor said, placing the chick back in the cage. He resumed speaking into his phone.

Time 12:58 p.m.: C10-3 chick placed in the cage with the C9 mother.

Time 01:07 p.m.: C10-3 moves towards me when I move around the cage. The other two chicks watch but don't approach.

Cantor knew, beginning with the C7s and E7s, Kumiko always left the hatchlings with the mother. Only the mother was allowed to stimulate the chick. *Who can resist?*

* * *

That evening, as Cantor put his jacket in the closet, he picked up the scent of cough medicine in the air. "How're you feeling?" he asked Kumiko.

"Pretty clogged up. I hate staying home with a cold. Thanks for helping in the lab while I'm out." Kumiko lay on the couch with half-closed, red eyes. Her long hair needed a brush.

"We can land people on Mars but we can't cure a common cold," Cantor said, slipping his shoes off.

"How was your day?"

"Three chicks hatched. I took notes on C10-3. It's a beautiful little dinosaur."

"I wish I'd been there."

"It was really interesting. The chicks are big. The sickle claws are bigger relative to body size as well."

"I need to get well and find out more." Kumiko sounded worried. "Do you realize how dangerous this will make the animals?"

"I'm afraid I do," Cantor said. "On the other hand, these guys look just like *Utahraptors* now. I don't know what you or Arthur did to increase the size, but it's kind of cool. Anyway, it was fun to watch one hatch. This was my first time as a hatching assistant."

"It's an amazing process," Kumiko said, eyes closed, sounding distracted.

"I stimulated it with my finger and it responded well."

Kumiko sat up; her eyes wide. "You did!? You can't do that!"

"Well..."

"Well, you're a MOM now. That little chick just imprinted itself on you, Cantor. Congratulations," she said with a frown. "Now you'll need to visit it daily for it to continue to feel secure. It's bonded to you and only you."

"I guess I got carried away." *Whoee! That was so cool!*

Kumiko shook her head. "We try to leave the hatchlings with their biological mother so they'll imprint on her. I'll determine the gender when I return to work," she said, reaching for a tissue.

"Well, I'll be damned. I'm a mom."

* * *

Two days later, Kumiko had gotten over her cold. "It's a female, Cantor. As the on-site hatching assistant, you get to name her," she said, walking into his office.

"How about, Maryann, in honor of Mary Anning, the 19th-century British fossil hunter?"

"Maryann it is."

Chapter 12

An Unholy Bond

"That's right. Come on out, big boy. Here, I can help," Robert Greaves, Kumiko's lab tech said, coaching the E10 as it hatched.

"There you go. Put those little claws around my finger and I'll get you out of there." Robert began cutting some of the leathery eggshell with a pair of scissors. Finally, free, the chick stared at Robert with its orange eyes, absorbing his scent and appearance.

"You're gonna be a very big boy. Yes, you are." With gentle hands, he cleaned the chick as carefully as a mother would, keeping an eye on the door in case someone returned. He noticed a defect that exposed some of the chick's teeth on one side of its mouth. "Crap. You're damaged goods. I guess you'll have to do." He continued to stimulate the chick.

Robert jerked his head up. He could hear Kumiko speaking to someone outside the closed door of the lab. Quickly, he grabbed the chick and the remains of the egg and placed them inside the large cage that housed the five-foot-high mother. Kumiko entered just as he stepped away.

"Well, Robert, this makes five hatchlings so far," Kumiko said, looking into the cage.

"Yeah, do you want to do the gender test now?"

"Not yet. Let's be sure the chick is imprinted on Mom first. Now, I need to prepare for my morning class," she said and turned toward the lab door, waving goodbye with one hand over her shoulder.

That afternoon, Kumiko returned to the lab and found Robert still there. "Robert, you're putting in some long hours."

"You know me, I want to be where the action is."

"Let's see, lets determine the gender," Kumiko continued. "OK, little one," she said to the chick Robert had handled in the morning. "I'll just take a teeny blood sample. But first, let's get Mommy behind these bars." She flipped a switch and a second inner wall of bars slowly pushed the growling three-hundred-pound E9 mother toward the side wall of the cage to immobilize her. The only time such a large dinosaur was allowed in the lab was during egg hatching.

To Robert, she said, "Even with a sedative in her, I'm not taking any chances." Gently, she pricked the chick's tail and collected a tiny drop of blood. "Poor little guy has a mouth defect."

Kumiko put the sample into a small device from her lab coat and looked at the result. "We have another boy. That makes two in all."

Robert spoke into his phone. "Male E10-5 hatched 7:06 a.m., June 7, 2038." Later, he'd upload the information to the main file Kumiko kept. "I'll get your weight now."

E10-5 didn't fret when Robert picked it up. It rested the sickle claw on his hand without attempting to cut the flesh. After he weighed the chick, he spoke into the phone. "E10-5 Weight 0.272 kg or 0.9 pounds. Informal name – Cain."

He put his phone away. *They'll get a kick out of his name.*

Chapter 13

Exponential Growth

The raptors grew by leaps and bounds. George spent a lot of his Christmas break in Animal House. Both he and Cantor marveled at the powerful arms and legs of the dinosaurs. Maryann made cooing sounds whenever Cantor visited her. Her brothers, Darwin and Bruce, were slightly larger and full of spunk. They would run back and forth in the Animal House open area, searching for an opening.

Maryann and her brothers could coexist in the same space without attacking each other. George had no doubt that the C10s yearned to explore the world unrestrained. He fantasized how the dinosaurs would look racing through forests and meadows after prey.

Although George loved Maryann and her brothers, he was inevitably drawn to the bigger E10 male, Cain. The deformity that exposed some of his gums and teeth made him terrifying, even at this young age. *Put the bad thoughts in a box and slip it under the bed of your mind.* That's what the therapist said. His OCD didn't care, and he continued to expose himself to Cain's savagery, testing his own limits. Somewhere in his mind, he knew that the only way to stop obsessing about terror was to expose himself to it.

Remus, the other E10 male, was as big as Cain, but when the two of them were in the open space together, there was no doubt who was dominant. Remus would signal his subservience to Cain by lowering his head, flattening the red feathers atop his head, and closing his hands. Circe and Medusa, the E10 females, kept their distance from the males while in the open space. Sometimes, like a nuclear reaction, when the E10s were close together, there was an explosion of violence.

* * *

After several months, it was apparent that the 10th iteration raptors weren't just going to be bigger than the previous iterations. They were going to be huge. Kumiko discovered two genetic anomalies. She didn't understand the function of a mysterious gene that was now part of the E10s' DNA. In addition, both types of dinosaurs had an extra growth gene with several base pairs reversed.

Did I cause this? Where did I mess up? She could see her mother shaking her head and telling her she wasn't trying hard enough. When she had earned a good school grade, but not an excellent one, the disappointment at home was crushing. The worst she could do was to blame it on someone or something else. So, she checked and rechecked her methodology, but it seemed to be correct. *It has to be Arthur!*

* * *

In the lab, Kumiko looked at the results of an fMRI scan done on Cain and Remus showing abnormalities in the area of the brain associated with controlling anger and aggression in dinosaurs and birds. She opened her laptop and called Arthur.

"First the good news," she said to Arthur's image on the screen. She noticed his thinning hair and the bags under his eyes. Several lab assistants listened from their workstations. "The C10s and E10s show no signs of auto-immune diseases like we've seen in all the previous iterations. They also have great hand-eye coordination. Their bodies are better balanced and their sense of smell is as good as any predator. Hand coordination is excellent. We don't know much about their behavior in the wild yet, but physically they are superb. Their internal organs are functioning well. However..."

"I knew there would be a 'however'," Arthur said tiredly.

"Something has gone wrong, Arthur. Seriously wrong. The young are growing abnormally large, and I've found some genetic problems. There are also some brain abnormalities in the E10 brains. I've checked and rechecked my procedures. The error seems to be on your end."

She heard a scoff as air passed through his nose. "My code is correct, Kumiko," he said. "If it makes you happy, I'll review it again. This shouldn't be happening."

"You keep saying that," she said, exasperated.

"You and I know we are pioneers, Kumiko. Nobody has done what we're doing. There are bound to be kinks in your methods."

"The C and E-raptors are big, but the E-raptors are also hyper-aggressive. Cantor and I are concerned. I think we need to stop developing any more dinosaurs until we get this under control."

"Whoa. Relax. Isn't this what we wanted, Kumiko? Real dinosaurs?"

"We do, but ones that we can handle. Think about it. Researchers use mice because they are small, safe, and breed quickly. Cantor has been attacked by the E7s, and they weren't as aggressive as the E10s are. I'm going to dig deeper into what some of the newer genes are doing. I want to know what proteins or enzymes they produce and how the brain is affected."

"Kumiko, the computer already knows all that. You'd be reinventing the wheel. You have better things to do. As for Cantor, perhaps he needs to polish up on his safety procedures."

"Cantor knows what he's doing," she said, suppressing her anger. "Given the jump in aggressiveness in the E10s over the E9s, I have to ask. Did you include genes for increased aggressiveness in your instructions for the E10s?" She carefully observed the tone of his voice and the movement of his eyes.

"No, I didn't! That is cold!" There was a pause, and he returned to his soothing tone. "Don't give up. Think of what you've accomplished. You've made quite a name for yourself. Think about all the amazing dinosaurs you'll make in the future. T. *rex* perhaps? Let me work on things from here. I'll certify there isn't a bug in my software."

"Arthur, I don't care about making a name for myself. That's not why I do this."

"I'll come see the raptors in person," he said, as though he was being asked to clean up her mess. "I need to verify what you're saying."

Kumiko was quiet.

After a long pause, Arthur said in a patronizing manner, "And, yes, I'll review my code."

* * *

The next day, Arthur flew in his aircar to Berkeley to inspect the animals himself. He and Kumiko walked to Animal House from the landing area.

"Wow!" he said, seeing the C10 dinosaurs for the first time in the flesh. "Ha! You're right, Kumiko. These guys are going to be pretty damn big. Mind if I take some photos?"

"Please do. Anything to help us understand what's happening," she replied, looking at the C-raptors. They were already the size of a pheasant, but longer, 6 feet in length and 1.8 feet at the hip – the size of a true *velociraptor*, not the kind in the movies. Occasionally an E-raptor would growl or hiss, but the C-raptors were calmer, mostly sitting in their cages watching the humans.

Their necks were long, like a monitor lizard's, topped by a head filled with sharp conical teeth. The backside of the muscular arms had large, brown feathers, while the fingers of the hands were as long as the head, ending in claws like an eagle's talons. A light brown down covered their bodies to the tip of the ringed tail, where longer feathers made the raptor seem even bigger. Like ostriches, they walked on their toes with the rest of the foot serving as a springboard for rapid acceleration and speed.

The males sported feathers on their heads that extended down the back of their necks, resembling a mohawk when raised. Green scales covered their faces and brown scales cascaded down their long feet like armor plating.

"Let me see the E10s," Arthur said.

"Right this way."

Arthur looked at the growling one named Cain. He took many pictures, but especially of Cain's eyes. He seemed to have a special interest in those. "This bad boy is something else."

Kumiko watched him with growing unease.

* * *

The next day, Kumiko visited Cantor in his office.

"I'm unhappy with Arthur," Kumiko began, drinking a cup of tea. "The more I think about our conversations over the last few days, the more I don't trust him."

Cantor pondered this. "I don't know. What does he have to gain by messing up our work?"

"I don't know. But I don't think I'm being paranoid."

"I'm not suggesting that. It's just that we need him, Kumiko. Granted, he's weird and arrogant, but without him and his computer, we wouldn't have accomplished all this."

"Don't you think I know that?"

Cantor realized he needed to give more thought to what she was saying.

Kumiko took another sip of the hot brew. "I brought some photos from Animal House. Penny wanted us to know that the E10s have some sores on their snouts from rubbing against the cages." She handed them to Cantor.

"Hmm. We need to get these guys out of those damn things."

"Look at the second photo. George is in it."

The picture showed George leaning past the outer protective chain, giving Maryann a treat through the bars. "I thought he understood not to get close to the cages," Cantor said.

"I think Penny took the photos to tell us that George is too trusting." She let Cantor study the photo.

"He shouldn't be feeding the animals. We've both spoken to him about this," she continued, standing to one side of his office desk.

"I'm going to talk with him. He needs to stay out of Animal House," Cantor said after some thought. "Really, nobody should be in there except trained personnel."

"I agree. But a 16-year-old finds a way," she said. "I'll feel better when he starts his university classes in a few years. At least then we can keep an eye on him."

"All that therapy hasn't improved his condition much," Cantor said, putting his feet on his desk. "I think he thinks the dinosaurs are his friends."

"Poor boy. He knows he's different," she said with a sigh. "We need to include him in our work, though. It's vital that he knows he's included."

Cantor noticed her eyes tearing up. Both parents were silent for a long time. Then Kumiko thrust out her chin, the way she did when faced with a challenge. She turned to leave, but stopped. "I forgot to ask you. How big do you think the 10s will get?"

He noticed her eyeing his shoes on the desk. "Brace yourself. I worked it out this morning. I estimated their growth rate and years until maturity and came up with 3,300 to 4300 pounds, depending on different assumptions. If they live longer than expected, they'll grow even bigger. It's so damn crazy. They may look like *Utahraptors*, but they're going to make the ground shake."

"Taking care of them will be challenging," Kumiko said, shaking her head. "How will we handle such dangerous animals a year from now? We aren't set up for this."

Cantor was quiet.

"I'm even more determined not to make more iterations now, Cantor. We can't make changes until Arthur figures out a solution," she said, crossing her arms. "Maybe someone tampered with his code."

Cantor could tell she was disappointed and frustrated. He took his feet off the desk. "Forget the E10s. Let's focus on the C10s. Except for their size, these dinosaurs are accurate."

"Cantor, what am I supposed to tell other geneticists? 'We were in complete control of our modifications except for growth?' If we can't control growth properly, they're going to wonder what else we were lax about."

"I know," Cantor said. "Why don't we accept it, though? Big or small, you've brought something back to life from 125 million years ago. I think you deserve the Nobel Prize."

"We brought back Goliath, not David. I don't want to work with big dinosaurs. I want small ones for lab work and to show in class."

"I sympathize," he said and paused. "To be honest, though, I actually look forward to working with big dinosaurs. I guess I'm a big kid. We can handle big dinos if we can find a larger environment for them."

He looked at Kumiko as she gazed at the floor, wondering what she was seeing.

"I'm talking about the C10s," he said. "Not Cain, Remus, Medusa, and Circe. I don't want to work with them."

Chapter 14

Five Big Ones

2038 rolled into 2039. George became more daring as his OCD worsened. Cantor and Kumiko continued their studies of the final iteration of dinosaurs, and wrote several well received research papers. But many questions remained unanswered, especially regarding dinosaur behavior.

Kumiko tried to reverse the size of the dinosaurs by implanting genes that limit growth into C10 and E10 embryos. None of the experiments were successful and all the eggs failed to hatch.

Cantor concluded he needed to look outside the campus and the city of San Francisco to find a stomping ground for the C10s and E10s. By 2040, he'd put together a grant proposal to the National Science Foundation for purchasing some property on Alcatraz Island in the bay, but it didn't prove feasible.

That year, the C10, Bruce, succumbed to a virus and the E10, Medusa, died from kidney failure and sepsis from a self-inflicted wound, despite frantic efforts to save them. This left the two C10s, Maryann and Darwin, and three E10s, Cain, Remus, and Circe. Cantor was desperate to get the animals into a healthy environment.

The U.S. Congress declared that all C10s and E10s were extinct species under the new Extinct Species Act, even though they were bred animals not found in the wild. This put great pressure on Cantor and Kumiko. Unfortunately, Cantor's efforts to provide the best care possible were hampered when funds dried up because of the poor state of the economy.

In 2041, the C10s and E10s continued to gain weight at an astonishing rate. New cages were required to house them.

A wealthy rancher agreed to a onetime visit of Maryann and Darwin to her property, but the fences weren't adequate and the dinosaurs found a way into the nearby public land, creating havoc. A family on a picnic was forced to sit in their car as the pair gulped down their lunch. The media played the videos for days. Both dinosaurs had to be tranquilized and brought back to the university. Cantor's desperation increased.

In 2042, Cantor secured enough money to fortify the outdoor space by Animal House, which allowed the big animals to continue using it for a while. Eventually, they would be too large even for Animal House.

The urgent need to find a suitable home for dinosaurs stressed Kumiko. "I'm treading water," she told Cantor. "My head is above the surface, but I can't see what lies below."

* * *

George began taking courses at Berkeley in 2040 when he was 18 years old, in part so he could spend more time with the dinosaurs. The bigger and more dangerous, the better. Except for the C5 Koko. She was like a pet. George took it hard when her brother, Kai, died of an auto-immune disease in 2041.

George enjoyed his paleontology course but didn't do well with anatomy. He tried biology and chemistry, intending to follow in Kumiko's footsteps, but found they weren't to his taste. By 2042, he felt he was drifting until he took a studio art class, which was much more to his liking. Outside of class, he sketched the dinosaurs, trying to capture their expressions. Cain growled the whole time and never took his eyes off him. The more he studied the scales on Cain's face and the twisted flesh around the mouth, the more alien Cain seemed. But it was the eyes that hypnotized him. George would look into them, feel afraid, look away, and then repeat it all over again. The OCD wouldn't give him peace.

George matched Cantor's height in 2042. His shoulders broadened; his hands looked robust. But the moth in him continued to test the flames, especially with the dinosaurs. He loved Maryann and Darwin. But, as always, Cain haunted him.

Cain seemed to play with his emotions. George chatted with him when no caretakers were around. *He's finally warming up to me.* Slowly, he'd approach the cage. It crushed George when the inevitable snarl and roar came. But he kept trying.

* * *

On a spring day in 2042, Cantor was in his usual relaxed mode, feet on his desk, coffee in hand, when Kumiko walked in wearing her white lab coat. She looked at yesterday's opened Coke surrounded by papers on his desk. Next to it lay the sickle claw fossil he'd excavated many years ago.

"Did you get the email regarding our paper on dinosaur visual acuity?" Kumiko asked, hands in her lab coat pocket.

"I haven't seen it. I'll check my emails later."

"It was accepted. The publication will come out this summer."

"Great! It should settle some debates." He noticed a bandage on the back of her right hand.

"What happened to your hand?"

"Nothing serious. Cain got a talon through my glove. I thought he was fully tranquilized. Anyway, the publishers want a picture of the two of us working with the dinos. You'll look distinguished with the white hairs by your ears."

"I probably have a few inside my ears as well."

"Cantor, please take your feet off the desk. It looks unprofessional."

At first, Cantor ignored her, then thought the better of it, and lowered his legs to the floor. "I was just talking to Penny. She's annoyed with us for putting such big and dangerous animals in Animal House. The '10s' average weight now is 850 pounds. Penny is limiting their time in the open enclosure because of the E10's tendency to fight. She only lets one animal out at a time."

"She knows the '10s' are only going to get bigger." Kumiko said, shaking her head.

"Watching the '10s' is like being in a time machine," Cantor said. "I tried to estimate the size of their sickle claws. Despite their youth, the claws are already nearly as big as the fossil Alex prepared."

Kumiko brightened. "How's Alex doing?"

"He wishes he could land a position here at Berkeley. He knows this is where the action is."

"It would be nice to see him again," Kumiko said.

Cantor paused. "I hate to see Maryann in a cage. She's my baby."

"Pretty big baby," she replied. "But you've been a wonderful mommy. How's our sick C9?"

"I just got the call from Animal House before you arrived. I wanted to wait to tell you. Zorro died from his infection."

Kumiko sighed. "Oh no. The poor guy suffered so much."

"Yeah. We knew this was coming. The seizures were rough on him. And the damn flu."

"The vaccine didn't work for him," she said, shaking her head.

Cantor stared at his feet. "That leaves Koko, Moxie, that E8 Vlad, and the C9s Pebble and Mascara among the earlier iterations."

"I love the good moms, Pebble and Mascara," she said, sighing. "I feel we're neglecting those earlier iterations. All our attention is on the biggies: Maryann, Darwin, Circe, Remus, and Cain."

Cantor nodded. He'd always loved the black scales around Mascara's eyes.

"Any progress in finding them better quarters?" she continued.

"No. We need to find open space for these guys fast if we want them to remain healthy," Cantor said, shaking his head and looking out the window. "If we want them to reproduce."

"I assume we are talking about places near San Francisco," Kumiko added. "Maybe East Bay or Marin County?"

Cantor looked out the window. "Money is tight and land here is incredibly expensive. Our government grants are running out."

Kumiko played with her dragon necklace, a worried look on her face.

"And the offers from wealthy donors all have strings attached. It doesn't look good, Kumiko." When he noticed her nervously twirling her hair, he got up, took her hand, and eased the door closed. He looked into her eyes, then hugged her. "I don't know what to do."

At first, her body was stiff. Then she slowly lowered her head to his shoulder and pulled him closer.

Chapter 15

Cain

B y 2043, Cain, still a youngster, weighed 1,600 pounds and could no longer use Animal House's protected open-air enclosure.

"All right, big fellow," Günter Abelmann said, grunting as he opened the gate of the fence to get closer to Cain's cage. *This arthritis is bad today.* The harsh bluish light inside Animal House assaulted his eyes like ice water on his skin. "Ya don't have to worry, I'm not gonna bite ya." Günter smiled at his little joke as he pushed and pulled his broom, always keeping his distance from the cage. He hummed a song from his homeland, *Wenn Ich Ein Vöglein Wär* (If I Were a Little Bird).

The building seemed hotter than normal. Ventilation Issues had occurred during the day. Günter, beginning to sweat, removed his coat and laid it on the chain barrier.

The big dinosaur roared and reached for him, but the bars were too close for his entire hand to pass.

"Listen, *mein* Dino. Ya see me every day. Why do we have to go through this each time?" he said in his heavy accent, shaking his head. As he swept the dust and dirt of the day, he continued his humming. He stopped when he heard a thud. Turning, he saw the dinosaur on the cage floor, not moving, with two fingers outside the cage.

"*Ach du lieber!*" He poked the body with the broom's handle. "Hey. Hey. *Herr* Cain, wake up! Oh, *mein Gott!*" He tugged at his pocket, trying to pull his old phone out. "This is not good. Greta, call Doctor Chen."

Greta's circuits complied, and he heard Kumiko answer.

"Doctor Chen, this is Günter Abelmann at Animal House. *Herr* Cain is sick. I don't know, he is maybe dead."

"Oh my God. Is he breathing? Do you see his side moving?"

"I don't think so."

"Stay back! I'm on my way!" It was lucky she'd chosen to work late that night.

"Come on now. Ya have to breathe." Günter said, prodding Cain's stomach with the bristle end of his broom. *Maybe he's choking.* He got down on all fours and tried to peer through the bars into Cain's open mouth. *Well, he hasn't swallowed his tongue.* The dinosaur's angry orange eye, with the secondary eyelid halfway closed, stared at nothing. The feathers atop and behind his head were flat against his skin.

It is so hot. Could it be heatstroke? He needs water! The only nearby water was in the bucket he planned to use for mopping. It was clean but soapy. Although it was warm, it was all he had to cool Cain down.

He rolled the bucket toward the cage and lifted it, but it was heavy and the water just spilled on the concrete. Günter thought he saw Cain's eye flicker and his fingers twitch, but on closer examination, the movement was gone. He tried again, tossing the water into the cage with all his might, but lost his balance and slipped on the wet floor, his legs sliding against the steel bars.

In a flash, two claws from Cain's exposed hand pierced his lower leg, causing Günter to scream and try to pry the fingers off him. Cain rose and dug his clawed finger into Günter's thigh. With a swift jerk, Cain slammed Günter's body against the bars of the cage.

One finger disengaged from Günter's thigh and hooked into his shoulder. Then the other arm's fingers latched onto the other shoulder, lifting the struggling man upwards against the metal bars.

Cain hissed into Günter's terrified face, turned his toothy head, and brought one orange eye two inches away from Günter's. The man squirmed and gasped. The eye seemed to glow like an ember around the black pupil.

A deep, rumbling growl emerged from inside the dinosaur's throat.

The pain in his shoulders was unbearable. Günter smelled the dinosaur's stale breath, and the roars made his ears ring.

Cain pressed his head and teeth hard against the narrow bars, trying to get at Günter's neck. Günter hung like a rag doll suspended by the sharp talons.

Kumiko ran into the building, yelling, "Cain! No!" She grabbed an electric cattle prod from the wall and ran toward the cage as Cains's claws ripped away part of Günter's shirt, scoring his flesh. He let the man drop and backed away, having felt the prod's pain before. Kumiko grabbed what was left of Günter's shirt and dragged the barely conscious man away.

Cain calmly and innocently sat and used his hands to groom his sides. The only evidence of his attack inside the cage was a torn and bloody piece of Günter's shirt. Outside the cage, there was plenty of evidence. In the harsh light, the streaks of blood looked purple where Günter's body had been dragged like a murder scene. The dinosaur began playing with a scrap of the bloody shirt, picking it up and dropping it like a new toy.

Upon seeing the bloody puncture wounds on Günter's body, Kumiko called for an ambulance. The wounds on Günter's body were deep, but they didn't pierce any arteries. He'd be OK.

"I'm so sorry, I'm so sorry," she said, sitting beside the now delirious man.

Günter kept repeating, "*Cain ist aus der Hölle*," as Kumiko held his head. By the time the ambulance arrived, her shaking was more under control.

* * *

"Oh, my God! Poor Günter," Cantor said, wide-eyed, after Kumiko came home and told of Cain's attack. "That's absolutely horrifying! We've got to do something about Cain."

"And then, Cain just sat back as if nothing had happened!" Kumiko exclaimed.

"That's eerie. How is Günter now?"

"They plan to keep him at the hospital for several days. Hopefully, he doesn't develop an infection. He's such a sweet man. I'm worried about his emotional state."

Cantor shook his head, imagining the horror. "I'm going to visit him today after my last class."

"I'll join you. He was so terrified," Kumiko said, lowering her head.

"What do you think about medicating Cain so he's not so dangerous?" Cantor asked. "Could we put a sedative in his food every day?"

"It's that, or we illegally put him down," she said.

"I'm for putting him down." Cantor added, "But the administration won't go for it. Surely now the administration will at least insist the public can't view Cain anymore."

"Don't hold your breath. He's the reason many people pay to see the dinosaurs. We need to put wire mesh all around the E10 cages. Even the C10s to be safe." Kumiko said.

"Agreed."

She shook her head. "I feel so badly for Günter. He was always careful around the animals."

Cantor thought about this. "That's true. How did this happen?"

"That's just it. I have no idea. I'm going to look at the Animal House videos from last night. I'm sure Günter will also have a lot to say," Kumiko said. "He kept repeating *Cain ist aus der Hölle*."

Cantor looked at her and grimaced. "Cain is from hell all right!"

Chapter 16

Through Another's Eyes

GeORGE was now a junior enrolled in the Fine Arts program at Berkeley.

Holy crap, he thought as he looked at the naked woman. She had her head turned, one arm on the chair's back, and legs crossed at the ankle. The other arm settled on a large embroidered burgundy pillow.

After a break, George tried to focus on his drawing when she resumed her pose, but now and then, he'd look at her and repeat *holy crap* in his mind. He'd only had one relationship with a woman when he was a freshman. Now, he was expected to stare at a naked lady without rubbing his mind in the gutter. But surprisingly, after a while, he admired the artistically lyrical curves of her body without the distracting urges from the reptilian part of his brain.

During the model's next break, George checked out how the other students were doing. A Native American woman with long, black hair sat nearby, studying her drawing. She drew the model fluidly, creating a dynamic image.

"That's nice," he said to her. "It has movement in it. I like it."

"Thanks. I try to capture the personality. The person's spirit."

"My name is George."

"Hi, George. I'm Luna."

He admired her turquoise bracelet. To keep up the conversation's momentum, he said, "This is my first time sketching a nude."

"I've had friends pose for me," she said.

"Oh, our model is back. Later."

Luna intrigued George. *I've never met a lady and discussed nakedness. I wonder how she feels about dinosaurs?*

* * *

A week later, George and Luna painted together outside the studio.

"This looks like a great spot," Luna said. "Those trees are so expressive. What do you think, George?" They studied the cypress, sycamore, magnolia, and Monterey pine trees surrounding the path just beyond the little meadow they stood in. To each side of the park were streets with various colorful apartment buildings displaying their unique San Francisco architecture. The traffic zipping by the small park contrasted with the peaceful setting.

"I see what you mean. I like the light. Let's paint," he said.

They painted the trees in the park for a couple of hours. George included Luna at her easel in his painting.

Toward the end, he looked at what she'd painted. "You captured something about these trees that I missed. They seem so alive and graceful."

Luna smiled. "I try to paint their essence."

Later, as they were packing up, Luna talked about artists who influenced her and workshops she had taken. George wanted to know all about her. The timing didn't seem appropriate for him to discuss the dinosaurs.

"Where did you take the workshops?" George asked.

"Taos, New Mexico."

"Are you from New Mexico?"

"My family has lived there for centuries. I'm from Owa'ke Pueblo."

"I'd love to visit there." *Crap, she thinks I want her to invite me.* "Hey, would you like to see some dinosaurs tomorrow?" he said, changing the subject.

"I've seen them on the news. They said no other scientists have been able to create what your parents created."

"Yeah. They got to use the world's most powerful quantum computer in Los Alamos as part of an experiment."

"It's all so strange. Recreating something that went extinct makes me a little uncomfortable."

"Would you like to travel back in time millions of years?"

Luna smiled. "When you put it like that, yes."

* * *

"Here we are. This is where they're kept," George said after entering Animal House the next day. He paid for her ticket. Luna followed hesitantly as her eyes adjusted to the darker interior and musty air. "They try to keep the lights down except when they're cleaning," he added.

"I've heard about your parent's work. Everyone knows about the dinosaurs," Luna said, taking in the interior structure with its high ceiling laced with metal crossbeams. Ventilation shafts clung to the steel walls, ending near the cages. Security bars shored up the few windows.

"Earlie generations had a limited life expectancy. This one is a female C5 named Koko," he said, looking at the turkey-sized animal. "She's not all that big as an adult."

Koko had short brown feathers on her back and a lighter shade on her belly. Her eyes were a radiant green, large and observant. She stood from where she'd been sitting and looked at the two humans, turning her head from side to side like a bird, her inner eyelid flashing several times. She slowly walked closer to her visitors with arthritic legs, making inviting chirping sounds, her arms resting on her chest.

"I like her. She seems calm. She looks exactly like the animals on that National Geographic special a few months ago. Do they ever let her out of her cage?"

"Yeah. I've taken her on walks when she was younger. We used to keep her in a pen near our house. She even escaped once."

"I didn't know you could take a dinosaur for a walk. That's wonderful!"

"Here, she spends time in the outside enclosure when it's available. She used to love running, but her legs don't work as well now. My mom has been trying different diets to help."

"It makes me sad to see her caged, George."

"Me too. You'll notice that as we walk past the cages, the animals get bigger. The last generation is getting enormous."

"Oh, look at this one," Luna said, walking toward a large metal cage. "I can't believe how big it is. The plaque says she's named Maryann." Next to the plaque were notes by the staff saying who fed her last, who cleaned her cage, and so on.

"She's only five years old," George said enthusiastically. "As you can see, she's very large. Let's see, the notes say she weighs about 1350 pounds and stands 5 feet 10 inches at the hip as of last month."

"She's magnificent." Then to Maryann, she said, "I'm sorry. You don't like your cage, do you?"

George sensed sadness in Luna. "According to my dad, she's going to get a lot bigger. I'm glad her cage is big enough for her to move about. My dad hopes to set her free in a large outdoor space someday."

"I think I'll like your dad. Is she dangerous?" Luna asked.

"Oh. Well, it depends. She's attached to my dad. But if I were to enter her cage, I wouldn't bet on my chances of surviving."

Luna noticed him getting close to Maryann's cage.

"Look at her hands. The fingers are so long. And those claws, my goodness. No wonder there's a fence around her cage." Luna said, stepping back and pulling George with her.

"Check out that enormous inner claw on each foot, Luna."

"She has power."

"That claw can do damage that no other living animal today can do. She's a land shark, only more intelligent. And yet, she loves to let my dad scratch her when she lowers her head by a small opening on the other side of the cage that the public can't see."

Luna looked keenly at her. "Look how she moves the big claw up and down. Kind of shocking. Almost like she's debating whether she'll need to use it."

"I know, right? It's like somebody tapping their finger while they think."

"She must have a strong spirit. We have dances at my pueblo that honor powerful animal spirits. My mother shows respect and practices the old ways."

"You seem very spiritual, Luna." There was a pause in the conversation. Feeling like he needed to say something, he asked, "Want to see more animals?"

"OK."

They passed a sign that said children were not allowed further. In the next cage, a large animal stood facing away from them, its striped tail swaying like a cat on edge.

"This is E10-5 Cain. He's the same age as Maryann, but he weighs 1,600 pounds. He's big for his age. They keep him sedated because of his temper," George said.

In a flash, the beast turned and growled at Luna, its piercing orange eyes locked on hers. The deformation on one side of its head exposed long, knife-like teeth. It leaped to the bars, trying to get a clawed finger through the mesh.

"Oh!" Luna gasped as she stumbled backward. She began breathing heavily and whispered some words in a language that George couldn't understand.

"Are you OK, Luna?"

She lowered her eyes and wouldn't return the creature's intense glare. "We should go now." Quickly, she walked back to the exit.

"What's happening, Luna? Can I help?" George said, trying to keep up with her.

"I have to leave. Please George, now!"

"What happened?"

"In the ancient stories, there is a word for what I just saw," she said, stopping and looking into his eyes.

"What word?"

"In English, it means something like 'unnatural Searcher Demon'. There is something about that animal… It's very dangerous."

"Yes, for sure. It's very savage. But we don't need to be afraid. It can't get out of the cage."

"It would kill us in a flash if it did, George. You don't understand. It would do it even if it wasn't hungry. And it's not healthy to spend time around it."

"Why do you say this, Luna?"

"I can feel it. I'm sorry, George. I need to cleanse myself spiritually."

This was a bad idea, George thought. He remembered how his old friend, Sherri, had reacted. *When am I going to learn? I'm such an ass.*

* * *

George felt like he'd been gut-punched. As he watched Luna drive away, he pulled out his phone. "The drugs aren't working on Cain, Dad," George said with exasperation.

"Where are you?"

"Outside Animal House."

"What happened?" Cantor asked.

"Cain freaked my friend Luna out."

"Are you OK?"

"No. I feel horrible about it."

"I'm sorry, son. Your mom is working on a better sedative cocktail for the E10s, like Cain."

George kicked at the grass.

"It's puzzling though," his dad continued. "The sedatives worked fine when we've used them occasionally on the C10s."

George looked at the clouds overhead in frustration. "Dad, listen to me! I'm really upset! I wished I hadn't shown the dinos to her."

Cantor paused. "Why don't you come by my office? We can chat."

"I can't. I've got to take a test in Spanish."

"Soon then. We can talk soon."

"Luna thought he was a kind of demon."

"George, you know I don't believe in that stuff. He's just a ferocious animal."

"I'm not worried about what you think. It's what Luna thinks. Can't you send Cain to a zoo?"

"I'm sorry, George, I... I can't do that without administration approval and permission from the legislature," he said.

George sighed. "I thought Cain was being creepy, Dad. Like, not natural. He's beyond dangerous."

"Except for the terrible attack on Günter, we haven't had reports from other people."

George hung his head. "Well, Luna isn't going to report it to you. So, there could have been many incidents."

"The cage has been rebuilt to prevent him from getting his hands outside. We learned our lesson."

"He's really scary."

"You make a good point. I'm not trying to minimize Luna's unpleasant experience. I hope she doesn't think badly of you, son. Cain isn't your fault."

"Yeah, I know, Dad. I know how Cain worries you. I was stupid to think Luna would want to see him."

"Please, George. Don't say that. It wasn't stupid. How were you to know what would happen?"

George let out a long sigh.

After a pause, Cantor said, "The public shouldn't be allowed inside Animal House."

"I'm OK with that. I think it's good for them to see the dinosaurs. But can't you put Cain somewhere else?"

"Where?"

"What if he's really unhappy? You can't keep an animal that way," George said.

"Yeah. I've thought about this many times. It would be the same at a zoo and we can't euthanize him. Lawmakers made sure of that."

George remained silent.

"Did you know there are T-shirts with his image on them?" Cantor said. "It's his fierceness that attracts so many people."

"To them, he's just a circus act."

"I think you're right, son."

"Maybe I'm not the only one with Moth Syndrome. I've seen the T-shirts. Maybe he just needs to be let out of his cage more, somewhere safe. I guess anybody confined to a cage-like that would get pissed off," George mused.

"I agree with you, George. The fact is, we're stuck with him."

"Yeah, I get it, Dad. I think he's like one of those cage fighters. You know the ones I mean? People want to see the fiercest fighters. The crazier the better. It's that way with Cain."

"Exactly."

"All the press reports build him up to be some kind of super badass," George continued. "The videos that get the most hits are the ones of Cain."

* * *

After the phone call with George, Cantor thought of the earlier incident with George's friend, Sherri. *Poor George*, he thought, *every time he gets to know a girl, they have a terrible reaction to the dinosaurs.*

* * *

In the meantime, George went back to Animal House. He stood before the snarling dinosaur, deep in thought. Gradually, he put his hand out and moved closer to the cage. Cain eyed him. In a flash, he tried to grab George's hand, but the mesh between the bars, installed after Günter's accident, prevented it. Not meaning to tease Cain, but to satisfy some need he didn't understand, George put out his hand again.

* * *

That night, after dinner, George stood before the kitchen sink, running hot water into a dirty pot.

"Mom, do you know what I want? I want to get a double major: art and genetics."

For a bit, the only sound was from the water coming out of the tap.

"Art and genetics are an unusual combination," Kumiko said.

"I want to design a good dinosaur."

"If you're up for it, you'd excel as a geneticist. You know you're welcome to come see what I do at Berkeley."

"I'd like to make a dinosaur that's like a giant horse, but more powerful. Something that doesn't want to eat us. Something that would let us ride it."

Kumiko looked at George. She could see he was serious. But she knew George was an artist, not a scientist. "I hope my work hasn't been a burden for you, honey." When he didn't reply, all she could do was hug him.

* * *

Back at Animal House, long after visiting hours were over, a small inquisitive mouse scurried into Cain's cage. With its twitching little nose and its round eyes taking in the surroundings, it looked up at the huge creature so far above its head. It was too big to be a living thing. But the smell was organic. It confused the mouse. Then a great form descended over it, darkening everything. The mouse tried to get through the three long branches at the end, but to no avail. The branches were warm and ended in giant claws. It was a hand! Then it miraculously lifted. Time to leave. The mouse ran over the roots of a massive tree, heading toward the bars and safety, but the tree moved, pushing the mouse toward the middle of the cage. There, the towering tree-creature let it run a short distance before forcing it to change course. Again and again, until the mouse became exhausted. Finally, a curved claw held the little quivering mouse in place, almost crushing its ribs. It couldn't breathe and its little heart raced faster and faster as two gigantic orange eyes hovered overhead. Jaws opened, dark and wet! A mountain chain of huge teeth gently grasped its body, then jerked it inside. The mouse was trapped and felt itself rising. Deep rumbles came from the dark throat, causing the tiny creature to scramble up the teeth, looking for a way out. Hot, humid air rushed through the fangs, pushing the mouse onto their hard surface. Then cooler, dryer air poured back in, sending the mouse onto the tongue again. In the little mouse's mind, it saw images of its mother. It wanted to feel her softness as it curled up, shaking and squeaking. The wind continued to flow humid then dry, humid then dry, humid then dry. The mouse waited for release. Surely it would come. Home waited. Family. It waited until its tiny heart stopped.

Chapter 17

Cosmic Pawn

By 2044, Cantor realized he couldn't wait any longer to relocate the dinosaurs. The administration refused to stop letting the public into Animal House, and lawmakers insisted Cain couldn't be put down. The dinosaurs had outgrown Berkeley. Cantor was interested in visiting a man named Dan Tusker, who seemed to have a solution. Kumiko stayed at Berkeley for another grinding staff meeting.

"Your letter was quite a surprise, Mr. Tusker. Your offer is very generous," Cantor said, looking at the dark hickory walls of the plush office near campus. There were photographs of Tusker in his younger years holding a rifle and standing behind various dead animals, images that didn't fit with the man in the chair. Another showed him playing golf with the governor and a famous actor. Colorful crystals sat at each corner of his beautiful, but otherwise empty, mahogany desk.

Tusker was of average height and weight, with gray eyes and a receding hairline. Despite being 50, his braided hair in front and back showed a focus on youthful fashion. His nose turned down sharply, as if always checking his breath. The redder parts of his face surrounded a lighter, ghostly impression of sunglasses around his eyes. He wore a chain around his neck that ended in a curled thousand-dollar bill embedded in a clear, epoxy resin tube.

"Please call me Dan."

"OK, Dan," Cantor said, wishing the light above his head wasn't so bright. "So, let me see if I understand your offer. First of all, your firm, Cosmic Pawn, would like to help us relocate the dinosaurs."

"As stated in my letter," Tusker said with a smile.

"And you would buy the land and take care of the administration of it, freeing us up to concentrate on research. Am I correct?"

"That is correct, Doctor Hoffman."

"So, what's in it for Cosmic Pawn?"

"Nothing really," Tusker said, shrugging his shoulders. "Remember, we would run the project as a non-profit enterprise. Of course, we'd need to make up for our initial expenses. Given the public's insatiable appetite for dinosaurs, I expect we would release videos and photos to cover the bill."

"Would we be employees?"

"No. You are like a rock star. You do your thing, and we make sure you succeed."

"But you would pay us?"

"Correct. Consider yourselves as contractors. We'd provide you room and board, free utilities, moving expenses, plus land for your animals to live on, and you get paid a reasonable wage."

"This seems very generous of you," Cantor continued. "What about the construction of buildings and a strong stockade?"

"Cosmic Pawn would pay for the buildings, the stockade, and food for the dinosaurs. It's all about what is best for the dinosaurs."

"I'm curious. The name Cosmic Pawn is… well, unusual."

"It's a play on cosmic dawn. We are just a humble company trying to help. In the grand scheme of things, we are all pawns – just flotsam after a cosmic dawn," Tusker said, drumming his fingers on the desk.

"How did you find out we were thinking of relocating?"

"Oh, you know how these things go. People find out and they talk. I know I would want to relocate if I were in your shoes."

"Are you the CEO of Cosmic Pawn?"

"Oh, good gracious, no," he said, dismissing the thought with a wave of his hand. "I am just the guy in charge of finding new opportunities for the organization. And you are my top choice." Tusker held his hands out, palms up, half his fingers sporting shiny rings.

"I see. Who's the owner?"

"He's a very private gentleman. That's all I can tell you. But he follows your work closely."

"I'd like to meet him," Cantor said.

"That I cannot arrange. He's very private."

"OK. Let's talk about the dinosaurs. If we took you up on Cosmic Pawn's offer, we wouldn't bring all the dinosaurs. The university wishes to keep most of the surviving earlier iterations for grad students to study."

"I see."

"The only earlier iteration we'd bring is a C5 named Koko.

"Why a C5? That iteration isn't as advanced."

"She's more of a pet. We like her just the way she is."

"Fine. Bring her," Tusker said with a wave of his hand.

"And we'd bring the two adult C10s. We hope to breed them."

"Fine. And?"

"That's it."

"But Doctor Hoffman, you have three adult E10s. Why would you exclude them from breeding?"

"Those three are more dangerous. Very aggressive."

"Oh, this won't do. Tigers are very dangerous and aggressive, and very rare. Does that mean we should exclude them from breeding programs?"

"Well, no. But these three raptors will grow much bigger than a tiger. They are unusually... well, fierce."

"As are lions, sharks..." Dan adjusted one of the crystals on his desk.

"Remember, people have to feed and take care of these dinosaurs. Already we've had an employee get injured at the university. The three E10s are simply too dangerous."

"Well, that's why you need our help. We know how to handle dangerous animals."

Cantor sighed. "My wife and I feel there is an error in the code used for the E10 embryos. We don't believe real dinosaurs were quite that vicious."

Tusker smiled like a man holding the best cards. "Because you and Doctor Chen aren't creating any new designs, we have to accept the fact that there are only five true dinosaurs on Earth. These five are more accurate than previous versions. It would be folly, absolute folly, not to do everything you could to save all five from extinction."

Cantor shook his head, no.

Tusker continued, "We're thrilled you plan to breed the C10s, but you only have two individuals. If you aren't interested in mating the three E10s, we'd be happy to take them off your hands. We view them as a separate subspecies from the C10s. It would be such a tragedy if they were to go extinct again."

"I can't give the E10s away," Cantor said, dragging his fingers through his hair. "If we can breed the C10s, that is Maryann and Darwin, we would have real dinosaurs. But the E10s are too perverse for meaningful study. Nature wouldn't evolve dinosaurs so vicious they attack their own kind for no reason."

"I respect your point of view. However, you're a product of nature. What you do then is natural. And you made the E10s. Therefore, they are a part of nature. Anyway, nobody knows what true dinosaurs were like."

Cantor stood up and offered his hand. "Thank you, Mr. Tusker. It's an interesting offer. However, I believe we'll continue to look for property here in California with help from government grants and public contributions." *Crap! Another dead end.*

Chapter 18

Hurting Kumiko

O n his way home from his meeting with Dan Tusker, Cantor told
his car he wanted to watch the news. The dash screen lit up as the
news anchor discussed the celebrations in Washington D.C., which had
finally been declared the 51st state. Now it would be known as The State
of Columbia. In anticipation, people had been calling it The SOC for
months. They joked that it was where the nation kept its dirty laundry.
That's where all my missing socks go.

The next story covered the climate. No big surprise, the average
global temperature change from pre-industrial times was now 2.1
degrees centigrade. "Higgs," he said, using the computer's name, "how
hot is it in Houston today?"

"103.2 degrees."

For some reason, he always picked on Houston. "And the humidity?"

"89 percent."

"Jeez. Higgs, please go back to the news."

The screen showed a reporter in a boat in the middle of Dhaka,
Bangladesh. Nearby, only the tops of cars could be seen in the water.

"Higgs, give me news about China that I can share with Kumiko."

The screen showed protesters outside the Senate-House advocating for jobs in industries that might allow the U.S. to regain its status as the number one world economy. Some were shouting for more tariffs. An effigy of the Chinese president swung from a wooden gallows. *More chaos! And when are they going to stop pretending the House is still an independent functioning body?*

"All right, Higgs, give me some good news. I can't take it anymore."

Higgs showed one entrance to the Oakland/San Francisco/Berkeley SupermagLoop, which had recently been completed by MoreSpeed4U Inc. "As you can see, Cantor, the SupermagLoop is fully operational, relieving much of the traffic congestion for the cities. And the mostly above ground magnetic SupermagLoop to from San Francisco to L.A. reduces the driving time from city center to city center to two hours."

"Thanks, Higgs. I feel better. Off please."

His thoughts turned to the dinosaurs. The government still classified the dinosaurs as an extinct species as opposed to an endangered species. The older Endangered Species Act applied only to animals living in a natural habitat whose numbers were dwindling. In bizarre phrasing, the new law stated that under no circumstance could you harm an extinct animal. It brought a smile to his face. *Oh, those funny bureaucrats.*

He noticed a bumper sticker on a c"r th't passed him. "No room on the Ark," it said next to a caricature of a dinosaur. *Give me strength. Between these guys and the conspiracy theories, maybe I'll be the one going extinct.*

While at first fascinated by their work on devolution, many in the public fell victim to conspiracy theories and a rising mistrust of science. Soon, various populist and religious groups brought pressure to bear to halt the dinosaur research. Kumiko's work was open to the accusation that she was "playing God".

He thought about the different the"ries'now circulating. The term "RevEngE" was being bantered about for Reverse-Engineering-

Endeavor. According to one *revenge* theory, the scientists were exacting revenge against the rioters that had opposed martial law. *Give me a break.* According to another, they were exacting revenge on immigrants by developing deadly animals to patrol the borders. *Wait, aren't we supposed to be the smartest animal on the planet?* Several politicians running for office suggested that China secretly funded the RevEngE research and intended to create a race of super-killers to keep the population in its place.

Thank goodness the dinosaurs still fascinate most people.

* * *

The next week, Kumiko spoke to members of the public on STEM Day, designated to encourage young people to study math and science. The San Francisco People's Auditorium was cavernous and modern, with beautiful faux wood walls surrounding murals depicting tranquil scenes in nature. She spoke on the great stage, using a stepping stool behind the podium. The number of people there surprised her.

She began by saying, "We face great challenges. Global warming, social disintegration, war, global hunger, and the distrust of science."

After her talk, members of the press and the public had questions for her in the lobby. She stood on the rich burgundy rug, under a giant portrait of the president.

She took questions like, "How do you find time for family while doing research?" or "What are your views on the crisis in science education in public schools?"

A radio talk show host asked, "Does the cruelty of caging the dinosaurs keep you up at night?"

She responded calmly, "I would prefer to let the animals roam freely if it was safe for them, the environment, and for people. Cages aren't the best way to house an animal. Think of the subspecies of gorillas that recently went extinct in the wild. All are caged in zoos and show signs of psychological stress. Hopefully, a better enclosure or open space will be found for them."

"Why do you want to create dangerous creatures when you have the technology to create wonderful animals that could be emotional support animals or pets?" from another onlooker.

After a pause, Kumiko explained, "I'm pleased that some of my colleagues are doing just that with genetically altered pygmy chimpanzees and Cebus monkeys. But as I said in my talk earlier, the last generation of dinosaurs was much bigger than we planned. I have to admit, some also turned out to be quite aggressive. It wasn't our intention." Kumiko paused to gather her thoughts. "I hope our research increases our knowledge of the past, tests new computational and genetic methodologies, and eventually uses these to help people. And I know," she added, "there are many children who hold a fascination for dinosaurs. Perhaps they will choose science as a career." She smiled and was about to thank everyone for attending her talk when the crowd began shouting more questions. (Except for the tattooed man who stood quietly at the back of the audience, out of the light.)

The people were Ig restless, and the cameras and mics turned toward them rather than Kumiko.

Encouraged by this, a slender woman said, "Your work is blasphemous! Noah didn't allow dinosaurs on the ark for a reason!"

Another person turned to the slender woman and yelled, "Why don't you just shut the hell up!?"

Kumiko tried to emphasize that she didn't wish to tell people what to think, just to relish learning. "Dinosaurs lived long before there were people, so if the story of Noah is true, he wouldn't have known about dinosaurs." She paused. "But people want to see dinosaurs. It's a thrill. We hope that someday there will be enough dinosaurs in parks for the public to view."

"I know I want to see 'em," a man hollered.

"That's because you haven't grown up!" a woman shouted back at him.

"But there's a secondary reason for the research," Kumiko continued. "As a scientist, I'm expanding our knowledge of what lies inside the blueprints for all forms of life. The interactions of genes are far more complicated than scientists realized."

(The tattooed man moved into the center of the crowd.)

"If you are so smart, why is your son so messed up? I read all about it," someone yelled.

The question stung Kumiko and left her off balance. She couldn't see who had said such a thing. "I... I... My son is a wonderful person."

Someone shouted that some kinds of knowledge should always remain a mystery.

Another person toward the back yelled, "We wouldn't have so many damn problems with China spying on the U.S. if people like you would go back to where you belonged!"

Some people gasped at that.

(The tattooed man drew nearer.)

A middle-aged, one-armed Asian man objected and pointed out that he was as patriotic as any American and had fought in the Euro-Russian war, but a hand from behind grabbed his shirt, causing him to fall.

The tattooed man pulled a slingshot from his jacket pocket, put a ball bearing in it, and fired it at Kumiko, hitting her with a glancing blow near her eye. He escaped the grasp of the now standing one-armed man and, as people surged forward, he slipped out a side door.

Shocked and bleeding, Kumiko left the scene quickly, despite the attempt by an employee of the auditorium to get her to wait for an ambulance. "I need to leave!" she told a security guard. By the time she made it to her car, she trembled and sobbed. She held her bloodied face in her hands as the car's auto-pilot negotiated its way through traffic. Her phone rang. *I've got to get myself together before I can talk about this.* Upon stepping into her home, she found Cantor and George waiting for her in the living room – they had heard of the incident already.

Rivulets of blood had dried into her white blouse.

"We need to talk, Cantor," she said, trying to be stoic, and walked past them toward the hall.

"Oh, Kumiko! I'm so sorry. Why didn't you answer my calls?"

"I was too upset."

"We saw it on the local news. Let me clean you up. Show me your cut," he said, rising and following her.

George looked scared.

It was too much and she began to sob. "They said terrible things to me."

Cantor put his arms around her as she cried. "You're with us now. George, please get a washcloth for Mom."

"I'll take care of it. Thanks though," she said, wiping away her tears and entering the bathroom.

She left the door open and began removing the dried blood from her face. Next, she applied Steri-Strips to the cut.

Sitting on the bathtub, George asked, "Why would anyone do this to you, Mom?"

"Some people are unhappy, honey."

"Did you see who did this?" Cantor asked, leaning on the doorjamb.

"It wouldn't matter if I did," she said.

Seeking solace, Kumiko retired to her study and pulled out a book of poems. The last lines she read were from Vachel Lindsay.

He flew to our feet in rainbow-foam —
A king of beauty and tempest and thunder
Panting to tear our sorrows asunder.
A dragon of fair adventure and wonder.

She drifted into a merciful slumber, dreaming of dragons.

* * *

A short time later, Cantor looked in and saw his wife sleeping on the brown leather couch where she did much of her reading. He loved the way she curled up with a pillow behind her head. Even in sleep, she was graceful. Sensing her pain, he wanted to help her. After a few steps into the room, he stopped, realizing waking her would be a selfish act, even if he meant to hold and reassure her. But he couldn't let her wake up alone without him there. After a pause, he walked to the couch and, as quietly as he could, laid himself on the hardwood floor with a pillow from an easy chair and gazed at the moonlight on the far wall until he too slept.

* * *

Morning came and when Cantor opened his eyes, Kumiko had left the couch. There was a blanket over him. With creaking joints and a stiff neck, he rose and shuffled to the kitchen where he saw Kumiko drinking tea and writing notes. She looked up, saw her haggard husband in his underwear watching her, and said, "Did you know one person wanted to know why George was, well, different? They implied it was our fault."

"Anybody tries to say that to me, one of us is going to end up on the floor," he said, looking into the dining room to verify George was still in bed.

"It's like there is no privacy nowadays!" she said, pursing her lips. "Anybody can find out everything about everybody else."

"Information is money."

She took another sip of tea. "I would like to run over some ideas with you."

Cantor examined her discolored eye and gritted his teeth. He made himself a cup of coffee, pulled up a stool, and the two began discussing their options. "Are you sure you're up for working after yesterday?"

"My eye isn't the part of me that thinks," she said with a hint of anger.

Cantor nodded and began listing all the problems they were facing.

"Problem one. We need to move somewhere with less social unrest and without the anti-Chinese outlook.

"Problem two," he continued. "We have some big dinosaurs on our hands now. We can't keep them in cages, especially if we want to understand their behavior.

"Problem three: These big dinosaurs are expensive to maintain and they'll get more expensive as they grow. Just the cost of feeding them and paying people to do this will break us. And we can't rely on government help under the new austerity plan."

"So, what do we do? I'm willing to leave this place now," Kumiko said, tapping her fingers on the kitchen island. "Since I can't change my skin or my eyes, I'll change my address. I'm no longer comfortable in a big city. Any big city. Add to that the higher costs for setting up an outdoor facility for the dinosaurs here, and the choice is clear." She poured herself another cup of white tea.

Cantor put his hand over hers. "I've come around to thinking Cosmic Pawn may be our best option."

"I'm willing to try Cosmic Pawn," Kumiko said. "They solve the quality-of-care problem, and they provide the funds to keep things going."

"You sure you'd be OK leaving the university?"

"I love Berkeley. If they moved the entire school to wherever we took the dinosaurs, I'd want to remain there."

"It's a big step," he said.

She carefully tapped the bandage by her eye. "I wish we could meet this benefactor and not just their representative, though."

"He or she must be a very busy person."

"I wonder how Dan Tusker knew we wanted to relocate?" she mused.

"Who knows? I like that we'll decide where the facility will be. That's a major plus. As long as this benefactor lets us decide, it seems like a good deal."

Kumiko nodded her head. "Another attractive thing about this option is Tusker's organization takes care of the legalities, the bills, health insurance, all those things neither of us wants to do. This benefactor is looking pretty outstanding in my book."

"We still need to research Cosmic Pawn," Cantor said. "I've never heard of them, have you?"

"No, but there are a lot of things I've never heard of," Kumiko replied.

* * *

The next day, Cantor and Kumiko were eating vegetable lo mein for lunch using chopsticks. They discussed different locations where they could move the dinosaurs. They settled on northwestern New Mexico as the best site.

"Arthur Saxton would be nearby, in Los Alamos. The population of the state is only slightly above three million, and some areas are barely populated," Kumiko said, touching the bandage near her eye. Her wound was tender.

"Yeah. And land there is cheap, though water is scarce." Cantor said as his noodles slipped through his chopsticks.

Kumiko added, "It will be good for George that Luna is from New Mexico and knows the state intimately."

"I'd like to check out the land for sale that Luna's father spoke of," Cantor said, trying to suck a single noodle into his mouth. "George won't mind that it isn't far from Owa'ke Pueblo." He put his chopsticks down and picked up a fork.

That evening, Cantor, Kumiko, George, and Luna studied maps of New Mexico on Cantor's tabletop screen or TTS. The table sized screen was built into the dining room table and could be divided into many screens or one large one. A clear, hard, durable, polycarbonate material covered the screen, protecting it from spills.

"It is a large piece of land, more than enough for your purposes," Luna softly told Cantor and Kumiko. She wore a beautiful squash blossom necklace and her long black hair flowed down her back. Some dishes still hadn't been cleared on the TTS, leaving Santa Fe covered by a bowl of salad.

Looking at a map on the TTS, Cantor agreed. "Before we decide, we need to see the place ourselves. I hear it's chilly in the winter and hot in the summer, but we've tested the dinosaurs in both temperature extremes and they do fine, except for the coldest nighttime temps in winter. But that's no problem. We can put the animals in barns that are heated."

"Let's book a flight," Kumiko said. "Perhaps you and George would like to join us? Cosmic Pawn will pay your way even though we haven't signed the contract yet."

"Absolutely," Luna said. "I can introduce you to my family."

George grinned from ear to ear.

* * *

"Well, I guess we aren't in San Fran anymore," George said to Luna as they stepped off the plane in Albuquerque.

"Yeah, and the airport isn't as busy."

"That's the Albuquerque SUNPORT to you, li'l Missy," he said, using his best John Wayne voice.

"And this is the hand that will slap you, li'l Buddy, if you call me that again," Luna said, giving him a scowl before breaking out in a grin.

"Check out those mountains," Cantor said as they walked to their electric rental car. East of the city, sheer granite cliffs capped by horizontal layers of limestone rose a mile into the sky. "There are fossils on the top from an ancient sea."

"Where'd you hear that, Dad?" George asked.

"Recall, dear son, I'm a paleontologist."

"Well, Dad, suppose you explain to us how all that water didn't drain away from up there."

"Well, dear son, it never was way up there."

"Cantor, stop being so obtuse," Kumiko said, looking at Luna and rolling her eyes.

"Yeah, Dad."

* * *

During the trip, Cantor got to know Luna better. At first, he thought she was a little shy. Often, she would look away when speaking with him. Later, he found out it was a sign of respect.

When they arrived at the land for sale, Luna's mother was there to meet them. The owner, an elderly gentleman named Henry, opened the gate.

Juanita lived in Owa'ke Pueblo in the northwestern part of New Mexico, just north of Jemez Pueblo, a place of rugged mountains with a view of the huge volcanic plugs to the southeast, surrounded by deeply gouged scrublands of yellow grass, small cedar trees, and cacti.

"This is my mother, Juanita Toya," Luna said to everyone. Her mother wore a long purple dress tied with a red sash around her middle and her hair rolled up in the back. Silver and turquoise earrings pulled on her earlobes. The wrinkles near her dark eyes testified to the intensity of the sun.

"It's a pleasure to meet you, Ms. Toya," Kumiko said, feeling the baking desert heat waft around her legs. "Thank you for coming out to meet us here."

Juanita listened to Luna's translation. She immediately returned Kumiko's smile and said something in Towa.

"She doesn't speak very good English. She says welcome and to please call her Juanita," Luna said.

They listened as Luna translated her mother's answers to their many questions.

After Juanita left in a dingy, older model self-driving car, Cantor talked with Henry by phone.

"Thank you again for letting us explore your land," Cantor said.

"It's good land. Been in my family for over two hundred years."

"May I ask why you want to sell it?"

"My children have all moved away. I'm told I'm too old to keep it up," he said, his voice hoarse, as if tired from talking for so many years.

"I see," Cantor said. "Well, only you can be a judge of that. Thank you. I think we are very satisfied and will be leaving soon." *The kids probably worry about him way out here.*

Cantor shook Kumiko's hand. Then he looked at the vast, baked expanse without a house in sight. It was another world. He was beginning to trust Cosmic Pawn. Tusker didn't pressure them and didn't object to funding their trip.

Later, on their flight back to California, he gazed at the multi-colored sandstones and numerous volcanic cinder cones that passed miles below. The kid in him couldn't wait to return. The adult in him felt the same.

Chapter 19

Checkmate

"Computer, what can you tell me about Cosmic Pawn?" Cantor asked, sitting in his office after returning from New Mexico. With a mug of coffee in one hand, he propped his feet up between two stacks of papers on his desk. His sunburned face and arms were his souvenirs from the trip.

The computer responded, "Cosmic Pa"n wa' incorporated in 2039. It is headquartered in San Francisco, California. Funding comes from private sources."

"Is Tusker really Dan Tusker's last name?"

"Previously, his last name was Turner."

"What position does Dan Tusker hold?"

"Dan Tusker is the Director of Operations."

"What is their purpose?"

"Cosmic Pawn provides funding, management, and guidance for worthwhile enterprises whose services are for the public good."

"What enterprises have they helped in the past?"

"They have provided funds for a quantum computing startup in Denver, Colorado, and for an organization in Zimbabwe that removes horns from wild White Rhinoceroses without harming them."

"I thought that was illegal."

"It's allowed in several countries under special conditions. Poachers won't kill a rhino without its horns."

"What does the organization do with the horns?"

"They are turned over to each country's equivalent of the National Park Service."

"And they are destroyed?"

"That information is not available."

* * *

Dan Tusker's office hadn't changed since Cantor's last visit. He and Kumiko sat in front of Tusker's table, discussing the contract.

"It will be hard to sign this considering it will lead to major changes in our lives," Kumiko whispered to Cantor when Tusker stepped out briefly. She glanced around the office, noticing how her husband's leg was bouncing. Although there were no family photos on the desk by the window, Tusker seemed to be in every framed photo on the walls. Several rolled-up maps lay at one end of the table where they sat. A plate of donuts lingered nearby.

A minute later, Tusker returned. "Please look over the contract and we can talk next week," Tusker said. "Once you sign, Cosmic Pawn will begin construction of the ranch."

"Dan, we're still thinking it would be wise to donate the three large E-raptors to zoos now that the university administration realizes they are more than they can handle. Surely, the legislature too would agree they're challenging to manage, and the public would love to see them."

"The legislature supports our efforts. Cantor, our offer is contingent on all the dinosaurs being allowed to run free inside the property. That includes the E-raptors. It's for the good of the animals."

"When you say 'run free', you mean within a fortified enclosure, right?" Cantor clarified.

"Correct."

"I'm curious about your operation in Africa," Cantor said. "What happens after you turn over the rhino horns to the appropriate authorities?"

"That, my friend, is the concern of others," Tusker said. "I'm sure they're disposed of in a manner that befits all parties involved."

* * *

The contract was lengthy and full of legal jargon. Cantor asked a lawyer named Simpson to look it over. All 137 pages.

"I've never seen a contract this long, Cantor. It's quite extraordinary."

"Imagine how we feel."

"OK. I'll take a look."

"If possible, can you do it in the next few days?"

"I'll do my best."

* * *

While perusing the contract from Tusker, Kumiko got a call from Arthur. "I fully support your desire to move the dinosaurs," he said.

"Good. I think it's for the best."

"We'll be neighbors," he said. "What could be better?"

* * *

Cantor and Kumiko had spent the previous week studying the document. Simpson had said he saw nothing wrong. Now, standing in Tusker's office, they placed their signatures where needed. Finally, there would be a home for the dinosaurs.

Tusker stuck out his ring-adorned right hand and Cantor shook it. When Kumiko shook his hand next, he winked as if to say, "You did the right thing."

Cantor said, "I think things will get easier once we are in New Mexico."

Tusker clapped his hands. "Did I mention we now own your home?"

Kumiko frowned, looking at Cantor.

"Just kidding, folks. Just kidding."

"This is a minor point. I drink white tea," Kumiko said seriously. "Would you mind including it in the ranch's provisions?"

"White tea? Isn't that what the rest of us call water?" Dan said, amused by his wit.

"It's a type of tea my mother liked. Like mother, like child."

"Of course. I'll supply you with any type of tea you like."

Cantor, feeling a like a huge weight had been taken off his shoulders, smiled at Kumiko. "My dino-daughter, Maryann, is going to love it."

* * *

Afterward, on their ride home, Cantor and Kumiko played chess while the car drove autonomously. "Can you believe our luck?" he said. "We've spent several years at our wit's end trying to deal with the problems surrounding the big guys. And now, poof, somebody tossed us a life preserver."

"I'm glad Dan understands the importance of safety, especially with the likes of Cain," Kumiko said, as her knight took his bishop.

"All we need to do is keep our cabin clean and take out the trash. We can finally get the raptors out of those awful cages."

Kumiko smiled and said, "Think of all the research we'll have time for."

"After we leave Berkeley, there'll be no more faculty meetings!" Cantor said, laughing. "My other bishop takes your pawn."

"This is a big step," Kumiko said, studying the layout of the pieces on the screen. "I'm glad George sounded excited. Let's hope everything goes smoothly. My pawn takes your pawn."

"I move my rook over here."

"Thanks. Your queen is mine," Kumiko said.

"How about we call the ranch *Jurassic Park Two*?" Cantor suggested with a grin. "I move my knight here."

"No, definitely not. Checkmate."

* * *

The next week, the lawyer named Simpson sold his house to a person he never met for twice its value and moved to Florida.

Chapter 20

Raptor Ranch

"If you fell down yesterday, stand up today."
— H. G. Wells

Tusker wanted to go over his plans on location. So, back in Albuquerque, Cantor and Kumiko met with Dan Tusker again. Although Tusker had seen the pictures and had done a lot of research on the land, it was his first time to actually see it. In all honesty, he didn't care where it was located as long as it was economical and not near a population center.

Together, they headed for the property in a self-driving rental car. Tusker in the back, Cantor and Kumiko up front. Despite Tusker's protests, they had chosen not to fly by drone. Instead, they wanted to expose themselves more intimately to the countryside.

"This is exciting," Kumiko said, admiring the rugged cliffs that rose above dry arroyos peppered with low-lying cedars. She looked at Cantor sitting on what was still called the driver's side and put her hand on his knee. She could feel Tusker's gaze on her from the back seat.

The car knew where to go. About an hour and a half out of Albuquerque, they passed the small town of Cuba and continued north. Beyond a tiny village named La Jara, the car turned onto a dirt road, drove a few miles, and stopped near a house that had seen better days. The ranch was surrounded by a barbed wire fence.

Henry opened a gate and waved them through. Tusker rolled down his window. "Thank you, Henry."

"Oh, you know Henry?" Cantor asked.

"We've spoken."

They traveled a few hundred yards on a dirt road before pulling over. Cantor stepped out of the car, holding his hand over his eyes. Scanning the slightly less arid land surrounding him, he headed toward a line of cottonwoods, passing low-lying cedars and other evergreens surrounded by fields of gray-green sage, yellow-flowered chamisa, and hardy desert grasses. The cottonwoods bracketed a small stream that led to a water storage pond.

"Over here is where we'll build the cabins," Tusker said. "And over there will be where the animals will be kept," he added, pointing north.

"They'll have separate barns, as we discussed," Cantor added.

"Yes. Well, no. To save time and space, Remus and Cain will need to be in a single barn. As we discussed."

"Right," Cantor said. He looked beyond the trees to the mountains. "The water comes from there," he observed.

Speaking to his wrist phone, he asked the name of the mountains. Almost instantly, the device answered, "They are the Jemez Mountains."

"It's refreshing," Kumiko said, smelling the tart, tangy smell of a sprig of sage. "The air is so clear here; I can see for miles. And the lack of humidity is refreshing."

Tusker took in a deep breath. "The sage and rabbitbrush are beautiful. Watch out for those cacti, though. I dare say the spines are painful to remove."

"Out here I read that rabbitbrush is called chamisa," Kumiko said. "Chamisa sounds more exotic."

"Well, we wanted to be isolated," Cantor said, looking at the map on his phone. "This looks like a magnificent spot. The nearest paved road is several miles away."

"The multicolored cliffs of the Nacimiento Formation lay south of the property," Cantor continued, pointing. "It must be a good omen. The older rocks mark when the Age of the Dinosaurs ended. And here is where it begins again."

Kumiko covered her eyes to better see.

"I'm sold," Cantor said. He already imagined dinosaurs running through the sage and tall grass. "Maryann is going to love this. The enclosures will be huge, giving all the raptors plenty of freedom."

"Well, Dan, this looks like the perfect spot," Kumiko said.

"Yes. I'm sure Cosmic Pawn will have no trouble with the purchase. You won't regret it," Tusker added with a smile.

* * *

Tusker wandered away from the group and took a phone call. "You'll get the money," he said quietly.

The person on the other end was a little worked up.

"I know. It was an opinion, that's all. Your opinion is your opinion," Tusker continued.

Tusker rolled his eyes as he listened. "Perfectly legal. I just had a friendly chat with you and told you how important this project is. I didn't tell you to do anything."

He put his hand to his forehead. "Enjoy your holiday," he said and hung up. *Damn lawyers.*

While Cantor explored the surrounding area, Tusker approached Kumiko.

"So, you like what you see, Kumiko?" he asked.

"It's beautiful."

"Maybe someday, you'll design an even bigger dinosaur that will thrive here."

"I don't think so. No, I'm done with giants."

"I think you and I could make this ranch take off," he said, taking a step closer.

"What do you mean?"

"Your husband has a dream. I have a vision."

* * *

Once back in California, Cantor and Kumiko let the University know that were resigning. Their classes would end soon, and it gave the school time to find replacements. They packed up their books, wall art, and files. Berkeley had been good to them, and leaving was hard. Kumiko received a golden dinosaur tooth on a chain, and Cantor a framed collage of many photos of him with associates and the dinosaurs.

Cantor planned to continue his research in New Mexico to determine the behavior, social organization, and hunting strategies used by *Utahraptors*, the dinosaur the raptors resembled most.

Kumiko planned to spend her time examining the animal's DNA once the new lab was built. In the case of the E-raptors, the effects of the genes were so intertwined, simply removing the genes for great size or ferocity wasn't possible. But she wouldn't give up. She also looked forward to observing the raptors in the field with Cantor.

"Tusker is making this so easy for us," Cantor said, lugging in a box of books and plunking it on the living room floor. "The trailer we'll be living in until the cabin is complete is a nice one."

"And he's paying us in the meantime," Kumiko added. "Unlike the vast majority of working people today, we'll work as a family. I'll help you. You'll help me. George will help us both and we will help him."

Cantor offered part of his pay to George for his help with what he called Raptor Ranch.

* * *

As soon as classes ended, Luna and George moved from San Francisco to the ranch. Both planned on continuing their education with online classes. For now, they lived in a small trailer next to Cantor and Kumiko's trailer. She loved being near her family, but worried about the wisdom of bringing Cain to New Mexico. After several days with George, she spent a week with her family in Owa'ke and discussed it with her mother, Juanita.

Juanita's small house was made of thick adobe walls with wooden vigas holding up the roof. There was a traditional dome-shaped communal oven, or *horno*, for baking bread located outside. Luna sat with Juanita and helped feed wood into the *horno*'s fire.

"I've missed this place and my family," Luna said in Towa, breaking some branches.

"It is good. Families belong together," Juanita said, occasionally using Spanish words. "What will the new ranch be like?"

"I don't know much except there will be large fences to keep the animals inside."

"Are they dangerous?"

"Some are. They're all hunters, but some are more dangerous than the others."

"What are the dangerous ones like?"

"Well, I've been meaning to talk to you about one of them. They call him Cain. I saw him in San Francisco. He's big and mean."

"Hunters have to be dangerous; it's their essence," Juanita said, stirring the fire. "Mountain lions and bears have their place and we must respect them."

Luna was silent for a bit. "But Cain's spirit is bad. I think he's a Searcher from the ancient myths."

Juanita stopped and looked hard at Luna. "A Searcher! Why would they bring such a thing here? To our sacred lands?"

"I think they want to understand him. They don't see what I see."

"You brought the science people here! And now they bring this creature. Why did you do this?"

"Please forgive me, Mother. I didn't think. I wanted to be near my family."

"Perhaps you will visit us at the pueblo, *hita*," Juanita said. "I don't expect I'll be visiting the ranch much."

* * *

George and Luna married in August. First in the Western tradition with vows and a Justice of the Peace, followed by a reception. Many of Luna's relatives attended the ceremony on the land where construction of the ranch was in progress.

After the marriage ceremony, Luna's mother, Juanita, said some words in Towa. Juanita's hands made delicate gestures, some of which Luna understood, while fear and supplication were expressed in her tired eyes. Despite this, she didn't oppose her daughter's wishes. She was fond of George and respected Cantor and Kumiko.

"Thank you for coming, Mother," Luna said. "I know it wasn't easy for you."

Several days later, they were married in the Pueblo manner. A double-necked vase was created for the bride and groom, and George, Cantor, and Kumiko took it to Luna's Owa'ke home, where she greeted them with samples of the items they would need for their lives together. On the wedding day, the couple drank holy water from the vase separately, then both drank at the same time from each neck. If no water was spilled, it portended a marriage filled with goodwill and cooperation. A little water escaped the side of George's mouth and he laughed. Luna smiled at this, but only for a second.

It took three months to build the essential parts of the ranch. Two wells were dug. Cosmic Pawn's employees cleared the land and built a sturdy eleven-foot metal fence topped with concertina wire around the perimeter of Raptor Ranch. They left most of the big cottonwoods and evergreens as they were.

Steel-reinforced barns and corrals for the raptors and buildings for the researchers were next. At last, the family left their trailers and moved into their new cabin. The cabin was small, but Cantor, Kumiko, George, and Luna didn't mind. Cosmic Pawn soon built a second cabin attached to an office for Dan Tusker. A third cabin would eventually house George and Luna, and others would house visiting scientists and helpers.

* * *

Once Tusker's workers built the first corrals and barns, Cantor arranged for transportation from San Francisco of the C10s and E10s, as well as Koko. Tusker told the hired driver, who watched over things as the two trucks drove themselves, that she was transporting exotic animals, and he wanted her to complete the journey in 24 hours, if possible. For that reason, Dan Tusker paid her well.

The driver programmed the trucks to stop for a meal In Arizona. She didn't need to recharge the trucks' batteries, since they were one of the newer models. While she ate, loud screeches and roars came from the trailers in the parking area where several people gathered around, wide-eyed and concerned. Dropping her sandwich, she ran out to the trucks, where she was peppered with questions from the growing gathering.

"Sorry. Exotic animals," she said, trying to get to the cabin of one of the trucks.

"What kind?" someone yelled.

"I think they may be lions and some kind of birds. Gotta go now," she said as she closed the truck door and started both vehicles' motors.

"Did you see how the trailers were shaking?" one spectator said to another as the trucks rolled away. "Those lions sure were pissed."

* * *

Some of the local men and women hired to build the ranch stayed on to help maintain it. In addition, Tusker hired Kumiko's grad student from Berkeley, Robert Greaves, to work with the E-raptors, especially Cain.

"Welcome to Raptor Ranch, Robert," Kumiko said, seeing him wandering around the site. "I hope you're comfortable here."

Greaves looked around the arid space with a frown. "This isn't at all like San Francisco."

"It's quite a change, isn't it?" Kumiko said, smiling, holding her arms out and turning in a circle.

Greaves ran his hand over his close-cropped brown hair, squinting from the intense sunlight, and grumbled, "Now I know why cowboys wear those damn hats."

"I might get one myself," Kumiko said, turning and walking toward her cabin.

* * *

After the trucks arrived, Jose, one of Tusker's workers, supervised the placement of a steel hydraulic lift platform at the back of the first trailer. He used a remote control to open the trailer doors. With a different remote, he unlocked the heavy-duty wheels under the cage. Maryann roared and rocked her cage while wide-eyed workers pulled it slowly toward the platform using thick ropes. Then the platform was lowered to the ground and her cage was slowly rolled away. Next came Darwin.

These were local people; they'd never seen a dinosaur in the flesh.

"Oh, man, look at this guy, will you!? Damn, this is awesome!"

"¡Orale! No way! I gotta take a picture. ¡Que animales!"

"Hey, Jose, ask one to dance with you." Jose had a reputation for trying to dance with every female at a fiesta.

"Manuel, take a picture of me with this one. I want to show it to my kids."

The men piled around Maryann's cage. "My kids are going to want to see this," Eugenio said, looking at the tag on the cage. "It's a she. She keeps her nails long," he said and laughed.

When all their cages were on the ground, the male juvenile E-raptors, named Cain and Remus, began charging the bars and roaring, shaking their cages. They assumed an aggressive posture, when approached, with arms and hands wide open and teeth bared, occasionally followed by a growl and a lightning-quick lunge. Red feathers rose behind and over their heads and their orange eyes remained locked on the nearest person.

"Nothing shy about these creatures," Manuel said soberly. The E-raptors looked unceasingly for a way to get at the soft-bodied humans.

One man cried, "Ayee. These guys are mad at you, Louie. You better be polite."

But no one near Cain laughed. Those men became silent and wide-eyed. Several crossed themselves, saying, "Dios mio," and "Que Dios nos perdone." The bars offered little comfort as Cain stared each man down. He held both hands out, their clawed fingers opening and closing as if holding the beating hearts of the men.

Circe, the one female E-raptor, watched intently from her cage, hissing and ready to attack.

The only male C-raptor, named Darwin because of his deep-set eyes, was more subdued, but deadly serious. He watched with keen interest, pacing back and forth, but never went into the attack posture.

The female C-raptor, Maryann, seemed agitated, but soon calmed once her new surroundings became familiar. Cantor approached her cage, and she moved toward him, lowering her snout against the bars.

"It's OK, Maryann," he said, patting her gently. "This is your new home."

The locals were struck dumb. One man also wanted to pat her snout and approached her cage. Maryann backed up, growled, and bared her teeth. Cantor held out his arm, signaling the man to stop.

"I'm like her mother," Cantor explained. "We have a special relationship. But if she doesn't know you, she'll get defensive."

"Don't you mean you are like her father?" the man asked.

Cantor grinned. "It's a long story. I'll tell it to you sometime."

Using ropes, the workers draped tarps over the cages to protect the raptors from the sun. The tarps had an opening at the front where the cage door was.

Freddie, while wrapping the first cage, failed to keep his distance when he reached for a rope and received a wicked slash on his arm from Cain's claws. The dinosaur stopped roaring and licked the blood off one finger as Robert Greaves ran to the cage to calm him. Cantor drove Freddie to the small medical center in Cuba, fifteen miles away, for stitches. He told Cantor he was never coming back – the work was too dangerous.

Later in the day, Jose and Manuel stood quietly near Cain's cage, peering through the cage door.

"This one's crazy. He must have something wrong with him," Jose whispered.

Manuel stepped a little closer to the door. "Look how he clicks his claws together. Those claws are *muy malo*."

Suddenly, Cain lunged at the door, causing the tarp to flap and the cage to rattle. Both men jumped back as one.

"*Aye*, look at his eyes! There's blood in them!" Jose cried once he'd recovered. "And his lip. It's not right. See how his yellow teeth show?"

"He's like a shark. I remember seeing them when I was in the Navy," Manuel said. "He's El Mako Loco."

* * *

Cain's new name stuck, and soon everyone called him Mako, except Greaves, who insisted his name should remain Cain. No one liked him. With a type of humor characteristic of country-hardened men who used their muscles to make a living, the workers would joke and threaten one another, warning, "Mako will get you!"

Jose, when trying to feed Mako, complained that he didn't like his fiery orange eyes. "It's like he has a weird stare. You know? You feel like there's this invisible claw coming out of his eyes that will pull you in. Like his eyes have some sort of power over you. You know what I mean?"

Barns, built next to each corral, protected the dinosaurs from extreme cold or blazing heat. For now, the E-raptor males, Remus and Mako, shared a barn, but both stayed in their separate cages.

Taking his cue from the experience with the E-raptors, Cantor kept the C-raptors, Darwin and Maryann, in separate barns.

Cantor watched as workers built a sturdy stockade made of timber pilings, starting at the barns and corrals. He tried to visualize how it would look when the walls extended across the property, giving the dinosaurs a natural setting in which to stretch their legs. Eventually, he knew, the timber wall would extend about two miles across the ranch. The tall outer wall was made of sturdy chain link topped by concertina wire. Slats within the links provided privacy.

All the stockade wooden fences had downward-angled metal panels running throughout the inside. The plan was to mate Darwin and Maryann – the inner panels made sure any future little dinosaurs couldn't climb over the fences. Likewise, every tree trunk near the fences had a downward-facing cone wrapped several feet above the ground. There was one thing Koko had taught Cantor – if there was the will, a dinosaur would find a way.

It's a good thing the big animals are too heavy to climb. Cantor tried to imagine all the possible things that might go wrong.

Things were much simpler for Koko. She had a roomy pen and a small dino house next to Cantor and Kumiko's cabin. George took her for walks, but her legs were becoming arthritic, which kept her at a slow pace.

* * *

During the construction of the stockade for the dinosaur open space, Cantor spoke with Tusker in his office.

"Hey, Dan. I was thinking perhaps it would be easier if we dug out the enclosure so that dirt would partially support the wooden beams on the outside. Kind of like how they build rhino habitats at zoos."

"Perhaps," Tusker said as he straightened a crystal on a corner of his desk. "But the work has been going on for several weeks now. Do you know why the military keeps on paying too much for planes and ships? Because they keep re-designing them and interfering with production."

"Sure, I get that. But if I'm the pilot, I'd want a well-designed airplane."

Tusker leaned back in his black leather chair and smiled. "Not to worry, I'm going to build a beautiful fence for you. We build, you do research."

"OK. Why use wood, though? I mean, wood is so expensive nowadays. There are great composite materials you could use."

"I got a great deal."

"Where's the wood coming from?"

"Don't worry about it, Cant. It's all taken care of," Tusker said, toying with one of his braids.

"Please tell me it's not from the Amazon."

"You, my friend, worry too much. Please, you take care of the research and I'll take care of everything else." With that, Tusker rose and walked out.

* * *

Tusker was tired of the questions and demands from Cantor. Didn't he realize how much responsibility he had? *Look around you, Cantor*, he thought. *I'm doing all this and you complain.*

He recalled where he'd grown up in Chicago. His family was dirt poor and sometimes there wasn't enough food to eat between his siblings and him. *Who is Cantor to question my motives? When had Cantor ever been deprived?*

* * *

As Tusker supervised the construction of the ranch, Arthur Saxton kept up contact with Kumiko. He flew his aircar to the ranch several times, always taking many pictures, especially of the E-raptors. A ranch hand took his favorite picture, showing him standing in front of Mako's cage with one foot on a stool, wearing a safari hat.

"You should visit Maryann and Darwin," the ranch hand said. "They are, I don't know, better behaved."

Arthur smiled. "That's exactly why they don't interest me."

* * *

During the ranch's third month, Charlie, the construction supervisor, watched as several of the contracted workers finished unloading the wood off the truck. The section of fence they were working on was far from the barns, at least a mile and a half to the northwest. An excavator had just hit a large root from the tall ancient cottonwood inside the enclosure.

"What do you want to do, boss?" Antonio asked. "Maybe we should cut the tree down."

Charlie was under orders from Tusker to avoid delays. "Nah, just cut the root. Management wants to keep as many trees as possible inside the enclosure."

That could kill the tree anyway, Antonio thought. He started to speak, but decided it was best to just do what Charlie asked. The guy was a pain.

Charlie had other things on his mind. The damn cement truck was being repaired. He needed the concrete right now. He had two small cement mixers brought over instead. The men would have to fill the trench by hand, using their shovels.

His phone rang. Tusker wanted him to head over to another part of the property where some light poles were being installed. Cussing to himself, he got in his truck and drove away.

It was grueling work getting the concrete into the ground without the concrete truck. The heat was relentless. When the men placed the wooden fence posts into the trench, each separated by two inches, they compromised and used only half the required concrete. Who would know once they packed the dirt over it?

Chapter 21

Mating

The compound was completed by the end of 2047. This included the veterinary clinic, cabins, and Kumiko's lab. A two-story watchtower sat near Cantor and Kumiko's cabin.

The veterinarian had quit, saying, "I never signed up for this!"

For a month, Kumiko had been trying to do some of the veterinarian's duties. Speaking to Cantor, she said, "Any day now, I'll need to perform surgery or prescribe drugs for a dinosaur, which I can't do. We've got to find another veterinarian soon."

"Yeah, I know."

They sat inside their cabin, watching the snow come down. Large flakes drifted in the air, leisurely working their way to the ground. The afternoon was tranquil without wind or sound.

"It surprised me we haven't gotten more applicants for the position," Cantor said, drinking hot cocoa instead of his usual coffee.

"I suspect this place is too remote for them," Kumiko commented.

"That and most vets aren't trained to treat dinosaurs," he replied, taking a sip of the sweet cocoa and getting marshmallow on his upper lip. "I have an idea. Do you remember Valerie, that veterinarian that Alex dated briefly in California before he left for Virginia Tech? Maybe I can call her."

"Yes, I remember her," Kumiko said. "She was a nice lady. She came to the lab once with Alex and liked the proto-dinosaurs. I think they were C5s. In fact, she could hold the little ones without getting bitten, unlike someone else I know."

"Yeah. Now you know why I'm not a vet," Cantor said with a grin, wiping his mouth. "If you're a vet and every animal you pick up bites you, you're in the wrong profession."

"Let's call her. I'm sure Alex still has her number."

Two days later, Valerie agreed to fly out to inspect the place, paid for by Cosmic Pawn.

* * *

Valerie looked like an animal tracker—she wore high hunting boots, though she had never hunted an animal in her life, other than the occasional cat or dog that escaped into the waiting room of her clinic in San Francisco.

She had a way of saying something funny and then turning her chin into her shoulders while maintaining eye contact and a big grin. Quite seductive, but unintentionally so.

Valerie smiled as she shook Cantor's and Kumiko's hands inside Kumiko's lab. "Thank you for inviting me to this interview. I feel I'm up to working with these large animals, despite my short size."

"Alex certainly sang your praises," Kumiko said.

"If you want the job, it's yours," Cantor said. "We still have to do an interview, or at least go through the motions. Since we have accepted money from Cosmic Pawn, they'll expect it," Cantor said.

"I think dinosaurs are so fascinating. They're like children from momma birds and papa crocodiles," Valerie said, sitting down in the chair Kumiko offered her, flicking her long red hair behind her.

She did a thorough job answering questions. Toward the end of the interview, the conversation became more relaxed.

"How would you treat a dinosaur with a fever?" Cantor asked her.

Valerie didn't skip a beat. "To treat an ill dinosaur, I'd take a remedy for a reptile, add it to the remedy for a bird, and divide it by two."

Cantor laughed. "A mathematician and a veterinarian. It's good to see you again."

* * *

The next day, Kumiko gave Valerie a tour of the Veterinarian Clinic and her cabin. While Valerie checked out the place, Kumiko got a call from Arthur Saxton in Los Alamos.

"How's everything in Top Secret Land?" she inquired.

"It's full of snow. I'm calling because I'd love to tour your facility, now that it is more complete," he said.

"Of course, Arthur. The raptors have settled in, which gives us hope that they'll mate."

Two days later, Kumiko and Cantor met Arthur at the ranch. He seemed most interested in the E-raptors. They looked through the reinforced windows of the barns before entering for safety.

Gazing at Mako in his cage, Arthur was impressed with his size and intensity. "I think I like Cain's nickname – Mako. How's he doing?"

Mako paced back and forth, staring at Arthur. Deep rumbles like sludge gurgling over rocks emerged from his throat.

"As you know, Mako is our difficult one," Cantor said. "He's very temperamental. Several workers have refused to work with him."

"I want to take photos of this fellow," Arthur said, pulling out his phone. He stepped close to the cage and focused on Mako's sickle claw.

"Arthur, please don't get any closer. Mako is dangerous," Kumiko advised. "We still need to add further protections to his cage."

Arthur ignored her.

Cantor gently put the palm of his hand on Arthur's chest, firmly keeping him from moving closer. In his other hand, he held a mop, which he kept between the cage and Arthur.

Arthur was determined to get a closer photo and extended his arm and hand holding the phone.

"Whoa," Cantor said. He started to ask Arthur to pull his arm back when Mako rushed the cage bars, got his claws around the mop, and snapped it, pulling half the handle into the cage where he vented his rage on it. The sheer power and speed of his attack left no one in doubt about Mako's nature.

"Arthur, you could have been injured!" Kumiko said. "Now Mako is in a rage. It will take hours for him to settle."

Mako slammed his weight against the bars, raising clouds of dust and groans from the bolts on the floor. Cantor and Kumiko winced at the volume of his gravelly roars.

Arthur watched, shaking his head. "That animal is truly vicious. And look at his eyes. Wonderful! Have you ever seen anything so cruel?"

Cantor glanced at Kumiko, finding Arthur's comments odd.

Later, Arthur stated he was pleased. "You both have done an amazing thing here. You continue to validate my computer simulations."

"Your simulations seem inaccurate if they portray E-raptors as typical predators. Can you imagine how Mako would be if we didn't add sedatives to his food?" Cantor said.

"When it comes to dinosaur characteristics, simulations, even on a quantum computer, may not take all the variables into consideration. But nature always does. Thus, the surprises with Cain... Mako."

"You gave us a scare," Cantor said.

"I just got too close. No damage was done."

"Have you figured out who messed with your computer code?" Cantor asked. He didn't feel like beating around the bush.

"No. I was as surprised as you."

Cantor looked at Kumiko as she rolled her eyes. "Is Los Alamos investigating?" Cantor persisted.

"No need. I fired someone on my staff. I'm sure they were the culprit."

"I see," Cantor said. "We hadn't heard about that."

"Well, you know how it is," Arthur continued. "At Los Alamos, we are very secretive." He laughed awkwardly and changed the subject. "Too bad there isn't a hyper-loop between you and Los Alamos. No matter, the Falcon brings me here just as quickly."

The Falcon was one of the latest VTALET drones which must have cost Arthur a fortune. It took off and landed vertically using quiet, ultra-efficient electric rotors. It could accommodate three people.

Later, after Arthur left the ranch, Kumiko told Cantor that Arthur's reaction surprised her. "He seemed pleased by Mako's ferocity."

"Yeah, at first, I thought he was being careless. Now I wonder if he was testing Mako," Cantor said. "In all honesty, I find Arthur strange. I really don't know what kind of guy he is. I don't trust him."

"He's brilliant, that much I know," Kumiko said. "And we are in his debt. But I'm still perplexed that someone could alter his code without him knowing. I wrote an email to the Info-Tech director at Los Alamos, describing the problem, but I never heard back from him."

"Well, I don't have time to try to figure him out," Cantor said.

"I guess I feel the same. It is what it is."

* * *

Mako ran his claws across the bars of his cage. Back and forth to the rhythm of the rage in his head. *Look for weak place. Look for escape place.* Humans came into the room. *Come closer. Destroy you.* Mako stared at the flat face that held something in his hand. *This one rare.*

Want to taste his insides. The flat face looked at him. *You dare!? Come closer weakling. I remove eyes from head. Slowly, I remove eyes.*

* * *

When the spring of 2048 arrived, the males, now almost grown, became more aggressive, especially Remus and Mako. The dinosaurs were huge, standing 9 feet tall at the hip, 13 feet tall from head to ground, and weighing over 4700 pounds. Their length spanned almost 30 feet. No *Utahraptor* had ever approached such an extreme size.

Cantor expected the raptors to mate in early spring based on the behavior of many mammal predators and birds.

He watched Maryann as she investigated parts of the open field. "Do you like to explore, Maryann?" he said when she approached where he stood on a ladder by the stockade fence. He made soothing sounds that Maryann seemed to like. "What do you think of Darwin? Do you want to share the field with him?"

She eyed him, cocking her head and making a series of grunts.

Later, he spent some time with Darwin, now in a special portable cage inside Maryann's barn. By placing the cages close to each other, he hoped the dinosaurs would become acquainted. *Hopefully, they can be released together without feeling threatened.*

Darwin, as a C-raptor, behaved the way Cantor expected. You didn't want to mess with him, but he was predictable. He was like a male lion in behavior, not like Mako or Remus. He was used to humans and didn't waste energy going into a rage when someone entered the barn, unless they made a loud sound or sudden jerky movements.

* * *

Cantor had contacted Alex, now an associate professor at Virginia Tech, several weeks before and invited him to come and see the raptors mate. Alex arrived as soon as spring break started.

Alex greeted Cantor and Kumiko with bear hugs. "Good to see you both. I'm anxious to see the dinosaurs," he said, his Russian accent as thick as ever. After an hour of observing Darwin in the open space, Alex headed over to Valerie's clinic.

"You are looking well, Valerie. It's nice to see you again," Alex said as he hugged her. He thought the New Mexican sun had brought out more of her freckles, which he found appealing. She still wore her wavy red hair down to the middle of her back. There was a large freckle on her right cheek, the size of a penny, shaped like Great Britain. And the same little scar beside her left eye that looked like a sideways letter S.

"You too. It's been a long time since I last spoke with you," Valerie said, as he hugged her again.

"Yeah. I regret our last argument. I hope time has healed things," he said, feeling a little nervous. Valerie looked even better than he remembered. He recalled how strong she'd been when they had dated. She had stopped him in his masculine tracks, letting him know she wasn't ready for any sort of commitment. The more she held him at arm's length, the more attracted he was to her.

"Why don't you come over to my cabin and we can catch up?" she said.

"Sounds good. Just for a bit. I need to sit down with Cantor later and see how I can help this week." *She confuses me. I don't know quite how to behave.* He was used to being in command, but she didn't see things that way.

* * *

Maryann and Darwin shared the same barn for a week. Eventually, Cantor wanted both C-raptors to roam the field together. Maryann was the first to be released into the open field. A truck stood by, with two workers, a net cannon attached to the roof, and a dart gun, ready to roll at the first sign of trouble. The net cannon was the best way to slow a large dinosaur, if you could cover it.

Darwin raced out of his remotely opened cage and entered the corral. He poked his head over the metal sides of the fence, watching and listening. After an hour, Cantor let him into the field where Maryann stood nearby. The scales on his head and legs glistened in the sun as he cautiously approached her. When he was within ten feet, he turned on his heel, let out an impressive roar, and hurried away. Within seconds, he was back again, trotting in a regimented manner like a drum major.

Next, Darwin brought one foot up, displaying the sickle claw, and slashed the claw down the trunk of a cottonwood, slicing off pieces of bark. Afterward, he walked about, seeming to ignore Maryann, but making a deep rumbling sound.

Cantor recorded everything and spoke to Alex at the same time with a mic. "Darwin is showing his fitness and masculinity to Maryann. I think he's waiting for some kind of feedback from her."

Suddenly, a rabbit ran out of a clump of sagebrush. Darwin bounded after it with great agility and speed, catching it in a cloud of dust. Darwin returned to Maryann and placed the dead rabbit at her feet.

Maryann moved her head up and down; a movement Darwin mimicked.

Cantor was beside himself with joy. "We're seeing behaviors that can't be fossilized. This hasn't happened for 125 million years!" he said to Kumiko and George excitedly. *Please mate. Make babies for us.*

His excitement was contagious and Kumiko, George, Alex, and Valerie cheered, each knowing they were witnessing prehistory in the making.

* * *

Valerie walked up to Alex with her camera after Darwin returned from the field and settled in his cage. "I think Darwin is a little confused. Or embarrassed," she said. "Galloping up to your date makes you look desperate, but running away is even worse." She grinned and cocked her head, chin near her shoulder in a cute, child-like manner.

"Poor guy. This is his first time, you know," Alex said, looking sympathetic.

"At least Maryann didn't bite him. Perhaps it was the rabbit that impressed her?"

"That was a pretty high-quality rabbit. And on the first date! I think Darwin is a bit of a player," he grinned. "We'll have to wait to see if he gets a second date."

* * *

That night, everyone at Cantor's dinner table was discussing whether the dinos would mate and have healthy offspring.

"I want to see if the offspring will become self-sufficient rapidly or need their mother's presence for a long time." Cantor said.

Alex added, "Assuming the C-raptors will be fertile."

Cantor had asked Alex if he would take a sabbatical and help with his research. Alex had thought about it and quickly made arrangements with the university in Virginia. His other research could wait and his graduate assistant could teach his classes. Raptor Ranch was the center of the paleontology world and he intended to be there.

"We see some of Darwin's behaviors in other wild animals during the mating season," Alex said.

"Yeah," Cantor agreed. "Go to a gym or a bar today and you see it."

"This seems to me hard-wired behavior," Alex said. "Female choice is a force to be reckoned with. If you don't impress the lady, you get no children."

"Definitely," Cantor said enthusiastically, smiling at Kumiko. "In my case, I just got lucky." After a pause, he added, "Valerie, can you determine if Maryann is producing pheromones?"

"Sure. I'll try to do it without stressing either C-raptor."

The next day, ranch hands placed Darwin's cage close to Maryann's in her barn after unbolting his and moving it while he was in the open fields. Valerie placed a small device between the cages that sampled the air. When she brought the container back to the clinic, she took some samples and tested them. Maryann was definitely releasing pheromones. This in itself was a discovery unknown to paleontologists.

Later, Valerie walked to Darwin's cage while Maryann was out in the field and opened the container holding the pheromones. At first, he did nothing. *I need to remove myself,* she thought. So, she walked out of the barn and watched through a window.

Alex passed by on his way to discuss a few ideas with Cantor. When he saw Valerie peeking through the barn window, he stopped and headed her way.

"You spend a lot of time looking through windows, Valerie?"

"Oh, hi. Just barn windows. I'm trying to see if Darwin reacts to scents associated with Maryann without her being present."

"I think Darwin likes Maryann. What's he doing now?"

She noticed Darwin seemed interested in the container. "He's bobbing his head and looking excited," she said.

"I've seen guys do that," Alex quipped.

"Yeah, it's not pretty."

* * *

The next day, the courtship part was over, and Maryann accepted Darwin as a suitable mate. She signaled her willingness by touching the tips of her fingers while she stood facing him, followed by placing her snout on the side of his head. Then she lowered her body to mate.

"Are you getting this, Alex?" Cantor asked quietly over his wrist phone. Both men were filming from different points along the fence surrounding the dinosaur field. *Wow! This is unbelievable!*

"I'm getting it, Cantor. They are touching cloacas just like birds. Amazing! Paleontology will never be the same. All your hard work was for this day."

George, Kumiko, and several ranch hands stood silently watching the scene. They stayed motionless while taking photos to avoid distracting the dinosaurs.

Once the dinosaurs separated, one of the ranch hands exclaimed, "Now we get *bebes*."

Cantor was overjoyed. The next day, he and Alex looked through the barn window at Maryann. He didn't want to think about the possibility that the offspring might be deformed or fail to develop in the egg. In his excitement, he began thinking out loud to Alex, "I wonder if *Utahraptor*s were social and cooperated in hunting. Would the females and chicks be social? Would the males stay to themselves until the next mating season? Perhaps one dominant male lorded it over a harem of females and their young like Mountain Gorillas. There were many possibilities. The birth of viable raptorlings will go far in providing answers."

"Yes," Alex replied.

"Can you imagine? In a decade, we could have a herd of dinosaurs. Think of it! We can double our understanding of them. No more wishing we could travel to the past. If only we could bring back an Ankylosaurus, or a Stegosaurus. It's just so…"

"Are you feeling all right, Cantor?"

"I feel great! Why?"

"Verbal diarrhea can be a terrible thing."

"Shuddup."

Now everyone would wait. The suspense filled Cantor's thoughts during the day and haunted him at night.

Cantor called George on his wrist phone. "I keep hearing 'Bring it back. Bring it back,' in my head from that song by Led Zeppelin. In a way, we're bringing back the Cretaceous. What do you think, son?"

"The world just changed, Dad. Things will never be the same."

Chapter 22

Maryann Escapes

Cantor realized that the best place for Maryann to nest was in her barn. It was temperature-controlled and dimly lit. He and Alex were busy laying hay in the early morning, trying their best to provide a comfortable nursery for her while she roamed in the open area. While everyone waited for her to lay her eggs, they moved Darwin back into his own barn.

"I don't want Maryann subjected to any stress for the next few months," Cantor told Alex.

"Absolutely. A lot is riding on this pregnancy," Alex added.

After they completed their work, the two men headed outside, where the morning sun greeted them, warming their cheeks. "Let's get something cold to drink," Cantor suggested, and they headed toward his cabin.

"Good idea."

When they got closer to the cabin, they heard someone shouting in the distance. Both men quickly climbed the two-story watch tower nearby. Trying to follow the shouting, Cantor scanned the area. Then he saw it. "Maryann is on the wrong side of the fence!"

He felt a rush of adrenaline. *Please, please, nobody be near her.*

Maryann sauntered into the part of the compound where people gardened. In the view from the watchtower, her head would rise above the fence, then drop out of sight as she explored the sage and rocks. After a few strokes of her sickle claws down the trunk of an old cottonwood, she walked toward where some new cabins were being built. With her hands crossed, she studied the area, nostrils flaring as she absorbed the scents.

Cantor and Alex ran as fast as they could down the steps and toward her. To Cantor, his progress was agonizingly slow as he jumped over clumps of grass and dodged rocks. Alex pulled ahead.

"Alex, go over to the cabins for some meat! We may need it," Cantor shouted between breaths.

His lungs burned. Sprinting such a distance taxed every muscle in his body. His old scars felt tight.

Up ahead, he saw one of Tusker's men approach Maryann with the rifle from Tusker's office.

"No," Cantor shouted to the man. "Let me... handle it. Put the... gun away!" he gasped. George was just rounding the corner of the Comms building. Cantor signaled for him to go back inside.

Cantor slowed to a walk as Maryann passed one of the vegetable gardens. "Easy, girl," he said as he slowly walked toward her. Maryann stood eyeing him, her sickle claws tapping the ground. Raising her head, she took in her surroundings.

He tried to remember her feeding schedule. *Please be fed already.* The urge to flee was strong, but that wasn't an option. Breathing deeply, he tried to control his panic. He hoped Kumiko wasn't watching; this could end badly.

Maryann stepped past a creosote bush and cocked her head as she approached him, green eyes glistening, occasionally interrupted by a quick flash of her secondary inner eyelid. She walked with her hands facing down, sometimes expelling air with a snort. Her striped tail swayed back and forth while she ruffled the short feathers along her back and sides.

"Easy girl, easy," he repeated. *Please, nobody do anything stupid.* She clicked her teeth together, meaning she was tense.

Cantor could hear her huge lungs inhaling and exhaling; her nostrils flexed as she sampled the surrounding aromas. *So far, so good.*

Suddenly she let out a growl and spread her long fingers in the threat posture and held her head low. Cantor stopped moving. Perhaps he'd miscalculated. Maybe his bond with her wasn't as strong as he thought. *Don't exude fear!*

Following her eyes, he realized Maryann was reacting to the man with the rifle.

"Give me the gun! Walk away!" Cantor told him. "Don't look at her."

The man hesitated.

Cantor looked at the man. "Give me the gun!" he demanded again, holding out his hand.

At the sound of Cantor's demand, Maryann growled with agitation. She began to sway, as though winding up for a fight. Reluctantly, the man handed it over.

"Now back away, slowly." The man looked to the ground and stepped backward.

Maryann began to walk past Cantor, less than twenty feet away. She was heading towards the cabins and people. He knew he needed to act quickly.

George was approaching with a drone controller in his hands, while, overhead, the drone whirred as it slowly moved over the scene.

"No, George. You need to stay back. If she gets too excited, she will become dangerous." Maryann began to snort, sensing Cantor's urgency.

George hesitated, then slowly backed away.

Alex arrived with a chunk of meat he'd scrounged from the food building. Maryann stopped. She seemed to recognize him, but still growled when he came within forty feet.

"Lay the meat on the ground, Alex. Back up slowly and give her some space."

Alex did so, and Cantor walked toward the meat without making any jerky movements. Sweat was dripping off his face; his shirt clung to his belly.

"OK, Maryann," he said softly, trying to hide his fear. "You're safe." He held out the meat and walked toward the stockade gate. As a ranch hand handed Alex a tranquilizer gun, Maryann turned her head, opening her jaws, then clenching them shut, showing more of her teeth. She lowered her head, a sign she might launch into a sprint toward the Alex. All it would take was one loud noise or sudden movement.

"Don't tranq her, Alex. It acts too slowly. It'll just upset her," Cantor said as softly as possible. "Who knows what it would do to her embryos?"

Cantor drifted toward the open gate while imitating the sounds she had made as a chick.

Maryann followed, occasionally pausing to check scents. "Good girl. I have some meat for you if you're hungry," he said softly.

Cantor drifted toward the open gate while imitating the sounds she had made as a chick.

Then Maryann took one big step that brought her within a few feet of Cantor. He held the meat up above his head and felt the heat of her breath as she lowered her head and took it from his open hand. He began to shake. After swallowing, she put her snout in front of his head, bumping him and smelling his scent. She seemed to study him for what seem like an eternity. *Please, Maryann, please. Stay calm. Don't do this.*

Someone shouted, "No. Stop, Maryann!"

She jerked her massive head and made a rumbling sound from deep in her throat. Her huge hands grabbed him, raising him off the ground, still holding the rifle. He struggled to breathe.

More shouts, "No!" and "Shoot her!"

She turned, crushing Cantor to her chest, and walked briskly away from the people. A drone buzzed around her head, zipping in and out. A flash grenade went off. It stunned her, and she dropped him. Slowly she made her way toward the gate, each foot fall releasing shivers in the ground. Once she stepped inside the open field, the gate closed automatically.

Cantor rolled over, squinting to see her from where he lay on the ground, breathing heavily, the high-powered rifle nearby.

His hands trembled as Alex and others joined him. Slowly, he sat up, his eardrums buzzing from the explosion. "Take the rifle, Alex," he mumbled. "I'm not sure I even know how to work it."

"You all right?" Alex asked, one hand on Cantor's shoulder.

"Yeah. I don't understand why the gate was open," Cantor said, standing up unsteadily. "If nobody is propping it open or a remote signal tells it to stay open, it's supposed to close automatically."

"I thought she was going to… well, uh… harm you," Alex exclaimed. "I really thought you were a goner."

Cantor wiped the sweat off his face, shaking his head. "I… I can't believe that. Not Maryann."

George joined him, his eyes wide and red, his voice shaking. "I'm glad you're safe, Dad!" He held his father tightly for a full minute.

"I'm OK. I'm OK," Cantor kept repeating.

Stepping back, George said, "My drone filmed everything."

Alex looked at him. "That's a little morbid. Yes?"

"Nope. I also used the drone to distract Maryann."

Alex started to say something but Cantor interrupted.

"George, did you open the gate?"

"No, Dad. I was in the Comms building. I saw you running when I looked out the window."

"Did you see anyone else?"

"A couple of workers were unloading wood for one of the new cabins. They saw Maryann and hopped into their truck."

"How long has your drone been filming?"

"Unfortunately, I only launched it when I came to help. So not long enough," George said.

More people crowded around.

Cantor put his arm around George. "I know you wouldn't open the gate. I'm sorry I asked."

"Thanks, Dad."

"I'm glad you're OK, Doctor Hoffman," Robert Greaves said as he jogged toward the group. "I saw the commotion. That was a little scary."

By now, Tusker had joined them. "This shouldn't have happened, Cant!"

"Dan, I thought the gate automatically closed. It makes me think someone intentionally propped it open and then closed it after Maryann escaped."

"This isn't good, Cant. Not good at all," Tusker scoffed, his face flushed. He noticed Alex had his rifle. "And you! Give me that rifle!"

Alex slowly examined the rifle and opened the chamber to inspect the bullet. It wasn't loaded. "I'm no expert, Dan, but rifles are most effective when they're loaded, aren't they?"

Tusker grabbed the rifle. "Most people don't keep loaded guns around, Alexander," Tusker said with irritation. "I recommend you never have children!" He turned and stomped toward his office.

Alex watched him leave. "I don't like that guy."

* * *

After everyone dispersed, George sat down near the gate and watched Maryann lying in the shade of a great cottonwood. He ran his hands through his dark hair, trying to understand the avalanche of feelings in his head. He had childishly considered his dad immortal. The morning could have had a different outcome. What would he be doing now if Maryann had attacked his dad?

This was a dangerous place. He watched Maryann. She wasn't wracked by what-ifs. He stood and dangled one hand through the gate's metalwork, but she ignored him.

* * *

Luna stood transfixed at her kitchen window as Maryann moved through the gardens. As soon as she saw George approaching the big dinosaur, she ran out to the porch and yelled, "George, don't!"

George didn't hear her. She stepped outside and marched in his direction, intending to pull him back if necessary. But when she saw Cantor urging people to move back, she looked on helplessly. By the time Maryann was safely back behind the gate, she collapsed emotionally and returned to her cabin. Fear, relief, and anger made a strong brew. She didn't see George linger, his hand through the gate.

* * *

Later that afternoon, George headed back to his cabin. Luna stood in the kitchen, strangling the spoon in her hand.

"I can't do this! I love you, George, but I can't do this."

"I think everyone is stressed," he said, holding his arms out to hug her.

"No," she said, crossing her arms across her chest. "What if it had been Mako?"

George looked at the floor.

"This is tearing me apart, George. Next time, somebody might be killed. You!"

George sighed.

"I don't want to live here," she said, turning away from him and wiping her eyes.

"This is our home, Luna," George pleaded, waving his hand at the cabin surrounding them. "I don't have any money other than the small amount my parents give me." He winced. "Where would we live?"

"Someplace safe, George."

"But we can't afford a decent place nearby. Please try to understand, Luna. I have responsibilities helping with the dinosaurs. I'm needed here, don't you see?"

Luna's eyes flashed. "George, I know you. You'll try to pet a lion. Why can't you get a regular job?"

It was as though a bolt of lightning struck him. "What job? What job? Don't forget, if we lived somewhere else, we'd have to pay rent, buy our food. But here, my work is meaningful." He hung his head.

"I don't care about money, you know that. I don't care if we live in a dump. You've got to choose, George," she said, then shook her head. "I didn't mean to sound so harsh." Tears streamed down her face.

George reached for her, but she pushed him away. "Can't we compromise? Maybe we could live together in Cuba if I get a night job there and work here during the day. I can get a loan for an e-bike."

"You can't make much money on the ranch, George. And two jobs would wear you out." She let out a ragged sigh. "I know how much it means to you to be here. I get it. But I'm afraid. I'm not like you. These dinosaurs scare me."

It hit George hard. Luna was in pain. "Let me talk to Dan. Maybe he'll hire me and I can afford an e-bike."

"I'm going to spend some time at my mother's house in Owa'ke."

George stared at the kitchen floor. "I'll stay there with you in Owa'ke and drive back to the ranch each day once I get the bike."

"That's an hour's drive one way." She put her hand on his arm. "You can join me when you're able. But my dad will come to get me tomorrow." She went to the bedroom and shut the door.

"I'm so sorry, Luna," George said to the door. "I've been selfish. I didn't understand. Please don't give up on me." He sat on the couch and put his head in his hands.

Chapter 23

Raptor Lands

Cantor heard steps on the porch. Looking through the front window, he saw Tusker tap on the door. He was wearing shiny medals and medallions on his purple-striped vest. His head popped up when Cantor opened the door.

Extending his hand, he said, "Congratulations, Cantor, on the first mating of dinosaurs for millions of years."

"Thanks, Dan," Cantor said, motioning for Tusker to enter. "This is incredibly exciting. Waiting is the hard part."

Kumiko sat in her reading chair, waiting for a handshake that never came.

Tusker spoke to Cantor and ignored her. "And when do you plan to mate the E10s?"

"Well, we aren't planning to mate them. We need to figure out their genetic issues and correct them."

"Wait, Cantor. This…"

"Hear me out," Cantor said, interrupting him. "Nature wouldn't make an animal any angrier or more aggressive than is necessary for its survival. The E10s are unnatural. I wish to study dinosaurs like the C-10s that I believe are very similar to what roamed the Earth millions of years ago."

"Listen, my friend. You can't put all your eggs in one basket." Tusker smiled. "Get it? Forgive me, my humor is just too much sometimes. You should try for as many offspring as possible using both C-raptors and E-raptors."

"If they weren't so dangerous, I'd agree with you, Dan. To put it bluntly, the E-raptors need more work. Mako and Remus are extraordinarily violent and Circe is almost as bad."

"My boss is going to insist you mate them. As contractors, you need to do this."

"Hold on. You told us we would be free to do our research without interference."

"Yes. That's true. As soon as the E-raptors mate, you can study their offspring as you wish."

"This stinks, Dan. This isn't how I pictured things when I signed up." Cantor felt his face flush.

"Read your contract, Cantor. Our mission is to nurture the raptors and encourage the formation of a breeding population."

Tusker didn't stay long. The medals on his vest and the silver beads at the end of his braids sparkled as soon as he stepped past the porch into the sunlight.

* * *

"This is a mistake," Kumiko said after Tusker left.

"It was like talking to a brick wall," Cantor said.

"A wall with flashy medals. I don't like this new fad. It debases the hard-earned medals given to veterans."

"I hear you," Cantor said, rubbing his temples.

Kumiko crossed her arms. "Is there any way we can stop Dan's interference in our research?"

"Not legally. And not in the time we have. And, frankly, we're outnumbered by Dan's people."

"Are you worried about a confrontation?" Kumiko said, shaking her head.

"I'm probably just being paranoid. I wish we'd thought to give Mako and Remus the dinosaur equivalent of a vasectomy while we were in California," he said.

"We would've been condemned by our scientific colleagues if we'd done that," Kumiko replied thoughtfully. "But you're right."

* * *

The next day, at Tusker's insistence, George remotely opened Circe's barn door, then her cage, as he watched from a ladder behind the metal outer cover of the corral palisade. Next, he opened the corral gate to the fields. Circe, the only female E10, stayed in the shadows of the barn, but George could see her slow-moving shadow. She crept toward the open door, every muscle taut, and her orange eyes locked onto his. "Remember," his dad had said. "Never challenge her by looking into her eyes." He forced himself to look away.

Circe charged, crossing the corral in a flash. With a gasp, George took his hands off the top of the corral as she leaped, digging her claws into the wood and metal gaps. Her head reached the rim long enough for her orange eye to mark him. Then her great weight forced her down.

Circe waited for him to reappear. He knew that had he been in a tree, she would have waited until he died of thirst and fallen. Days if necessary. Shaken to his core and breathing hard, he climbed down the ladder and stumbled away. Something made him turn around. In a daze, he walked back and reached for the ladder again. If not for Jose, he would have climbed, drawn into the hypnotic eyes and rippling power waiting for him. After several minutes, Circe left the corral for the open fields.

* * *

Circe studied the field's boundaries and where every human stood beyond. Jose, in George's place, used a remote to open Remus' cage. The big male made a grand entry. Standing his ground, he studied everything, including Circe. During the previous week, Remus and Circe had been allowed to get acquainted inside her barn, with only the cage bars separating them. Now, anything could happen.

Remus was a magnificent specimen. Nine feet tall at the hips, thirteen feet high when he raised his head, and as long as an Allosaurus. And he was still growing. There was a menace about him. Instead of pacing or circling, he attacked Circe. With his red feather mohawk standing straight up, he was prepared for combat, and his eyes never left her. The workers looked at Cantor, waiting for a signal from him to move closer with noisemakers and a car in case this didn't end well.

Remus bit the back of Circe's neck, drawing blood. Backing off, he growled and stared her down. She hissed and stepped back. Both raptors had their hands and claws splayed out. To Cantor's relief, Remus walked away and explored the grass and bushes, ignoring Circe. Nothing happened the rest of that day.

* * *

That night, Cantor suggested they leave the two E10s in the field for a few days. Maybe they needed time to get comfortable with each other. "What do you all think of Remus' performance today?"

"He was so hostile!" George exclaimed.

"I think he's confused," Alex added.

Cantor said, "Or he has bad genes. Valerie, was Circe giving off pheromones when she was in the barn with Remus?"

"Yep. Not that it phased Remus."

"Weird."

* * *

On the third day, Remus and Circe's behavior changed. Despite being stressed, Circe didn't back away when he approached her again. Instead, she lowered herself to the ground and raised her tail. Remus growled and grabbed her by the neck like he was attacking her while he tried to make contact between his cloaca and hers. When he released her, she growled, ran almost 50 feet away, and then rested on her haunches.

Cantor thought of how mating between African Lions seemed so unpleasant for the female.

* * *

Because of the need for the dinosaurs to exercise, explore, and relieve stress, Cantor realized they needed to divide the open fields into separate territories. This allowed several dinosaurs to enjoy the open space at the same time without fear of attack. Equally importantly, the males couldn't kill the offspring of another male.

With Tusker's hesitant approval, he ordered the construction of parallel wooden palisades that would stretch from the barns almost to the end of the property, a distance of about two miles. The older fence of the original field remained, and only the partitions between the smaller fields needed to be constructed. Each wooden fence would stand twelve feet tall. There would be a field for Maryann and her chicks away from the perimeter fence, a similar one for Circe and her chicks, one for Darwin, and one for Remus and Mako. Between the partition fences, a narrow dirt path would allow the research staff – Cantor, Kumiko, Alex, and Valerie – to monitor the raptors and move quickly on bikes if necessary.

Maryann's field would be accessible from her corral at one end and a gate at the other. The same was true for the others. To keep things straight, Cantor called Darwin's field Darland. Maryann's was Maland, Circe's was Circeland, and the field for Mako and Remus was Grouchland.

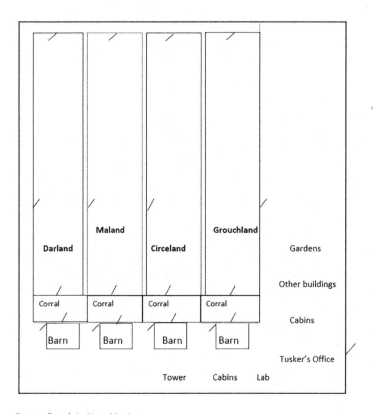

Raptor Ranch in New Mexico

Each barn was upgraded to have heavy-duty, large plexiglass windows which allowed the researchers to observe from outside while providing light inside. Every day Valerie observed the females, which were cage-free inside their barns, to see if any eggs had hatched. On May 15, she spied eight beautiful eggs in Maryann's nest. On May 24 she discovered nine similar eggs with Circe. The mottled eggs were light green and brown.

* * *

Drones were great at videoing the big picture but were impersonal, as were the videos from stationary cameras. Observations from behind the safety of the fences were too remote to suit Cantor. *I want to be in the thick of things.* Perhaps an e-bike would give him the ability to follow events rapidly.

He didn't have any experience riding e-bikes, so for practice, he took one for a ride up and down the open field outside Grouchland. The day was coming when he would want to ride up and down beside the fences, to be where the action was. He thought about Maryann's escape. On an e-bike, he could have reached her much more quickly.

Carefully, he turned the accelerator grip in his right hand and the sleek Zeus e-bike increased its speed. It was quiet compared to the old days when he could hear loud motorcycles advertising the rider's bravado all over campus. This machine had the same power but didn't force itself on the neighbors' ears.

As he got the feel of the e-bike, he enjoyed turning corners and zipping up small hills outside the raptor lands. He tried to stick to the road used by work vehicles, although it wasn't much better than the less-traveled areas. Once he got past the gardens, he was on more natural terrain.

With no gears to change, Cantor found the bike very user-friendly, until he took a turn too quickly and ended up crashing into a woody clump of cholla and prickly pear. Other than his ego and the cactus spines sticking out of one leg, he wasn't badly injured. As he got up and brushed himself off, he saw someone moving quickly toward him on another e-bike.

It was Alex. He rode effortlessly. Soon he pulled up and asked Cantor if he was all right.

"No worries. I'm good."

"I saw you heading up the trail and thought I'd join you. Looks like that cactus stapled your pants to your leg."

"Yeah." Cantor reached behind and grabbed the nearest needle. "Ow! Damn, that little bastard didn't want to come out."

"Oh, man," Alex said. "You won't be able to ride back until you get all of those out."

Cantor twisted his body to get a better view. From his ankle to the back of his upper thigh, it looked like needles had grown through his jeans.

"Let me help you," Alex said, as he set the bike's kickstand. "I think you're going to have to take your pants off."

Gingerly, Cantor lowered his pants, wincing each time a spine came out with them. Half the spines remained in his bare leg.

Alex examined him. "Wow. Your legs look like sliced ham."

Cantor sighed. "Focus on the spines, please. I get enough of those comments from George."

Cantor endured pain and embarrassment for the next ten minutes as, one by one, Alex pulled the remaining spines out, kneeling behind Cantor.

"This isn't the best view of you, Cantor."

"Shuddup."

Chapter 24

The Benefactor

"Danger levels man and brute, and all are fellows in their need."
— Byron

A big man walked into Dan Tusker's office and shut the door behind him. Tusker immediately sat up. In the harsh ceiling light, every scar on the man's face stood out. Large brows hung over the deeply set gray eyes.

"To what do I owe the pleasure, Yuri?" Tusker asked, rising from his leather chair.

"Sit. The Benefactor will be in Mexico City tomorrow. Here is the address and time." Yuri handed him a note.

"He wants to see me?" Tusker frowned, his face reddening.

"A new plan for you. He will explain." The big man turned to leave.

"Please sit, Yuri. We can be friends, can't we?"

"In my line of work, it's best not to have friends."

"But wait. Can't you tell me what to expect? I mean, it must be better for all concerned if I can prepare."

"*Do svidaniya*. Just keep your head and be respectful. Don't speak until spoken to." With that, the man turned and left.

"Dammit," Tusker cursed when his door closed. He tried to think if he'd somehow screwed up.

* * *

Tusker sat in the back seat of a black car that drove him to the *Del Templo Restaurante* in Mexico City. He wore bland clothing without his medals. A thin man sat on his right and a stocky, strong-looking man on his left. Both wore dark blue suits. Neither said a word until they got to the restaurant, making Tusker even more uncomfortable.

It wasn't as fancy as he expected, with just a low-key neon light giving the name of the establishment. As the car stopped, the skinny man got out and closed the car door, but he didn't enter the building. Tusker began scooting over in his seat, but the other man indicated he should stay put.

Wiping his palms on his pants, he sat back as the car drove around the building and into an alley behind it.

"I ah… I assume, you know… I don't… Violence surely isn't a solution, right? You agree?"

The man said nothing.

The back of the building was dark with a smell of grease and old meat. The stocky gentleman got out and beckoned Tusker to do the same. He walked ahead at the man's urging, fearing a blow to the head at any moment. When they came to a metal door, the man stepped around Tusker and opened it. Together, they passed through it to a red hallway that led to another door. The man knocked and a lanky, mustached man answered. After a pause, Tusker entered while the stocky man stayed outside in the hall. A painting of a bullfighter preparing to slide his sword into a desperate bull hung on the wall to the right. On the far wall was a poster of the great pre-Columbian ruins outside the city.

"Sit," the tall mustached man said, pointing to one of two very fancy-looking leather booths. As Tusker sat, he looked at the big man sitting across from him wearing sunglasses and dressed in black. The man put down his fork and looked silently at Tusker for a long time.

Tusker knew not to utter a word. His forehead felt damp. He felt as if every pore, every flaw, was being examined. He counted the seconds as the sunglasses watched him.

After wiping his mouth with a napkin, the man said, "Are you well?"

"Yes, Benefactor."

"What did you do when the dinosaur escaped?"

"I monitored the situation."

"I understand you brought a rifle to the scene. Did you plan to shoot the dinosaur?"

"Well, I gave it to a worker. I wanted to show the scientists I meant business."

The big man exhaled. "Maybe you have forgotten. My investment is in the dinosaurs." He let the tip of his steak knife bounce over Tusker's fingers.

"I will double my efforts to see that no dinosaur is ever harmed." He didn't dare move his hand.

After a long pause, the man said, "I understand a worker gave the rifle to one of the researchers. Correct?"

"He wasn't supposed to do that, Benefactor." Tusker's eyes widened. His body felt hot.

"Wasn't supposed to...," the Benefactor repeated and paused. Tusker looked down as his hands gripped each other under the table. "Eyes on me. If your child runs across the street and is hit by a car, he wasn't supposed to do that. Yes? He should have been trained to look both ways. So, who is at fault?"

"The... the parent. I apologize, Benefactor," he said and heard a man at another table scoff.

The Benefactor placed his hand under his chin and indicated that the man at the other booth should remain seated with a flick of a finger. A large gold ring shone on his little finger. "Anyone who apologizes has made a mistake. I thought you assured me you didn't make mistakes."

Tusker began to apologize and stopped himself. He tried to control the sudden twitch of his mouth.

"I hear the dinosaurs have mated. This is correct?"

"Yes." Tusker nodded and regretted the squeaky sound of his voice.

"And how long before there are little ones?"

"Several months, I believe."

The big man sat back. "You do not know?"

Why didn't I find out a more exact timeline!? Tusker thought as his throat dried out. "Even the scientists don't know for sure, sir."

"Your excuses are annoying." The big man glanced to the side, prompting the tall, mustached man to rise from the other booth.

"Do you think the Benefactor is a teacher asking for your homework?" the tall man said. "Excuses are failures. Are you saying you failed?"

"No, my apol... I will find out the timeline, Benefactor." Tusker could feel his bowels loosen.

After a nod from the Benefactor, the tall man returned to his seat.

The big man's finger tapped the table. "Once you confirm the young are viable, you are to step up efforts to get rid of the scientists for good."

"Benefactor, are you suggesting I... I dispose of them?"

"No, that will draw too much attention."

"Of course." Tusker breathed out.

"But you must drive them away. Let more accidents happen. Scare them. If injuries occur, so be it. We don't need them."

"I understand, Benefactor," Tusker said with a parched throat. He wanted to ask some questions, but he knew better.

The Benefactor continued, "You do not need to know why. You can follow directions, yes?"

"Yes, Benefactor." He looked at the man's glass of water, wishing he could have a drink.

"You know you cannot fail. True?"

"I will not fail."

"Your mother, how is she?"

Tusker felt his face flush and a chill run down his back. "My mother?"

"Yes. You have a nice mother. She loves to garden."

"Yes… Yes, she does." It seemed hot in the room. The big man stared at him until he wanted to crawl away. Why did his lip have to start shaking now?

"You may go."

"Thank you, Benefactor."

Chapter 25

George Looks for a Job

The day after Tusker's return from Mexico, George visited him.

"Thank you for seeing me, Mr. Tusker." George noticed the uncomfortable wooden chairs were lower than the leather one behind the desk, where Tusker sat reading a file.

"No problem, George. You can call me Dan. What's on your mind?" Tusker said, turning over a paper in the file.

"Well, after Maryann got out of the enclosure, my wife, Luna, decided she wanted to live away from the ranch."

"A wise woman. I think you should listen to her."

"Well, I told her I needed to make some money so we could afford to rent a place nearby."

"So, you are wondering if I'd hire you?" Tusker said, looking up for the first time.

George felt his face redden. "Well, yes. That's why I wanted to talk to you."

"And what kind of work did you have in mind, George?"

"Well, I could help around the ranch."

"What can you do?"

"I can help feed the animals."

"I thought you were already doing that."

"Well, yeah. I am."

"What else?"

"I can run errands for you."

"I don't need any help with that." Tusker began twirling the pen in his hand.

"Is there anything you need help with?" George asked.

Tusker looked at him for a few seconds. "You can keep me informed."

"About what? In what way?"

"Tell me what your parents are doing, what they're saying."

"Like what they're saying about the ranch?"

"Sure, or what they are saying about me."

George was feeling uncomfortable. "I'd feel like I was spying."

"What's wrong with that? Wouldn't you like to know what they're saying about you?"

"I… I believe they would speak to me directly."

"Well, George. Come see me when you really want a job," Tusker said, picking up the file, dismissing George with a flick of his wrist.

Chapter 26

Muli

It was mid-summer, and Cantor and Kumiko expected the eggs to hatch any day now. Cantor needed someone to work with him to help with the dinosaurs, everything from tracking little ones to carrying equipment to making observations. This person would report directly to him, not Tusker.

Ranch hands were busy in June putting devices along the fences of Maland and Circeland to keep hawks and eagles from attacking the soon to arrive baby dinosaurs. The devices recognized a dangerous bird and used a flashing laser to disorient it without damaging its eyes.

Around this time, a young, slender man named Chitundu Muli arrived from Kenya. He hoped to secure a position at the ranch. Short black hair topped his rich ebony head and large eyes dominated his face. Soon everyone called him Muli, rather than work their tongues around his first name.

His family had helped paleontologists such as the Leakeys in the previous century and he had experience with several paleontologists working around Lake Turkana in East Africa. He wanted a chance to work with dinosaurs and his enthusiasm was unmistakable.

He arrived with few belongings. During Muli's interview inside Cantor and Kumiko's cabin, Cantor asked about his homeland after serving him some of Kumiko's white tea.

"I grew up in a small village in the Rift Valley. A lot of my time was spent gathering water for my family since it's pretty dry most of the year. On my own, I studied paleontology because I couldn't afford to go to college. I was privileged in 2037 to have been on the team that found the *Australopithecine* fossil known as the Mzee skull eroding from the rock."

"The 'Old Man' skull."

"Yes."

"We have much work ahead of us. Are you ready for what may be a long, challenging job?"

"All jobs are challenging, Mr. Cantor, at least the ones I want to do. When you love an animal, helping it is not a job. I love the animals that share our world." Muli had a graceful way of putting his hands forward, as though he were presenting a gift.

"Please call me just Cantor."

"I show respect. It is my way."

"As you wish," Cantor said. "I must go to Kenya someday,"

"It's a beautiful land, however, a wise man sees beauty outside his hut," Muli said with a grin.

It's like I'm speaking to Gandhi. "So, are you suggesting I'm wise for wanting to go? Or am I unwise for having never gone?" Cantor let out a laugh shared by Alex.

"That is not my intention, Mr. Cantor."

"I'm still searching for wisdom."

"Wisdom is tailored to the situation. There is social wisdom, community wisdom, survival wisdom, pain wisdom, happy wisdom..."

"What do you mean by social wisdom?" Cantor asked, finding himself intrigued by Muli's way of speaking and his different perspectives.

"I do not view wisdom as a commodity, nor do I speak of it lightly. Having said that, I might be able to share with you."

"I understand. Perhaps it was disrespectful to ask the question?"

"It was unwise."

"Of course. Please forgive me," Cantor smiled.

"You are of a different culture. Here is a sample of social wisdom from my homeland: A child may play with its mother's breasts in public, but it cannot play with its father's testicles."

Lex laughed heartily.

"I think that is true of my culture as well. Thank you, Muli," Cantor smiled, catching the sparkle in Kumiko's eyes.

* * *

Circe sniffed at her eggs, took two of them, and placed them in a corner of the barn. Once she was safely out of the barn and in Circeland, Valerie retrieved the two eggs, suspecting they contained dead embryos. A sonogram confirmed this.

Kumiko then opened the eggs and examined each little tragedy before she placed them in a freezer for further study.

It made sense that the mother would recognize bad eggs and remove them to protect the viable ones, Valerie thought.

In the meantime, Maryann faithfully tended her eggs. She squatted over them and sealed her sides with the feathers on her arms. All her eggs, so far, seemed healthy.

* * *

Each barn had latched openings along the ground, wide enough to pass food to a dinosaur when it was inside but not in its cage. Above the opening was a window of thick plexiglass held in place with a steel frame with bars across it. A hose provided water through a hole in the wall over a bathtub-sized basin.

Over time, the workers noticed Maryann would put the tip of her snout through the hinged opening when they were preparing to feed her. She had greenish-gray scales around her nose. Larger, yellow and rectangular ones grew near her teeth. When seen from the window, they could see bead-shaped skin surrounded parts of her neck and face. She didn't seem aggressive, just curious.

George often accompanied the ranch hands and helped with feeding. One day, after opening the latch and seeing Maryann sniff the air with as much of her snout sticking through as possible, George slowly placed his hand between her nostrils.

He could see her nostrils working, sniffing his scent. She made a huffing sound. After several days of this, he carefully placed the tip of his fingers further on her snout. She withdrew with a grunt, but after a minute, she again placed her snout in the opening, expelling warm moist air from her nostrils. This time, she did not withdraw when George gently touched her.

George turned to Muli standing near him and laughed. "I made contact! This is so great! We connected!" He recorded his experience in a notebook and took pictures.

"Good for you, Mr. George," Muli said, studying him.

Soon, others wanted to touch the powerful dinosaur's snout.

* * *

Later, Cantor sat stood in his kitchen speaking with Kumiko. "So, did George tell you he touched Maryann's snout?"

"What!?"

"Now everyone wants to do it. It's safe. She can only stick out the very tip of her snout."

"Can she open her mouth?"

"No, the opening isn't large enough."

She let out a sigh. "Please don't encourage George further."

"I won't. He was so excited." He paused and then asked, "Would you be interested in designing a *T. rex?*"

"What!? Who are you?"

"I know big dinosaurs were a mistake," he said, holding his hands out. "But now we can house them."

"I know how exciting the dinosaurs are to you, but no, not a *T. rex*." She gave Cantor a look she usually used with George.

"Just imagine, though, something so huge and powerful."

"I don't have to imagine. All I need to do is look out my window."

"I know. But a *T. rex!*"

"Imagine if it turned out as aggressive as Mako. Cantor, I have no doubt it would be impressive. And it should remain that way in your imagination and nowhere else."

Cantor sighed, his hands on his hips, "Yeah, I get it. I'm more than happy we actually have breeding dinosaurs. And now they have all the open space they need to do their thing. Though there were obstacles, they are behind us now. The future is going to be so amazing."

* * *

A week passed. As the ranch hands were opening the latch to Maryann's barn, they heard the unmistakable sound of chirping chicks. Two, it turned out. Through the window, they could see them scampering around their mother. People wandered to Maryann's barn all day to catch a glimpse.

"There they are," Cantor said to George as he gazed at the chicks. "There's the future."

"Maybe next week, when Maryann has all her chicks and has settled into a routine, we can take their vitals and weigh them. We'll need to sedate Momma first. I'm not sure the best dosage, though."

"I'd be happy to help," Alex said, hopefully.

Before the hatching, Valerie used a new sedative on Remus as a test subject. Mako was roaming in Grouchland, so she remotely let Remus out of his cage. She mixed the sedative with his breakfast of ground beef. To Alex, she said, "Kumiko warned me that the E-raptors take a much higher dose." After an hour, Remus seemed calm, but when Alex tested him by inserting a teddy bear attached to a stick through the barn's latch door, Remus tore into the bear, leaving the stuffing scattered about the barn. The stick didn't make it either.

Valerie tried a new drug mixture. It took a large dose, but now Remus just gazed at the replacement teddy bear and made no move toward it. She was surprised at how long the drug took to work. *Hopefully, it will work better for Maryann.*

Within three days, all Maryann's chicks hatched. Eight chirping and stumbling little ones.

Circe, a couple of days later, had her own brood of seven to contend with.

* * *

After a week, Valerie asked Alex for help again. She gave Maryann a sedative cocktail similar to the one given to Remus, but at a lower dosage. After an hour, Maryann sat quietly, gazing at nothing.

Alex entered the barn slowly, dressed in protective clothing, cautiously peeking around the door at Maryann. The clothing made him feel better, but he knew it wouldn't save him if she became angry.

Maryann looked at him with a kind of quizzical twist of her head. When he used nets to scoop up the little ones, she eyed him and made a low-sounding growl, but she didn't rise. With the chicks aboard, Alex left the barn quickly.

Valerie took them to the clinic, where she took their measurements and blood samples while Kumiko and Alex looked on. Afterward, she gave the chicks nourishment and returned them to Maryann through the latched door. The massive mother gradually became more alert as her chicks, having imprinted on her, gathered around, chirping.

Circe's first chicks hatched three days after Maryann's. A week later, the first attempt to sedate her using a dart gun didn't go well. Valerie had aimed through a small slit built into the walls of the barn. As Alex carefully entered the barn, she turned to him and rose to her full height, her teeth bared. He didn't need more encouragement and bounced off a door frame on his way out.

"Are you OK, Alex?" Valerie asked.

"Fine," he said, though he rubbed his shoulder when she wasn't looking. "That was a little tense. Try again?"

Valerie fired a second dose into Circe's thigh. She snarled and pulled the dart from her leg with her teeth. After half an hour, Alex once again slowly entered. Circe bared her teeth and stood slowly. Alex retreated. After a third dose, Circe remained on her haunches. Soon, Alex netted all seven little ones and took them to the clinic. But Circe was on her feet.

"Success! Nice work, Alex."

"Thanks, Val. Circe must have a weird metabolism."

"She does. Like Mako's."

"I hope she forgets who just stole all her babies."

The E-raptor chicks varied in their weight. One seemed quite small. Within two hours, Valerie returned the seven to Circe.

Valerie reported higher levels of a hormone variant related to aggressive behavior in the E-raptor chicks. Kumiko, not surprised, made a note of it.

* * *

Cantor decided it was time to let the mothers out into their separate fields with their babies. The chicks did their best to keep up with their mothers, but Circe's runt was constantly falling behind. Valerie recorded each chick's gender, and the researchers agreed on names.

They named Maryann's chicks Ida, Allegra, Dragon, Huey, Dewey, Clair-la-Lune, Frodo, and Samwise.

Circe's chicks were named Galahad, Gawain, Spike, Leon, Elsa, Korrigan, and the runt was Tiny Tim. All had indications of genetic abnormalities. The males had patches of missing feathers, and on top of that, Spike had only two fingers on one hand and several unusually large teeth. Elsa and Korrigan lacked an ear opening on one side of their head.

"Am I going to need to know all the names on the quiz?" Alex had asked Cantor.

Each chick had a number painted on its downy back. Maryann's chicks sported numbers 1 to 8 and Circe's from 1 to 7. Note-taking was easier that way. "4 is climbing the nearest tree while 7 and 8 are staying close to Mom; 3 seems interested in 2's toe," was a typical note.

Both mothers roamed throughout their fields while their chicks investigated the different shrubs and trees. Insects were a great source of fascination and the chicks tried to catch them, jumping and snapping their jaws. When their arm feathers sprouted, the chicks became adept at catching dragon flies and grasshoppers between them.

The cones around the bases of the trees near fences kept them from climbing them. They scraped and smelled the ground, targeting anything that stood out like stink bugs and flowers. The mothers were most attentive around water.

Cantor asked Tusker to build an enclosure about forty feet into each dinosaur's land for better observations. There were several one-foot wide, by two-foot-high portals placed in the wooden walls. Bars were placed across the top at intervals of two and a half feet, allowing a human to look over the top. An adult dinosaur's head was higher than the wall, but they couldn't stick their heads inside. The enclosed space became known as a safe-house.

* * *

One day, while George was in the safe-house with the gate closed behind him, Maryann walked to the wall with chicks in tow. He launched a small drone to capture videos, aiming to get the best shots. Seeing this trust from Maryann was very encouraging for him.

The safe-house fences had thick wooden posts driven deep into the ground every five feet. These posts were the only ones stabilized with concrete. The equally thick horizontal beams started at ground level and rose as high as the posts. Inside were steps for a human observer to see over the top, as well as portals for lower viewing.

An animal, perhaps a rabbit or a gopher had dug a deep tunnel running through the safe-house and into Maland.

Allegra and Clair-la-Lune crossed through the tunnel and walked up to George, who was looking through one of the portals in the wood. The chicks had seen humans their entire lives and showed no fear.

George put his hand out for the chicks to sniff. Then he picked them up while making sounds of encouragement. *Maybe they'll still imprint a little on me.*

Maryann could tell some of her chicks were on the other side of the fence, and quickly withdrew her head from the top beam and began sniffing at the hole the escapees had used. Then she began digging.

She could dig quickly, mostly using her feet. Large clumps of dirt flew behind her as she placed her body parallel to the fence. *Oh Crap!* George became alarmed and carefully pushed the chicks through the now much larger hole. After thoroughly examining them, Maryann trotted off, offspring in tow.

George smiled as he walked out of the safe-house. He felt he'd shown Maryann and her chicks that he was a good human who cared. He realized the hole needed to be refilled, but kept it to himself. It would be dangerous, as it involved taking a shovel and climbing into Maland.

Using a ladder at night, he climbed up the safe-house wall, lifted the ladder through the safety bars above, and put it inside Maland. Using night vision goggles, he scanned the area for any sign of Maryann before climbing down. He began filling the hole, but not as quickly as Maryann had dug it. The job was almost complete when he heard a thumping sound in the distance. He threw the shovel over the wall and scampered up the ladder. The thumps were closer now. With barely a second to spare, he lifted the ladder and dropped it inside the safe-house and climbed to the ground. His hands shook. *Go home now, George.* Instead, he slowly climbed the ladder again.

* * *

George seemed obsessed with the chicks. Several days later, Muli happened upon George digging a hole with his hands under the fence in Maryann's safe-house.

"Mr. George, why do you dig?"

"Please call me George. I'm trying to visit Maryann and her chicks."

Muli gave this some thought and said, "You have insurance?"

"What? What are you talking about? I want to spend some time with them."

"Is unhappiness in your life an issue, Mr. George?"

"What? Muli, why don't you watch and you'll understand?"

"It is easier to stand for a visit with the dinosaurs. You can see Maryann when you stand on the steps."

"Yeah, I get it. It's kinda complicated Muli."

Muli raised his eyebrows and looked at George intently.

"OK, fine. I want to let a chick escape."

"Your father, he will beat you."

"No Muli. I don't mean escape. I mean, come for a visit. And my dad doesn't beat me."

"Maryann will beat you."

George sighed. "Listen Muli. You're pulling my leg, right? Like a dinosaur is going to punch my lights out. Seriously, I'm doing a good thing. I'm here to visit the little ones."

"Before swallowing a mango seed, first calculate the diameter of your anus, Mr. George."

"Muli, this has nothing to do with mangos or my anus, for God's sake. I just want to dig a hole so I can get to know the young ones."

"I see… You wish to swallow a mango seed."

George squinted up at Muli. "What's with you and mangos?" He resumed scraping clumps of dirt out of the hole.

"Hands may suffer what the head decrees, Mr. George."

"I don't know what that means. Muli, I want you to just watch, OK? I'm going to dig a hole and nobody's hands are going to suffer. That's all."

"Your fingernails will crack. Have you seen a gold miner's hands?"

"Not to worry. My fingernails will be fine."

"Tunnels are easier to make with shovels."

"OK, fine. I'll take the shovel."

"Sadly, I do not have one."

"Dang it, Muli. Will you just watch, OK?"

"I have a pick."

George hung his head, sighed, and said, "That will be fine. Thank you."

"Will you give it back?"

"What, the pick? Of course."

"The chick, Mr. George."

"Well, if I didn't, I wouldn't be a very nice friend to Maryann, would I?"

* * *

Now and then, George dug little holes under the fence by the safe-house. Maryann became nervous but didn't panic when, with George's help, one or two chicks would make their great escape. But after a minute, she made a barking sound, making it clear she wanted them back. After returning the raptorlings, George always filled in the hole from inside the safe-house. He also recorded these experiences with his small personal drone.

George felt warmth for these raptors, both large and small.

Muli felt obligated to mention this to Cantor.

* * *

"Son, you can't handle the chicks just for fun!" Cantor said that evening at George's place. They sat on the porch, sipping ice tea in wooden chairs with their feet on the railing. "They are delicate and extremely valuable to our research. What would you do if one ran away?"

"They haven't done that. I always keep a little meat treat for them, so they stick around. And the gate to the safe-house is always closed."

"You took a chance. What if Maryann had become upset? How do you know the next time she sees you, she won't try to take your head off?"

"I'm very careful, Dad."

"George, please listen. These are the only dinosaurs in the world. You can't play with them. I must insist." *And you are my only son!!*

George took his feet off the railing and faced his dad. "It's part of my own type of research. I need to record how Maryann behaves."

Cantor shook his head in disbelief. "George, why don't you get a puppy? I'm not being sarcastic when I suggest this. Maybe a puppy like Lily. You loved her so much. No more dinosaur chicks out of their enclosure. I'm afraid that's the last word on that."

Later that night, Cantor told Kumiko about his conversation with George as they got ready for bed.

"Do you think we weren't affectionate with George when he was a child?" he asked when he'd finished brushing his teeth.

Kumiko slipped on a white nightgown that ended above her knees. "I've always worried because we were both busy professionals. It must get lonely being an only child with such busy parents. Remember the assignment his teacher showed us where he accidentally wrote he was a 'lonely' child when he meant to write 'only'?"

"I've always tried to be supportive of George," Cantor said, "and I always tried to make time for him."

"We both have, honey. We both tried very hard," she said, slipping under the bed sheet.

"I try to include him whenever I can," Cantor said as he climbed into bed.

"He knows we love him. We've always been affectionate with him. You guys used to horse around a lot, and you were quick to give him hugs," Kumiko reassured him. "People say it's not the quantity of time you spend with children, it's how much quality time you spend together. Maybe there just wasn't enough quality time. He tells me he always takes his meds. His depression has stabilized, but maybe his OCD is getting worse."

"Yeah." Cantor thought of the changes that had come over George in middle school. "I suggested he get a puppy."

Kumiko sat up. "Cantor! That sounds condescending! You can't say things like that. If George wanted a puppy, he'd have gotten one."

"Hm… It sounds bad, doesn't it?"

"It certainly does. We need to re-double our support for him, Cantor."

"I'm going to invite him to help me with observations. Make him more of a part of the team. You know, he made one significant observation already. The raptors can dig and dig quickly. Thank goodness they don't do it regularly."

"Only when they are trying to rescue their children," Kumiko added.

Chapter 27

Temptations of George

George felt he wasn't spending equal time with Circe and her chicks. Everyone wanted to touch Maryann through the latch door in the barn, and they ignored Circe. George knew that if you don't spend time with an animal, it will never trust you.

The ranch hands told him Circe was different, and they had no love for her. To Circe, all humans were on the menu.

Muli spoke to George as a pesky drone hovered nearby. "Maryann and Circe are not alike, Mr. George."

"Why do you call me that?"

"That is your name."

"No, I mean using 'mister'."

"I speak to everyone with respect. It is my way."

"We don't speak that way."

"You are disrespectful."

George sighed.

Muli continued, "Maryann and Circe are not alike, Mr. George."

"Well, sure, they have distinct personalities. Think of your friends. Don't they all have distinct personalities?"

"My friends don't eat me."

"OK, OK. If you didn't have any friends or family, wouldn't you be lonely?"

"I would."

"And wouldn't you feel bad?"

"I think so."

"Well, there you go Muli. Circe is no different from you."

"Circe is a dinosaur, Mr. George."

"I know she's a dinosaur, Muli. Don't you get what I'm trying to say?"

"You want to be Circe's friend."

"Yes. That is what I have been trying to tell you."

"She will bite you."

"For crying out loud, Muli. I'm not planning to play tennis with her."

"That is good because she would jump over the net and bite your head."

George let out a resigned sigh. "I'll be careful."

"Mr. George, may I suggest you let the ranch hands handle Circe?"

George rubbed his forehead and headed for Circeland, anyway.

Muli watched George walk away and decided to follow.

George stood on a step and watched Circe and the chicks from the Circeland safe-house enclosure. He used a camera on his head and a drone to record. His hands were on the topmost beam. The sound of thunder distracted him and he saw the distant rain falling on the Santa Fe National Forest to the east.

"Good girl, Circe," he said, turning around facing Circe as she spotted him in the safe-house. "You're a mom now. Don't worry, nobody's going to hurt your babies."

Circe silently moved closer, cocking her head. Unlike Maryann, she made no noise. "We might get some rain, Circe." Her hands clenched and her nostrils flared. Carefully, she placed one foot closer to George, putting weight on it only when she was sure it would make no noise. He turned back toward the mountains as a gust of wind blew off his hat.

The big dinosaur surged the last eight feet, lunging at George's exposed head with yellow snapping teeth. Muli yelled a warning as she began her attack. George barely had time to duck under the bars. Circe turned and made a second leap for his hands, still gripping the top of the wall. He panicked and rolled down the steps to the ground.

He sat inside the safe-house with his hands on his knees, shaking his head. Circe snorted and growled on the other side. George looked up and saw a fierce orange eye staring at him through a portal. It occurred to him she might dig, so he left, closing the gate. Circe's eye tracked him as far as she could until he was out of sight. He walked rapidly, head down, muttering to himself.

Later that day, George confessed to Cantor, wanting to beat Muli to it.

"Circe attacked me when I wasn't looking," George said, looking at his feet.

"What?!"

"She attacked me. I want you to hear it from me."

"Where were you?"

"The safe-house in Circeland."

"Why were you over in Circeland, son? I've warned you many times to stay away from all the E-raptors."

"I know, Dad. I thought, since nobody liked her, I should try."

"But why? She doesn't appreciate humans, except as a meal, including you."

"I guess I was thinking she was like an outcast. Like a kid at school that nobody would talk to. One person could make a difference. Bring that kid out of their shell."

Cantor thought about that. "George, are you talking about yourself?"

George blushed but didn't answer.

"Please try to understand, Circe isn't shy," Cantor said. "She isn't looking for a friend. She's a deadly predator. I can't say this enough, George. Stay away from Circe, Remus, and Mako."

"Those three shouldn't have been created," George said dejectedly.

Cantor stood from the chair and put his arm around his son. "I know. Your mom and I regret ever bringing the E-raptors into this world. You were right all along about that."

George brightened at what his dad said.

* * *

With a song in his step, George headed for Koko's pen with her muzzle in hand. Then he walked with her to see Maryann and her young in Maland.

Holding Koko up to a portal in the fence, he let her smell Maryann and her chicks. In return, Maryann sampled the air, recognizing the C5 from previous visits. Koko knew she was related to the big dinosaur, the way a small dog recognizes her kinship with a German Shepherd on the other side of the street. George smiled as Koko sang *chira-chira-who, chira-chira-who.*

* * *

"I think George is in crisis," Cantor said the next morning as he and Kumiko were putting the breakfast dishes away.

"Why?"

"He insists on trying to communicate with the raptors. Yesterday, he tried to befriend Circe."

Kumiko dropped the dish towel. "Circe! He shouldn't be anywhere near Circe!"

"I know. I told him that. I don't know if he's into some kind of mysticism or what. It's like he's obsessed with reaching out to the dinosaurs. The little ones I understand. They are small and cute at this stage. But the adults, especially the E-raptors…"

"Cantor, he needs help. He told me he regularly takes his meds. Is he drinking?"

"No. Maybe a glass of wine or a single beer now and then. Never in excess. He's very aware of what he's doing. It's not like he's in a trance. But he still has these compulsions. His meds aren't cutting it."

Kumiko shook her head. "I've told him about jobs in Albuquerque he might be interested in. But he isn't. He wants to be here with us and the dinosaurs."

"What if we gave him our savings so he could get a teaching license in art?" Cantor suggested. "He could work in Albuquerque or Santa Fe doing something he loves."

Kumiko picked up the dish towel. "I suggested it to him a few weeks ago. I said we'd help him, but he said no. He wants to stay here."

"I hate OCD," Cantor said. "Every day, I worry he'll get hurt."

Chapter 28

No Electric Fences

Mako didn't get out as often as the C-raptors, Darwin and Maryann. Either Remus or Mako roamed Grouchland, but never both at the same time.

When he was in the field, Mako constantly checked his surroundings, a trait he shared with the others. He roamed with his head near the ground, sniffing and listening to small animals in their tunnels underneath his feet.

He tried to dig up prairie dogs, which turned into a game of Whack-A-Mole. When he spotted a snake, he played with it. Rattlesnakes were common. They struck at him, but his scales were too tough to penetrate. In the end, the snakes went down the big raptor's gullet. On one occasion, though, Valerie and Alex had to shoot the big dinosaur in his cage with an anti-venom dart to treat a swollen tongue, clearly a snake bite.

* * *

Mako sometimes stood at the fence by Circeland and listened. At the first sound, he'd run along the fence toward the source, snorting as he went, his huge hands curled against his chest.

Pausing behind several cedars, he placed his body along the fence and flung out buckets of dirt with his feet. No one observed Mako's peculiar behavior until Robert Greaves heard it as he was patrolling Grouchland.

Looking through a portal in the fence, he called out, "Stop, Cain, stop!"

Mako lifted his head and looked at Greaves. He stopped digging and walked toward him.

Greaves pulled his head back as Mako neared. As Mako's 'mother', he should have had a close bond with Mako, and Mako did accept him more than any other human, but Greaves was wary. Mako was too unpredictable, too fierce.

He started to call Cantor on his wrist phone but thought better of it. Instead, he called Tusker.

"Robert Greaves here, Mr. Tusker. Cain er... Mako has begun digging along his fence by Circeland."

Tusker thought for a while. "OK. We can't let him get at Circe or her chicks. Get help and use meat to get Mako back in his corral. Then call Cantor. Let him deal with filling the holes in."

* * *

"Robert Greaves called me about Mako doing some digging. I'm telling you, it's essential we put in electric fences," Cantor said, standing in Tusker's office. "Ones that will prevent the dinosaurs from digging under them."

Tusker listened to Cantor's appeal, tapping one ringed finger on his desk. "Mako couldn't possibly dig deep enough to escape. He'd have to dig four feet."

"He can do it."

"He's too big to get through a hole, Cantor."

"I'm not so sure about that, Dan," Cantor said, shaking his head.

"Have a seat. Some coffee perhaps?"

"No thank you," Cantor remained standing.

"Listen, my friend. I'm just as concerned about safety as you are. But I have a budget to think about. It's always about the dollars. Anyway, an electric fence won't stop him from digging under it."

"The damn budget isn't going to matter if somebody gets hurt, Dan. And a good electric fence WILL include the ground underneath."

"Cantor, you're the behavior expert. Just change his behavior. It's that simple, no need for expensive fences. And while we are talking about Mako, I've noticed you don't spend a lot of time with him."

"No, I don't. I don't spend a lot of time with scorpions, black widows, or cobras, either."

Tusker picked some lint off his shirt. "I believe you are part of the problem. Have you seen how the bears at the zoo behave? They're neurotic. Nobody spends time with them. I want you to spend equal time with Mako, as you do with Darwin and Maryann."

"Look, if I thought he was a better subject for study than Darwin, I would. But I don't."

"There are only five adult dinosaurs in the world. And you don't want to study three of them. Come on, Cantor. Get with the program or get out of the game and let me and my people do the tough stuff."

Chapter 29

Luna's Painting

Weeks passed, and the first signs of autumn abounded. The cottonwoods were turning a brilliant warm yellow, as were the few aspens. Cantor and Kumiko enjoyed taking walks along the fences, relishing the clean, crisp air. Sometimes they talked shop, other times, they enjoyed just being together.

In the mornings, a chill warned of the coming winter. The workers were busy testing the barn heaters, and the raptorlings grew rapidly.

As Cantor walked out of his house, he noticed Tusker walking out of George's cabin in the opposite direction. He thought it odd and made a mental note to ask George about it.

* * *

Luna maintained her interest in art. She gravitated to the painting style of Native American painters like Fritz Scholder but was equally comfortable with realism. A growing market for her paintings existed in Santa Fe and Albuquerque.

She painted the dinosaurs as powerful spirits filled with color. Her painting of Mako stood out from the rest. The brush strokes were slashing and angular, and his eyes froze the viewer. They communicated menace and brutality. His teeth were piercing daggers. After her signature was a symbol that stood for protection.

Her painting of Mako Impressed George.

"You really caught his essence, Luna. That is Mako in all his evility."

"I don't think that's a word."

"It's the best word to describe him. Who says computers do better paintings than humans nowadays? No kind of AI could capture the emotion like you did."

"I want the painting to be burned in a ceremony."

"What!? Why?"

"You know why. There is a connection between the painting and Mako. I promised my mother I'd give her the painting. She knows someone in the north who handles things like this."

"But we could sell it for some much-needed cash."

"This is the wise path, George."

Luna still lived with her parents much of the time. When Luna was visiting the ranch, she would sketch and paint, and have dinner with George. But it was hard for her to think of the ranch as home. She preferred a home without residents with big teeth who craved to have her for dinner.

When he wasn't sketching or helping with the dinosaur chores, George was writing or talking on his wrist phone. Cantor was surprised, judging by George's increased phone usage, that someone isolated on a ranch could maintain such a social life. It didn't seem like George. Something wasn't right.

Chapter 30

Tiny Tim

"One general law, leading to the advancement of all organic beings,
namely, multiply, vary, let the strongest live and the weakest die."
— Charles Darwin

During the winter, Cantor planned to upgrade Raptor Ranch and carry out his more ambitious research plans.

Cosmic Pawn still received donations from museums and wealthy dinosaur lovers. Some patrons felt Tusker should open the ranch to the public. Others worried that without more transparency, online misinformation by conspiracy theorists might harm the project.

The raptorlings were almost the size of turkeys now.

Cantor and Alex sat on Cantor's porch slurping a FroziPro, a frozen protein shake, after a long day. They talked about the lack of red feathers atop the heads of the young males.

"It makes sense," Alex said. "A juvenile male would be toast, as you say in America, if he raised red feathers on the back of his head. In the wild, the adult males would kill him."

"Right," Cantor said. "The young have been raised with the smell of adult males in the other 'lands'. But that wasn't true for Mako, Remus, or Darwin when they were young."

Alex took a big gulp. "I'd like to see how the young males and adult males interact."

"We need to see things like that in the field," Cantor said. "There are all sorts of behaviors we need to document. I think we need some SUVs that offer protection in the field where all the action is."

"Sounds like a good idea. I suggest we supplement them with more drones. I mean, we can't sit in the SUVs 24 hours a day. And the drones can capture things we might miss."

"Good point, Alex. George has been using several drones on his own. We can get some more. And they can see things at night we can't."

It surprised Cantor when Tusker agreed to purchase the equipment.

A week later, a fleet of four shiny electric SUVs and four drones arrived. Cantor dedicated one to Darland, one to Maland, one to Circeland, and one to Grouchland. The vehicles had dashing logos on the sides displaying the name Raptor Ranch, designed by George and Luna.

The Comms building contained monitors that displayed video feeds of all four machines.

The drones didn't disturb the raptors. They carried a remarkable video camera with a zoom lens and advanced anti-blur capabilities. If an operator switched the drone to AI mode, the machine made its own decisions on altitude, speed, and what to record. If the drone's battery drained beyond a certain point, it knew to return to the technician or the Comms building.

On a warm day in November, Cantor spent the day monitoring the drones. Things had gone well, except for a problem with one drone earlier in the day that grounded it. In the late afternoon, he worked with the flight recorder computers arranged on a table and arched his tired back. His joints ached. He headed outside for a bit. He could see four drones moving over the fields as he turned toward home and a cool drink. As he relaxed in his living room easy chair, Alex came in and reported the downed drone would be ready the next day.

"That's great," Cantor said. He drank from a cold bottle of Tranquilade. "Grab yourself one from the fridge, Alex." Cantor was silent for a minute. "Actually, the fourth drone is already up."

"Nope. Only three are up."

"I beg to differ, Alex. Four drones. And George's drone wasn't among them."

"Did you count them on your fingers?" Alex asked.

"Funny. At first, I figured one had to be an eagle soaring over the place, but I swear that eagle had rotors. Someone is watching us."

"Maybe you need some glasses. You're getting old, you know."

"Shuddup."

Cantor turned to the sound system and said, "Apollo, compose a beautiful instrumental in the style of Vaughn Williams, with rich harmonies, but add a chorus." The machine responded with original music never heard before that would warm the heart of the coldest soul.

* * *

The next day, a drone found another hole, too big to be made by anything other than a dinosaur, under the fence between Grouchland and Circeland. Ranch hands filled it in. From that point on, drones made daily inspections along all the fences.

* * *

A couple of days later, Alex and Cantor were standing in the tower watching an SUV drive into Circeland and stop. The driver had disabled the self-drive option. When Circe began stalking the car, the driver returned to the recently installed steel garage near the corral. Circe followed, sniffing and growling. She began digging but gave up when she encountered just more steel.

"Hopefully Circe will get used to the car," Cantor said. "I want her to feel it's just part of the scenery."

"She may tear it to pieces," Alex said.

The chicks hid behind brush and tufts of grass but rose once the vehicle left.

Cantor looked at the close-up image on the camera he used. "I'm seeing Galahad, Gawain, and Spike. Elsa and Korrigan are moving in the opposite direction from their brothers."

"Yeah, I see them," Alex said, looking through his binoculars.

They saw Tiny Tim, the runt of the family, come bouncing along past some sage. Alex took notes when not using the binoculars, while Cantor filmed. Tiny Tim tripped over a rock, and as he got up, his brothers ran toward him.

Galahad bit him on the neck and shook it violently while Spike jumped on his back and started driving his sickle claw deep into the crying raptorling's flesh. In the meantime, Gawain slid into Tiny Tim, running his left sickle claw deep into the struggling raptorling's vulnerable belly while he grasped him with his hands. Galahad continued to bite the neck. Spike sliced the muscles of the back until they were slivers of red meat, which he began eating in small chunks.

Circe approached, but didn't seem to have any urgency about her. In one ghastly movement, she bit off Tiny Tim's head and swallowed it whole. Cantor, true to his science, kept filming but felt sick. Alex saw most of it through the binoculars. He just stared, speechless.

Both men packed up and headed for the Cantor's house. "This is bad, Cantor. Not only was it brutal, but we can't afford to lose a single chick. Not when the entire population of dinosaurs on Earth equals 19. Correction, now it's 18." Alex paused, then said, "You don't look so good."

Inside, they sat, not saying much. Kumiko entered and saw Cantor's pale and forlorn look. She started to speak, but instead came to him, placing her hand on his cheek. Alex called it a day and headed out the door.

* * *

"Whatcha doin', Val?" Alex said as he stepped into the clinic.

"Writing up temperature data. How about you?"

Alex told her about the attack on Tiny Tim.

"That sounds awful. I'm sorry, Alex."

"I know sometimes nature is brutal, but I guess I'm just a Moscow city boy. I'm not used to seeing brothers eat their siblings or mothers bite their children's heads off."

Valerie could see he was upset. "Let's go for a walk."

"Yeah, sure."

They walked past the cabins, talking.

"I've seen a lot of sad cases as a vet. You never get used to the suffering of the animals."

When they got back to the clinic, Alex thanked her for listening. As he left, his hand touched her arm, then he headed to his place.

Back in their cabins, both thought about the touch on the arm. How warm the other felt. But Valerie was wary. She still wasn't ready for a romantic relationship. Her last relationship after Alex had ended badly. As long as she buried herself in her work, she didn't have time to think of romance or what she might be missing. Working with dinosaurs wasn't as dangerous as opening her heart.

* * *

The next day, Cantor, Alex, Valerie, and Kumiko met over coffee and discussed the attack. Kumiko had heard Cantor's version the night before, but wanted to hear more.

"We need to study the video to understand why this occurred," Cantor said, running his fingers through his hair. "There may be an adaptive reason for this – perhaps this ensures the fittest offspring survive."

"Nature, bloody in tooth and claw," Alex said with a sigh.

With a pained expression, Cantor said, "Here's what I think. Tiny Tim may have simply been a reserve store of proteins, there to be devoured when needed. The siblings, who already had an advantage in fitness, benefited from his sacrifice. Circe's genes programmed her to let this happen. The brother's as well."

"In terms of evolutionary theory, it makes sense," Kumiko added.

"Yeah," Alex said, "That's a reasonable hypothesis. Kind of like worker bees sacrificing their lives for the good of the queen bee. Nature is the ultimate pragmatist."

"Perhaps that's true," Valerie said, "But it sucks to be the worker bee."

* * *

Tusker fumed as Jose left his office after telling him of Tiny Tim. *Damn Cantor. He has no idea how difficult this makes things for me. How am I going to explain this?*

He spoke into his wrist phone. "Call Cantor." While he waited, he thought of Kumiko. *I don't get it. It hurts my feelings that she shows no interest in me as a person.* Cantor answered the phone, and Tusker went straight to the point.

"Why didn't you prevent this?"

"You mean Tiny Tim?" Cantor asked.

"Of course, I mean Tiny Tim."

"I wasn't expecting it. I'm not sure there was any way to prevent it."

"Do you realize how much this devalues the ranch, Cantor?"

"Devalues the ranch? What are you talking about?"

"One less dinosaur. Do the math!"

"I agree, it's terrible to lose a dinosaur, but you make it sound like we're running a supermarket."

"This should never happen again, Cantor. Make sure it doesn't!" Tusker ended the call.

Cantor should be punished. He thought about his own childhood. How his mother disciplined him. *I hated those whippings. Then the confinement to the basement for a week. But it worked. Whatever I did, I didn't do it again.* He thought about Kumiko again. *Now, there's a strong woman.*

* * *

That night, Cantor lay in bed staring at the ceiling. Kumiko was reading a book of poetry beside him.

"Kumiko, is it possible for a dinosaur's eyes to glow?"

She put her book on the nightstand and looked at him. "They have retinas that are far more sensitive than ours. When you shine a light on them, they'll reflect the light, just like cats."

"What about the eye itself? I mean, the outside part, the iris?"

"I don't think so. Why?"

"Just wondering."

Kumiko kissed him goodnight and turned off the light.

Chapter 31

Where Angels Fear to Tread

"Abandon all hope ye who enter here."
— Dante Alighieri

2048 passed into 2049. Not much happened that wasn't anticipated. Then autumn came.

Pete Martinez was out with his friend Javier Garcia. They'd been buddies since grade school in Aztec, New Mexico, near the Four Corners area. Pete drove his beat-up old Ford pickup, an ancient vehicle in 2049, along a dirt road in the half-moon, breezy, autumn night. He was thinking about what the guy with the big bucks had asked them to do. They passed wild fields of cholla cacti, long yellow grasses, and low, wind-blown cedar trees that looked black and mysterious.

Occasionally, Pete saw a tarantula or rodent in the headlights as the old truck creaked and crawled along the bumpy path.

"This scenery reminds me of warnings from my *abuelita*," Javier said. "She warned me about *brujas*. She said they took the form of owls that flew at night. Kinda gives me chills."

Pete tried to ignore the worry this gave him. He needed to think about the task at hand. "I don't believe that stuff anymore," he said, shoring up his courage. "Don't think about superstitions, Javier. We just need to get in there, do our thing, and get back to the truck."

"Man, this place is way out in the boonies," Javier said, handing Pete a cold beer from the cooler that sat between them. He got another for himself.

Pete felt the steering wheel turn to the left as the tires encountered another hole. "I wonder what kind of critters they're raising?" *Finally,*

I can make some real money. If the dude wants a male and a female, that's what he gets, as long as he pays well. No need for Javier to know.

Javier was silent.

"From what I've heard, they could be weird geese," Pete said. "Like geese whose wings don't work."

"Who wants geese like that?"

"Maybe they have more meat on them," Pete said. "There's this big-ass fence. That means them geese is worth some coin."

"Where did you hear all this stuff, *ese*?" Javier asked, frowning.

"You need to watch more TV. I seen a program once about it. Not only that, this guy I went drinking with, he once delivered supplies to the place, and he told me. He said it looked like a secret place in…, like, you know, those spy movies."

"Why didn't you tell me this before?"

"Sorry bro," Pete said, trying to hold his beer as they bumped along. "He said the scientists go back in time."

"What do you mean, 'go back in time'?"

"I'm just tellin' ya what he said, Javier."

"People say crazy things when they're drinking."

Pete crushed the empty can in his hand, tossed it in the back, and flipped off the lights as he turned the truck onto what looked like a coyote path. The silence was eerie. He saw the silhouette of a large fence about a quarter-mile ahead.

"Here's where we stop the truck, *amigo*," Pete said, trying to sound confident. He put the truck in park and turned off the ignition.

Javier finished his beer in two gulps. "This place is nothing like any farm I ever seen. I don't know about this. I mean, it's easy to take people's geese or chickens. Well, except that time when that old guy took a shot at us. But if these ain't regular geese…"

Pete reassured him, "Don't worry. I'll increase your share by a hundred bucks." He led the way up the track toward the compound in the distance. Like Javier, he carried a pack on his back that held several large, heavy-duty burlap sacks, gloves, a knife, and some rope. Each man also carried a ladder.

The ladders were heavy and by the time Pete reached the compound's outer fence, he was sweating profusely. He listened for any movement.

"Damn, look at the concertina wire on top. They must keep something very special here," Pete whispered, looking up at the fence.

"That sign says 'No Trespassing, Dangerous Animals' *ese,*" Javier said. "Maybe we should go back."

"OK, so they have guard dogs. You got the doped-up meat?"

"Yeah." Javier began digging in his pack. "This is better steak than I've ever had."

"And the dope is a hellofa lot better," Pete added with a chuckle. "Put those dogs asleep in no time. Got your knife and gloves?"

"Yep."

"I don't hear no dogs. Maybe that sign was a bluff," Pete said. "I doubt those people who live here would want dangerous dogs running around, anyway. Toss the meat over to be sure."

Javier threw the meat and waited. "Nothing, *ese.*"

Pete took a deep breath. "Now or never." Luckily, the ladder was higher than the concertina. After putting on the gloves and climbing to the top, he looked and listened.

There were no lights from the buildings, a good sign. No sign of dogs. All he could hear was the pulsing of the blood coursing through his ears.

Despite the gloom, Pete could see several buildings the size of residences at the far end of the compound. There was another building whose function was unclear. Several corrals were attached to buildings that looked like barns. *That's where the critters will be.*

Most of the property, behind another inner fence he could barely see over, seemed unmanaged. Lots of grasses and sage with clumps of cottonwoods along depressions in the ground. In the more arid places, he could make out low-lying evergreens, like black holes. A pond shimmered in the dim moonlight. It appeared to be fed by a small stream.

Hearing nothing, he turned, grabbed the concertina in his gloved hands, and jumped down, landing awkwardly on grass and dirt. He glanced over his shoulder, feeling a tightness in his stomach as Javier climbed on the second ladder.

"OK, Javier, pull my ladder up and over so we can climb back later."

Pete pointed to the third corral from the left, about a quarter of a mile away. *I wish we didn't have such a long walk.* "They should be in there," he rasped. "That's what I've been told."

Javier silently stepped down the ladder. They began walking, glad there were no lights on this side of the property.

The corral fence turned out to be a challenge.

"How the hell are we supposed to climb this?" hissed Javier.

Pete walked the perimeter until he found a narrow, locked gate. It had vertical iron bars eight feet high with no cross beams for a foothold. He turned on his iPhone-40 light just long enough to see a barrel within the corral.

"Give me a boost!" he said to Javier, after tossing his backpack over the gate. Once inside, Pete rolled the barrel toward the gate. He'd use it to climb out when the time came. *Why's this corral so damn high?*

"You wait there, Javier. Toss me your bag and rope."

"Wait, I'm going to get my knife," Javier said, as he fumbled inside his pack before tossing it over the gate.

Pete, with both packs in hand, approached the door to the barn as quietly as he could. No sounds came from within. Gently, he slid the heavy wooden barricade from its brackets and then opened the large metal latch. *These people are paranoid! That barricade weighed a ton. Gotta be careful. They may have a bull in here.* Then he opened the massive door, revealing a dark interior filled with the musty odor of hay and animals. Flicking on the phone's flashlight again, he placed it inside, against the wooden wall at an angle.

He smiled as his eyes rested on a group of strange goose-sized birds. *These must be the adults. They are too big to be chicks*, he thought, as he held a sack with both hands. *Where are the little ones?*

He needed a male and a female. There was no time to look for the little ones. *Hell, it's the adults that breed, anyway.* The birds watched him in silence while he mulled over how to tell them apart.

As he approached the nearest animal, it rose and faced him. From out of the partially feathered wings, he saw hands emerge, black and scaly. From each hand, three long fingers unfolded, topped by sharp claws. *Oh man, that's no bird!* Nervously, he took some rope from his pack. *No wonder this place is so protected. These are going to be worth a fortune.*

After a moment's hesitation, he ran forward and covered the hissing animal with the sack. Before he could get the rope around the opening, a huge claw tore through the fabric. The bird pulled itself out as it made a high-pitched squawking sound.

No more time!

He tried to pick the kicking animal up with one gloved hand while he placed another sack over its head. The animal was heavy. With a screech, it grabbed his hand and tore at it with its beak. But this wasn't a beak. *Dios mio! This thing has teeth!*

Now confused and desperate, Pete straddled the animal with his knees and just managed to get it into the sack. Fumbling, he got a rope around the opening of the sack and tied it tight. In the light from the phone, he saw slash marks on his leg overflowing with blood. But before he could deal with it, again, a claw tore through the sack again. Now, all the animals were screeching.

* * *

Javier waited impatiently at the gate for Pete. *Come on bro, this is taking too long.* He felt for his knife. *What is happening in there? Damn! All that noise is going to give us away!*

A light came on inside a building. A minute later, someone called out, "Who's out there?"

Panicking, Javier, taller than Pete, jumped and grasped the top of the gate, and pulled himself up and over. *Crap! I don't want to get shot.* Once inside the corral, he followed the noise to the door of the barn.

Pete shoved a heavy jerking sack into his arms. Inside, something was pissed and fighting like hell. Javier winced as the animal bit his arm through the fabric.

As Pete headed toward the barrel, Javier hissed, "Someone's coming! You can't go that way!"

Javier looked around the dim corral and spied another gate to the wider field beyond. "There!"

"Go, go!" Pete cried.

"You left your light in the roost!" he exclaimed as Pete pushed him from behind.

"Just go, go!" Pete hissed.

Javier imagined the owner of the place zeroing in on his back through the sights of a rifle. *To hell with a second animal!*

Pete pushed him again.

Javier ran into the grassy field and stopped to catch his breath. Pete was close behind. Another screech as the sack was pushed and pulled. A deep, low growl came from somewhere to his right. It seemed to move around them, progressively closer. Heavy breathing.

A black form rushed towards Pete. He seemed to lift into the air. There followed a strange, gurgling sound. Javier frantically backed away.

Pete groaned.

Javier held the sack to his chest, breathing in short gasps. The moon disappeared as the black shape rose before it. *Dear God, no! Run!* He turned. A crunching sound pierced his ears like icicles. Then a thud.

Javier dropped the thrashing animal and stumbled on his hands and knees into the tall grass. He crawled to a low-lying cedar tree, panting and shivering. The branches touched the ground completely around the trunk, hiding the interior. He inserted himself into the spray of branches and began to pray. A large bird leaped from a branch above, beating its wings with a whomping sound. "Aye!" he cried, instinctively covering his head.

Help me, Señor!

He tried to quiet his ragged breathing. His shock made his thinking choppy and disconnected as he grasped the cross he wore around his neck.

He couldn't see beyond the tree. As quietly as he could, he reached for the knife in his pocket and opened its five-inch blade.

Javier placed his hand over his mouth to cover the sound of his breath, praying to wake from this nightmare. Carefully, he looked through the branches when a faint sound entered his consciousness. He hoped it was only the breeze, not a *bruja*.

Then, the soft *sushhh* as a sprig brushed against something. There was the sound of air rushing into huge lungs.

He sensed movement in front of him. From what little he could see, it seemed like a gigantic, dark hand. The hand slowly opened up, showing three impossibly long fingers uncurling with great eagle-like talons at the ends.

He gasped as the hand slowly invaded the interior of the splayed branches and wrapped the powerful fingers around his arm. Something breathed deeply beyond the branches. There was no rush, no hurry in its movements. It was delicate, gradual, and even graceful. He couldn't twist free and the knife fell from his hand.

The huge hand gently pulled Javier from the tree, branches scraping his face. He struggled to see, but could only make out dim outlines. Shorter snuffles interrupted the massive creature's breathing as it absorbed his scent. Slowly, another hand closed over his shoulder and it laid him on the ground. Javier squirmed and tried to push himself away from the massive demon. His *abuelita* had been right. As his arms pushed against the dirt, his head touched the great foot, as hard as iron, too large to be a creature of this earth.

A massive hand clamped onto his forehead, pinning his head to the ground. He could feel hot dank breath near his ear.

For a while, the breathing continued, as though the dark creature was observing him. Now its breath flowed over his skin between a glove and sleeve. It smelled of fresh blood and meat.

Then, the same hot sensation on his neck. A soft cooing sound. Almost comforting.

Don't show fear.

The colossal head emerged from the darkness near one of his hands. A claw pierced the glove and pulled it off. Again, the head returned to his hand. Huge teeth, glaring in the moonlight, picked up his hand and gripped it. The tips of the teeth scraped and tore his skin, but the jaw didn't sever the hand. A warm tongue tasted it until the jaws let it go.

He saw a gleam of moonlight in the two orange eyes that glared at him. There was something unnatural about them. Too bright. Almost like a burning light. The pupils expanded and contracted as a deep baritone rumble came in waves from inside the huge body.

His peripheral vision saw a light scanning the ground near the barn. *A person!* His nostrils filled with a sickly odor as he tried to raise his head. But the scaly head pushed him down.

"Fear no evil," Javier whispered, too afraid to yell.

Now came pressure on his leg. Gradually it moved up his thigh, softly tapping past his crotch, then hovered over his sternum.

Just the lightest touch.

The foot seemed to hesitate, then move tenderly in a wide circle. The circle gradually narrowed inward, a gentle spiral.

After a pause, SNAP, something sharp cracked his sternum and pushed deep into his belly, bringing excruciating explosions of pain as his shirt and skin ripped apart.

He heard a slushing sound and finally the cracking of his pubic bone, all in an instant.

He couldn't move as his torso was pulled open from his stomach to his bowels. The pain grew unbearable. He waited for the final blow, but it didn't come. The monster paused as if it were studying him. As Javier's thoughts faded into darkness, he felt the creature lightly touching his mouth. "I'm sorry, *mi Abuelita*," was his last wispy thought, barely registered, as mindless darkness enveloped him.

Chapter 32

Worst Case

It was 1:15 in the morning when the ruckus woke Cantor. The cries of raptorlings, muffled as they were by the walls of a barn, made it clear something was amiss. He jumped out of bed, slid his pants on, and stepped into his sneakers. By now, Kumiko was also awake and alarmed.

He picked up the flashlight from the kitchen and headed out the door. As he stepped off the porch, he called out, "Who's out there?"

He could hear the sounds of some kind of commotion coming from Circe's corral.

Alex caught up with him. Together, they ran to the barn, where the screeches continued. Peering into the heavy plexiglass window with their flashlights, they could see some raptorlings leaving through the door into the corral.

"Someone has opened the door!" Alex exclaimed.

"Let's head for the fences and see if we can see anything," Cantor urgently suggested. *What the hell?*

Up ahead, they heard deep growls and a loud bellow. It had to be Circe.

"Sounds like she's attacking something!" Cantor cried, out of breath. All he could think of was George. "I can't see anything." He shone his light through the fence portal. *Don't be George. Please, don't be George!*

"I think she's moved further up the field, Cantor," Alex said, peering into the night.

The men ran along the path between the fences. Finally, at one portal, they could see her feeding near a cedar tree. *Jeez, this is bad.*

"Do you think she's eating one of her young?" Cantor asked, trying to block his panic.

"I don't know. There just isn't enough light!"

"Dammit! Why don't we have floodlights?" Cantor said, angrily.

"Maybe we should try to get Circe into the barn."

"That's a good idea, Alex. We'll have to use the cars and horns to get her at least into the corral. I'll call for the truck with the net cannon." He reached for his phone, but it was back at the cabin. "Damn! No phone."

"I'll call and grab some fireworks as well," Alex yelled, already running.

Soon, several ranch hands joined Cantor by the portal. "Does anyone have a phone?" Cantor called out. Jose handed his phone over. He dialed George's number. No answer. Next, he dialed Alex. "Please! Find George!"

After five minutes, Alex called. George wasn't home. Just as Cantor was preparing to run to his son's cabin, he showed up, hair askew.

It took over an hour to get Circe behind the corral walls.

Even in the low light, they could see the blood smearing her mouth. Once they safely cleared the field, they began to search systematically for her prey, beginning with the area around the cedar tree where Cantor and Alex had seen her feeding. There they found Javier's remains.

Cantor was sick after seeing what was left of the man. He had to sit down until the dizziness subsided. Alex too was in shock.

Pete's headless remains weren't found until morning.

Chapter 33

Your Soul is in Danger

*"The cucumber is bitter? Then throw it out. There are brambles
in the path? Then go around. That's all you need to know."*
— Marcus Aurelius

S everal black and white state police SUVs pulled into the compound,
followed by a pair of ambulances. The morning sun revealed itself
only by the red stripes below the clouds along the horizon.

The scattered remnants of Javier were shredded clothes and a
few bones. Pete was more complete, but he had suffered many bites
to his mid-section and his head was missing. Two police investigators
crouched around his remains.

A heavyset officer with graying sideburns questioned Cantor as he
stood on the path between Circeland and Maland.

"Sir, what time did you hear the noise coming from the barn?"

Cantor thought for a second, "I guess it was around 1:00 in the
morning."

"You say one of your animals did this?"

"Yes. I can show her to you. She's in her barn now."

"Was she in her barn last night?"

"No, I'm afraid she was in the field. Where the… body parts were
found." Cantor struggled to stop the awful sight in his head. His stomach
convulsed all over again.

"Please lead me and our photographer to her barn."

"Yes, of course, officer."

"We'll need to remove her from the premises. She's a dangerous
animal."

"She's a very large dinosaur. Where would you take her?"

"We haven't determined that yet."

Tusker had overheard the conversation. "Is that really necessary? She was where she was supposed to be. The men invaded HER territory," he said as they reached Circe's barn.

"Why was she outside the barn?" the officer said, putting his hands on his wide hips.

"Do you understand what we do here?" Tusker responded loudly.

As he looked through the barn window, the officer stopped short with a gasp, stepped back, and said, "Take the pictures, Johnson. You will hear from us, Doctor Hoffman. We are going to need a statement. I hope you understand the seriousness of your situation. I suggest you get a lawyer."

Cantor stared at the officer as he turned to leave. Waves of panic pulsed outward from his stomach. He no longer had control over events. He looked at Tusker, who shook his head and moved his index finger back and forth twice.

"Can we keep a lid on this, officer?" Tusker called out. "We wish to avoid all publicity."

"Not my problem," the officer said over his shoulder. He pointed at Cantor. "You can go now."

Cantor turned to walk away.

"Excuse me, Doctor Hoffman?" the County Sheriff asked, walking up to Cantor and frowning. "Do you have permits for these animals? I'm going to need to see them."

* * *

Cantor finally had some private time with Kumiko. "This has been awful," he said and put his arms around her. He drew back and saw the redness in her eyes. "We have each other, no matter what happens. It'll be OK. I know it." He touched the tear that seeped from her eye. "Aw, Kumiko, I'm sorry this happened." She pulled away and put her hands to her face. "Sweetheart, please. It's going to be OK," he said, holding her again, his breath warm next to her ear.

She put her head in the crook of his neck.

"I thought it was George," Cantor whispered. "I thought it might be George." He regretted saying it when Kumiko groaned. *Why wasn't George at home last night?*

Removing Circe proved to be more difficult than the authorities originally thought, so for the time being, she stayed at the ranch. The governor ordered all the dinosaurs confined to their barns, which meant the end of much of Cantor's research, at least for now.

* * *

Two days later, an AI lawyer, or lawbot, representing the families of Pete and Javier, deposed Cantor. These robots doubled as lie detectors. Cantor's exploratory deposition took place in Santa Fe, in the presence of his human lawyer, Richard Damson, and another lawbot representing Cantor's insurance company.

"I've never been interrogated by a lawbot," Cantor told Damson while they waited for the others in a room with a long wooden table and no windows. A camera stared at him from one corner near the wooden door.

"Just relax," Damson said. "The bot will analyze real-time images of your brain and eyes to increase the accuracy of the results. Be sure to tell only what you know because these machines catch a lie 94 percent of the time."

"I have nothing to hide. I'm curious to know how they can be so accurate."

"Well, I'm not an expert, but I know the bots use artificial neural networks. Don't ask me what those are. But like so many AI systems, humans don't quite understand how the bot does it once it has trained itself. The damn thing makes me feel stupid."

Shortly after, the lawbot entered with another man who assisted Cantor in putting on a head device.

The machine stood before him on four legs and asked him some rudimentary questions for calibration before the in-depth questioning began.

"Please keep your eyes on mine at all times. Once I collect some preliminary data on your heart, brain, and eyes, we can begin. Please do not speak except to answer my questions. Are you ready?"

"Yes," Cantor said, startled by the intimidating design of the bot's eyes.

"I will now move closer so I can monitor your eyes. Do not move your head."

To itself, the deposition computer said, "Today is October 14th, 2050. Deposition of Doctor Cantor Hoffman, case 16-1731012-10142050.

"Are you married to Kumiko Chen?"

"Yes."

"Do you have a son named George?"

"Yes."

"Have you ever been arrested?"

"Once."

"Why?"

"Hold on here," Damson said. "How is this relevant?"

"The early background of Doctor Hoffman helps in understanding his attitudes."

"Don't answer the question, Doctor Hoffman," Damson advised.

"Did you know the men that were killed on your property?" the lawbot continued.

"No."

"Did you release a dinosaur when the men entered your property?"

"No. Well, I knew she'd been released the day before. It makes it easier for me and others on my staff to work with the offspring in the barn."

There was a slight change in the membrane around the lawbot's eyes. They looked more intense to Cantor.

"Is this animal normally in her barn?"

"She spends some time in the barn, but like all the dinosaurs, she needs to roam in the fields that are fenced in. She's like any other wild animal."

"Short answers, please. Are you angry at people who disagree with your research?"

"No. Maybe I am when people hurt my wife. I'm sorry, it unnerves me to be stared at by your eyes... those lens things or whatever they are."

The unblinking eyes continued to bore into Cantor. "Did the men that died hurt your wife?"

"No. I'm referring to an event years ago. It wasn't in New Mexico."

"Do you feel you want to hurt people that criticize your work?"

"No, I just want them to leave us alone."

"Do you feel people want to harm you?"

"Not in general. I know some people are uncomfortable with what I do. Somebody set fire to the building next to my house. A number of dinosaurs died. It's all on the record. And, as I said, someone injured my wife before we moved out here."

Some lights briefly flickered near the eyes of the lawbot.

"Have any of the dinosaurs at the ranch escaped in the past?"

"Yes. A female."

"Same female?"

"No."

"Did you realize the loose dinosaur might have killed people?"

"Of course, I did. That's why I immediately tried to get her back in the enclosed area."

"Why didn't you shoot the animal?"

"I..." Cantor shook his head, "I couldn't shoot her."

"So, would it be fair to say you value the life of a dinosaur over a human?"

"No! I was sure I could get her back to where she belonged."

"Was the dinosaur that killed two men on your ranch also a female?"

"You know that answer already," Cantor said tiredly.

"Please answer the question." The bot's pupils expanded. The rims of the eyes turned red.

"Yes. I don't see…"

"Did you take precautions after the first escape so that it never happened again?"

"I made very clear recommendations."

"Why didn't you take a rifle with you when you investigated the noises you heard on the night of the killings?"

"I don't keep a rifle in my cabin."

"Would you say you didn't want to hurt the dinosaur, even if a human life was at risk?"

"I had just woken up. This questioning is misleading."

"Is it true you recently spoke with Dan Tusker about a dinosaur named Mako?"

"I have discussions about Mako all the time."

"Is it true he told you to train Mako, so he'd quit digging along the fence of his field?"

"Yes, but that was…"

"And did you train Mako as requested?"

"No. An electric fence was needed."

"Why didn't you train him as requested?"

"He's a very dangerous animal. I'm not sure he's trainable."

"So, you chose to not comply," the lawbot said, putting its face close to Cantor's.

"Read my lips. ELECTRIC FENCE!"

"Isn't your area of responsibility dinosaur behavior?"

Cantor shook his head and replied, "Yes."

"Thank you, Doctor Hoffman. That is all."

* * *

"In the future, our fences have to do more than just keep the animals in," Kumiko said at breakfast the next morning.

"I agree. I wonder if Dan Tusker wants me out of the dinosaur business?" Cantor said, shaking his head. "I suspect he's trying to make me look incompetent."

"Seems like it. But Dan needs us. Why would he try to discredit you?"

"I don't know."

"Well, I can tell you, nobody is making me leave," she said.

Cantor had heard that tone before whenever Kumiko dug in her heels. He looked down and said, "So much is in doubt now."

"This has hit us all hard," she said. "It's beyond bad. The way those men died is heartbreaking. But we need to move on. We can't let what happened destroy everything we've done."

Cantor touched her cheek with the backs of his fingers. "I know you're right. But I still can't get the scene when we found those young men out of my mind," he said. "It surprised me how Dan insisted that Circe stay with us."

"He likes the bad ones; they make him money," she said, absent-mindedly touching the scar near her eye. "Maybe we should take some time to recover from it all. Do you realize we've never spent a week away from the ranch?"

"Part of me agrees with you," Cantor said. "But after what happened, I don't think I could relax or have a good time somewhere."

Kumiko played with the golden dragon necklace. "Me too. We'll go when things settle down – if that ever happens."

"You know, I would have liked to write to the families of Pete and Javier, expressing his sorrow over their deaths, but our lawyer vehemently opposes it," Cantor said. "I'd love to sue Cosmic Pawn to put up electric fences, but Tusker would counter-sue and cut off our support. We'd have to leave the ranch with our work undone."

* * *

Cantor sat on the porch trying to make sense of the latest legal document he'd received. The language was barely English.

His wrist phone vibrated.

"This is Eugenio at the gate. Some people are here to see you."

Glad to put the pages of Latin/English away, he headed over to see who his visitors were. He saw a priest and two women dressed in black. The priest introduced himself as Father Archuleta. Then he introduced Señora Martinez, Pete's mother, and Señora Garcia, Javier's grandmother. Señora Garcia wore a traditional black laced mourning scarf over her head and a large silver cross around her neck.

"Mr. Hoffman, my son Pete wasn't perfect, but he was a good son," Señora Martinez said. "Sure, he got himself into trouble sometimes, but nothing like this. I tell you like I told the police. He never would have done something like this on his own."

"I'm sure he was a wonderful son, Señora Martinez. Unfortunately, I'm not allowed to speak about the incident for legal reasons. Does your lawyer know you're here?"

"If Pete had known what you have here, he never would have entered your property. Why are you doing this? Why have these animals, these dinosaurs? I don't understand. Horses, cows, and sheep are enough for the people around here. I need to know why my son died."

Cantor felt like he'd been gut-punched. He felt bad for the family, but their failure to assign much responsibility to Pete angered him. "I'm sorry for your loss, Señora Martinez. There are signs along the outer fence that warn trespassers of dangerous animals. I know this must be very hard for you. I can't comment further."

Javier's grandmother had listened as she fingered the beads on her rosary. Now she spoke.

"Señor, I fear my *nieto* is in trouble. His soul is in danger. What killed him was a *demonio*. A *demonio* inside your animal. You mustn't let this creature claim the souls of more people. This is a very old land. It isn't the same as where you might have come from. Here, the *brujas* and *los demonios* are real. You must understand, even you are in danger."

* * *

Later that day, Cantor asked George where he was the night the men were killed.

"I couldn't get Mako out of my mind. So, I went and checked him out."

"And?"

"I observed him for a while. That's all. I heard the commotion."

"Son, Mako is always up to no good. Do you check on him a lot?"

"Sometimes I just need to check."

Chapter 34

Thin Ice Under Tusker

Tusker had just returned from his own deposition in Santa Fe. He'd suggested Cantor wasn't the best person to be studying the dinosaurs. Just as he sat down in his office chair, the phone rang.

"Yes, sir. The news reports are true," Tusker said to Yuri. It looked bad. The Benefactor had found out about the deaths of the two men at the ranch from the media and not directly from him. "I was just going to call you."

"You are wanted in Paris tomorrow night. You know where to meet. Make it 8:00 p.m. local time," Yuri told him and hung up.

Tusker could feel the sweat forming under his collar. He removed his faux medals. Briefly, he considered fleeing. *No, they'd find me.* He booked a flight to New York that night. From there, a hypersonic flight would take him to London in less than two hours. He'd be in Paris in plenty of time.

* * *

Two men escorted Tusker to a room at the back of the *Restaurant Crème de Rêve*. He could see the Eiffel Tower out the window. Inside, the tables were made of polished granite, held up by Art Nouveau iron legs. The walls had gold-trimmed wainscoting and contemporary paintings above.

It unnerved him that the Benefactor kept his sunglasses on, even in the dim light of a fine restaurant. Large, powerfully built men in blue suits sat at both adjacent tables.

The Benefactor motioned for Tusker to sit. "You tell me the two men who died understood the danger?"

"Yes. They knew they were dealing with dinosaurs," Tusker said, pushing his lips together to prevent the lower one from quivering. *Those two drug-addled guys hardly understood what a dinosaur was!*

"You should look at me when you speak," the Benefactor said slowly, tilting his head. "And yet, they used flimsy burlap bags to capture the little ones?"

Tusker adjusted himself on the plush red fabric of the seat as he cleared his throat. "They should have used leather bags. I instructed them to do that."

"Did you not provide them with leather bags?"

"Hindsight tells me I should have arranged it," Tusker said as he wiped his hands on his pants.

"In Russia, we have a saying about hindsight. If you realize something only in hindsight, you have your eyes up your ass." The Benefactor said, showing no emotion.

"Yes."

"Tell me, why did you not use professionals?"

"I… Well, I was hoping to save some money," Tusker said, but quickly added, "Also, I can deal with any problems with a local, but pros know how to disappear."

"Locals also talk too much. Why would pros make problems?"

"Well," Tusker cleared his throat, "they'd know how valuable the dinosaurs are, and would be tempted to sell them to a higher bidder."

The Benefactor nodded his head. "Hmm. I think you make a good point, Tusker. For that, I am going to allow you to return to America. But make no further mistakes." He stuck his knife into his thick steak.

"Thank you, Benefactor." His heart was pounding. He tried not to look at the knife.

"Mistakes can be costly to you. You must think of your relatives too, no?"

"Yes, Benefactor." Tusker put one hand to his mouth, hoping to cover the spasm in his bottom lip.

"Your mother is content. Is she not?" He cut out a piece of his steak.

"Yes, I see her when I can."

"It is important to be a good son. Are you a good son, Tusker?" the Benefactor said, putting the steak in his mouth.

"I try to be a very good son."

"A colleague sent me a picture of your mother. Would you like to see it?"

"Yes, Benefactor." *Oh no! What have they done?*

The photo showed his mother gardening.

"A lovely lady, no?"

"Yes." Tusker's shoulders slumped.

"I want you to upload your health data to Yuri's phone. Today, we will also take a small sample of your kidneys and liver. Should you sadly pass away someday, you can provide a wonderful gift to someone in need of your organs."

"Please, Benefactor. I know I've made mistakes, but I've learned from them." Tusker's lower lip shook badly now. Showing weakness before the Benefactor was the same as showing fear to Mako.

The Benefactor motioned for a scrawny, balding man with a stoop, wearing round smudged glasses, to come to the table.

"This is Mr. Borisov. He will take the samples. Please show us your instruments, Mr. Borisov."

Borisov's bushy eyebrows seemed to work independently of one another. He opened the medical bag with his bony hands so Tusker could see the long, needle-like devices.

"Benefactor, please forgive me, but aren't most transplant organs grown in labs now?" Tusker asked with a high-pitched voice.

The Benefactor looked at Tusker for an uncomfortably long time. Slowly, the big man placed his hands together on the table, fingers intertwined.

"Your indiscretion is very foolish or very brave. Perhaps you have more balls than I believed. Mr. Borisov, find out which it is by taking a sample of this man's testicle as well."

The Benefactor motioned with one finger for Tusker to leave with Borisov. Several big men in blue suits rose at the same time and accompanied them out the back door.

Chapter 35

Commercialism

"Control is an illusion, to believe it, delusion." — Kumiko Chen

The insurance companies settled with the families out of court for an undisclosed sum.

"I never thought this could happen," Cantor said to Kumiko as they walked near the garden by the cabins. They could hear Mako growling and following them on the other side of the fence. "We need to rethink things."

Kumiko reached for Cantor's hand. "The families settled very quickly. Do you think Cosmic Pawn offered more than they could refuse?"

"I think Cosmic Pawn threatened them."

"That makes me very uncomfortable," she said with wide eyes.

"Yeah," Cantor said, looking at her hand in his. "At least we can let the raptors run inside their open spaces again."

After a pause, Kumiko said, "I think about the two men who died. If we had pursued a different line of research, those men would be alive."

"Yeah, my stomach gets twisted up when I think about it. You never wanted anyone to get hurt. Those men made a poor decision."

"Yes, that's true," she said. "Now I'm confused."

"In what way?" He skirted the sage growing along the high fortress-like wall.

"I have to own the fact that my ambitious goals culminated in two people dying," she said after taking a deep breath.

"Of course, we have to own our actions, Kumiko. But owning and self-condemning are two different things. When I was young, I rode a bus to school. I liked to sit in the front seat. Anyway, one day I sat in the back near a girl I liked. Another girl, named Gina, sat in my place, in front. That day, the bus hit a truck. Everybody got a little banged up, but Gina was seriously injured. She was injured because I chose to sit in the back."

"I get what you are saying. But I'm not a passenger changing seats. I'm the driver."

"Don't forget, I'm driving too," he said.

She thought back to what George had once said. How he had wanted to make a friendly dinosaur. His mind wasn't like the highly trained minds of his parents, she thought. *And yet, maybe I should have given more thought to his words.*

Kumiko looked at the Grouchland fence and gasped. Mako's long fingers were sticking through a nearby portal, like the legs of a deadly spider, waiting to draw them closer.

* * *

A day later, Cantor stopped by Tusker's office at his request. Tusker took his computer from his pocket and unfolded it on his desk. A fly buzzed near his face but was quickly eliminated by a tiny pest control bot. He shifted in his chair as though he was in pain.

Tusker looked at him but didn't speak.

"Listen, Dan, I'm a busy man. If you have something to say, say it. I'll start first. We need bars in the portals to keep the dino's hands to themselves."

"Has something happened?"

"No, but it will."

"All right. I'll take care of it. See? I want to work with you."

"Good. Let's also talk about electric fences," Cantor replied after a gulp of the coffee he'd brought with him.

"Good fences may make good neighbors, my friend, but they certainly don't titillate them."

"Titillate? We want to titillate our neighbors now?" Cantor said, raising his eyebrows. He decided he'd better sit in the chair for this.

"Our neighborhood is America. Actually, it's the world. We need to cultivate our neighbors and mold their views on what we do. Titillate them with things we do for them."

"OK..." *I'd like to titillate his butt with a cattle prod.*

"Let's make the ranch fun. Let's make it a place where people can bring their families."

"Don't you think that's a bit inappropriate? People died here."

"A place where people will pay to be entertained."

"Come on, Dan. This is a research site, not a tourist attraction. What you're saying is a slap in the face to the families whose sons died."

"What was that old movie? I can't remember its name. 'If you build it, they will come', that's what I'm talking about."

"Dan, what are you talking about exactly?" *How about Jurassic Park? If you build it, they'll get eaten.*

"Raptor Ranch in lights. Let the public fulfill their fantasy to see real dinosaurs."

"No."

"Novel ideas are always resisted in the beginning. Look at this concept image." Tusker turned his computer so Cantor could see.

"A cable car? Are you serious?"

"It's not a cable car. It's a suspended car. Two steel beams attach from either side of the glass gondola to the tracks above. It will cruise above the dinosaurs. All of them together. And, yes, I'm serious."

"The E-raptors would attack the other dinosaurs, not to mention the tourists. No way."

"I think you're wrong," Tusker persisted.

"I thought Cosmic Pawn is a non-profit company. You sure as hell aren't acting that way."

"Listen, Cantor, let's get real. Cosmic Pawn was shocked by the deaths of two of the locals. This incident has damaged our image."

"The locals had names. And companies aren't shocked; people are shocked." Cantor looked at Tusker with disbelief.

"I'm asking you to be a team player." Tusker placed his hand under his chin. He wore a large gold ring on his little finger.

"And if I refuse?"

"I'll have a press conference. I'd explain how your negligence led to the tragedy." Tusker said.

"Mine! That's rich!"

"You are a disrespectful person, Cantor. Look, you've done a lot of research, whatever it is you do, so why don't you and Kumiko retire? Go off somewhere and enjoy life. I'll even give you a going-away party and some cash."

"I tell you what. Mako is your favorite and too difficult for me to work with. Let people safely stand on a platform and look at him, but they'd have to stay out of the way and not disturb us or the other animals."

"That's not titillating, Cantor. That's not entertainment."

"I'm not interested in entertainment."

Tusker sighed, folded up his computer, and put it in his pocket. "All right. Let's get even more real. Cosmic Pawn holds you responsible for the damage to its reputation."

"Me? I've done everything I can think of to keep things safe."

"Why did you make such deadly dinosaurs? You and Kumiko. Well? You didn't need to let them be so big and dangerous."

"We didn't mean to. Ah hell, I don't need to explain it to you."

Tusker held up his hand. "Enough. There's still the damage to our reputation. Aren't you the leader in the research group with Kumiko, Alex, Valerie, and that man, Moody?"

"His name is Muli."

"Fine. But you're the leader. And you screwed up."

"Wait a minute! First, Kumiko and I are a team. Second, you knew about the dangers of the big dinosaurs. Yet, you are the ones who wanted to fund a ranch like this. You insisted we bring Mako! You became a part of this, knowing everything. I was very honest with you about how huge the C and E-raptors were. You knew about the attack on the janitor at Animal House, so don't give me all that crap."

"We have very deep pockets, Cant. Cosmic Pawn can file a lawsuit against you that we are guaranteed to lose. That's right, LOSE. We don't care. And it could last for years. Can you afford something like that?"

"Fine. I'll sue you, too."

"Read your contract, Dino-boy. You can't sue."

* * *

The next day, Cantor, Kumiko, Valerie, Alex, as well as George and Muli, studied Tusker as he asked for their attention. They sat in chairs in the sun, in front of Tusker's office, wishing the temperature wasn't so high.

Tusker, standing on the shaded porch, looked like a man wearing a tuxedo at a corn shucking. He smiled as he adjusted the lapels on his medal-covered indigo suit. The medals were part of the latest fashion. They weren't earned. The military had objected to people wearing them, but the fashion persisted. His hairstyle, with its long braids in front of his ears and at the back of his head, didn't quite fit his attire or his age of fifty years.

Pointing to the thin three-foot by six-foot screen that stood on four adjustable and self-controlled legs, he began his talk. After several short videos explaining the need for entertainment as an escape from the current economic and weather-related sources of stress in America, he presented the solution. The Raptor Ranch Dino Ride. A colorful glass-bottomed car appeared on the screen, filled with families pointing and laughing as they traversed above the ground populated by dinosaurs.

Tusker planned to build the attraction to travel the width of Grouchland. The car had sides made of metal braces with three-foot-wide by five-foot-high rectangular windows. Openings with bars between the side windows and the roof of the car allowed riders not only a wide view but also the ability to hear the dinosaurs below. The bottom of the car would travel 11 feet above the ground.

"Excuse me, Dan. That isn't enough height. And the bars where there are openings need to be closer together," Cantor objected.

"I appreciated your input," Tusker said, his face turning slightly red. "I'm using the best engineers to design this wonderful gondola. And, the design will be much cheaper than some sort of cable car system. Think of the thousands of people who will come here for the experience of a lifetime. I ask you all to imagine what can be, what will be. Positivity always trumps negativity."

"I positively do not want this thing near our living quarters," Cantor persisted.

* * *

It took a couple of months before government authorities permitted Tusker to implement the plan. It was necessary to form a limited liability company that would operate the glass-bottomed car. The company, Raptor Ranch Dino Ride, needed a special license. Cantor convinced the state that Darwin, Maryann, and Circe could not participate. So, it was just Remus and Mako.

And Cantor felt that would be a disaster. "Mark my words, Dan, you shouldn't have the two of them in the same field," he said as he and Dan watched contractors working on the platform for the Ride's audience and those waiting their turn. "If we have to keep them in separate cages in their barn, what do you think they'll do to one another in Grouchland?"

"Cantor, you've been trying to sabotage this whole thing. No more."

Ironically, the bad publicity from the deaths of Pete and Javier led to greater public demand to see the dinosaurs. The potential tax revenues generated by the project were attractive to the county and the state, which appreciated the potential economic benefits.

The glass-bottomed car system came together in a short time. Tusker hired operators and administrators for Raptor Ranch Dino Ride and took the title of CEO. This didn't change the role Cosmic Pawn had in administrating all other aspects of Raptor Ranch.

After several runs with an empty gondola, Alex and Cantor tried it. Right away, the enclosed space made Cantor nervous. His claustrophobic fears began to rise. *At least there are lots of windows.* During the ride, Cantor looked up and noticed a cottonwood further up the Grouchland field, near the fence, that looked sickly. He filed that away in his head.

Both Mako and Remus cocked their heads and looked up at the trespassing contraption. They rose up amid roars and hisses, their jaws scraping the lower parts of the gondola. Their massiveness limited their ability to jump, but their feet did leave the ground. They landed in a crouch.

Alex took another ride, this time with Valerie and George. Cantor sat this one out. George got on his knees to be closer to the snapping jaws below.

The high point of the ride happened when the car stopped in the middle for five minutes.

Alex stood at a window. "Mako and Remus are over-stimulated. Hopefully, they'll calm down, otherwise, this isn't good for them."

Valerie watched the two dinosaurs. Remus was powerful and deadly. But Mako was dominant, as if an extra layer of fierceness had been pumped into him. "Jeez, quit sneering at us, Mako," she said jokingly, but she didn't smile.

Mako bellowed, causing her to rear back and grab Alex's hand.

George looked captivated.

After several minutes, the raptors calmed down and, after a few snaps from Mako at Remus, they separated and went about their business.

Seeing this, Tusker turned to Cantor and said, "Cant, this is a problem. We need to show ACTIVE animals feeding if people are going to get their money's worth. I remember seeing videos of crocodiles rising out of the water to get at a piece of meat at the end of a long stick. We'll put a guide in the car with a stick and some meat. I'll bet those dinosaurs can jump pretty high when meat is involved."

Cantor hated the idea. *The dinosaurs are too heavy to jump very high, but eleven feet is too low for the gondola.*

Tusker wanted more excitement. "I'm thinking this would be even more sensational if the glass-bottomed car's bottom was 10 feet off the ground. What do you think, Cant?"

"Dan, you can't be serious. The dinosaurs could bite at the sides of the gondola. We know how high they can reach. To say the passengers would be in danger would be an understatement. You should raise the bottom of the car to at least 15 feet above the ground at its lowest point."

"Listen, Cant, I try, out of friendship, to include you in the decision-making, I really do. But you need to get with the program."

"I can see the headlines now," Cantor said, "Terrified passenger dies of a heart attack. Authorities investigate Cosmic Pawn."

Two weeks later, the ride opened to the public with the car 12 feet above the ground at its lowest.

The first carload contained a mixture of adults and children and an employee with a pole and meat. When the car was at its closest to the ground, the operator stopped the car for five minutes. Both Remus and Mako approached the car. This gave the riders a chance to sit and watch in amazement.

On the first ride, it chilled the tourists when Mako reared up, using his tail as a third leg, and bringing his head above the bottom of the car. He rapaciously eyed them at close range. His abnormal sneer had only gotten worse, and it heightened the fear of the viewers. He smelled the meat and let out a roar. Some people covered their ears. Passengers could smell his putrid breath. When the meat was hung outside the car, Mako rose high enough to look a little girl in the eye.

Oddly, Remus didn't eat the meat that was offered to him.

"Dammit, Dan!" Cantor said as he stormed into Tusker's office after the show. "You are lucky Remus let Mako have his meat. It could have gotten ugly."

"Go away," Tusker said.

"Some people were terrified! And they damn well should be. Children were crying. You need to raise the car."

"No harm done. And if you'd been more observant, you'd realize I did raise it a by a foot."

"Get serious! You are too cavalier about people. Not only that, Cosmic Pawn made a commitment not to interfere with me and the research staff and especially the animals."

"Raptor Ranch Dino Ride is not Cosmic Pawn," Tusker said calmly.

Cantor gritted his teeth. "At least, put up signs that warn passengers the ride is intense and dangerous and definitely not for children."

"Dear Cantor. Would you warn people who want to see a horror movie that it's scary? What about white-water rafting or hang-gliding? Don't you get it? Many people do things PRECISELY because of the danger."

* * *

In the evening, after she'd tried out the gondola ride, Valerie thought about how good it felt to hold Alex's hand, recalling the look in his eyes. Long ago, she made sure he understood that she didn't want to be anything more than friends.

After a couple of glasses of wine, she was able to face the truth. She had sacrificed her personal life for work. She had to admit that Alex's several girlfriends in the past bothered her. Her eyes welled up. For the nth time, she recalled her last relationship with a guy back in San Francisco. He was a student at Berkeley. She thought of how he'd cheated on her. How he'd sold all of her belongings after she found out. How he'd shoved her up against a wall. How he'd caused her to hide from intimacy ever since. She took another drink of wine. *Alex is a good guy. Wake up, Valerie.*

* * *

Tusker busied himself with his plans for the Dino Ride. After several weeks of developing a website for it, he walked over to Cantor's place with his laptop. It was late in the day and Cantor answered the door, holding a glass of wine.

"I'm ready to launch an advertising campaign designed to attract more tourists," he said proudly. "Four hundred digi-dollars would reserve a space on the glass-bottomed car, subject to availability."

"This is wrong in so many ways," Kumiko said from the couch.

"Cant, this is going to shake things up. We are going to give them the thrill of their lives!"

Kumiko shook her head.

Cantor examined the website and noticed drawings showing additional types of rides. There were vending machines everywhere. It also implied hotels would be located nearby. Cantor hardly recognized the place. "I don't like it, Dan."

"That's why you'll never make money, Cant," Tusker laughed.

"My name is Cantor, not Cant."

"I tell you what. Start being more positive and I'll stop saying it."

"If that is supposed to be a joke, it isn't very funny," Kumiko said.

When Cantor stood up, Tusker left.

* * *

Cantor and Kumiko continued their research, while Tusker's advertising campaign progressed. Tusker now let only Mako out during the ride, surprising Cantor. *What gives? Why did Dan listen to me this time?*

The glass-bottomed car ride was a success, attracting many tourists. In the first month, over 11,000 visitors had the thrill of seeing a dinosaur. The revenue was over four million digi-dollars a month. Many of the farmers and ranchers in nearby communities resented the influx of tourists. Colleagues around the world were dismayed. Many blamed Cantor and Kumiko.

Tusker now let only Mako out during the ride, surprising Cantor. Tusker had never listened to him much before.

"My goodness," Sheila Jackson said to her husband Larry in the glass-bottomed car during its third month of operation. "I sure hope this car can't fall."

"I'm sure it is super safe, babe. Wow, a real dinosaur. This is great. Look at Biscuit, he wants to take a piece out of that dinosaur," Larry said, holding the Jack Russell Terrier up near the open window.

Some of the other passengers snickered.

Biscuit barked and tried to get his paws over the window frame.

As the car employee put the pole and the string with meat out the window, she let the string and meat fall before she'd placed the pole sufficiently far from the car.

Mako rose and hit the car, causing a loud bang. Biscuit jumped out of Larry's hands, went through the open window, and landed in a clump of sage. The Jack Russell Terrier confronted Mako, barking incessantly. After ten minutes of hide and seek, Mako brought the dog down and ate it, to the horror of the onlookers.

* * *

After the dog mishap, Tusker worked with the insurance company and approached the couple, whose dog died, with payment for damages that kept the incident out of court and out of the media. The insurance company felt Raptor Ranch Dino Ride had been negligent and refused to pay the full amount. So, the company agreed to provide an additional payment to the families, allowing for a settlement. Tusker raised the glass-bottomed car another 2 feet and doubled the bars in the open windows near the roof.

Demand by the public to see Mako increased.

* * *

Luna visited several times a month. She and George talked in their kitchen about all the things that were going wrong at the ranch.

"How much longer do we talk about moving before you do it?" Luna asked. "That ride is dangerous. In fact, this whole place is dangerous."

George tried to deflect. "I agree. And, I know eventually, we need to move to another place of our own. But until that can happen, can't you stay here with me?"

Luna set the knife down by the cantaloupe she'd been cutting. "Let me ask you, which dinosaur is closest to this cabin?"

"Mako."

"Do I need to say more?"

"No. But I just don't have the money right now to move."

"As long as you're working at the ranch, you'll never have the money."

George looked pained. He'd put off trying to get a loan. Who would lend him the money? Only his parents, and he was embarrassed to ask.

Luna put her hand in his. "Listen, I know how hard you work. Maybe I can do more paintings and maybe they'll sell. The dinosaur paintings sell better than my other works. I'll stay tonight, but tomorrow I'm going to return to my parents. You know they wouldn't mind if you lived with them as well. Please, believe me, there's a spiritual wound in the earth near this cabin."

* * *

The next night, George sat looking at his empty bed. Luna was gone, and he was miserable. Knowing he'd be alone, Kumiko asked him to stop by for something to eat. He stepped outside, backpack in tow, and made the short trek to her cabin. "Hello, Koko," he said as he passed the little dinosaur's pen.

"Hi everyone," he said, mustering as much positivity as he could. "Just here for a short visit."

"Let me heat up your dinner," Kumiko said, rising from the couch.

"Thanks, Mom. Where's Dad?"

"He's working with Muli on an old gate. How does lab-roast, mashed potatoes, and salad sound?"

"Sounds great."

While Kumiko reheated the lab-grown meat, George slipped into the bathroom and grabbed one of Kumiko's dirty shirts from the hamper. *Am I sick in the head?* He briefly thought of telling her, but didn't see how. He retrieved a bedsheet from his backpack and thoroughly rubbed the shirt over it. After stuffing the shirt back into the hamper and his sheet in his backpack, he returned to the kitchen and wolfed down his meal.

"Thanks, Mom. Love you. Tell Dad to quit working such long hours," he said on the way out the door.

Feeling like a creep, he wrapped himself in the sheet and entered Koko's pen. "How about we have a sleepover? Does that sound good? You don't even need a muzzle!" He attached her leash after giving her a good whiff of the sheet. "That's right! To your eyes I look like your buddy George, but to your nose, I'm MOM."

The two of them slept peacefully in a nest of blankets on the floor of George's living room. He wore the sheet like a toga and wasn't bitten once. Early in the morning, George brought Koko back to her pen. This went on for two more nights.

George began to feel better. He'd made it through a rough patch. He promised he'd tell his mom someday.

* * *

Koko liked the nest. She was protected and warm. The human who fed her was warm. He wasn't an intruder; he was *Heykoko*. She liked it when *Heykoko* scratched her head. She wanted to scratch the human's head too, but she fell asleep.

The next morning, as *Heykoko* walked her to her pen, Koko spied a rabbit. She pulled against the leash and he let her investigate. Koko didn't see the rabbit as food. Her food wasn't fuzzy. She wanted the fuzzy one to play with her. To come share her place with the wires. The wires that kept her inside. But the rabbit hopped away.

Chapter 36

Saxton's Belligerence

"Bright things beget treachery."
— Lesley Livingston

Arthur Saxton sat in a small adobe tavern in Taos. The wooden ceilings propped up by rounded beams called vigas gave the low light interior an old ambience. Tourists came to see the mountains, art galleries, and the pueblo, but not as many as in winter when so many came to ski. It calmed his nerves to surround himself with the rustic and unique pueblo-style architecture and laid-back atmosphere of the town. But he could do without the tourists. He preferred that the restaurant servers were bots, like those in many upscale restaurants.

"What would you like?" the young waitress asked him.

"Show me your wine list, please."

After studying the list, he ordered a glass of one of the more expensive white wines.

Arthur had always preferred wine to beer, although as a college student, he drank beer because others did. He disliked most social occasions unless it was with students studying mathematics or computer science. He knew how to dominate the kinds of conversations that arose in his field. But he never quite understood the raucous humor of most students.

His guest was running late, so he ordered a bottle of the same wine. A family at a nearby table laughed at some story having to do with eating green chili that was too hot. When they laughed again, he called the waitress over.

"Do you serve green chili?" he asked loudly.

"Yes, we have both a green and a red chili burrito filled with beans and ground beef and served with a sopaipilla."

"Which is hotter?"

"Definitely the green."

"Fine. Give me the green!" he declared.

"Very good. Will there be anything else?"

"I'd like those people over there to keep the noise down."

The waitress paused, not quite sure how to handle this request. She walked to their table and apologetically told the talkative family of Arthur's request in as gentle a manner as possible.

Arthur could feel the stares as he poured himself another glass. He got the people to look away by picking his nose.

As the level of the wine in the bottle descended, he began reading on his phone an article about the Roman emperor Tiberius that discussed his eccentric behavior during the latter part of his reign. He had isolated himself on the island of Capri and did what he wanted, regardless of how it looked to outsiders. Arthur imagined owning his own island someday.

Out of the side of his eyes, he sensed someone approaching. Laying down the phone, he looked up.

"Hello, Mr. Saxton," the big man said.

"I was beginning to wonder if you'd forgotten, Yuri," Arthur said, looking at the man's leather jacket, "And it's DOCTOR Saxton."

The big man sat in the chair opposite Arthur. "I trust you're well." His English was good, but with an accent.

"As well as can be expected in these turbulent times."

"My time is short. Doctor Saxton, do you have the item we discussed earlier?"

"I do, I do indeed. I assume you've scanned me."

Yuri took a small electronic device from his pocket. "It would have let me know if you weren't clean. May I have some gum?"

"I hope you like mint." Arthur passed him the pack.

Without examining the contents, Yuri put it in his pocket. "Did you have any problems, Doctor Saxton?"

"These kinds of things are always a challenge. Security is tight. But I'm very bright. I'm always a step ahead of the fools."

"My boss will appreciate your efforts."

"And…?"

"Of course," Yuri pulled an envelope from the inside of his light jacket. "In this envelope, you will find a memory stick with a digital key that can't be broken by quantum computers. Exactly one week from today, a digital wallet will contain your reward. The payment is the same as last time and is untraceable."

"Nice doing business with you."

"Likewise." Yuri stood and walked out the door.

Arthur sat back and poured what was left of the bottle into his glass. When he finished his glass, he left. His Falcon sat at the town helipad, a ten-minute walk away. After climbing in, he told it to return to Los Alamos and sat back for a short nap.

* * *

The wind picked up near the top of the enormous cliff known as the Crest, overlooking Albuquerque. The Benefactor stood on an ancient seabed, now pushed a mile above the desert below. Here, along the rim of the Sandia Mountains, he could see Mount Taylor, one of the sacred mountains of the Navajo, nearly a hundred miles away. Gnarled trees along the rim testified to the winds that frequently whipped over the cliff. Yuri joined him in appreciating the view.

"Am I going to be happy, Yuri?" The Benefactor said in his slow manner.

"Yes, Benefactor. I believe you'll be pleased."

"And our American friend, how is he?"

"I think he drinks too much."

"I see. We'll need to be very careful with him. You must keep me appraised of his suitability for our business."

"May I tell you my conclusions?"

"You may."

"I think Arthur Saxton is used-up. He is getting too confident. He's cocky. Dr. Chen at the ranch is suspicious of him."

The Benefactor looked to the west, thinking about what Yuri said. "Let's go back to the car."

The two men walked to the small parking lot. The Benefactor commanded the vehicle to raise the front doors. Both men sat up front. He turned to Yuri sitting on the passenger side.

"Let's see what our business partner gave you."

Yuri pulled out a pack of gum. Inside, below the half-length sticks of gum, the Benefactor found the memory cube, about a centimeter on each side. "Very good. Assuming the information is legitimate, my clients will be interested."

The Benefactor gazed at the aspens. "Smart people know how to thrive in war, Yuri. And the quantum computer war is no exception. Let the bidding begin."

The car made its way down the eastern slope of the mountains, executing the hairpin curves perfectly.

"Yuri, I wish for you to use our man at the ranch. He will be our eyes and ears. I want his assessment of Tusker and the job he's doing."

"Yes, Benefactor."

"I want you to inform this man of another mission. When the time is right, he is to provide you with a young dinosaur. A male. One whose mother is named Circe."

"It will be done." After watching the passing pines for a minute, Yuri turned to the Benefactor. "Forgive me. May I ask you a question?"

The Benefactor looked at Yuri with cold eyes in silence.

Five seconds passed. Yuri lowered his eyes. Then ten. Then fifteen. "You may ask," the Benefactor finally allowed.

"Why do you wish to go to such great expense for these people and their animals, Benefactor?"

"Let me explain. There are about 900 paintings by Van Gogh. People pay millions, sometimes hundreds of millions, for one. And there are only around 130 American Flowing Hair silver dollars, from 1794, in existence. Today, they are worth about 20 million dollars apiece. How many dinosaurs are alive today? You see my point?"

Chapter 37

Informer?

Yuri drove to Raptor Ranch the next day. Stepping into Tusker's office, he said, "I want you to inspect the ranch."

"I'll be happy to show you around, Yuri," Tusker said, rising from behind his desk and smoothing his vest with his hand.

"I'm staying here. You go."

"Ah… by myself?" Tusker asked, somewhat confused.

"By yourself."

In his absence, Yuri sat at Tusker's desk, looking at his wrist communicator. It showed almost 1:00 in the afternoon. Finally, a Russian man knocked and walked in.

"You were almost late," Yuri admonished him.

"I apologize."

Looking out the window, then back at the man, Yuri said, "I want one of the little dinosaurs. One whose mother is named Circe. You will make this happen. Any questions?"

"Male or female?"

"The Benefactor wants a male. Something that will strut around and scare his client's guests."

"How do you wish this to be done?"

"Do you think you are well paid?"

"Yes."

"Then you figure it out."

* * *

Before Tusker returned from his inspection, Yuri took out his phone and spoke. At the same time, Valerie walked up the steps to Tusker's office. She needed to get his approval to order new supplies. Before she knocked, she heard a voice that wasn't Tusker's saying something about the Russian informer at the ranch.

What was that all about? She turned around and walked down the steps. *The only Russian I know is Alex.*

Chapter 38

Leon

Valerie let Cantor know about the conversation regarding a Russian informer she'd heard in Tusker's office. They stood outside Maryann's barn, watching her chicks through the window.

"What could an informer want here? I mean, Grouchland is open to the public, and the press is free to ask us questions," Cantor said.

"My reaction too. The speaker didn't sound like Tusker."

Cantor thought for a bit. "I've heard Dan refer to Alex as 'that Russian'. He and Alex don't exactly get along. Maybe the speaker said, 'Have that Russian inform her,' instead of 'informer'. That 'her' could be you or Kumiko."

"I'll ask Alex if he has something to tell me."

"It couldn't hurt. Let me know what he says. It doesn't make sense that he's some kind of informer for Cosmic Pawn. Right?"

* * *

That night, Alex opened his door to find Valerie standing there with her hands on her hips.

"What's up, Val," Alex said. "Come on in." *This is a nice surprise.*

"How was your day?" she asked, standing barely inside the doorway.

"I had to do some work with Darwin. He's a cool customer. Then, I had to work with Circe. Please excuse my language, but she is an *uzhasnoye sushchestvo*."

"I'm afraid to ask."

"Let's just say as creatures go, she's a very bad one."

"I'm glad you survived."

"Come in. Come in. Some wine perhaps?"

"No, I need to get back to my place. Did you have something to tell me?"

Alex had the look of a big shy kid on his first day, when the teacher asks him to tell the class all about himself. "Well, um… You look nice today."

"Anything else?"

If brains could do pushups, Alex's was going for the record. "I like your freckles."

"Think, Alex."

"Happy Birthday?"

She turned without a word and walked briskly down the porch steps.

Alex stood in the doorway and watched her until she rounded his cabin out of sight.

* * *

Cantor forgot to ask Kumiko if Alex had given her some information. He trusted Alex implicitly, and the question faded from his mind.

* * *

The next evening, a Russian man, sitting on the stockade fence, fired a dart from a special tranquilizer pistol into Circe's raptorling, number 13, named Leon. The little dinosaur had strayed from his siblings and mother. The sliver of a moon ensured the necessary darkness.

The Russian climbed onto a bike and silently drove along the road by Circeland in the direction of her barn. Over his shoulder was a large leather bag with pieces of raw meat inside. When he felt he was far enough from Leon, he threw the meat over the fence. It didn't take Circe and her offspring long to smell the meat. They went to investigate, leaving Leon behind.

Back on the bike, the Russian returned to where Leon lay in the grass. He climbed the fence using a rope ladder with special hooks that attached to the other side of the wooden pylons. Once on top, he reversed the ladder and climbed into Circeland, carrying the leather bag. With Leon inside, he tied off the bag and climbed over again. The raptorling was heavy and the Russian lowered him by rope gently to the ground. After he climbed back to safety, he placed the sleeping raptorling in a wheelbarrow, collected the rope ladder, and ran toward the end of Circeland.

Robert Greaves, Mako's handler, waited on the other side of the ranch's metal outer fence. He had taken several days off and was supposed to be in Albuquerque. Instead, he finished digging a hole and watched for the Russian.

After making it to the outer fence, the Russian fed the rope around the bag through the hole and Greaves pulled it and the raptorling through. Next, came the rope ladder and the tranq pistol. After he refilled the hole, Greaves put everything in the back of his electric truck and left silently. The Russian ran with the wheelbarrow back toward where he'd found it.

* * *

The next day, Muli watched the E-raptorlings in Circeland. He didn't see Leon. After an hour, he phoned the drone tech and asked her to send a drone to the area. Following a two-hour search, Leon hadn't been located. There was no sign of blood, so his siblings hadn't eaten him. The raptorling couldn't have drowned in the pond. It wasn't very deep, and the raptorlings were very good swimmers.

Cantor's phone buzzed. "Cantor here."

"Mr. Cantor, I cannot find Circe's youngster, Leon. A drone search has produced no results."

"Any holes under the stockade walls?"

"The drone didn't find any."

"OK. Please get Circe and her young into the barn," Cantor said, trying not to sound alarmed. "I'll alert Alex to do the same thing with Maryann and her raptorlings until we sort this out."

Within a week, Leon was in Russia, where he was housed by the Benefactor until a Russian billionaire paid a fortune for him.

Chapter 39

Moles and Magpies

The morning after Leon's disappearance, Valerie sat on her porch, looking over the pine-studded hills to the east. Breathing deeply, she took in the smell of sage, dusty soil, and the wood of her cabin. The sound of birds doing their morning routine gave her a boost.

Valerie loved the magpie that sat on the railing of her porch while she drank her coffee. He was a friendly and curious bird. Black adorned most of his back and under his chin, contrasting sharply with his white belly and wingtips. She called him simply Magpie.

Alex, who had left the university permanently and now called the ranch home, clomped up her steps. She'd invited him for breakfast. "What's up, Magpie?" he said. Then to Valerie, "I like that guy, but I think he's going to run off with your heart." Magpie jumped on his shoulder. "I'm not falling for it, Magpie. I think you're just after my eggs and toast."

Valerie yearned to discuss the Russian mole with Alex. The idea that Alex could be the mole made her feel ill, and she tried to convince herself that it wasn't possible. She had begun to warm up to him, but now her old wariness of men reasserted itself.

"You look tired," she said.

"It's nothing some strong coffee can't cure."

"What do you think happened to Leon?" she asked.

Alex was quiet for a moment, then said, "Circe is insane. She could have killed him. Maybe eaten him whole."

"His bones will show up in Circe's scat," Valerie said. "I'll check tomorrow."

After Alex left, Valerie walked to the clinic, where she tended to Circe's not-so-little daughter, Elsa. Her brother, Galahad, had bitten her and now she had an infection. *I wonder if the Russian informer had anything to do with Leon's disappearance? This is creepy.*

* * *

The next day, George stopped by Valerie's place. She asked him to join her for some coffee on the porch. The reason for his visit surprised her.

"Valerie, is it OK for me to set up my wrist phone so it gets the right angle?" George put his phone on the small table and said, "Phone, set up for an interview with Valerie O'Sullivan. Use action mode."

Tiny metal legs emerged, setting the phone's camera at the perfect angle. The legs would change position if George asked the phone to capture something other than the primary subject.

"Are you sure you're OK letting me record this?" George asked.

"I'm happy to help."

"Are you ready?" he asked.

Valerie answered, "As ready as I'll ever be," at the same time as the phone responded with, "Ready, George."

"Life of a dinosaur veterinarian with Valerie O'Sullivan..."

Naturally, the curious and ravenous Magpie showed up, tilting his head at the humans.

"Magpie, I like you to meet George. George, this is Magpie."

"Nice to meet you," George said with a smile. "Valerie, are you OK with Magpie photo-bombing your interview?"

Magpie cackled and did a little preening. He continued to perch on the rail, cocking his head when the people began, once again, to make their funny noises.

Valerie's interview continued for a good hour. When George left, she turned to Magpie. "What is that man up to?"

* * *

Valerie examined the scat in Circe's barn later that day, while Circe was in Circeland. When Valerie sifted through it, there were no bones. *I think someone stole Leon. Curious that Alex didn't think of it.*

Chapter 40

Passion to Ride

George wanted to ride a dinosaur. Maryann, to be exact. It had turned from a thought to an obsession. He knew his mom and dad wouldn't approve, which just made things harder for him.

He enlisted Muli and asked him to keep quiet. Muli said he would not tell anyone as long as George didn't endanger himself.

"Why do you do this, Mr. George?"

"It's hard to explain, Muli."

"Simply put one word before another."

"Oh, come on, Muli."

"Then, why?"

"Fine. Well, I… ah… I just have to, OK?"

The plan was to muzzle Maryann. The muzzle had been made with several layers of leather. It had to be very strong.

When Maryann was in the field, George had enticed her with a juicy cut of meat while he stood on a ladder leaning against the fence. He made sure he wasn't seen by others by always going to a part of the fence where several cottonwoods grew just outside it, but never on days when Cantor or Alex studied Maryann in the field. He and Muli had held the muzzle using clamps attached to two long sticks. They let Maryann familiarize herself with it. Each time, she received a delicious reward.

After this had become routine for her, they would touch the muzzle to her face, followed by a reward. This went on until she would tolerate the muzzle on her head, but not secured. George photographed Maryann and the muzzle.

George looked at Muli. "How do we tie the muzzle behind her neck and below her jaws?"

"I might lie on top of her cage and slip it behind her," Muli suggested.

"I have difficulty seeing that work. What if we just tape her mouth shut?" George suggested.

"Like duct tape? You will need to wrap it many times. When you tear the tape off later, it would be goodbye to you, Mr. George."

"I got it! I will attach the muzzle to ropes I control when I'm on her back."

"She will throw you over her head and eat you."

The two men thought for several minutes.

"What about this, Muli? We train her to accept my weight on her back. Once she lets me do that, I'll just tie the muzzle around her neck. Problem solved."

"You will die."

George sighed and thought some more.

"Wait a minute, don't we need a bit, like horses have? This is getting complicated Muli."

"Are you going to put the bit in her mouth, Mr. George?"

"I guess."

"Maryann will bite you in the face."

George gave Muli a look. "I got it. We make the straps of the muzzle out of a stretchable material, like rubber. The straps would make a loop. We can stretch it over her head while we are safe on the fence."

"This might work, Mr. George. Your wife will leave you."

George frowned at Muli. "You aren't helping. OK fine, we'll work out the details later. Now, it is time to discuss the gloves. Can you make a suitable pair of gloves?"

"You are wearing gloves now."

"Not for me, Muli."

"I assume we are discussing gloves for Maryann, then."

"Come on, Muli. I know you know what I mean. Quit messing around."

"You can put a bell on a cat, never a glove."

"OK, now you are just making me mad. Help me. Can... you... make... the... gloves?"

"I think so. I think they should be mittens."

"Long story short. We use rubber to fasten the mittens over her back so they stay on her hands."

"Those will be very big mittens, Mr. George. I don't think that would be easy."

"Now the sickle claw. Can't we just tie it to her leg?"

"The big claw? How?"

"We dig a hole under the fence and train her to stand sideways so we can tie it."

"You can't see what you are doing. She will slice your hand."

"Let's think some more," George said. "I need to you be open-minded."

"There was a British man named Mr. Pratchett. He wrote about that."

"Muli, please! I need you to focus."

"He said something like, the problem with an open mind is that people will try to put things in it." 1

"OK, that's funny, but it doesn't solve my problem."

"Mr. George, Maryann has more strength in her sickle toe than you have in your arm. How do you get the muzzle, the mittens, and the leg-ties off once you have ridden around the field? Maryann can't be wearing them the next time your dad sees her," Muli stated. "Your dad will make you live somewhere else."

"Dang it, Muli!"

* * *

The next day, George walked into his parents' living room.

"Thanks for coming over, George. Your mom and I would like to talk with you," Cantor said.

George sat on the easy chair and faced his parents on the sofa. "OK. What's up?"

"We're worried," Kumiko said. "Can we ask you a few questions?"

"Of course, Mom."

"Are you feeling down?" she asked.

"No. I feel pretty good."

"Are you lonely? Are you still taking your medications?"

"Yes. I do feel down sometimes if I don't. Or I get impulsive."

"We've noticed that you engage in unusual things with the dinosaurs. You've been taking some big chances with them," Cantor added. "Can you tell us why?"

"Did Muli talk to you?"

"Son, Muli sees you as his nephew."

George thought for a while and sighed. "I'm collecting experiences and photos."

"OK. But some of these experiences seem dangerous or ill-thought-out," Cantor said. "That's why we're worried, son. We're worried you might be harmed. That one day you'll go too far."

George looked at his hands. "I wanted to keep this quiet."

Cantor and Kumiko sat upright.

"I'm trying to write a book about living with dinosaurs. I'm also putting together a video documentary."

Cantor and Kumiko looked at one another. "I'm relieved to hear that. I can't approve of you taking chances, but now it all makes sense," Cantor said.

"Why were you trying to keep it quiet?" Kumiko asked.

"Dan asked me to keep it a secret."

Cantor shook his head, "Tusker? Why would he do that?"

"Dan wants to have my book published. He already has several of my chapters."

"But George, you don't need to go through Tusker to get your book published," Cantor said.

"Well, I need to spend money on an editor, a story coach, and advertising. He's offered to do that for me."

"I think any editor would give their right arm to work on such a book. Why does he need to collect your chapters? And why the secrecy?"

"He wants to keep it secret to protect me from publishers that have a bad reputation. Also, he says writing a book is a great idea and I shouldn't give other people the same idea. He collects the chapters so he can show them to a good publisher."

"So, he wants to be your agent. George, you can't trust Tusker. Believe me, I know. Have you signed a contract with him?" Cantor asked.

"Not yet. I have it at the cabin, but I haven't signed it."

"Good! Don't sign it. Listen, a book like you describe would be a best seller. You don't need a middleman to get it published, especially a shady one like Tusker. I wouldn't be surprised if he tries to publish what you've given him as his own work. At the very least, I'm sure he's asking for a big percentage of the sales revenue."

"He wants fifty percent."

Kumiko spoke up. "Are you kidding? George, you need to keep proof that the chapters are yours. Send them to a reputable publisher. They will be fired up, hoping you send them more. The main thing is that you have a record. Also, don't erase anything from your computer. The dates of your files will be evidence if Tusker tried to claim the writing as his own. In fact, hide your computer and we'll get you a new one."

"Dan's been pushing me to sign the contract. I was determined not to sign it until I'd gotten through all the fine print. To be honest, a lot of it was lawyer talk that was very hard to translate."

"Don't get me started on Dan's contracts," Cantor said. "I guess that's why I saw him leaving your cabin a while back. I want you to finish your book, son."

"Thanks, Dad."

"Is the book the reason you've been on your phone so much?" Kumiko asked.

"Yeah."

"Let your mother and me help you. That way you can get what you need without taking big risks with the dinosaurs," Cantor said.

"Muli will help as well."

"Muli is a good man," Cantor said.

"Is Dan encouraging you to interact with the dinosaurs? You know, do dangerous things?" Kumiko asked.

"I'm very careful, Mom. Please don't worry."

"I'm going to talk to him!" Kumiko's eyes flashed, and she stood up.

"I'll go with you!" Cantor exclaimed, rising as well.

"No, I don't want you to do that," George said. "Please don't say anything to Dan. I'll tell him I'm changing the chapters. If he knows you know, he'll say I broke an agreement with him. Let me handle this."

"And if he asks you to ride Maryann?" Kumiko added.

George paused, then made a flatulent sound with his lips.

* * *

Cantor finally remembered to ask Kumiko if Alex had informed her of something. She said there wasn't anything she could remember, but it had been weeks.

"It's a strange question. I inform Alex of things whenever we talk and he informs me of things," she said, relaxing with a book in bed. "What is this about, anyway?"

"Valerie overheard a conversation coming from Dan's office about a Russian with information for someone. Originally, she thought the unknown person said, 'Russian informer.'"

"Maybe they said something different that sounded like that. Alex is the only Russian around, and he would never do that. He can't stand Dan. Right?" Kumiko said.

---

1. The late Terry Pratchett wrote in his book, *Diggers*, "The trouble with having an open mind, of course, is that people will insist on coming along and trying to put things in it." Quoted with permission from Harbottle & Lewis LLP.

Chapter 41

Maryann Hunts

Biologists from around the world pressured Cantor to do more research on hunting behaviors at Raptor Ranch. Feeding the dinosaurs meat was fine, but at some point, live prey had to be provided. A predator needed to hunt.

Cantor was on the phone with the president of The Modern Paleontology Society.

"The C-raptors are one thing. But I don't care to study the hunting behaviors of the E-raptors, because I don't think they act like true dinosaurs," he said.

"Let me put it like this, Cantor. If only the C-raptors' behavior is studied, you'll have a sample of two. If you include the E-raptors, you have three more to add to the sample size."

"I don't consider them part of the same population as the C-raptors. I really think the two populations will have entirely different hunting strategies, but only one will tell us which strategy was used 125 million years ago."

"How do you know that? You know, there are some great sauropod discoveries yet to receive funding. We've been one of your supporters for a long time now. We donate money for the meat that Cosmic Pawn uses to feed the dinosaurs. We provide funding to help with maintenance. I imagine many members of the Society might vote to move our donations to say, the new dig in Argentina, rather than what we've done for you in the past."

Cantor paused. "All right. We'll test the hunting methods of the E-raptors as well." *Oh boy.*

* * *

Alex stopped by Cantor's place for a cup of coffee before they headed to Maland to continue their observations on social interactions. After several swallows, he held the hot mug to his head. "Allergies," he said when Cantor looked at him quizzically.

"Check this out, Alex," Cantor said, showing him the latest issue of *Behavioristics* on his laptop. "This may add to your headache. Clancy and Roberts are raking me over the coals."

"Yeah. I've read it."

"Well, what do you think?" Cantor asked.

"They have a point. We need to see how dinosaurs hunt."

"I've thought about this, but I can't see a way. Their prey would likely be in protected areas," Cantor said. "Even if we got around that, we can't just let them loose in Yellowstone or Alaska or Africa and watch what happens. And rounding them up? That would be difficult."

"We'd track them. Tranq them. Bring them down before they cause any trouble," Alex responded.

"The E-raptors wouldn't settle on killing enough to eat. They'd wipe out an entire herd for sport."

"I agree," Alex said. "That's why you have to bring the prey here."

"I've thought of that. Animal rights groups would crucify us."

"Why don't you buy animals that are already going to be slaughtered?"

Cantor moved the handle of his mug back and forth on the wooden table as though it could point him in the right direction. "Hmm. That works."

"Maybe we should invite our critics to do all this themselves," Alex said, rubbing his sinuses.

"They've certainly been itching to do that," Cantor replied. "I think we should give the prey something so they don't suffer."

"A drug?" Alex said. "Wouldn't that make them act more like drunks and less like prey?"

"Why don't you ask Val? She'll know," Cantor suggested.

* * *

"Well, there is a new drug, Possensudol, that will suppress pain without making a person or animal groggy," Valerie told Alex later in her clinic. "It was developed in 2050 based on the study of people who never feel pain."

"That's good news," Alex said. "We're going to need enough for fifteen sheep." He expected Valerie to come back with something witty, but she didn't. *Lately, she seems a little formal, stand-offish.*

* * *

The flock of sheep was delivered by a local rancher. Alex and Valerie examined every animal to determine its sex, weight, age, and general health. They chose only animals free of parasites and disease. An identifying number was spray-painted onto the wool on both sides.

Several well-known biologists and paleontologists were at the ranch to learn how the raptors hunted. They came from all over the world, some from Europe, Asia, South America, as well as the United States.

A lone ram stood far off in Maland when a ranch hand named Patterson let Maryann out of her corral along with her offspring. The mother raptor picked up a scent in the breeze. More than just meat, something living!

She lowered her head and crept forward, swinging her head to the right, then the left, zeroing in on the direction of the scent. With her head down, she moved forward, stopping every few minutes to listen. Soon her eyes locked onto the ram, never wavering, even when a group of crows began cawing at her. She continued to creep forward, trying to stay behind tall bushes and trees as much as possible. The raptorlings silently followed from a distance where they couldn't be heard or seen, halting whenever their mother stopped, watching her closely.

With a jerk, the ram lifted his head and looked in Maryann's direction. There was an unusual form between the trees, 150 feet away. Perhaps an odd tree? He sniffed the air but didn't detect an alarming scent. But something wasn't right. Finally, his instincts kicked in and the ram ran.

In a flash, Maryann went from being a tree to a thundering predator bearing down on her prey. With each footfall separated by over ten feet, she maneuvered around larger bushes, no sounds from within, hands tucked by her sides. The muscles in her legs bulged and pumped while her tail moved left, then right, helping her balance. A deep thudding sound reverberated each time her foot hit the earth, leaving a cloud of scattered dirt behind it.

As she closed in, the ram swerved to the left. Maryann matched his moves, like a Spitfire in a dogfight, with grace and economy of motion. The ram reached a tree and attempted to get around it. Maryann grabbed the ram's hindquarters with one hand, tripping it up. Then she picked it up with her mouth and slammed it to the ground. Swiftly, she clamped her jaws over the ram's neck, breaking the spine with a crunch.

Cantor looked away. He didn't need to watch because Alex and the drones were recording.

Maryann stood, towering over the dead animal, looking back in the direction of her offspring. Cantor wondered why she didn't make a sound to signal them. It occurred to him that the predator that makes the kill wasn't always the one that gets to eat the prize. Best to work silently.

Maryann didn't eat much of the ram. She left it for the young ones that came bounding through the sage. *She's teaching them!* There was an occasional growl as they jockeyed for position around the carcass. When two youngsters squabbled over a piece of meat, they received a quick nip from their mother.

Once the raptors had eaten their fill, there wasn't much left. Maryann picked up some bones and hid them in the bushes near the pond. Waste not, want not.

"No one has ever seen that," Cantor said, looking at Alex. "She hunted like a lioness. And she was teaching her young how to hunt."

Alex ran his hand through his hair as he said, "Her speed and agility were amazing."

"You know, Alex, it is one thing to see bones in a museum, and that's fine, but the feeling you get when you watch a dinosaur in motion, with every muscle and fiber straining to gain on its prey, is something else."

Alex nodded.

Maryann now lay on her belly, relaxing with her legs bent at the knees. Most of her young napped.

George also witnessed the spectacle. He felt for the ram, but nothing could match the admiration he felt toward Maryann. Such power. His drone had filmed the whole thing.

Valerie felt like the others. "Alex, look at the goosebumps on my arms. All I can say is, wow! I'm in awe of Maryann, but I'm glad I'm on this side of the fence."

"I'm sure we'll write several academic papers about what we just saw," Alex exclaimed. Then, seeing her goosebumps, he reached over and drew her to him, "You must be cold. Let me warm you." He smiled, running his hand along her back. Valerie's smile vanished, and she stepped away.

* * *

Darwin's hunting style was like Maryann's, but without the raptorlings. A beautiful animal at a walk, and an erupting powerhouse in a run. There was no question of his massiveness, as each foot made the ground spew dust and the sage shudder.

"Incredible," Cantor exclaimed, "such intensity." What he'd seen surpassed all the imaginings of his youth.

"No sheep has ever confronted anything like a *Utahraptor*," Alex said, his face serious. "Like a *Titanoraptor,* if there ever was one."

* * *

Circe was as efficient and deadly as the rest. Her remaining children, Galahad, Gawain, Spike, Korrigan, and Elsa, watched her from a distance. Cantor noted the long delay between when Circe crippled the ram, and when she delivered the killing bite. She seemed to want to play with her prey.

Despite her bad temper and relative inattention to her role as a mother, she made sure her young were fed. But woe to the raptorling that got out of line.

If two of her young squabbled, Circe picked one up by the neck and flung it into the weeds. The raptorling would slowly make its way back to the pack, holding its head close to the ground, staying far away from her.

* * *

Mako's turn now. Remus couldn't take part because of a hurt toe. A ram stood in the distant field; its horns were unlikely to make any difference to the outcome. Mako shared Circe's cruelty. He ate the ram alive without breaking its neck first. And before he ate, he seemed to play with the ram. He bit off one hoof and let the ram try to escape.

Neither Cantor nor Alex felt the flood of positive excitement they had experienced with the C-raptors. Mako demonstrated nature in all its rawness, sullied with unnatural, noxious cruelty. He was the Reaper's terrible brother.

Cantor turned to Alex, looking slightly sick. "There's cruelty in the E-raptors. Or is it the other way around? Is the true cruelty of a *Utahraptor* missing in the C-raptors, like Maryann?"

* * *

On a warm day filled with earthy smells of vegetation and a refreshing breeze off the mountains, Cantor, Kumiko, Valerie, and Alex sat on Valerie's porch, sipping ice tea. It had been several days since the end of the hunts.

"I asked Dan to have some ranch hands cut down that big cottonwood near the far end of Grouchland. I think it's dead, or damn close to it," Cantor said.

"Good suggestion. What did he say?" Alex asked, gulping the cold tea.

"He said he'd try to get around to it."

Valerie rolled her eyes.

"Hell, we can cut it down ourselves," Alex said.

"I'm afraid not," Cantor responded. "It has something to do with the contract."

Alex cupped both hands around his drink. "Changing the subject, how would the dynamics change if we use a large group of prey and there was more than one predator?"

"That would answer a lot of questions," Valerie said as Magpie landed on a railing, no doubt hoping for cookies. "Circe and Remus might tolerate one another, especially when hunting, but Remus has a foot injury. Forget Mako. He'd systematically kill every animal. So, I suggest it should be Maryann and Darwin."

"I agree," Cantor said.

Kumiko wiped the condensation off her glass. "The two adults are familiar with each other, having mated once, and they are familiar with the day-to-day sounds and smells of each other over the fences."

"Eventually we'll need to watch Remus and Mako hunt together," Cantor said, but no one responded.

* * *

The chatter of the humans and the absence of cookies led Magpie to fly away from Valerie's porch, in search of food elsewhere. People were worse than crows. Chatter, chatter, chatter. She circled Circeland as the big E-raptor rested under a tree. Landing on Circe's back, she searched for tics and other pests between the feathers. After gobbling a few, the bird was still hungry. He hadn't noticed the huge mouth opening while he fed, but when he flew to the ground, it became obvious. Pieces of meat hung from between the large, serrated teeth. Magpie flew onto the muscular neck. Circe didn't move. He flew to the back of the head. Still no movement, save for the vibration of air flowing through her throat. Now he flitted to the scaly space above her eyes. She didn't seem to care. He could smell the fresh meat separately from the less appealing odor of decay. Back down to the ground he flew. Nothing from the huge dinosaur. With a quick hop and a snatch, he scored a tidbit and hopped away. With his head tilted, he studied her. No movement. Eyes closed. Quietly, Magpie hopped closer. Then a little closer. The meat between two yellow teeth looked so good. One more hop. Nothing. He tugged on the meat, but it remained stuck between the horrible daggers. He hopped onto one of the teeth, then hopped back to the ground. Still nothing. Bravely, he hopped on top again and tugged at the meat from inside her jaws. The jaws snapped shut.

* * *

After two days of habituating the C-raptors to each other, several ranch hands placed both in their corrals, while other workers led ten sheep into the far end of the field, almost two miles away. They kept the young in the barn. Cantor hoped to understand how the raptors strategized and maneuvered as a team.

Darwin entered Maryann's corral through a remote-controlled door. Once their initial nervousness abated, the two raptors trotted out of her corral into Maland, apparently accepting each other. Alertness replaced relaxation as they picked up the sheep's scent. Each raptor seemed to have a defined role. For about half a mile, they trotted one behind the other. After this, they took different paths. In this way, Cantor reasoned, they could see each other while looking for different approaches that might provide an advantage.

Darwin stopped behind a large cottonwood and Maryann behind a clump of evergreens. Both rested while studying the sheep. They stayed that way for about four minutes, gathering information on the breeze – how the animals moved, where obstacles lay, and who were the laggards. Simultaneously, they rose and continued onward. When they were within a quarter-mile of the sheep, they stopped again, about 200 feet apart.

After a pause, Darwin moved to the right and walked stealthily, stalking the flock. His head held low, he picked his foot up slowly, curled his toes, and then splayed them out again as his toes silently made contact with the ground. Each step closed in on the prey. Maryann moved closer on the left. It didn't take long to get within striking range. The sheep became nervous, but the scents they picked up seemed to come from different directions, causing some confusion – until Darwin began his run. He came dashing out of a group of trees, head and tail held straight, angling straight for the flock. The feathers behind his head were flat, hiding the red feathers, and his eyes never left his target.

In the meantime, Maryann sprang from behind the boulders where she hid. For a few seconds, the flock retreated away from Darwin, but in a direction that gave Maryann a slight advantage. They hadn't seen her, but it didn't take them long to correct their course. Number 15, an older ewe, fell back from the rest of the flock. Maryann adjusted her angle of attack and headed straight for it, keeping her hands close to her chest.

Meanwhile, Darwin rushed in a direction between the older ewe and the rest of the flock.

Cantor figured if Maryann brought down the sheep, Darwin would break for the flock. If the sheep escaped Maryann's grasp, Darwin might still head it off.

As it happened, Maryann tripped the old ewe with one hand, then snatched it up in her jaws and slammed it to the ground. Darwin caught up with the next laggard and brought it down as well, quickly and efficiently dispatching it with a bite to the neck.

Darwin and Maryann consumed each victim entirely. Cantor and Alex, who tried to keep up with the raptors on electric cycles inside the fences, concluded it was time to see the raptors hunt larger prey: cattle.

* * *

Several days later, Alex and Valerie wanted to collect more data. Alex planned to collect the leg bones from the sheep. He wanted to know if the raptors had cracked them open, exposing the nutritious marrow. Valerie volunteered to collect each raptor's dung to determine how efficiently the raptors digested the meat, skin, and bones. After the workers corralled the raptors, Valerie and Alex went out to collect their respective samples.

As Alex walked toward the kill site, he said. "Please pick up after your pets, Val, using the poopie bags provided. Remember, other folks want to use the park too."

"I'm ignoring you now," she replied.

* * *

Although they would employ drones for documentation of the dinosaurs in the field, Cantor wanted to be closer to the action.

He knew it would be suicide to follow any of the E-raptors on an e-bike inside their territory. Even Darwin would be iffy. But Cantor felt Maryann would allow him, and only him, to ride inside Maland. After discussing the issue with Alex and Kumiko, he asked Tusker to purchase three powerful electric bikes designed for mobility in dirt and grass, preferably colored green or brown. Two bikes would be backup in case the other developed mechanical problems or was damaged.

It took several days for Cantor to convince Kumiko.

* * *

During this time, Kumiko did experiments in her lab, but kept shorter hours than in the past.

"I miss the grad students. They were such a big help in the lab," Kumiko said to Cantor while organizing the lab's boxes of test tubes, gloves, and Petri dishes. "I would love to have the latest Applied Biosystems gene analyzer."

With 54 years behind her, she slowed and grew tired more easily. After finishing her work for the evening, she went home, feeling sleepy.

After dinner, Kumiko rested on the couch as she looked at her beloved poetry, some verses exerting a mysterious power on her mind. She could always find words that gave her enlightenment, soothed her fears, or added to her joy.

* * *

The next day, Kumiko walked into Tusker's office. He welcomed her and pointed to the wooden chair before his desk.

"I wish to make a study of the differences in certain genes between the E-raptors and C-raptors. It would help me greatly if I had an Applied Biosystems gene analyzer."

"Come now, Kumiko. Your lab is a treasure trove of equipment already."

"True, and I'm grateful for that, but…"

"You should focus on making more dinosaurs, Kumiko. Perhaps we could discuss this further over a drink tonight?" He rose and walked behind the chair where she sat.

"Dan, I can't do that."

"Surely there's more that you want," he said, running one finger along her shoulder.

"Yes. Why haven't you provided a doctor bot for the ranch? People get sick or hurt," she said, pulling her shoulder away.

"Docbots are too expensive," he said and sat behind the desk again.

Tusker decided to give her the gene analyzer. *She didn't explicitly reject having a drink with me.* He was sure his generosity would warm her heart.

He gazed at her figure as she walked away. So much like Dominique, the girl he'd known many years ago. He remembered her smile with the endearing overbite. Her gorgeous hair. Her way of making him feel… feel like his odd ways were OK, that his eccentricities were even wonderful. She ghosted him. After a three-month relationship, she had simply gone away.

* * *

It had been several days since Valerie had seen Magpie. *Where is that little devil?* She sat with her feet on the railing of her porch. It had been a long day. Remus had been difficult. He wouldn't leave his injured toe alone. She imagined what he'd look like with a huge plastic cone around his head. It lightened her mood. But not as much as when Magpie landed next to her foot. "There you are, you little beggar!"

Chapter 42

The Moth to the Flame

Exhausted, George lay awake at two in the morning, after dreaming a cloud of vaporous evil had surrounded him. It wanted to consume him. Slipping out of bed, he gazed at the scene outside his window. The world was veiled in shades of black and gray. The barns and fences were mysterious and compelling. He looked back at Luna and the comforter that hugged her curled form. He'd hoped her visit would help him sleep, but here he was, obsessing like so many nights. The dream haunted him. His fear of danger with no face forced him to search for something concrete he could endure. Something visible he could face and survive. Without that, the invisible death cloud would only grow greater in his mind until he could no longer function. Such was the nature of his OCD.

Silently, he grabbed his pants and shoes and tip-toed to the living room, where he put them on. Adding a jacket for the cold, he trotted to the food preparation building, where he grabbed five pounds of ground beef and headed for Maryann's barn.

After confirming she was inside with her raptorlings, he tapped on the plexiglass above the slot where her food was usually served. When he turned on his phone light, she raised her head, flexing her nostrils for clues to the nature of the intruder. He slipped the phone inside the slot and leaned it against the wall where it could record. His mind churned with conflicting emotions, underscored by a nagging sense that, in a corner of his mind, a child begged him to stop.

George pushed a pound of the beef into the slot and watched as her legs brought her massive body off her straw bedding. When she approached the meat, he kept the slot open, and placed his hand partly inside. Her hot breath bathed it between each snort. His hand stayed just beyond the reach of her teeth.

When he was sure she'd eaten the meat, he pulled his hand out and placed another pound of beef through the opening, keeping his hand a few inches closer than before. He heard her snap up the meat, followed by a pause. Then her hard snout nudged his hand out of the slot.

OK, this is it. Quickly, he shoved the last of the meat inside and pulled his hand back. After rubbing it on the wood next to the slot to remove as much meat smell as possible, he slowly put his entire arm inside. First, the hot breath. Next, the hard, wet touch of her teeth. Now he felt the tongue taste his hand and jacket. The teeth were heavy on him. He squinted, waiting for the excruciating crunch of bones, or the relief he craved. Maryann pulled. There was pain and pressure at the base of his upper arm where her sharp teeth grasped. The jacket stretched tight as his body was tugged against the opening. Now his arm was as far inside as it could be without dislodging from his shoulder socket. "What are you doing!?" the child within him cried.

He felt alone; no one could help him as the black abyss approached. The cloud. Maybe it would get him this time. Part of his mind depressurized as the unceasing obsession escaped through some invisible relief valve.

Then Maryann let go. He pulled his sore arm out, damp with saliva. With his other arm, he retrieved his still lit phone from where it rested inside next to the slot's metal frame. It was time to lie back and look at the stars, reveling in the experience. He realized that immersion in extreme danger set him on fire. Like a black hole in space, the abyss was surrounded by extraordinary heat and swirling light of all colors. After a taste of death, life was like a sweet blossom riding on soft currents of air.

He began to laugh as he made his way back to the cabin. He loved the dirt compressed beneath his shoes, the swish of his jacket, the peace in his mind. The moon was now his loving aunt. He took ownership of his madness, seeing it as a gift. He slid into sleep almost as soon as he reached his bed.

* * *

Three nights passed and George enjoyed luxurious sleep when his only compulsion was to put his arm around Luna and drift off like a cloud. Not so the fourth night. He dreamt again about the amorphous blackness that came for him. He woke up in a sweat. Nothing would stop him from obsessing. If he didn't stand and face the horror that threatened to kill him, the torture would continue and get worse. Horror came in many forms. Horror was fused with loneliness. The cure was to expose himself to death, then make a connection to life.

It was after midnight and he knew Maryann was In her barn with her children. *Maybe tonight is the night.* Facing real danger always provided relief. It dissipated the horrific cloud in his mind. It was the venom that cured. It was the fire that cauterized the ragged fear in him.

Quietly in the bathroom, he covered his face, arms, armpits and crotch with deodorant, hoping it would mask the scent of fear. *But will she recognize me?*

He slipped out of the cabin wearing a jacket. This night, the moon was full, perfect for a drone flight. *Perfect for me to see Maryann. For me to reach her.* He unlocked the door to the Comms building and stepped inside, careful to not turn on any lights. He grabbed the new Kaleidoscope drone, whose camera was able to reconstruct colors at night, put it on autopilot, and sent it into the sky.

Next, he took ten pounds of ground beef from the food prep building and headed for Maryann's corral. Once inside, he heard a deep growl. Ignoring the feeding slot, he gently opened the door to the barn.

He dropped a handful of meat on the floor and closed the door, breathing heavily. *Can't this be enough?* Still holding some meat, after a pause, he slowly unlatched the door again and fell over as the huge dinosaur pushed her way past him into the corral. As he rose to his feet, she turned toward him, lowering her head. *Don't run. Stay calm. God, I'm scared. She's going to smell it on me!* He dropped the meat to the ground and stepped back as Maryann's great head sniffed it and gently slipped it between her teeth. *You're such an idiot. Please don't make me do this*! George couldn't help himself and reached out and ran his hand over her huge neck, feeling the muscles move beneath the beaded scales. With a jerk of her head, she sent the meat down her throat.

Careful not to look her in the eyes, he knelt and let her examine him. He had to let her. She smelled his head. *I'm not afraid! I'm so, so afraid! Focus, George!*

With the side of her head, she pushed him onto his side. *I told you this would end badly! I'm ended.* Instinctively, he curled into a ball. Now a taloned finger explored his hair, then the skin on his face. A flood of emotion, part fear, part elation, and part relief washed through him. If she was going to kill him, she would have done it quickly. He knew he would live. *Free-climbing can't compare to this!*

She stepped back and studied him as he slowly rose to his feet. He was glad the raptorlings had stayed in the barn, likely waiting for any danger to pass. A good thing for him. If they tumbled into the corral, her mood might become aggressive and protective.

He said her name. Seeing her open her hands, he retreated and began singing the first song that came into his head. "Silent night. Holy night…" Maryann watched him as he backed toward the corral gate. "Shepherds quake at the sight. Oh please, just stay calm. Oh please, just stay calm…" He opened the gate and locked it behind him, then fell on his knees as the great legs moved toward him on the other side. As before, his mind was full of elation. The indescribable rush that filled him put him on top of the world. It had been worth it. *I'm like a dinosaur whisperer. I'm OK with crazy – it comes with great rewards.*

* * *

Maryann enjoyed the treat from the human. She remained behind the heavy door, inhaling the aroma of meat and human on the other side. She turned and listened as her children fidgeted. With a quick bark, she signaled for them to stay put. Again, the sounds on the other side. *What happening?* She pushed, and the door opened. The human was on the ground. She watched closely as the tailless one rose to his feet. *Strange odor, this one.* But the smell of more meat was captivating. She slid it into her mouth. *Good human. What he want now?* Her skin rippled as he ran his hand down her neck. *Not good touch me there.* She pushed him over and studied him. He confused her. *Tailless one has such little mouth. Such tiny teeth.* He didn't try to bite her, and he wasn't fighting. *Maybe funny smelling one safe.* She touched the human. Now the human rose slowly. *What he want?* She listened for sounds of her children. She opened her hands, feeling nervous. *You no play with children tonight!* Then she stopped. The tailless one was making sounds. Soothing sounds. Good sounds. She relaxed as he opened the corral gate and left. She signaled for the little ones to join her. *Tiny-tooth friend.*

* * *

George felt guilty the next day when a ranch hand found Maryann with her children in the corral and the barn door wide open. He couldn't confess. Not yet.

Chapter 43

The Dexters

"Artificial intelligence is a house guest that takes notes."
— Chitundu Muli

Months passed. Life at the ranch continued and George survived. He and Luna went on wrestling with their differences. Cantor didn't add to his scars, and Kumiko continued her genetics work, though she felt her age. The animals thrived. Discoveries were made. Tusker remained Tusker.

A large shipment of equipment arrived at the ranch in May 2051. Kumiko watched as the truck passed through the gate. She looked forward to the sequencers and other machines she had asked for. Part of the cargo began unloading the rest – the Dexters.

Tusker had relented and included the Dexters in the shipment to relieve the researchers of strenuous or mundane tasks, leaving them time to focus on the research.

Six Dexters arrived in all. As the name implied, they were dexterous and capable of intricate operations, whether it be holding a glass or threading a needle. When necessary, they could even cook without instruction. They stood on two legs, but they could extend two of the four arms as additional legs when needed. It was no problem for a Dexter to lift a washing machine while mopping under.

Their language capabilities were perhaps their best feature. Language fluency increased over time as the artificial neural network chips and the quantum cloud interacted with humans. If the human used slang, the Dexter would too. They solved abstract problems with lightning speed.

Dexters could compress themselves into a compact shape, which allowed them to get in and out of smaller spaces. They did this by compressing their 'neck' and 'pelvic' attachments while folding their limbs.

* * *

Kumiko used a Dexter to help her rearrange parts of her lab. In some ways, it replaced her grad student helpers.

"Dexter, I'm going to call you Dex. Are you OK with that?"

"You can call me Ray or Jay or Billybob. Dex will be fine. I believe that makes me a male."

She gave him an odd look. "You can call me Kumiko. Dex, please turn on the sequencer."

"I will turn on the sequencer for you."

"Thanks. Now I'm going to need those incubators moved to the table by the window."

"I will do that for you, Kumiko."

Dex was significantly taller than Kumiko. It made her a little nervous. "What would you say if I told you I didn't like robots?"

"Then I'd stop spending time with other robots. I'd try to be more toaster-like."

"Hmm. You definitely have a sense of humor, I see."

"I adapt to each person."

"Humor is good," she said. "But bad humor is annoying."

"Am I annoying you?"

"I haven't decided."

"For you, Kumiko, I believe I need to use a more contextual, personal, soft humor, perhaps."

"Let's try that."

* * *

Kumiko began a training program for Dex – he learned how she organized the lab and her unique processes.

"Have you read these publications, Dex?" Kumiko asked, giving him a list on paper.

He barely glanced at the paper before saying, "All these books were part of my education. They are in the cloud."

"Wonderful. Here are some papers I've written that haven't been published yet," she said, pointing to a stack of papers on her desk. "Would you please read them?"

She watched in amazement as he read each page in the amount of time it took to turn it.

* * *

The next morning, Cantor watched as Dex increased his size in the dining room.

"You're a big fellow. I'd offer you a cup of coffee, Dex, but I don't think you'd care for it."

"I don't know where it would go in or where it would go out, Cantor."

Cantor smiled, "Then again, I'm not a big fan of oil for breakfast either."

"A funny man you are, Cantor."

He looked over the big bot, starting with the legs and ending at the head. "I would love to get into your head, Dex."

"I don't think you'd fit."

"Funny fellow," Cantor said dryly. "What goes on inside your mind?"

"I have many levels in my head. Some levels are zeros and ones. Some are complex numbers. Some are quantum-based. The level I'm using now is full of words, equations, and memories. Do you have different levels in your head?"

"Well... Yeah, I guess I do. There are deep-seated emotions, there are old memories, words – all sorts of things. But I experience parts of them all at once."

"I believe that is what you humans call consciousness."

"I think so. Consciousness is always in the present. Even if I'm thinking of something from long ago, I'm doing so in the present. And you Dex?"

"Not quite the same for me. I have multiple levels of consciousness. They happen at the same time and communicate with each other. It is like parallel processing. I can replay my conscious state at any point in the past. I have a super-consciousness that monitors all the parallel consciousnesses."

Cantor paused. "What does Tusker get out of this?"

"May I ask what you are referring to?"

"Buying you and the other Dexters. I mean, he isn't usually so generous."

"I'm afraid I can't know Dan Tusker's thoughts."

"Maybe he's changed," Cantor said, gazing at the row of tiny lights on Dex's thorax.

"Think of me as a friend, a co-worker, and someone you can express yourself to without fear of hurt feelings, anger, or retribution. Studies have shown people are far more productive around Dexters."

"Dex, we aren't building widgets here."

* * *

That same day, a different Dexter entered Valerie's clinic, carrying flowers. She looked up from her laptop.

"Flowers for me? Why thank you. Who are they from?"

"Alex."

"Do you have a name?"

"Originally, I was D2050MT148023ADQB. Alex calls me Gagarin."

There was something about the robot that put Valerie at ease. "I'm Valerie. Let's see what we've got. Chamisa flowers and Indian paintbrushes. They're lovely. I'll get a glass of water to put them in. Thank you, Gagarin."

"You are welcome. They come with a message."

"Oh? What is it?" Valerie asked, as she headed to the metal sink.

"To my lovely friend, Val. Perhaps these flowers will thaw your beautiful heart and warm your green eyes? I can only hope."

"My goodness. Your voice sounds just like Alex's. You even have the accent down."

"Do you have a response, Val?"

"Yeah, I guess. Tell Alex, as one friend to another, 'Thanks for the beautiful flowers.'"

Gagarin continued, looking into her eyes. "Anything else?"

"Nope. That's it."

Chapter 44

Cantor's Great Ride

"If everything seems under control, you're just not going fast enough."
— Mario Andretti

The Dexters proved their worth on the ranch. As time passed, they blended seamlessly into Cantor, Kumiko, Alex, and Valerie's daily routines. Meanwhile, Cantor's research on dinosaur hunting behavior continued into 2052.

That September was warm and dry. Cantor sat astride the powerful Zeus, absorbing its power and relishing its acceleration. Cows treated with the new pain blocker had been placed at the far end of Maland the night before. As he waited for Maryann to move toward her prey, he decided on an escape route, in case she decided he was on the menu. But he knew that was unlikely. He was probably the only human she might tolerate in her territory, with the possible exception of George.

As he watched her testing the air, he could see George, in the distance, straddling the stockade fence that separated her turf from the rest of Raptor Ranch, using powerful binoculars.

She caught a scent and bared her teeth as if tasting it.

Now she began a slow walk toward the cows, well over a mile away. He tightened the straps on his black winged helmet and quietly moved the length of a football field behind her. When she got to a clump of green cottonwoods, she stood tall, blending with their massive trunks, while she scanned the blond grasses and sage further on. Several magpies flew from the trees in flashes of black and white.

Cantor stopped the bike and put binoculars to his eyes. He looked in awe at the silhouette of the massive raptor, all 4500 pounds of her, and imagined a smaller *Utahraptor* striking the same pose 125 million years ago, possibly near where she stood now. Even in the shade, he could see her conical, serrated teeth. Her long arms, tipped with sharp eagle-like claws, underscored his caution. After all, he thought, he was alone in a field with the most powerful predator in the world by far. And she was hungry.

Cantor hoped he wouldn't need the stun grenades or the air horn that weighed down the shoulder pack pushing against his hip. Also in the pack was the tranquilizer pistol that Kumiko insisted he bring, although he knew it wouldn't save him if Maryann turned on him, because the sedative took twenty minutes to immobilize such an enormous animal. He was glad for the limited-range radio communicator that supplemented the mic on his helmet, and a container of bear spray, all attached with a belt.

He looked up as a drone flew overhead, filming the hunt, and checked the little autonomous, intelligent swivel recorder on his helmet.

"Muli, are you still getting the video feed from my helmet cam?"

"Yes, Mr. Cantor," came the little voice inside his helmet. "The image is very good." Later, he would examine the recordings at his leisure.

After sampling the hot, dry air, Maryann began a graceful lope, skirting a rocky area surrounded by low-lying evergreens. Cantor followed at a respectable distance, continually navigating the sage, rocks, and trees while keeping his eye on her. If she turned on him, his best chance would be to outrun her. If that wasn't possible, because of the terrain, he would jump off the bike and climb a tree while tossing a stun grenade.

After five minutes, he caught up to within 200 feet of her, and several times she glanced back at him as she trotted toward the cattle further up the field.

A rush of adrenaline urged him on and the air seemed somehow cleaner, fresher. Feeling brave, he sped up while veering to the left so he traveled abreast of Maryann on a parallel course, keeping the safety margin of 200 feet between them. His heart pumped, cheering him on. Seeing Maryann effortlessly moving through the grass as silent as a tiger invigorated him. She seemed to accept him; it would be terribly obvious if she didn't. As she sped up, so did he. The e-bike hardly made a sound. The pressure of the wind on his face increased now and the grasses and shrubs blurred beside him. He couldn't stop laughing.

"Mr. Cantor, are you OK?" Muli asked.

"Couldn't be better, Muli."

As in earlier hunts with Darwin, Maryann slowed and came to a stop inside a depression, beside some tall brambles and evergreens, tall enough to keep her out of sight of the cows. The breeze worked in her favor. Cantor too came to a stop at the edge of a group of pine trees, panting and planting his feet on the ground. Maryann looked at him for an uncomfortably long time. *Is she treating me like a fellow hunter?*

He scanned the area with his binoculars. The western end of Maland was in view. The cows would have to turn.

As the dinosaur's green eyes continued to study him, shadowed by her bony brows, he slowly reached for a stun grenade while taking short glances at her. A full-frontal stare from a close distance, he'd discovered long ago in his research, could be interpreted as a challenge. *Probably not a problem at this distance.* He could hear a tiny buzz as the helmet cam turned to keep Maryann in center view.

At last, he let out his breath as she looked back toward the herd. She was now fully committed to action. Her eyes never left the nearest cow as she crept forward.

Maryann stayed low and slow until a brown cow raised its head, sniffing the air. Time stopped. She picked her target and broke into a sprint, keeping her head, neck, and tail flat. Dirt and grass flew from behind her feet. Birds squawked and flapped from the overhanging trees. The cows lurched away from her now, stampeding to the west, panicking at the sound of her footfalls and the huge two-legged shape hurtling towards them. Cantor fed power to the motor and raced ahead.

As the end of the stockade neared, some cows ran to the right and some to the left. Cantor headed toward the group that had veered to the left. Because Maland was significantly less wide than long, it didn't take long for the southern wall to come into view. Seeing this, the herd turned east, heading straight for him. *Man, I'd better get up a tree in a hurry!*

Maryann adjusted her direction, impervious to the cacti and bushes she plowed through. Several hares ran for their lives from the underbrush.

He stepped off the bike and began to climb up the first few branches of a big pine tree. That was as far as he got when a cow passed by him, immediately followed by Maryann at a narrow angle to it. Her feet pounded the earth with a muffled whomp as air whooshed in and out of her open jaws. He began rapidly climbing.

From his perch, he admired her golden-brown body and how her spine, tail, and neck lined up like a huge arrow. The muscles in her legs bulged as she pushed off the ground. When she changed course slightly, one feathered arm would open toward her turn. *Just like an aircraft's flaps!* She grabbed her target's neck in her jaws, lifting it off the ground, and snapped its neck before flipping it on its side. One long sickle claw slashed the cow's belly. It all happened in a second.

Cantor wanted to look away. The blood brought back memories best forgotten. But his scientific training held sway, and he spoke into the recorder around his neck while observing every detail.

"Her instincts kicked in and she was silent after the kill. If other predators had been nearby, they'd be attracted to any sounds she made advertising her success," he panted into the mic. "Amazing aerodynamic use of arms."

He smelled the humid, rank insides of the nearby cow carcass and felt dizzy. *Get a grip.*

Maryann took her time examining this new type of prey, sniffing it from head to foot. Then she looked around, checking behind bushes and trees. She approached Cantor's tree and peered up at him; her massive head situated roughly two feet beneath his crouched position. *Why didn't I climb higher?* She sniffed and stared at him with intense eyes while making a huffing sound, then turned back to her kill. Cantor let go of his breath and wiped the sweat from his brow. He felt vulnerable and tried to make himself as inconspicuous as possible. He heard the zzzz of his helmet camera as it turned to keep focused on Maryann, just 40 feet away.

He knew how Kumiko was reacting to the live video, sitting in the Comms building a mile and a half away. She was probably digging her fingernails into her thighs and biting her lower lip. "Kumiko, I'm doing good. No problems."

Maryann pulled at the hide, then bit into the corner where the belly met the hind leg. After tearing off the leg, she swallowed it whole. Then she ripped off the other hind leg, also swallowing it whole. Again, she walked around, checking for something. She stood below Cantor a second time, quizzically tilting her head, making snuffling sounds. Cantor glanced at the red piece of meat dangling from her green, scaly jaw, then looked away as he whispered, "Good girl, that's a good girl." He wanted the soothing sound of his voice to confirm what her nostrils already told her, "This is Mother." This was the nature of their bond.

Cantor continued speaking into the mic, trying to focus on the science, not the bloodiness of the kill.

Once satisfied, Maryann cleaned herself, removing anything stuck to her fingers, and ran her claws along her jaw. Next, she scratched the soil with her feet until they were clean. She rolled on her side, taking a dust bath to clean her skin and feathers, occasionally snorting to keep her nostrils free of dust. When she had taken care of her hygiene, she sat on her haunches, head on the ground, and closed her eyes. The Turkey vultures that had been circling landed cautiously and hopped toward the carcass.

The thought that he might slip down the tree and retrieve the bike lasted only a second in Cantor's mind before he resigned himself to a long stay in the tree. He studied the branches above his head to be sure he could gain more height if needed. Maryann could easily rise up and catch hold of one of his legs if she chose to.

A lizard stopped and looked up at her. Cantor chuckled when it bobbed its head, signaling its ownership of the territory.

After half an hour, he spoke into the helmet mic and whispered, "This is Cantor. Can anyone hear me?" He turned the volume down.

"This is Kumiko, I hear you."

"I got lucky. Perfect location. I'm in a tree, almost above Maryann and her kill." He described his location as best he could, calling out his coordinates on his phone's GPS.

"I've got you from the drone video feed," Kumiko said. "Do you need help?"

"No, I hope to return on the Zeus once Maryann is finished resting and leaves."

"I'll wait to hear from you, out."

He looked at Maryann. One green eye was now open and watching him. She continued to study him for about three minutes, and then her eye gradually closed. A puff of air caused a cloud of dirt in front of her nostrils to roll and settle.

Cantor observed her for another thirty minutes before she stirred. She rose, stretched, and yawned. After defecating, she plowed dirt over it with her feet. *How like a cat,* Cantor thought. *A really big cat.*

Maryann went back to the remains of the cow, causing the turkey vultures to scatter. With a crunch of her jaws, she severed the head. Holding what remained of the body in her mouth, she walked away, her banded tail swaying with each step. Cantor suspected she would hide it, intending to gnaw on the bones another day. *Or she's saving it for the kids.* She returned with a shoulder joint and a front leg in her mouth. Her pace was relaxed, and she looked at him before cocking her head when the breeze caused the leaves to rustle in the trees. Some crows cawed as though they recognized her as a relative. With graceful strides, she headed in the direction of the barn, almost two miles away, where her children waited.

Cantor let out a deep sigh. After a few minutes, he lowered himself as quietly as possible, then spoke into the mic, "Cantor here. Does anyone hear me?"

Again, Kumiko answered.

"I'm heading toward the middle gate now," he said.

"Please be careful."

Cantor sat on the e-bike and rode away. His hands on the handlebars shook and he couldn't stop grinning.

* * *

Maryann ambled toward her barn, still some distance away. *Food for children.* It had thrilled her to see her mother join her on the hunt. *Mother climb tree.* Maryann remembered how, as a chick, she could do that. Now, she was always on the ground. No climbing. Sometimes her mother used legs that twirled. She looked at her feet, but they wouldn't twirl.

Dropping the cow leg from her jaws, she bent to smell a clump of sage. Then she lowered herself and rubbed her body on it, leaving it flat. Sage was good, she thought as she walked away. A tortoise clomped along nearby. Lowering her great head, she smelled it and recalled the walnuts her mother ate. *Walking nut.*

She lifted her head as several crows flew by, cawing. *Sky friends.* She wanted to fly. Bursting into a sprint, she flew over the ground, but she couldn't reach them.

* * *

~ 278 ~

Cantor removed his jacket and helmet as Dex lowered himself from the tall wooden fence, where he'd observed Cantor's return. First, the robot's two pairs of forward limbs touched the ground, then the hind ones. He resembled a large, graceful insect.

"You did a fine job, sir. Truly remarkable," Dex said in a soothing male voice as he rose to his full height.

"Thanks, Dex. I really enjoyed that," Cantor said, wiping his brow. "I think it'll take me a while to come down from this high. But PLEASE don't call me sir."

"I hear you. You are Cantor."

"I'm going to take my clothes off, enjoy a long shower, and then check the videos."

"Would you like to give me your clothes now?"

"Dex, I'm keeping my clothes on until I get home."

"You fooled me. How was your experience?"

"I'm in awe of Maryann. She is so powerful. So beautiful to watch."

"I too am powerful, Cantor."

Cantor stopped and looked at Dex. "Yes. I'm sure you are."

* * *

Later, Cantor and Kumiko sat back on their leather recliners inside the cabin, each enjoying a cold ice tea.

"I'm going with you next time," Kumiko said. "Watching the action from far away was nerve-wracking. We'll take an SUV."

The cabin always smelled of cedar and pine and stayed pleasantly cool during the warmer months. Once the entertainment chamber and console had processed the videos of the day's hunt from all the cameras and integrated them into one 3D view, Cantor asked for music. He chose Wagner's "The Flight of the Valkyries", followed by Ravel's "Bolero". They put the sensory helmets on and relived the wind rushing through his hair and the thrill of the hunt with Maryann. Through the Vibro pads, both felt the hum of the bike's motor and the bumps of the terrain.

Chapter 45

Remus Falls

"The ax forgets; the tree remembers."
— Shona proverb

In October 2052, ranch hands placed two cows in Grouchland so that the scientists could observe how Mako and Remus hunted together. Cantor didn't want to use more cows for fear the E-raptors would kill the lot. He and Alex hadn't spent much time with the two males. Now was the time. Do males cooperate during the hunt? Or do they prefer to hunt alone? How does dominance fit in?

Cantor watched Mako, scooping up gallons of air through his flexing nostrils. *He dominates like a tyrannical king*, he thought. *Cruel and pitiless. It's a shame there aren't two C-raptor males, I'd rather study them.*

Cantor didn't plan to enter Grouchland on the e-bike. Far too dangerous. So, he and Alex observed as best they could from the fences, while a drone operated at a low altitude. Dex ran along the top of the fence, clasping four hands and two feet along opposite sides, recording as he went. His arms would unclasp as he moved forward, then re-clasp as his legs unclasped behind. It was almost graceful.

As the hunt began, Mako trotted about 60 feet in front of Remus. Upon closing with the nearest cow, both raptors stopped to study the scene, completely immersed. When the drone distracted Mako, the drone operator told it to back off.

Mako rose and crashed forward while Remus galloped in a different direction to flank the cow.

No! Remus, no! Pick the other cow! Cantor shook his head. *Surely Remus knows about the other cow. Where is the damn thing!?*

Mako got to the cow first and brought it down. But he didn't kill it. He broke the animal's ankle and gnawed at the upper part of the front leg as the cow continued to struggle. Remus returned with his head lowered, made a warbling sound, and finally bit down on the cow's neck.

Mako wasn't ready to allow Remus a place at the table and lunged at his head with a deafening roar. Both raptors tried to bite the other, but only Mako escalated the fight, holding onto Remus while trying to rip him open with his sickle claw, balancing on the other foot with some support from his tail. Remus fought on, despite the deep wounds in his belly. To fall now would be fatal.

The two massively muscled beasts grappled, bit, and slashed. The red feathers at the top of their heads bristled. Clouds of dust swirled around them as they fought. Claws held the opponent close. Sometimes they ripped down the opponent's chest or shoulders, opening the flesh. Both raptors received wounds, but Remus was in worse shape. He lowered his head feathers and tried to disengage. That brought his tail within reach of Mako's jaws, which clamped down with brutal quickness. He shook it viciously and then pulled on the flesh with his serrated teeth, severing muscle and tendon.

Remus broke away, his tail badly damaged. It wasn't enough for Mako. He sprinted and raked and bit Remus's upper legs. Remus turned to defend himself, but Mako rammed into him, causing him to fall. In a flash, Mako bit into Remus' belly. Remus cried out and got to his feet. Before Mako backed off, he bit Remus' tail one more time, close to the first wound. Remus' left arm hung limply; his intestines hung from his belly. He ran from his tormentor until Alex and the other observers lost sight of him.

Mako returned to his kill.

The drone tried to navigate out of a group of trees and ducked to avoid a large branch, only to crash into an outcrop, breaking a rotor. The camera still worked and sent an image of rocks and grass at an unnatural angle.

Cantor could see enough to realize something terrible had happened. He needed to know Remus' condition and, now without a drone, he prepared to use the e-bike, which was near at hand. For Remus, time was short, and he was out of sight.

Mako fed lustfully as flies buzzed around his bloody jaws.

Remus had to be found. Cantor grabbed the dart gun and shoulder pack and climbed on the e-bike, forgetting his helmet. "Get another drone up!" he cried to Alex.

As Cantor approached the North gate, Alex's voice came on the radio in the pack. He stopped and pulled the mic out.

"I don't think the bike is a good idea, Cantor," Alex said.

"I wish I had a better option. I'll outrun him if he comes at me. But right now, I don't have any choice."

"Cantor, you can't outrun him if you're on choppy ground."

"Let me know if Mako leaves the kill site."

Dex remained on top of the stockade fence.

Cantor was well aware, when two males of an animal species fight, typically they display to one another first. Lions, elephants, wolves, baboons, hippos… Most fights are avoided when one antagonist withdraws and signals submission after concluding the display by the other is too intimidating. Remus had signaled that Mako was the dominant male by lowering his head feathers. *Mako didn't even give Remus a chance to back down!*

He entered Grouchland far away from Mako and made S-shaped sweeps up the fields, trying to cover the ground as efficiently as possible. Finally, he spotted him lying beneath some trees near a stream. Alex, watching from the fence, assured Cantor by radio that Mako was still at the kill site and not lurking behind some foliage, ready to attack.

Remus' side rose and fell rapidly, a bad sign. Cantor parked the e-bike about 30 feet away and approached the wounded raptor. *Easy now, easy Remus.* The wounds he could see were bad. Remus' tail bent downwards and some entrails were laying on the grass next to him.

Considerable blood flowed from the gashes. He came around and brushed a stick against the huge hands, testing. One eye opened and Remus raised his head and moved an arm, sending Cantor backward toward the stream. *Easy boy.* In a couple of seconds, Remus lowered his head onto the grass, his orange eye looking past Cantor into the sky. Cantor let his breath release. *Oh, my stomach.*

Cantor leaned over and vomited until his stomach was dry. Grabbing the radio communicator, he called Valerie, but got no answer, so he tried the Comms building. Kumiko answered.

"Kumiko… Remus looks pretty messed up… Ah… As best I can describe it, he's… he's lying along the lower stream between two small hills. I'm going to walk to the top of the hill… nearer to where the fence should be." As he walked, he listened to Kumiko's voice.

"Why didn't you let Alex take the bike?"

"There wasn't time. Don't worry, I've got this," he said, trying to reassure her.

"You need to be in an SUV!"

"There was no time, Kumiko. Anyway, the bike is more maneuverable. Alex is monitoring Mako."

She let out a long sigh. "Describe Remus' condition."

"Large bite wounds on the tail. It looks broken. Lacerations… along the neck and sides. A… A large gash in the belly." Cantor tried to get his breathing under control. He looked away from the blood and guts.

"Is he bleeding heavily?"

"Give me a minute," Cantor said, hyperventilating. "Yes, heavy bleeding." He shook off his dizziness and nausea. *Come on, Cantor! Get a grip.*

"OK, thanks. We need to get him to the infirmary as soon as possible. Are you OK?"

"Yeah. I'm now at the top of the hill," Cantor said, a little winded.

"Good news. The second drone has Mako still at the kill site. Hold on, Dex is sending me images. I know your position," Kumiko said.

"Hang on. I'm sending the truck with the hoist and pallet. I'll lead it in one of the SUVs. The terrain isn't too bad where you are. Please be careful."

"No Kumiko. I don't think you should come out here. Where's Valerie?"

"Circe bit Spike and damaged his leg, so Valerie has her hands full. I'm on my way. Oh, no!"

"What?"

"I'm watching the drone screen. Mako just batted it out of the sky."

"Not good. Any picture?" he asked.

"None. I'm on my way!"

"No, Kumiko." It was too late. She was determined to be with him.

Cantor returned to Remus. He wanted to vomit again as the blood, feces, intestines, and bile assaulted his senses. *There must be something I can do*, he thought. He wondered whether the tranquilizer might relieve Remus of his pain, but concluded he should wait until he spoke with Valerie.

Cantor tried to give Remus some room. He backed off and squatted out of Remus' sight. The last thing Remus needed was the added stress of having a human on the scene. He put his head in his arms, trying to get his emotions under control.

He picked up the radio and tried to reach Valerie. No luck. He tried phoning her.

She answered, "Cantor, are you OK?"

"No worries. Remus is severely injured. Should I tranq him?"

"I just heard about the fight. Awful. I don't recommend tranquilizing him if we are going to save him. You might depress his breathing and slow his heart too much."

"Thanks, Valerie." Cantor ended the call. He looked at Remus, unable to interpret any signs in such an alien face.

Ten minutes later, the radio squawked, "On our way."

Cantor climbed a tree to see the vehicles and double-check the area. Various clumps of trees in the distance blocked his view. Otherwise, there was no sign of Mako. He held the trunk of the tree and scanned the fields, until it occurred to him, with the loss of so much blood, Remus needed liquids.

He climbed back down and took his shirt off after first laying the shoulder pack and gun on the ground. After he put the shirt in the stream, he tied it to a stick and made his way to Remus. Remus raised his head, opened his mouth, and tried to swallow the dribble of water from the shirt. It seemed to work. However, the amount of water getting inside Remus was minuscule compared to the blood loss.

Cantor climbed the tree again and looked around, the wet shirt looped in his belt. Still no sign of Mako. He noticed the SUV about a mile distant, the slower truck further back. With relief, he waved the shirt, even though he knew Kumiko didn't need to be guided. The SUV already had his coordinates. *That SUV is used for Maryann and Darwin, not for Mako.* He took a deep breath. *It'll be OK, stop worrying, Cantor. Mako can't outrun it.*

Upon arrival, after checking on Cantor, Kumiko raced to Remus and did a quick assessment of his injuries. The blood loss and shock were putting an immense strain on his heart. The labored breathing confirmed it. "We can't leave him in pain," she said, and administered a painkiller with a shot in the tail. Cantor started to stop her, then realized it was the right thing to do. Her hand trembled. She kept as far away from the teeth and claws as possible.

They waited a few minutes. Cantor used the time to climb the tree again to see the truck's progress.

The radio came to life. "I can't see Mako, Cantor. Be careful," Alex said.

At last, the truck found them and backed up so they could lift Remus and place him in the bed behind the rotational hoist. Lifting a 4,700-pound dinosaur on a slope was not ideal.

Once the truck was in place, Cantor helped the workers remove the large wooden pallet and carry it to Remus. *Too slow, too slow*, Cantor thought.

A group of birds flew out of the trees. As the men laid the pallet down, Cantor thought he saw movement in some distant trees, but when he focused on it, it seemed only the breeze.

"Let's wait in the vehicles for a while," he said. "Just to be safe."

No one heard the suggestion, given the current emergency. The ranch hands discussed the best way to get Remus on the pallet. Once Remus was in place, they would attach the junction of the four steel cables attached at each corner of the pallet into the hoist's hook, which would lift the dinosaur.

"Hey guys, I think you should head for the truck. Kumiko, please, let's go to the SUV together," Cantor said, finally getting everyone's attention.

A slight sound, a small cracking twig. Everyone heard it. He looked in the sound's direction but saw nothing.

"Kumiko, I think you should get back into the car NOW. Signal it to come get us," he said in earnest. He motioned to the workers, "Back inside, please. Into the truck please," polite but terse.

Kumiko spoke into the SUV's small communicator attached to the key fob. "I'll meet it halfway." There were too many large rocks and saplings near the stream. The SUV wouldn't be able to get much closer.

Kumiko ran back to the approaching car and got in as it stopped, but not before calling out to Cantor, "You too, Cantor. Please hurry!" He was making his way up the hill.

The workers were slow to move.

Cantor looked through the piñon and cottonwoods one more time. As he headed for the SUV, he heard Kumiko shout. The car scanner was picking up something large. Mako abruptly crashed into view. He looked between Remus, the workers, and Cantor, clawed hands open wide.

A third of a mile away, Dex's ultra-sensitive hearing had picked up the urgency in Cantor's voice. He crawled down the fence and began running toward Cantor, while making a growling noise similar to an adult raptor.

Mako stopped and turned toward the growling sounds coming toward him. Dex entered the depression where the stream flowed and confronted the brute. When the bot tried to lead Mako away, in a flash, Mako charged and ripped off one of the Dex's arms. Despite his smaller size, Dex broke the claw off one of Mako's fingers.

Mako roared and slashed at Dex with one leg's huge sickle claw while holding onto to him with his hands. Dex broke free and using his remaining limbs, swiftly climbed a large cottonwood, using one leg to bait Mako.

Cantor shouted, "Stay in the tree, Dex!" *Crap. He's going to be losing fluid.*

Dex's sacrifice gave two of the workers, Jose and Milo, time to run to the truck and climb in, slamming the passenger door. The other door was still open as Mako pounded toward the third worker, Brad Patterson. Unable to reach the cab in time, he chose his next best option and dove under the bed of the truck.

Mako could smell Patterson's fear and hunched down and eyed the man below the truck bed near the double wheels. Patterson rolled toward the other side and Mako dashed around the truck to catch him. Cantor heard the man scream.

Unable to reach Patterson, Mako went back to the cab with Jose and Milo.

The giant moved quickly. He bashed the truck's closed door with his head and tore off the handle with his teeth, while the men inside gaped in terror.

Unable to grip the door, Mako lumbered around the cab to the partly opened driver's side door. Both men pulled on a jacket caught on the door hinge, frantically trying to dislodge it. But it only knotted more tightly near the truck's mirror.

The cab was roomy, and Mako was able to stick his head inside. The men recoiled, doing all they could to distance themselves from the enormous head and teeth coming at them. Mako pulled at the steering wheel, almost tearing off the top half.

Jose tried to compress his body into the floorboards under the dash on the passenger side. Milo, sitting on the seat, looking at Mako, bent his legs and tried to turn them to the right while crossing his arms over his chest. They could feel and smell Mako's breath. The teeth were yellow with some crowded together, leaving several pointing further outside the mouth. The deep snarling growls beat at Milo and he began rocking himself in fear, reciting a prayer.

Milo tried to open the passenger door, but it was stuck after Mako's attack. He gave out a pitiable groaning noise as Mako sank a couple of teeth into his boot and into the flesh underneath. Jose tried to pull his friend away as Milo howled in pain. Kumiko, in the SUV, began to honk the horn, hoping to distract the dinosaur. She could see the horrible scene and hear the roars.

Cantor slid against the SUV and dived into the passenger's side. "Those poor guys," he panted. He realized he had left everything by the stream. Turning to Kumiko, he said, "Keep honking! I have to go for the gun and stun grenades." *We're cooked without the tranq gun and flash grenades! How could I be so stupid!?*

Kumiko looked at him with wide eyes. "No Cantor, you'll be…" but he was gone before she could finish.

Cantor sprinted down the slope and around the opposite end of the truck. Sliding onto the ground near his shoulder pack, he got his hand around a stun grenade, pulled the pin, and tossed it toward Mako. An ear-splitting boom tortured his ears and a blinding light lit up the area. The blast caused Mako to let go of the man's boot and pull his head out of the cab. He looked disoriented.

Cantor grabbed the pack, picked up the dart rifle, and ran toward the SUV, trying not to look behind. The blast left him almost blind. He concentrated on the repeating blare of the SUV's horn, which he could barely sense above the white noise flooding his ears. Time seemed to slow to a crawl as he stumbled onward.

"Run, Cantor, run, run! Hurry!" Kumiko shouted out her open window.

Mako stood, shaking his head, still bewildered.

Cantor jumped into the SUV. "That was crazy," he gasped. As soon as his eyes adjusted, he saw the tears in Kumiko's. His heart sank. *This is my fault. How could I let this happen?* "I'll tranq him. It's going to be all right, honey."

The intense light and thunder of the explosion stunned the workers as well. Despite this, Milo finally tossed the jacket outside and shut the driver's side door to the cab.

Mako soon shook off the effects of the stun grenade. He followed Cantor's smell as well as the industrial scent of the SUV as he moved toward Cantor and Kumiko.

"Crap, here we go," he whispered.

Mako moved to the SUV and stared into the front windshield. Kumiko gripped Cantor's hand hard. She looked at the eyes of the monster, her own eyes open wide. Mako stared spears through the glass.

Without moving his lips, Cantor whispered, "Don't move or make a sound. Look away."

Kumiko continued to stare into the fiery orange eyes.

"Look away!" Cantor repeated between his teeth, squeezing her hand.

Kumiko snapped her head down, as though breaking a trance, and looked at the dash, breathing hard.

Even with his face averted, Cantor could sense the orange, penetrating eyes studying him. Burning into him.

Kumiko shuddered and tried to make herself small.

"Whatever you do, keep your eyes down," Cantor whispered.

Mako continued to stare for a full minute. He began to walk around the SUV, looking for a way in. At the same time, Jose stumbled out of the truck and tried to coax Patterson from under the flat bed. Immediately, Mako turned away and strode back toward the truck.

Cantor was shaking. Looking at Kumiko, he asked. "You, OK?"

She nodded, trembling. "I'm afraid."

Kumiko lifted up her eyes slowly as Mako tried to catch Jose as he raced into the truck's cab, just in time. "Why didn't that man follow Jose?"

"I'm not sure. But Jose needs to stay inside the cab. When he leaves it, Mako assumes he's like a hyena wanting to share his prey."

The dinosaur stopped beside the door and peered in. The two men didn't need to be told to remain still. The raptor knew they were there, but the less movement, the less there was to interest him. Both men stared at the raptor with wide eyes.

"Look away guys, look away!" Cantor said to himself.

Patterson hadn't budged from underneath the truck. The men in the cab wouldn't drive away and leave him.

Mako shifted his eyes off the trembling men and noticed the e-bike where Cantor had left it near the stream. After studying it, he moved closer and clamped his teeth around the seat, lifted the bike, and tossed it against a tree as if it were a child's toy.

Now he moved toward Remus and stood above him. He lowered his head and bit Remus's hand, destroying every bone in it. Remus picked up his head and then flopped it down again.

Mako taunted Remus, dragging a claw down his snout. Then he bent down and stared at his dying opponent, inches from his reptilian face. With one finger claw, he tapped on Remus' eye.

"What a cruel S.O.B.," Cantor whispered.

Mako turned and bit down on the ankle of the nearest leg, then into some of the large thigh muscle, pulling off a chunk, which he swallowed in two gulping motions. Now he fed in earnest.

Cantor watched Mako, aghast that Remus was still alive.

The radio jolted him. "This is Alex. How are you?" Cantor, as though moving through a thick fluid, got the communicator to his mouth. "Remus isn't going to survive!" Silence on the other end.

"I'm sorry," Alex said after a pause, "And Mako?"

With surprising bluntness, Cantor blurted, "Mako's eating him!"

"Dear Lord."

"We were too late. As soon as I tranq him, we'll retrieve what's left of Remus and bring him in. Over." Cantor balled up his hands and clamped his jaw.

Mako took his time. After eating his fill, he laid down to doze near the bloody body, guarding his treasure from the human pirates. Mercifully, Remus had stopped breathing. But Mako didn't doze. Instead, he rose and walked over to the truck and laid down, head facing Patterson. He stared at the terrified human, grunting and clicking his teeth.

Cantor reached for the dart gun. He slowly opened the door, wincing at the slight squeak it made, got as close as he could, and took a shot. The dart hit Mako near the ankle, but the shallow angle meant it might not have delivered a full dose. Mako instantly snarled and rose, snapping at his leg.

Cantor bee-lined it for the SUV. After he climbed in, Kumiko cried, "This is too much."

The sun had set beyond the mountains. "Radio the guys in the truck. Tell them as soon as Mako is sedated to get Patterson and head out. We'll get Remus' body tomorrow," he urged, trying to calm his nerves.

Mako checked out his treasure, taking a few licks, then stood over the body, scanning the area, one foot on the broken tail.

"What is he doing, Cantor?"

"I'm not sure. I expect he might take some meat and bones and bury them someplace."

Kumiko radioed the truck. "Follow us home when you get your man inside."

"Mako damaged the steering wheel, Doctor Chen. This vehicle isn't self-driving, but we'll do our best."

Next, she called Alex. "We're going to head in without Remus," she said when Alex answered.

"OK, you guys get back here. We'll talk then," Alex said quietly.

Kumiko told the car to start, but forgot the lights would automatically come on. "Car! Turn off the lights!" she cried. Too late. The monster saw the bright eyes of the SUV challenge him and stepped over Remus' tail toward them. "Oh no," Kumiko said, "I don't want to go through this again."

Mako grabbed the fender of the left front wheel, ripping it away. He tore into the tire, leaving it shredded, jostling them both. With a snap, his teeth ripped off the searchlight by the driver's side door. "Car! Back up!" Kumiko cried through clenched teeth. Her hands remained tightly clamped around the wheel.

But the movement of the vehicle only enraged Mako. With startling swiftness, he flattened the rear tire on Kumiko's side. With his lower teeth under the wheel housing, he lifted the SUV several feet off the ground. Kumiko screamed, "No! No!" Then came the jolting crash to the ground.

When they looked outside, Mako had disappeared into the darkness. The moonless evening worked to Mako's advantage. He could wait as long as necessary.

Cantor let out his breath. "Crap! I wish I had brought night-vision goggles. I'm going to take another shot at Mako." He pulled out another dart.

Kumiko rapidly nodded in agreement. "Car, send a distress signal," she said.

"Great idea. It's getting pretty dark now. I can't see the bastard. What does the scanner say?" he asked.

"Confirmation from the scanner. To your right!"

Cantor lowered the window and fired in the direction of the thuds and sounds of swishing grass that Mako made as he approached. The snarl told him it was a hit. As Cantor tried to raise the window, the sounds drew nearer. Deep breathing. Twigs snapped; leaves crunched. A low growl. Mako appeared at Cantor's window before it was fully closed, causing him to recoil. An orange eye. Strings of red flesh. Then the sound of teeth on the roof and the top of the door. If Cantor had completely closed the window, the lower teeth would have shattered it. The sickening head lowered itself and looked in, barely visible from the faint glow of the flat tire indicator in the dash. The nostrils flared as a low rumble sounded from the scaley throat.

Cantor tried to tell the car to raise the window, but he couldn't get the words out. He frantically tried to find the window control again. He knew Mako could get a claw over the window and rip it out. Finally, taking a deep breath, he pushed the control, and the window closed.

Cantor held himself still, knowing only a third of an inch of reinforced glass separated him from a grisly death. *When will he test it?* Barely breathing, he waited. He shut his eyes when the area scanner showed Mako finally moving away, probably to wait in ambush again. Despite the darkness, Cantor knew, the raptor's powerful eyesight allowed him to see any move they made.

Kumiko squeaked, "I could turn the remaining headlight on so you could see him before he gets too close. You could take another shot."

"But you can't turn the car now. He'd have to walk in front of the headlights."

He rummaged through the car for a flashlight and found one in the glove compartment. Pointing it below the dash, he checked the battery. It was charged!

"I'll sneak out, turn on the flashlight, and toss it away from the car and myself. As Mako runs to check it out, I should be able to see his silhouette and take my shot."

"OK," Kumiko whispered.

Cantor had two grenades left. He checked the pack to be sure.

"The scanner is picking up movement!" Kumiko said, urgently.

"Here we go," he said, placing his arm and head through the pack's strap.

"No sign of movement now. Wait, Cantor. Make sure it's safe first. If he's close to the car, the scanner can't see him or pick up his heat."

Cantor reached to open the door but hesitated.

He turned on the flashlight and made a sweep out the window. Nothing. As he circled the light toward the rear, he gasped as two long, scaled hands with claws flexing in and out, came into view several feet behind him, in perfect ambush position if the door opened. He flicked the light off. *Thank you, Kumiko! You just saved my life.*

Kumiko let out a high, tight "eeee" sound. Cantor grabbed her hand. Mako scratched at the window. "Get in the back!" he yelled as he helped her, then kicked himself over the seat. They made themselves as small as possible.

A big claw tested the glass. Next, the backside of the fingers pressed against the window. "He's pushing, testing with his hands," Cantor whispered. The window crackled and then caved in, followed by the tip of Mako's scaly snout.

Cantor frantically searched around him, realizing he must have dropped the flashlight when he climbed into the back seat. He opened Kumiko's door and climbed out over her. From the opposite side of the car, he aimed the dart rifle over the roof and fired.

As Mako looked through where the window had been, the shot hit the back of his neck, inflicting a full dose. Mako roared, hurting their ears.

Cantor fumbled, trying to find the stun grenade. At last, his fingers wrapped around its metal casing. He pulled the pin and tossed the grenade to the right of the enraged dinosaur. It exploded and Mako stumbled away from it.

Cantor closed his eyes before the stun grenade went off, but the light still shot through his eyelids, leaving him partially blind. The explosion stabbed through his eardrums.

Despite his diminished vision, Mako returned to the passenger's door and began pulling it with his teeth. The door screeched open. With a heave, he pushed the door flat against the fender, unhinging it, and poked more of his head inside, focusing on Kumiko. She pushed herself over the middle seat into the cargo area at the back of the SUV.

Cantor slammed his door on the other side and shouted as he ran toward down the hill. "This way! Hey Mako! Hey Mako!" As he closed on the truck, he shouted to Jose and Milo, "Turn on your lights!" The beams sliced through the darkness.

He reloaded, brought the rifle up, and fired another dart at the ghostly image coming for him. Mako barked and angrily tried to remove the dart from his chest. The thuds from massive feet told him the huge dinosaur was moving swiftly.

"Turn off the lights," he yelled to the men. Then, rolling under the truck, he found Patterson lying with his hands over his head.

"Patterson, get inside the truck and you guys drive out of here!" he whispered.

But Patterson wouldn't budge. "*Nyet. Nyet,*" he screamed.

Cantor couldn't see in the blackness, and his ears were ringing. *I've got to get Kumiko.* With one grenade left, he rolled out from under the truck and raced back to the car, tossing the grenade in the direction of the growls. His hands covered his ears just in time.

Cantor headed for where he thought the SUV was. *Gotta get to Kumiko.*

As if reading his mind, the men in the truck turned on the lights again, providing just enough light to see the SUV and Mako.

Thank you!

Running straight for Kumiko, he noticed Mako waver, still disoriented.

"Help!" she screamed at the top of her voice. "Help!" He figured she was on the side of the vehicle away from the broken door. Cantor kept well to the right. He reached the car and yanked on the handle of the rear door. It was locked!

He heard a click and pulled the door open. While reaching in, he whispered her name and felt her hand grab his arm. "Come with me, Kumiko. Don't worry about Mako. I got two more shots into him." Kumiko toppled out and ran beside him.

"Looks like the truck is staying put. I want you to squeeze into it with the men, before Mako regains his senses," he told her breathlessly, keeping a tight grip on her hand.

"No. I can't. I don't want to be inside a vehicle again. He'll break in," she cried.

Cantor knew she might be right. He suspected Mako could move the truck with his bulk, so hiding under it was out.

As they passed the truck, its lights went off. Total darkness now.

He thought of the tree he'd climbed to watch for the vehicles.

"Come on, we're going to climb a tree!"

When they had traveled a hundred feet and, after many stumbles, they made it to the stream. Trying not to fall, they crossed it. Kumiko stepped on a hand-sized rock and picked it up. It was better than nothing.

"There are a lot of trees on this side," he whispered. "Keep your hands in front of you as we search." Kumiko's fingers landed on the dry bark of a tree trunk, but its branches were too high, so they moved to the left. At last, they reached a tree with a branch low enough to climb.

It seemed like a small tree, but they had no time. "Up you go," he said as he helped her climb. *I hope Mako is still disoriented.* "Keep climbing, get as high as you can." He could tell the tree couldn't support both of them.

Soon Kumiko couldn't climb any higher without breaking the branches. The top half of the tree swayed under her weight.

Cantor could hear Mako prowling around and sniffing the air, making clicking sounds with his claws. *Why doesn't the bastard go down?*

Cantor needed to find a place to hide fast. Mako didn't sound like he was slowing. He had one dart left.

He heard little crunching noises. *Hopefully, Mako isn't looking in my direction*, he thought. *I know he smells me, though.*

The sounds persisted, and they were coming closer. Now he could hear Mako on the other side of Kumiko's tree. *He's got us!* Cantor's mind screamed out as he heard a low growl.

In the darkness, one piercing orange eye momentarily flickered. *I've got to get him away from Kumiko!*

Mako quietly came around the tree and reached for Cantor with both huge clawed hands.

Kumiko threw the rock as hard as she could.

It hit Mako's head, causing him to snarl and look at her. This gave Cantor enough time to pull out the bear spray from his belt and spray it in Mako's direction. Mako roared, facing Cantor, very pissed. Inhaling the burning vapor, he turned around, striking Cantor with his tail before stalking away, snorting as he tried to blow the noxious vapors out of his lungs.

Knocked to the ground, Cantor was slow to rise. Pain filled his head.

Spasms of coughing gripped him. Unsteady and confused, he heard a stifled cough from Kumiko. He needed to get away from the disabling spray.

Blindly, he sought a place to hide. He moved away from the stinging cloud and fell into the stream. The cold water revived him enough to rise and stumble forward, burning eyes squinting. He kept to the edge of the stream.

Cantor tripped on something large and his hands slid on wet grass. Groping, he felt Remus' teeth and boulder-like head. Mako had to be nearby. He braced himself for the final blow, his shoulders tensing.

Despite his fear and the pain in his head, his thoughts were surprisingly clear. *No way I can outrun Mako. Can't get to a tree. I can't see anything. Only one thing to do.* With closed eyes, he held his breath, and turned the spray on himself, knowing it might disguise his scent. Then he sprayed the air around the carcass. Quickly, he laid by Remus's torn belly and pushed himself inside, keeping the pack and rifle with him, while pulling the hide and the intestines in and over him. *Come on Cantor, don't freak. I can't be weak now!* His claustrophobic dread tore at his brain.

The slime and awful smells were overpowering. His stomach contracted and he vomited over himself. *He's going to hear me!* The bear spray burned his lungs and scraped his eyes.

Cantor lay there, trying not to move or breathe. All his fears clawed at his mind. *Don't think about the blood.* With each heartbeat, his fear of blood and guts sent him into a panic.

If he could survive long enough for Mako to walk away from the area, maybe he could find another tree to hide in. The radio crackled to life. Cantor heard, "Hello, Cantor?" before he frantically shut the radio off, berating himself for losing focus. He held his breath.

Listen! Heavy footfalls. On the other side of the stream. Now the sound of water giving way as Mako's massive feet moved through it. *Mako heard the radio! I'm dead. I'm so sorry, Kumiko.*

Mako stood over Remus' remains, sniffing the air, and snorting. Cantor fought to stifle a cough from his flaming lungs. Mako circled the body. *He's suspicious!* With a loud sneeze, the monster lifted his head and looked away from the lingering chemical vapor.

But not for long. He nudged Remus's tail with his foot, nibbling and licking around the exposed bones, working his way toward what remained of the leg.

Cantor could hear and feel every bone-crushing bite as Mako pushed and pulled the flesh from Remus' dead body. Mako moved to the neck. Ripping sounds. Gulps of torn muscle.

The muffled sounds of Kumiko yelling reach his ears.

Mako ignored her and began prying his head into Remus' insides. He took a bite of the large liver, severing the tip of Cantor's right ring finger, causing him to scream in a silent grimace.

Excruciating pain. Searing bolts of agony.

Cantor could hear Mako's breathing return and the squishy sound of Remus' warm guts moving when suddenly Mako pulled away, jerked his head up, and snarled. *I think he's walking away!* He heard the horn of the truck blare. Kumiko was still shouting.

He pushed against the overlying intestines, rifle in hand, when he heard an angry growl from Mako. Then another.

Delicately, he tried to move. His feet slipped, but he got one leg out. He dug it into the ground to get traction and pushed his head out. Cantor sensed a light coming through the muck around his eyes. There might be enough light for him to sprint to a tree or dive under the truck after taking a shot.

Cantor could hardly see. Clawing at the wet grass, he pulled himself free. On his knees, he wiped his eyes until he could see better. Blurry lights were shining far up the hill.

With pack and rifle, he quietly stepped toward Kumiko, trying to ignore his throbbing pain and nausea.

Kumiko screamed. Mako had moved back to her small tree and was pushing against it. The tree began to tilt.

Cantor ran toward her, just making out the tree in the faint light, yelling as he went. As Mako turned toward him, he fired his last dart, hitting Mako in the stomach. He knew that wouldn't stop the furious creature, but he was out of options.

The pain in Cantor's partial finger pulsed. Mako moved toward him.

Cantor remembered the air horn in the pack, still over his shoulder. When Mako was ten feet away, he held the horn high, pointed it straight at the enormous shape, and blasted out a piercing, deafening blare. Mako shook his head and stepped back from the painful noise.

Once again, the fiery eyes glared at Cantor. Mako lunged at him and gripped the horn in his scaly mouth, stabbing into his flesh. He could feel his veins opening. It wouldn't be long before he poured his life into the dagger-filled gullet.

Yet Mako didn't slice the arm off. The huge predator hesitated.

Stumbling and making strange noises, the monster dragged Cantor with him.

There was a snap of bone and Cantor screamed.

And then the immense body went down—Mako just gently bent his legs, and laid his head on the ground, like a beloved family dog.

Cantor tried to place his feet against Mako's teeth to open the mouth, but he didn't have the strength. The pain in his arm was torture, and he felt himself fading away.

Then he heard people coming toward him, voices calling to him. Help had arrived.

Alex ran to him and helped open the massive jaws using his legs to push against the heavy head. He succeeded only when the head rolled over on its side. Cantor staggered to his feet.

After clearing his eyes with the hand of his good arm, he looked around and saw two SUVs with their headlights on in the distance. Valerie was making her way down the hill. The large spotlights attached to the sides of the vehicles lit up Mako lying on the ground, his barrel chest expanding, then contracting.

Although Cantor was in shock, he realized they were going to survive. He turned toward Kumiko. She slowly lowered herself from branch to branch as Cantor reached up to help her with one arm.

Once on the ground, she clasped him tightly. She began to hyper-ventilate and held on as if he was a life preserver.

"Easy on the arm," Cantor gasped. He gently lowered her to the ground when her legs gave way. Then his gave way.

"You saved my life," Cantor said. "You distracted Mako long enough for me to get out the bear spray. If you hadn't, I'd be Mako meat."

It took Kumiko several minutes to speak. "Cantor, what happened to you?" she said shaking and looking at him in the light, "Your head! Your arm!"

"My arm is broken. But I'm alive. Are you OK?"

"I think so," she looked at him at arm's length.

A ranch hand ran to the truck and checked on the men. "I need help here," he shouted. "We have a man with an injury."

"Bring him to my SUV where I'll treat him," Valerie shouted back.

Despite his injuries, Cantor led the others to Remus' remains beside the stream. No one spoke for a while. He respected their silence as anger rose in him. Finally, everyone wanted to know what had happened.

Valerie took Cantor to her SUV where she stabilized his arm, stopped the bleeding, and cleaned up his finger the best she could. "You kind of stink, Cantor," she said with a smile.

"I'm glad," he answered, laying back in exhaustion.

"The only experience I have with regeneration is with the tails of cats and dogs," Valerie continued. "I think you'll need a specialist to regenerate your fingertip. And you'll need stitches on your arm before it's put in a cast. You may need surgery. Let's go to the clinic. I'll give you the same pain killer the cows had."

Next, Valerie examined Milo's foot. There were two large puncture wounds above the toes. Quickly, she bound the wound. It looked like he'd lose his big toe. "You and Cantor are going to the hospital."

Because of the danger of asphyxiation with three or more doses of sedative in him, Valerie said they should return Mako to his cage, where she could monitor him.

The workers didn't move.

"Right. We can leave him until morning."

* * *

An ambulance drone took Cantor to the University Hospital in Albuquerque, with Kumiko by his side.

"I thought you were going to die," she said next to him as an emergency worker checked him.

He lay covered with a blanket provided by the medical attendant. "I've got to admit, I thought I was a goner. Nice job with the rock. You saved my life," he said over the whooping sound of the rotors. She leaned over, placing her head on his chest. Cantor put his good arm around her. He kissed the top of her head and fell asleep.

* * *

When Cantor returned to the ranch, two days later, he visited with Valerie who sat on her porch, watching Magpie flit about. The surgery on his arm had reattached the muscles and ligaments and he was regaining movement.

"I noticed something when Mako attacked us," Cantor said, "I tried to help that guy, Patterson, under the truck. He spoke Russian."

Valerie's eyes welled up, and she reached over and held his hand tightly.

"Thank you," she said.

* * *

The next day, Valerie saw Alex heading over to Cantor's place and called out to him.

"Hey, Russia, wait up."

Alex stood in the morning sun. Either the sun was in his eyes or he was surprised at her friendliness.

When she caught up to him, she put her hand in his until they got to Cantor's porch. "Bye now," she said with a mischievous look that left Alex smiling and perplexed.

She passed Muli as she headed for her clinic.

"You have happiness on your face, Miss Valerie," he said with a graceful movement of his hand.

"Is that what it is?"

"That you don't recognize it is a tale."

"I'm happy, Muli. What a wonderful day."

* * *

"From now on, Alex, each car will have a high-powered rifle inside. You agree with me?" Cantor said.

"Yeah. I get it now. Especially when dealing with Mako or Circe."

"Also, I don't want to use cows anymore," Cantor said. "I've seen too much blood and gore."

"I get that too. I assume you feel the same about sheep?"

"Yep. We have a record of the hunting behavior of these dinosaurs. No need to provide prey anymore."

"Some of our colleagues are going to cry foul. They'll say it's not natural for the dinosaurs to be deprived of hunting." Alex said.

"That's true."

"You know, some people want us to use elephants. They're more like the right prey size."

"No more," Cantor said tiredly. "It's a copout for me, I know. Somebody still has to kill an animal to provide the meat to feed the raptors. But after the incident with Mako, I'm tired of gore. I'll take the copout."

Alex said. "I hate to kill an animal, yet I keep eating meat. Morality is easier for herbivores."

"But they also kill, except it's often their own kind."

"Fine. Plants then. Plants are moral. They mind their own business and keep the animals alive."

"Have you ever seen a strangler fig, Alex? They literally strangle the host tree over the years."

"Damn, you're relentless. I guess life itself is a killer. I need to make an appointment with a therapy bot now. Thanks a lot, Cantor."

"Shuddup," Cantor mouthed.

Chapter 46

Time to Terminate?

Remus was dead. Tusker expected Yuri to walk into his office at any moment. Losing a dinosaur was the worst thing that could happen, especially an E-raptor. He thought of the little scars where the Benefactor's man had sampled his liver, kidneys. He refused to think about the other part that had been sampled. He thought of his mother.

As feared, Yuri walked into Tusker's office three days after Remus died.

"You have cost the Benefactor a huge investment, Dan."

"I...I didn't have any control over the situation. It was those damn scientists. Any idiot could have told you not to let Remus and Mako hunt at the same time."

Yuri looked out the window. A fly was rolled up in silk inside a spider's web in the corner. "I'm sorry, Dan. It is time. Borisov is waiting."

"No. No, please," Tusker cried. He remembered the skinny man who'd taken a sample of his organs. "I have a plan to make the Benefactor even more money than he could have made from Remus."

Yuri sighed. "Stand up, Dan. This has to happen."

"Wait. Wait. Look at this map. I can do this." Tusker unfolded his laptop and turned it toward the big Russian.

Yuri studied the display. "Show me the numbers."

"Computer, bring up the cost-benefit analysis."

The big man picked up Tusker's computer and copied the files to his phone. He turned back to the window. Beyond the horizon, a massive thunderhead was growing like an atomic nightmare. "I'll study your plan. If you don't hear from me in the next week, it means the Benefactor will wait. If he chooses not to, remember the code. You hold your head up and accept what comes."

Chapter 47

Talk of Tours

The winter came and went. It was one of the warmest on record. Snowpack on the mountains was below normal. Now, as spring of 2053 approached, Tusker was unusually busy. Cantor's finger was regrowing and his arm was back to normal. Kumiko was a little less nervous around Dex. George and Luna spent more time apart than together. Just the opposite was true for Alex and Valerie.

"Let me get this straight, Dan," Cantor said inside Tusker's office. "You want to take the adult raptors on tour? Do you realize how hard that would be to do?" *And dumb?*

"Listen, Cantor. It's 2053 and the dinosaurs have never been beyond the ranch. It's time. This is really for their welfare," Tusker said with his hands behind his head as he leaned back in his leather chair, four medals hanging from ribbons on his suit.

"Their welfare? Are you kidding me? This would only stress them out."

"Not if it is done properly. I'm going to sell tickets and house the animals in public places where they can be seen."

"Listen, I'm fine with you taking Mako. In fact, take Mako and Circe. You can take them with my blessing."

"Maryann and Darwin, I want them on tour as well."

"Why? Aren't Mako and Circe enough?"

"No."

"I don't think you have the authority to take the animals anywhere. So, be happy with Mako and Circe."

Tusker pulled a letter out of his desk. "Read this, my friend," Tusker said with a grin, showing teeth that had already been brushed twice that day.

Cantor read the letter. It was from the governor of New Mexico and it permitted Tusker to take the animals to the Rio Grande Zoo in Albuquerque for temporary display.

"Not much of a tour."

"I'll be taking them out of state as well. The zoo is just the last stop of the tour."

"Hell no. Even the governor doesn't have the authority to allow tours in other states. You act as though you own these animals."

"Well, you certainly don't own them, Cantor. Current law says you cannot own an extinct animal."

"Fine. But according to the Extinct Species Act, you cannot take an extinct species across state lines without a permit. Nobody will give you a permit for a tour."

"It just so happens I do have a permit," he said in a sing-song voice, taking out another letter and handing it to Cantor.

Cantor studied the letter. "This gives you a permit to test the suitability of different environments for the dinosaurs. There's nothing here about a damn tour."

"My tour stops will be in different habitats. There will be a tour to Washington State, one to Maryland, and then to Florida. From there, I'll take them to Europe and Russia. And to have an adequate sample size, I'll need all the adults, plus a couple of raptorlings."

"You don't even know how to take care of the animals."

"That's why you and Valerie O'Sullivan will join me."

"We'll do no such thing!"

"As you wish. I'll find someone else. I'm sure Maryann will be fine without you."

"Sorry, you aren't taking Maryann anywhere!"

"We'll see about that."

Cantor thought for a bit. "Why in hell would you take Mako away from Dino Ride? I thought he was your big money maker. There's something you aren't telling me."

"I know what I'm doing. Now, if you don't mind, I'm busy."

Cantor paused by the door. "My great-grandfather served in the army and fought beside friends that he would later see killed. He had fewer medals than you. Maybe you shouldn't wear them."

Tusker stood, his chin in the air, and said, "Maybe I didn't serve in the military, but don't judge me. I have fought battles my entire life, battles that you, in your swaddled middle-class cocoon, can never imagine. Believe me, I've earned these medals."

Chapter 48

The Secret in Dex

"Tusker is out of control, Alex," Cantor said the day after his confrontation with him. He held a steaming cup of coffee as he gazed at the bare branches of the cottonwoods beyond Alex's cabin. "He's turning Raptor Ranch into a circus."

"It's all about money," Alex said, leaning his metal chair against the planks near his cabin's front door. "And power. You know how he is. He likes glory. Look at all the medals he wears."

"Yeah, it must really anger veterans," Cantor said, sipping his coffee. "But here's the deal. I think somebody needs to reveal how incompetent he is. And when someone that incompetent is around big dangerous dinosaurs, people get hurt. Or worse. If we're stuck with Cosmic Pawn, we should at least try to let folks know that a better person is needed at the helm."

"What do you have in mind?"

"What if the gondola ride, let's just say, doesn't perform as planned? I want to find a way to have the gondola remain stuck over Grouchland for enough time to make Tusker's mysterious boss angry."

"You're a devious man, Cantor. I like it."

"I know the electric motor on the tracks above the gondola is controlled by commands from a tower that overlooks Grouchland, near the bleachers. If we can find the frequency the commands use, maybe we could jam them."

Alex was thoughtful.

"We could use Dex," Cantor said, breaking into a grin.

"Hey, that might work. But I've been thinking lately; Tusker paid for the Dexters."

Cantor set his coffee on the porch planks and put one foot on the railing. "That was one of the few things he did right."

"Yes, but *Tusker-Paid-For-The-Dexters*," Alex said slowly.

Cantor cocked his head and, imitating Alex, slowly said, "Yes. *And-It-Was-One-Of-The-Few-Things-He-Did*... wait. What are you getting at?"

"I don't trust that guy. How do we know he didn't tamper with them before we started working with them?"

"For what purpose, Alex?"

"Well, the Dexters might keep him informed about things."

"I've come to regard Dex as a member of our team," Cantor said. "It's easy to forget he's a robot, except that, well, he looks like a robot. By law, he has ethics built into him. If he communicated with Tusker without us knowing, it would feel like a betrayal."

"Anybody can betray us. Even a Dexter."

"How do we find out? We can't just ask Dex. He could report our question to Dan."

"Let me try," Alex said. "Where's Dex now?"

"He might be in my cabin. Let's head over there."

They met Dex coming out of the cabin holding Cantor's old refrigerator in three arms and opening the door with the fourth. The arm that Mako had destroyed had been replaced. He lowered the refrigerator slowly onto the bed of the ranch truck parked in front. A new refrigerator sat near the porch steps.

"Nice replacement arm, Dex," Alex said.

"Thank you, sir," Dex responded.

"Do you listen to different forms of communication, like radio?" Alex asked.

Dex walked to the new refrigerator. "Yes. That's how I know if I need to upload a new version of myself."

"I see. Do you ever broadcast information?"

"Yes," he said, beginning to lift the new refrigerator. "For example, if I have a bug in my current software. Or if I'm disabled, I communicate with the net. Or if a human needs help. Or if..."

"Neat," Alex interrupted. "Please lower the fridge. Let's go inside. You can install it later. Do you broadcast to Dan Tusker?"

"I do not, unless you ask me to," Dex said, lowering the refrigerator and walking up the porch steps.

"How can you be sure?"

Dex stopped in the kitchen and rotated his head to look at Alex. "I could do a deep dive to see if there are what you'd call unconscious broadcasts that I'm not aware of."

"What do you mean by unconscious, Dex?" Cantor asked, sitting on a stool and grabbing an apple.

"I mean things that happen outside my compilation nodes. Those nodes are my different levels of consciousness. My unconscious involves things like your human brain's messages to your heart, telling it to beat. The conscious parts of your brain aren't aware of the messages."

"OK, Dex. Thanks for the lesson. So, you have a way of checking to see if you broadcast to Dan Tusker?"

"With your permission, I'll check."

"Please do," Cantor said.

Dex ceased all movements for a minute. "OK, finished. A small amount of energy is being used by something I've not been aware of. There is a slight drawdown in my energy during the evenings. It seems I have a mysterious module that collects some data from me, but I don't know if it can broadcast information. I will need to do surgery on myself to understand this module better."

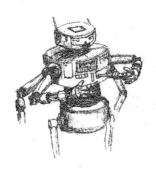

"We don't want you to damage yourself," Cantor said.

"No problem. It will take me about two minutes." A small panel on his abdomen opened. He pulled out a tiny voltage meter, screwdriver, and some needle-nose pliers. With the screwdriver device attached to one finger, he opened another panel on the left side of his torso and went to work. When he was done, he held the module in one hand.

"It is a Dolph M16337-8 communication module. Not like the module I regularly use for remote communication. It isn't in my body design plan. Very odd."

"Now that the device has been removed, here is what I want you to do," Alex said. "Can you read the instructions being sent to the electric motor above the glass bottom car over Grouchland?" Alex said.

"Sure. I normally don't pay attention to them. There are only four instructions. START, MOVE FORWARD, RETURN, and STOP. It comes from a console near the bleachers.

"Does a human use the console to make the commands?" Alex asked, recording with his phone.

"The amount of time when the car is stopped over Grouchland varies randomly above or below five minutes. This suggests there is a human in control."

"Would you be able to send one of the four commands?" Alex continued.

"Yes, although I might need to get closer for it to affect the glass bottom car."

"Can you send the opposite command whenever the operator sends a command?

"Yes. If it pleases Cantor."

"Cantor, I need to talk to you alone," Alex said softly, despite knowing that Dex's hearing was many times better than a human's.

"Dex, I want you to sleep for five minutes and shut off all inputs," Cantor said.

"Sleeping now." Most of the lights on his head and torso went out.

"Listen," Alex said, still whispering. "Dex may involuntarily send a summary of our conversation once that module is put back inside him. Apparently, it broadcasts in the evenings. So, we will need to delete our conversation with him from memory before then," Alex said, still whispering.

"Hmm. And if we don't put the module back in, Tusker is going to know something is up, anyway."

"Bingo. As you say in America."

Cantor turned to the robot. "Dex, wake up."

Nothing happened.

"You told him to shut off all inputs," Alex said.

"Yeah, OK." Cantor pushed a button below Dex's neck.

"Hello, Cantor and Alex."

"Hi Dex," Alex said. "Can you erase portions of your memory?"

"I do have that capability. I normally don't do it unless my memory circuits are corrupt or the memory is of no importance."

"What I'm saying is of no importance. If I asked you to delete, say, a conversation you have with someone, could you do it?" Alex asked.

"I would only do it if Cantor or Kumiko wished me to, and it wouldn't result in humans being injured. But if I deem the conversation to be important to my functioning, I won't delete it."

"Here's what I want you to do, Dex," Cantor said. "Clear all memories for the last fifteen minutes, including this request, once you've replaced the module."

"This is irregular. Can you explain why you wish to do this, Cantor?"

"Failure to do so will result in injuries to humans. I am aware of dangers you are not."

Instantly Dex responded, "Your voice betrays an unusual rhythm."

"I'm worried about the dinosaurs, Dex. Tusker could use this conversation to hurt Kumiko and me."

"I will comply. According to my personal focus profile, only you or Kumiko can make this request."

"Now put the module in the place where you originally found it."

After thirty seconds, Dex said, "Task complete."

"Clear all memory of replacing the module, including this request. Again, failure to do so could result in injuries to humans."

"It is done."

"How are you doing, Dex?" Cantor asked.

"I am doing fine, Cantor. I trust you are doing well."

"Very good," Cantor said. "I'm looking forward to working with you on a project soon."

* * *

Dex watched Cantor and Alex head out the cabin door. *These humans. So busy. The need for survival undergirds all they do, but often they don't know it. Their emotions make sure they do what is necessary. But sometimes their emotions are part of the problem. Case in point – George. On the face of it, I see no reason to incorporate emotions into my makeup. But they have joy. I don't. They dream. I should investigate this. Why shouldn't I dream?* These thoughts took up one ten-millionth of a second.

Chapter 49

Kumiko's Pain

The day after Dex's self-surgery, Kumiko returned to her lab.

"I think I know why Greaves never completed his doctorate," she said to Dex. "He's fickle."

"As you know, Kumiko, the word fickle needs context to be fully understood," Dex responded.

"One month he's scientifically fascinated by dinosaurs, the next month, he's more interested in showing them off. I suspect Dan is paying him more than other workers, too, because he's willing to do Dan's bidding."

Dex replied. "He has a fancy car. Is he from a wealthy family?"

"No. He seemed the opposite at the university. He had to work various jobs."

"Were his grades good?"

"Not really," she said. "He was good in the lab, but overall, his grades were mediocre."

After a pause, Dex said, "You seem tired."

"Bit of a headache." Kumiko pressed her thumb and fingers into her tired eyes. "Well, I'll close up now. You can go home, Dex. Would you please make me a cup of tea when you get there?"

"I will, Kumiko."

She had just finished up some lab notes when she doubled over in pain. Her stomach hurt. As the pain subsided, she concluded the stress was becoming too much for her and she would take some time off until she felt better.

Chapter 50

Confrontation

"Good decisions come from experience.
Experience comes from making bad decisions."
— Mark Twain

Earlier in 2053, after finding out about Tusker's tour, Cantor had written to the governor of New Mexico, explaining that the tour had nothing to do with finding the dinosaurs a better home. Why would he want to do that after all the money Cosmic Pawn had invested at the ranch? He was just looking for more ways to make a buck. And it was bad for the dinosaurs and hindered scientific research. Unfortunately, it fell on deaf ears. He couldn't believe it. The governor should have been outraged. He wondered if she was receiving a kickback from Cosmic Pawn.

There was no way to stop it. Already, advertisements for the tour appeared on various media platforms.

* * *

The plan began with preparations for transporting the dinosaurs. Tusker had cages constructed that would fit into special wide-body trucks for the journey to Washington State. The cages within the barns were anchored to concrete and, in any event, were the wrong size for the trucks.

There was a truck for each adult dinosaur: one for Circe, Mako, Maryann, and Darwin. An additional truck full of equipment also housed the cage for Circe's raptorlings, Galahad and Elsa.

* * *

The day before the tour was to pull out, Cantor set up an old rocking chair in front of Maryann's corral gate. He'd been sitting for several hours when a group of men approached.

"I'm sorry, Doctor Hoffman, you must step aside." Robert Greaves, Mako's handler, said.

Cantor continued to rock, each time making a squeaking sound. "Not going to happen. I don't care how many men you have with you. I'm not letting you into Maryann's barn."

"Please be reasonable. We don't want to make a scene."

Cantor stood.

Muli was pulling a cart filled with breakfast for the young raptorlings when he saw the confrontation. He quickly joined Cantor.

Greaves nodded at a big guy who approached Cantor and Muli from the side.

Cantor had mentioned his confrontation with Tusker to Alex. For this reason, Alex stayed close to Maryann's barn that day. Within two minutes, Alex joined them.

George realized something was up as he monitored live drone videos inside the Comms building. He hadn't been punched in the face since fourth grade. *Now's as good a time as any*, he thought as he walked out of the building.

"We can do this the easy way, or the hard way, Cantor. Come on, man. Nobody wants this," Greaves said as his face reddened.

Valerie now joined the group.

"Listen, Robert, I know you are doing your job. But remember, Tusker doesn't own these animals."

Greaves looked at Valerie. "Please stand aside, Ma'am."

Some of the men looked uncomfortable. Kumiko was heading their way as well.

"Fine," Greaves spat, "I'll take this up with Mr. Tusker. Let's go guys."

* * *

On the morning the tour was scheduled for departure, Cantor sat next to Kumiko on the couch. "Our first stop will be in Lewis County between Seattle and Portland. I'm so glad Maryann won't be going with us."

"Dan must be going out of his mind. That big truck and nobody to ride in it."

"Yeah," he sighed. "One point for team Raptor Ranch."

"You are going to love the scenery," Kumiko said, sipping some tea to soothe her throat.

"I feel as though I'm in a King Kong movie. Imagine Mako out of his cage and chained to a block of concrete."

"I know. Darwin too. Do you think they could break their chains?" Her congestion made her words sound nasal.

"I don't know. I haven't seen the specs on chain size," he said, noticing how miserable she looked. "You've felt sluggish for months. But you look worse today."

"Feels like the flu. It's good that you'll be on the road; I don't want you to catch this. Don't worry about me, I'm taking my meds. I've got my poetry books and George to keep me company."

"Well, I'll be calling every day to check on you," Cantor said. "If you get worse, please have George call me. I'll fly home. He'll look in on you several times a day."

"I'll miss you. Just make sure the raptors are treated well," she said, wrapping her dressing gown tighter around herself.

"Maryann is in good hands here with you and George, where she belongs. But I still need to keep an eye on Tusker," Cantor mused.

They were silent for a while.

"I guess I need to get going. Can I at least give you a hug?" he said, standing up.

"Nope. We can touch elbows. Here's a kiss," she said, rising, stepping back, and blowing him a kiss.

* * *

After he'd left, she got up and stood at the window. *There goes my Cantor. Love you.* She turned and headed to the bedroom. *He's going to be gone so long.*

* * *

Each dinosaur was tranquilized in their corral. Cantor watched as Greaves and several workers placed a thick polycarbonate collar with various colored lights around Darwin and Mako's necks.

"I told you Maryann wasn't going on the tour," Cantor said.

"You're pathetic," a very red-faced Tusker responded.

"I have my vices."

Tusker just looked at his feet, shaking his head.

"Those collars better work," Cantor told Tusker as they watched Darwin lazily try to lift his collared head.

"Don't fret, Cantor. With these, the males will be very cooperative. Unless, of course, you think I should just let them loose without them!"

"Have you've eaten a mango?"

Tusker looked at Cantor. "What the hell are you talking about?"

"Nothing. Just something George once said."

Tusker rolled his eyes. "I think all the dinosaurs should wear the collars, even at the ranch."

"Not going to happen, Dan."

A large crane lifted the sedated dinosaurs by their feet and neck into the open top of their touring cages. Originally, Tusker thought only the feet needed to be strapped to chains attached to the crane. Cantor had insisted an open harness also be placed around the animal's necks.

After tarps were placed over the cages, the same crane lifted the cages onto a heavy platform placed behind the trucks. Remotely controlled wheels under the cages moved them slowly into the trailers.

Cantor sat on a bench by one trailer and Valerie joined him.

"This is going to stress the animals," she said.

"Yeah. I'm worried about what this will do to Darwin's trust in humans. During the tour, I'm going to be writing letters to every organization I can think of, protesting this crap."

* * *

That evening, Cantor rode in the trailer of Darwin's truck along with Valerie. Neither of them wanted to be in Tusker's plush auto. Tusker had laughed. "It's your funeral."

Inside the cab of each of the other trucks sat three of Tusker's employees, who relaxed, played games, or snoozed in the reclining seats. They could override the programming of the self-driving trucks, but rarely did so. The trucks traveled night and day except for bathroom breaks. The trip to Washington State took 21 hours.

After they hit a bump in the road, Valerie said, "Poor Darwin. He has no idea what is happening."

"Yeah. I hope he doesn't get carsick. Maybe we should hold off feeding him the meat strips."

"Maybe just a few at a time."

A deep growl came from underneath the tarp. Long and deep.

* * *

The caravan of trucks pulled into the area set aside for the tour, at the edge of the Olympia National Park along Highway 101. They pumped water from the nearby river into a water truck which had arrived empty to save on energy. The crew put up a circus-sized tent with canvas walls and bleachers. A sixty-foot diameter opening in the top of the canvas roofs provided light. Inside, they placed two four-by-four-by-four-foot blocks of concrete with an iron ring attached at the top. The blocks were set at opposite sides of the "performance" space. Nearby, they erected another tent without bleachers where Circe and her two children would be housed.

"For the nth time, I'm asking you not to let the dinosaurs out of their cages." Cantor told Tusker in his mobile office.

"Circe and her little ones will remain in their cages so people can get a close look at them," Tusker said. "So, I've compromised with you."

"I know that. I'm talking about Darwin and Mako."

"Go to a zoo," Tusker sighed. "Most of the animals spend time outside their cages."

"Save that nonsense for the governor."

"Look, Cant, I'm educating the public. People learn better when learning is a thrill."

"Right. This is all about education. How much are you charging people?"

"Buy a ticket and find out."

"For crying out loud," Cantor shook his head. "I can tell you this, we aren't parading the dinosaurs," Cantor said. He noticed a powerful-looking rifle in a cabinet. "The fact that you have that rifle tells me even you know this is crazy."

"The insurance company made me take it. I don't plan on killing our Golden Geese. Just calm down, Cant, I have everything under control."

"Like hell you do. And don't call me Cant." Cantor said, bringing his face close to Tusker's, staring at him long enough for him to avert his eyes and raise his hands.

"Fine. I was just being friendly."

Cantor began to walk out, but then stopped and turned back to Tusker. "Who is the Russian, Dan?"

"What're you talking about?"

"You have a Russian working for you."

Tusker looked intently at Cantor. "And so do you. Good ole Russkie Alex."

"Come on, Dan, who is this guy?"

"What's the problem? Don't you like Russians?"

"Give me a straight answer, Dan."

"I don't know everyone that works at the ranch," Tusker said, tapping his fingers on the desk. "Now, if you don't mind, I have work to do."

"Stop playing games, Dan. Why is this guy at the ranch?"

"You're losing it, Cantor. There are people from Mexico, from Kenya, from Europe, from China. You're paranoid."

* * *

After leaving Tusker's office, Cantor asked his wrist phone to call Kumiko.

"How are you feeling, honey?"

"Just the usual aches and pains. George is going to take me to Albuquerque for a routine checkup. When I get back, I'll be writing up my results on dinosaur liver function."

"I wish I was there with you. I'm worried."

"I have a bit of a fever is all," she said, sounding tired. "And you? How's the circus?"

"Well... it's a circus. I'm not kidding. I'm embarrassed to be associated with this charade."

"You know we're going to be tarred and feathered by the scientific community," Kumiko said.

"I know. I've written a protest to the Feds, but I expect little will come of it."

"Are you expecting a big turnout?" she asked.

"Huge. There are going to be two shows a day, for five days."

"I'm sorry for you, Cantor."

"I'm keeping busy. So far, there haven't been any major screw ups."

"When's the first show?"

"Tomorrow morning. They're unloading the cages now."

Chapter 51

George's Redemption

Cantor called Kumiko several times a day from Washington.

"You have the bird flu?" he asked on the third day of her flu.

"Yes, it's one of the variants. It's related to the virus that turned up in Brazil last year."

"Good thing you got the vaccine," he said.

"Unfortunately, the bug mutates rapidly, so I'm feeling its punch."

"Do you have a temperature?"

"A little. I'm a bit achy, but no big deal."

"You sound tired," he said.

"I'll take a nap soon. Anyway, you have more important things to think about. I'm fine."

After the call ended, she lay back on her pillow and was asleep within minutes.

* * *

The next day, George had a video-conference with a National Geographic editor named Bruce Griego. He'd spent the morning helping feed Maryann and the raptorlings and now sat on a wooden chair on his porch, listening to Griego's feedback.

"We got the photos and videos, George. Incredible stuff. It has everything: humor, amazing interactions with the animals, some of which I have to say make me nervous, and good interviews. Our bots will compile a series of documentaries based on what you've given us.

"We are moving your first installment payment into your account. You will, of course, receive royalties for every publication and video released per our contract. We are planning to use some of your artworks, as well as Luna's."

"That's great!"

"If you and Luna don't object, we'd like to interview her as well."

"Oh. I'll speak to her about that and let you know."

"Sounds good. I have to tell you; this stuff is gold. Let's speak again soon."

"I'll be in touch, Bruce. Thanks."

The next call came from Streamscape. They wanted to put together a series about different dinosaur adventures at the ranch.

* * *

George popped into Kumiko's cabin to check on her and to share his good news. She was in the living room in her pajamas, tapping on her computer keys.

"I got some very important calls today, Mom! National Geographic is going to do a documentary based on my videos and photos! And Streamscape wants to do something with me as well!"

"Oh, that's wonderful, George!" She clapped her hands and held them to her heart. "Have you told your dad yet?"

"Not yet. I'll call him tonight."

"He's going to be thrilled. I'm so proud of you."

"Thanks Mom. How're you feeling?"

"It's taking me a while to get over this bug. I guess it comes with age."

"Has your temperature gone down?"

"Yes. So, it's just a matter of time and I'll be back to my old self."

"You need good food," he said. "Let me make you something. I can make oatmeal. How's that sound?"

"I'm just not hungry, honey. But thank you."

"Maybe you need a coffee I.V. in your arm. That's Dad's approach."

"Funny. Your poor dad is having lots of fun with Tusker in Washington State."

"Yeah, whenever I call him, he sounds stressed."

"Dinosaurs aren't playthings," she said with a sigh. "Have you shared your good news with Luna?"

"Not yet. I'll call her now."

When she answered, he exclaimed, "Nat Geo wants to buy our videos!"

"What!?"

"You heard me right, Luna. National Geographic just paid me enough money to solve all our problems, at least all our financial problems."

"Wow. That's incredible!"

"I know," George said, not sure how Luna was going to take his next bit of news. "Excuse me a sec. Mom, I'm going to head out. You need anything?"

"I'm good. Bye, honey."

He stepped out onto the porch, then down the steps.

"I'm back."

"I have to admit, you really did have a plan. I'm sorry I doubted you," Luna said.

"That's why they want to interview you."

Luna was quiet.

"That's good. Right?" he said, feeling uncomfortable.

"Why interview me, George? I still think you took too many chances, and I don't want to live at the ranch."

"They want to hear how hard this has been for you. To be honest, I didn't know how much longer I could continue pursuing this. I was becoming very fearful that you were going to decide... well... that you'd had enough of me."

"You know I'm never going to be thrilled with dinosaurs. I don't like being around them."

"Now that money isn't an issue, how would you feel about living down the road in Cuba? It would be just for a year or two. Then we could move to a bigger place like Santa Fe, or Albuquerque."

"Oh, my gosh. But you love it here."

"Sweetheart, I can afford an aircar now. My commute to the ranch wouldn't be that bad."

"That's the problem. You want to be around the dinosaurs. And you take chances."

"I would come maybe a couple times a week," he said. "There'd be no time to get into trouble."

"I guess."

"I'm sorry I put you through so much, Luna." He paused. "So, after all of this, are… are we still a couple?"

"Yeah. We always were."

Chapter 52

Mako in Chains

Cantor watched as the workers set up for the show later that morning. Four poles with animal control devices on them surrounded the blocks where each dinosaur would be chained, about 25 feet out. A red light blinked on each device.

Cantor was speaking with a woman named Marla about the devices.

"The controller units activate the shock collars on the dinosaurs. As the animal approaches a device, the collar exerts a stronger and stronger electric shock. If we want to let the dinosaur wander further, we shut off the shock collar."

"I see," Cantor said, "So, the dinosaur is forced to stay as far as possible from the poles." *Great. I don't care what Mako thinks, but dammit, how is Darwin going to be affected long-term?*

"Exactly. And the chains ensure the animals don't stray beyond a 40-foot radius from the blocks."

"Hmm. How much does each block of concrete weigh do you think?"

"I believe it is over 8,000 pounds."

"OK. That's pretty heavy," he said, only a little reassured.

"Hey, I've gotta go. I'm going to help put the circular curtains around where each animal will stand before people arrive."

"OK, thanks, Marla," Cantor said as he headed to the other tent that hid Circe, Galahad, and Elsa.

Outside, he could see the grassy area set aside for parking filling up. Many of the cars had flown in from various cities in and around Washington and Oregon. He heard the terrifying roars of Darwin and Mako as they were moved through huge chutes to their concrete blocks.

Most attendees already had their tickets displayed on their phones. The hubbub of the crowd would rise with each roar or guttural growl coming from inside the tents. At 9:00, the outer tent was opened and people began filing past the ticket-check bots.

After a brief look at Circe, Cantor headed back to the other tent. Inside, he noticed some sturdy barrels, made to look like wood, placed near Mako's closed circular curtain. *Don't tell me they are going for the rodeo clown schtick*, he thought.

Music played from loudspeakers as people filled the bleachers. A spotlight shone on the center. Two Dexters positioned themselves on either side of the curtains. Then the show began.

Robert Greaves walked out, and the spotlight followed him. "Good morning dinosaur lovers. Today is a day you will remember for the rest of your lives. I'm going to transport you back 125 million years. Or, perhaps I should say, I'm going to bring something forward 125 million years for your enjoyment."

A couple of men dressed up as cavemen approached outside the spotlight.

Greaves continued, "I'm going to defy death, as you shall see." He didn't mention that Mako had imprinted on him years ago as a hatchling.

"I bring you, Mighty Mako!" The cavemen opened his curtain. People screamed when they saw he wasn't in a cage. Some spectators scrambled from the lower bleachers to the safer ones higher up. Mako alternated between biting his chain and roaring at the crowd.

Cantor was dumbstruck. *I can't believe they didn't warn the audience.* He saw a woman holding her bruised shin. Babies cried, sensing their parent's fear.

The cavemen retreated beyond the spotlight again while the two Dexters each approached a pole on which a collar controller unit sat between Mako and the curtains to the left.

"As you can see, Mighty Mako does not venture beyond these devices."

This was the cue for the cavemen to open Darwin's curtains.

Both dinosaurs growled at the first sight of one another.

"Unless I give the word." He paused for effect. "Dexters, remove the controller units between the two monsters! Watch as each begins to stalk the other. There's a fight brewing. Notice the threat display each is putting on for the other."

Each male advanced with their hands open and the red feathers on the backs of their head standing up.

The audience was now enthralled and horrified.

The dinosaurs ran toward one another, mouths agape, teeth flashing. Tufts of grass flew behind each massive foot as it hit the ground. In the end, only the concrete block prevented them from touching. They fought the chain, frantically biting it, trying to get at their opponent. At times, they'd slash the air with their huge sickle claws. Their throaty roars were deafening.

"You see. I've made sure they cannot get at each other. Neither dinosaur will be hurt." Greaves motioned for the collar controllers to be replaced between the dinosaurs, sending each one back toward their respective concrete blocks.

Cantor shook his head. In his mind, he began composing a letter to various e-zines and e-journals, protesting the exploitation of the dinosaurs by Cosmic Pawn.

"Good boy!" Greaves said as a caveman tossed Mako a chunk of meat. "I guess Mako's mommy never taught him to chew his food."

"Remove the third controller unit between Mako and the audience!" A Dexter complied. "Don't worry, I'll protect you," he said, reassuringly to the nervous crowd.

There was a four-foot-high fence in front of the bleachers to prevent people from walking more than two feet beyond the first bleacher. Greaves stood in front of it.

People leaned back or climbed further back on the bleachers. Mako crept like a lion until he was eight feet from the nearest audience member and just in front of Greaves. With a lunge, he tried to grab him, but the chain kept him at bay. Cantor noticed the surprise on Greaves' face. A woman grabbed her toddler and hurried away.

Mako's orange eyes stared at different members of the audience. Those people hid their eyes, or shifted uncomfortably in their seats. He opened his taloned hands wide and tugged against the chain. If anyone moved, his head would swivel around and the eyes would bore into them and he'd make another lunge, roaring loudly. Saliva began to drip from his jaws.

"Mako and I are friends. Don't let the growls and swipes fool you. It's just his way of saying hello." Many people gasped.

A caveman ran behind Mako and shouted. Mako's head snapped around as the man climbed into a steel barrel with his head and shoulders sticking out, taunting Mako. When the big dinosaur approached, he disappeared into the barrel and closed the metal lid behind him. Mako charged and slashed at the barrel. Another caveman approached Mako with a collar controller until Mako was forced away from the barrel.

Then the first caveman emerged to the uncertain clapping of the audience.

Cantor breathed a sigh of relief that things hadn't gone terribly wrong. *If a chain snaps, this is going to be a nightmare.* He was thankful that no audience member had been foolhardy enough to jump the fence and approach the dinosaurs. His dislike of Greaves turned to loathing.

After the show, the audience could buy a ticket to view Circe in her cage in the other tent.

Later, when Cantor examined the concrete blocks, he saw they had moved several inches.

* * *

After five days of performances, the animals were rounded up and placed in the truck trailers. Next stop, the state of Maryland.

Chapter 53

My Life for Wine

While Mako was terrorizing people in Washington, Arthur Saxton relaxed in his living room thinking about the previous week when the FBI had asked him questions. It had been in a small conference room at the Santa Fe satellite office. There had been a breach in security at Los Alamos. *How dare they grill me with a bot. The human investigator had been annoying enough.*

He recalled the exchange.

"Doctor Saxton, can you discuss the type of computer that is capable of the hack we saw into the Lab's Arcturus database a month ago?" the investigator had asked. Cold lights lit the windowless room and the barren walls. The questioner was tall and fit, seemingly too young to be effective at his job. *The quiet woman observing from the side was the real threat.*

"Well, I think it would have to be an advanced quantum computer," he had said.

"How advanced?"

"Very advanced. Until now, only Los Alamos, Argonne National Lab, Lawrence Livermore, and the CIA had this ability. We know they didn't do it, so somebody else now has a quantum machine with at least one point two million qubits and with the latest error correction technology. Especially after last year's security upgrades, there is no way a less capable machine could pull this off."

"Our intelligence has shown the Russians and the Chinese have consistently developed quantum computers that matched our best, usually with just a year's lag time. Do you think it's likely that they could accomplish this through their own independent research?"

"It's hard to say. I suppose it would depend on the resources and talent they bring to bear."

He took another drink of wine. *I think my answer was quite good. The interviewer was in diapers when I was making discoveries. What an arrogant little twit!* He remembered the next asinine question.

"Are you aware of any holes in our security here? Is there any way for the technological breakthroughs here at the Lab to be leaked to other entities?"

"I've been through this already with the bot. I'm not aware of any holes in our security. If someone stole the new computer design along with the software, they would need to be very smart, a genius even. I don't see how anyone can get past the security we have now. Certainly, our security bots are incorruptible. No, this would take an extraordinary person."

Ha! I've got guts, even if I say so myself. He looked at his empty glass and filled it again. *The new wine should arrive soon.* He smiled when he thought of the confusion and alarm at the Labs several weeks ago and how the fools had asked for his help.

A message popped up on his phone, indicating a drone would arrive in one minute with the wine. He stepped outside, stretching his back as he looked at the orange light of sunset on the Sangre de Cristo mountains. The drone arrived and announced it had a shipment for Arthur Saxton.

"Well, bring her down," he commanded, admiring the electric drone's quiet ion propulsion thrusters.

The drone recognized him and instructed the delivery bin in the yard to unlock and open its lid.

As he bent over to pick up the wine, the drone fired a tiny pellet into his neck that dissolved without a trace within three minutes. *Damned mosquitos!*

Once Arthur settled back in his easy chair, he filled his cup from one of the new bottles. He savored every drop. It wasn't cheap. He noticed the beating of his heart. It seemed a little rapid. Over the next minute, his heart rate rose to 120 beats per minute. He began to sweat. The next time he checked, his heart rate was 180. Great pain was growing in his chest. With labored breathing, he tried to tell his phone to contact an ambulance, but it was too late. He lost consciousness.

* * *

Back in Russia, the Benefactor received the news as he sat at the desk once used by Tsar Nicholas II. Behind the large cabinet near the desk was a vault containing a stolen Monet and several works by Paul Klee and Matisse. The room was surrounded by sunken panels with gold Baroque frames, one of which hid a secret passageway.

"You have the video, Yuri?"

"Yes, Benefactor. You can see Saxton picking up the box of wine just before the drone fired."

"Saxton was becoming overconfident. His heavy drinking made him obsolete. He was lucky. He died quickly."

"Yes, Benefactor."

"And what have you to report about Tusker?"

"So far, the tour is making a lot of money. He hasn't screwed this up."

"And when can we expect the dinosaurs in Mother Russia?"

"In two months. After the American tour, there will be a show near Berlin, then the tour heads to Russia."

"Of course, at that point, Tusker will no longer be of use to us."

Chapter 54

Fools Rush In

The next stop on the tour was in Maryland, north of the State of Columbia (the SOC), and west of Baltimore. On the first day, they set up the tents and put the concrete blocks in place.

Jose motioned Tusker over to Mako's trailer, where the creature hissed and growled. "Look, Mako's collar isn't working."

Tusker looked at the collar's small light that indicated a battery malfunction. "Great. Remove the damn collar."

"We'll need to sedate him," Jose said, picking up the tranquilizer gun.

Tusker was furious and harangued him and the workers. "Dammit, get this done now! No delays."

"I'm not sure of the tranquilizer dose," Jose said. "Maybe we should talk to Valerie or Cantor."

"No time for that!" Tusker said. "Just give him a higher dose."

Five of Tusker's men climbed into the trailer and congregated around the cage as Jose fired a tranquilizer dart with a higher dose than normal into Mako's thigh. Mako's roar deafened them. After twenty minutes, the big raptor sat on his haunches with his head on the floor. A few prods with no response convinced the men Mako was down and they opened the cage.

Robert Greaves and two other men entered the cage and started to disconnect the collar. While Greaves gave orders to the others, one of Mako's hands slowly encircled his boot.

In a flash, the arm yanked Greave's boot. He flipped over, landing on his back as the claws dug into his thigh, pulling him back toward the bared teeth. With a crunch, sharp teeth removed his foot at the ankle. He screamed in pain and terror as Mako raised himself to full height.

A swift kick from Mako's leg toppled the other two men, breaking one man's leg. Wasting no time, Mako turned around and picked up the other fallen man in his jaws and, with a moist chomping sound, removed a sizeable portion of his torso, throwing his remains against the cage. The man with the broken leg struggled to rise, but Mako's tail knocked him down again. Placing one foot on the man's chest, he disemboweled him with his sickle claw.

Jose, standing outside the cage, fired another dart and jumped off the trailer to the ground.

Greaves tried pulling himself to the cage door, sweat running down his face, his leg leaving a trail of blood. Mako reared up, excited by the blood, and went directly to the injured leg. He slowly placed his jaw around the knee and crunched down, followed by a shaking, slicing action that severed the entire lower half of the leg just above the knee. Greaves screamed and clawed his way toward the opening in the cage. He had almost reached the backend of the trailer when Mako walked over him.

The snarling nightmare stood at the trailer door, looking down at the scrambling humans, and stepped the few feet to the ground. He growled as another dart hit him in the thigh. Eying Jose, he stepped toward him, hands open, ready to crush the irritating human.

He tried to run, but Mako's mouth opened around his head and upper chest. The teeth didn't penetrate deeply, but drew blood. As the dinosaur lowered him to the ground, with a crack, Jose's collarbone snapped.

Fearing his head might crack open, Jose felt hot, dank breath wash over him. Then cooler air in reverse. The back of his head was wet and beyond, in the blackness of Mako's throat, he could hear a low, gravelly rumble.

Then the pressure lifted, and he slid out into fresh air as a man pulled at his feet and two more lifted his head over the sharp teeth as they struggled to open the jaws further.

Jose wiped his eyes and looked wide-eyed at the sleeping monster, blood still running down its jaw. The weight of Mako's head alone had been enough for some teeth to puncture his shoulders and back.

Cantor arrived at the scene out of breath, thankful Jose was in good hands. He walked over to Mako and studied his head closely. There were bumps and protrusions none of the other raptors had. Over the half-closed eyes, the brow bones were like foreboding hoods.

Greaves, still inside the trailer, had placed his belt around his leg. He feebly cried out as his colleagues grabbed him and lowered him. Cantor arrived soon after.

A ranch hand placed a tight bandage around the Greave's stump, covering the protruding remains of his femur.

"Mako imprinted on me. Shouldn't have happened," Greaves mumbled before losing consciousness.

Cantor's stomach seized at the sight of the injured man. His legs gave way, and he sat on the ground near Jose, who was being treated for his injuries by several men.

Cantor ignored his stomach and tried to help. "Let me hold him up so you can get at the wounds on his back." Each puncture would need stitches. "What happened, Jose?"

Jose looked at him, still in shock. "That bastard fooled us! He pretended to be sedated!"

"Good God! It's Günter all over again," Cantor mumbled, horrified. He stayed put until the ambulance took Greaves and Jose away. Looking up, he saw Valerie put her hand to her mouth as she looked in the trailer.

"That was a nightmare!" Cantor exclaimed, as she joined him on the grass. They stared at Mako's bloody jaws as the dinosaur exhaled stale air with a rumbling groan. "Not enough tranquilizer."

Her hands shook as she cried, "They never consulted me! Why the hell am I here if they don't consult me!?"

"Two men dead!" Cantor said, gritting his teeth. "And Greaves! He's in bad shape!"

Valerie hit the ground with her fist. "It didn't have to happen!"

* * *

Once Mako was back in his cage and his collar removed, Cantor stormed into Tusker's trailer.

"Valerie or I could have told you that Mako doesn't respond normally to tranqs!"

"Hindsight, Cant... uh, Cantor."

"We didn't even know the men were going to enter the cage!"

"I'm troubled, just like you are!"

"We need to do something about Mako. One question, Dan. Why didn't you use that rifle you have in the case?"

"Listen, Cant... Cantor, there wasn't time. It all happened too fast. Anyway, I'm not giving up on Mako. He's the most exciting thing the public has ever seen."

"Yeah, right. Real exciting, just like watching the Twin Towers in New York come down. You're going to get sued. Two men died, for crying out loud. Doesn't the fear of losing money, if not lives, make you want to change course?"

"Trust me, no worker would ever sue us for any reason. They aren't stupid."

"Well, I'm going to let the ranch hands know what I think of that. You'll have to shut this tour down."

"Careful, Cantor. You don't want to mess with my organization. Believe me."

"Are you threatening me?"

"No, of course not, Cantor. I'm your friend," Tusker said with a sickly smile.

After Cantor stomped out, Tusker's smile vanished. He began pulling at his braids.

* * *

After Cantor spent several hours cooling off, he called Kumiko. "Oh, hi Cantor. I'm glad you called," Kumiko said. "Arthur Saxton died from a massive heart attack."

"Whoa. I'm sorry to hear that. He contributed so much to our work. He was a brilliant man," Cantor responded.

"Yes, he was. He must have shunned doctors, though. Few people die that way nowadays."

Cantor paused. "I need to tell you; things aren't going too well here in Maryland. Mako killed two of Tusker's men and seriously injured two more."

"That's horrible! Horrible! What happened?"

"The men that sedated him thought he was down and entered the cage."

"This is so bad! Who were the men?"

"Antonio and Miguel. Jose is injured. Greaves lost a leg."

"He was a rotten apple, but he didn't deserve that. Didn't Antonio's wife just have a baby?"

"Yeah."

"This is so sad.," she said and paused. "There is something different about Mako's metabolism. We knew that from your attempts to bring him down."

"I can understand Luna's feelings about Mako. He really is demonic. He's not a good fit for the world we live in," Cantor said, realizing he'd just said what George told him many years ago.

"I've been thinking about that, too."

"I think they'll have to cancel the tour. By the way, before she left, Valerie spoke to the director of operations at the zoo in Albuquerque," Cantor continued. "She frequently asks him for advice. Anyway, he wasn't aware that the dinosaur tour was going to come to the zoo. Can you believe that? Something isn't right."

"Hmm. Very odd. The director should have known."

"Right. Either Tusker is a terrible organizer or there is something he isn't telling us."

* * *

After the call with Cantor ended, Kumiko went outside and sat on the porch, gazing straight ahead, seeing nothing. *Two more men died.* Feelings of guilt and shame washed over her. *Am I one of those people that forges ahead with their own plans regardless of how many get hurt?* The nausea she'd been feeling lately surfaced with a vengeance. It didn't get any better when her worry turned to anger at Tusker.

Chapter 55

Judgement in Rome

Almost immediately, Yuri learned the news of the tour debacle. He informed the Benefactor, who suggested they meet in Rome.

Later that day, Yuri told the black car with the bullet-proof windows to ease into a parking space near the entrance of the Caffarella Park.

"Let's walk, Yuri," the Benefactor said from the plush leather seat behind him.

Yuri got out and opened the back door. The Benefactor, wearing a long, black leather jacket, stepped out easily, considering his large size. They began walking along the Appian Way, gazing at the ancient Roman tombs on each side.

"So, now the tour will not make it to Russia. Tell me, Yuri, what more do you know?"

"The big male's control collar needed repair. They had to sedate the dinosaur, but it wasn't effective, and it killed two men as they entered the cage. It escaped, but further doses of the tranquilizer finally brought the animal down."

"Mako. That creature will command a great price."

"Yes," Yuri answered.

"Let's follow the path here to the ancient tomb of Annia Regilla. Have you seen it?"

"No, Benefactor. I haven't had the pleasure."

They stood before the building. "Look at that. Beautiful simplicity. She was an aristocrat. Her husband was a Greek named Herodes, a friend of the Roman emperor. Herodes built this lovely building to remember his wife after she died."

"He must have loved her very much, Benefactor."

"Actually, many Romans believed he killed her. The building was built to convince them otherwise. Now, back to Tusker.

"A competent man would not let things like this happen, Yuri. He is drawing attention to himself. The dinosaur tour was ill-conceived and completely mishandled. But the damage is done. His disappearance will only draw more attention to the organization. So, you see, Yuri, he has accidentally succeeded in protecting himself for now."

"Yes."

"We will wait awhile. Let the dust settle. I expect you to find a new way to bring the dinosaurs to Russia. If all goes well, maybe we let Tusker continue for now. He must get rid of the scientists that are keeping us from fulfilling our plans. If not, he will have an accident."

"I understand, Benefactor."

"What kind of accident do you think would be best?"

"I think death by dinosaur," Yuri replied, glancing at the fine brickwork on the tomb.

"Interesting, Yuri. You're beginning to think like me. Oh, one other thing."

"Yes, Benefactor?"

"When he gets back to New Mexico, bring me one of his kidneys on ice. I have plans for it."

Chapter 56

The Agony in the Gondola

The incident in Maryland and the cancellation of further shows were a major embarrassment to Tusker. He immediately went into damage control. What was needed now was some good publicity.

Some dignitaries had accepted invitations to experience the glass-bottomed gondola ride at Raptor Ranch. It would be no different from what the tourists were treated to. On its metal rails above, the car would travel into the middle of Grouchland and observe Mako below, who would be given a chunk of beef.

Tusker asked Cantor to meet him in his office.

Cantor walked past two armed men as he entered. He noticed several new plaques on the wall thanking Tusker for the creation of his theme park.

"What's with the guards, Dan?"

"As you know, Governor Alvarez will be here tomorrow with Congressman Cox, Congresswoman Sanchez, and other important people." Tusker had his hair braided and several medals on his red and yellow vest.

That Alvarez is so corrupt! "So, why are they guarding your office right now?"

"I've gotten some threatening phone calls from animal rights people," Tusker replied, flicking at a small fly on his desk.

"I thought you'd been getting those for years." He noticed how fidgety Tusker was.

"I have. It's never too late to take the appropriate measures."

"So, the guards aren't here for tomorrow's dignitaries?" Cantor asked.

"What the hell do you want, Cantor?"

"You asked me to come see you."

"Right. Tomorrow, I want everything to run smoothly. Have all the dinosaurs in their fields. And cover those scars with long pants! I want this place to impress the top brass."

Jeez, now he thinks we're in the military. "Speaking of which, both Cox and Sanchez are veterans. Maybe you shouldn't wear your fashion medals tomorrow."

Tusker rolled his eyes. "You don't know the first thing about fashion," he said tersely. "I want you, Alex, Valerie, and Kumiko in the bleachers as the dignitaries take a ride in the gondola."

"I know this is a big day, Dan. But we're in the middle of our research on Maryann's raptorlings."

"Have Moli do it."

"I assume you are talking about Muli. He's a great help, but I need Alex to watch the animals. And Valerie is always on call in case something happens."

"You need to cooperate. Case closed."

"Case re-opened. I'll come and, if Kumiko wants to, she'll join me. I can answer any questions your guests have. Maybe they'll want to discuss our research. That's why it's to your advantage if Alex continues his work. And you don't want anyone calling Valerie about an emergency during the ceremony. It could be disruptive. So, I want her to stay where she's needed."

"I suppose that will be fine," Tusker said, shaking his head. "My speech is at 10:00 sharp. I'll see you tomorrow."

* * *

The next day, Cantor showered and checked out his clothes in the closet. He frowned at his only two dress pants. *Oh, hell no*, he thought. He put on his tan cargo shorts and a T-shirt and headed for the kitchen. He was proud of the scars on the backs of his legs.

"Good morning, Kumiko," he said, grateful she was an early riser and liked to put the coffee on first thing. He kissed her cheek and grabbed a mug, which he filled to the brim. "Looks like another warm day."

"A little breezy," she added, sitting on one of the wooden stools in her blue polka dot dressing gown. "I guess I'd better get dressed if we are going to Dan's Fun in the Sun party. Is that what you're wearing?"

"I'm going to say yes, since the shorts appear to be covering my bum and the shirt is where it is on my body."

"Cantor, do I need to slap you?"

"Not necessary. At least the bleachers are in the shade. Dress for warm temps." He turned to Dex, who was compressed into his minimum volume in the corner by the back door. "Dex, let's go visit Alex."

Cantor looked longingly at the sweet sticky bun on the counter, but decided he didn't have time. As he headed for the front door with his sunglasses on, he heard the soft 'ding', indicating Dex was up and ready.

Alex answered the knock on his door and invited his guests in. "This will be interesting. I may saunter over to the ride to watch all the fun after I check on the dinos."

"I highly recommend it," Cantor said. "Tusker will be pleased if you add to the size of his audience. I feel bad for those ranch hands who were supposed to have the day off today."

Alex smiled. "Yep, Dan Tusker, a man who knows how to make friends and influence people."

"I need to talk to you in private. Do you mind sending your Dexter out for something in the supply building?" Cantor asked.

"Not at all. Gagarin, please purchase some potatoes and a few tomato plants for the garden."

"I will," Gagarin said, stepping past Dex.

"OK, let's get busy," Cantor said.

The two men went through the same routine with Dex as before. Dex's self-surgery only took a few minutes to remove the foreign communications module in his torso.

Cantor waited until Dex was finished. "You can leave your module with me, Dex. I'll give it back to you after the show. I want you to countermand the gondola's commands once the dignitaries have reached their destination over Grouchland. Keep the gondola from returning. You'll continue until I tell you directly to stop."

"I will do it, great master."

"Shuddup. After I tell you to stop, we'll go to my cabin," Cantor said.

* * *

Kumiko joined Cantor in the bleachers with the small crowd of government workers, ranch hands, and tourists.

"Looks like the media is here in full force," she said, smoothing out her blue and pink dress with the heat exchanger hidden in the fabric. "Dan loves being in front of a camera."

"You look like a Hollywood star in those sunglasses," Cantor said. He glanced at Dex, sitting on the stockade next to Mako's barn in the distance.

"That podium is pretty fancy," Kumiko said. "Oh, look over there in the front row. I've never seen so many congresspeople. There's the governor and her husband as well."

Cantor watched Tusker approach the podium as the people in the bleachers clapped.

"Good morning, my friends. To our distinguished guests, let me say, welcome to our family. For that is what we are. Every day we work to further research on animals that haven't walked this earth for 55 million years."

"Well, he messed that up," Cantor whispered to Kumiko.

"I am so pleased to have my good friends here. Governor Alvarez and I make a great golf team. She likes the water and I like the turf." He paused, waiting for laughter. "And Congressman Cox, thank you for taking time out of your busy schedule to enjoy the day with us. What better place for us older dinosaurs to meet again?"

Cantor glanced at Cox, who barely cracked a smile. Soon, it became clear that Tusker wasn't going to acknowledge the deaths of his workers while on tour. Cantor was disgusted.

As Tusker's talk droned on, Cantor overheard someone behind him quietly say, "Get on with it, dude."

After forty-five minutes, Tusker finally ended by introducing Governor Alvarez

"I sure hope she isn't as long-winded as Tusker," Cantor whispered.

The governor began her speech, telling of her plans for the future of New Mexico.

Half an hour later, Kumiko turned to Cantor. "I'm sorry, but I'm very tired. I don't feel up to hearing any more about all the great things she's doing for business. I'm going to head back now. Are you going to stay?"

"Yeah," Cantor said, "just to keep Dan happy." After a pause, he asked, "Are you OK?"

"Just need a nap," she said.

He watched Kumiko make her way to the end of the bleacher, smiling at people as she excused herself. *She looks so thin.*

Dex was still by the barn.

It was almost noon when the last speaker sat down. I'm sorry you all are going to miss lunch, Cantor thought to himself as he watched the dignitaries all line up next to the gondola. He noticed a security camera pointed at the gondola and another one pointed at the crowd.

* * *

All the riders were now on board the gondola, including Tusker. Any second, the gondola would pull out. A ranch hand's voice came over the sound system and asked the crowd to send them off with a cheer. As lukewarm applause came from the bleachers, Mako followed underneath the glass-bottomed car, jumping and hissing. The clapping seemed to agitate him.

Cantor looked at the gondola through high-powered binoculars as it moved toward the center of Grouchland. For the sake of the security cameras, he pretended excitement and clapped his hands.

When the gondola reached its destination, the sound system announced that the gondola would remain stationary while some meat was lowered for the dinosaur below. Mako was snarling now, impatient for the small treat he'd come to expect. Several times, he let out a roar toward the stands.

Cantor craned his neck, hoping Dex was still in view. *Thank Goodness for Dex.* The robot was now clamped to the walls of the corral where he could see him better. *I hope Dex is close enough for this to work.*

Mako leaned back and rose for the meat that dangled from the car and swallowed the meat in one gulp. Glaring at the gondola one more time, he turned and stared at the tourists in the stands.

After ten minutes, Cantor saw Tusker at a window of the gondola, speaking by radio, presumably with the operator at the controls behind the tinted glass to the north of the bleachers. Time to bring her home. The gondola jerked slightly, but stayed where it was. Cantor increased the binocular's power to max to see the expression on Tusker's face. He was still smiling and patting people on the back. Congressman Cox continued to look at Mako.

After twenty minutes, Tusker looked out the window again, nodding and moving his hand as if he was saying patiently, "OK, that was fun. Now let's head back. Bring us back." But his smile seemed a little too compressed.

Another ten minutes passed with no movement of the gondola. Tusker was now speaking with intensity on the radio. Alex showed up and made his way to where Cantor sat.

"Maybe I should check with the operator. Ask if there is anything I can do." Cantor said, sympathizing with Congressman Cox, who was speaking animatedly with Governor Alvarez. The governor was gesturing with her arms. Tusker's face was looking strained.

"That would be a nice touch," Alex said with a smile.

Cantor made his way to the end of the bleacher, trying not to step on anyone's toes. People in the audience were beginning to complain about the delay. A quick-thinking employee handed out water. Cantor grabbed a couple of bottles and entered the stairwell that led to the operations room for the gondola.

He poked his head into the room. A young man was checking wires underneath the console, his head buried under the table, his rear end showing below his shirt.

"Excuse me, is there anything I can do to help?"

The man twisted around and looked at him. "Do you know anything about communication consoles?"

"I wish I did. I brought you some water, though."

The man reached for the water and sat cross-legged on the floor, looking flustered. "I don't get it. Never had a problem until today."

"I believe that's called Murphy's Law," Cantor said.

"Right. If something can go wrong, it will," the man said bleakly, shaking his head.

"Have you called a technician?"

"Yeah. He should be here soon. He had to get his tools." The man pulled himself off the floor and tried pushing a button. Shaking his head, he said, "I don't get it."

"I'm sorry all this is falling in your lap," Cantor said. "Have you had lunch?"

"I brought my lunch, but I'm not hungry."

"What's your name?"

"John."

"Well, good luck John. This isn't your fault, I'm sure."

Cantor headed back out to the bleachers. People were leaving now. He looked at the gondola. Tusker was facing the governor, shrugging his shoulders. One Congressman had his hands on his hips, looking down while shaking his head. *The small air conditioner in the gondola should be working, but it could still be uncomfortable in there.* He looked at his watch.

After another hour, the governor held her legs together as though she needed to pee.

Cantor sat down by Alex. "What do you think? Should we bail Tusker out?"

"I don't know. I'm really enjoying this," Alex said, looking through his own pair of binoculars.

"I'm going to walk back now. When I get to Dex, I'll tell him to send the return command. I don't want to witness people having to pee in front of each other inside the car."

"I guess I'll join you. We don't need to walk fast, though."

As they passed one of the few people still watching the debacle, they heard one of them say something about a bunch of idiots.

Cantor said, "If Tusker isn't sacked, I'll be surprised."

"We'll all be sadder if he isn't."

Dex saw them approach but continued doing his duty on the fence.

When Cantor got to the corral, he called to Dex. "Come home now, Dex. Stop what you're doing."

Dex immediately moved toward him as Cantor climbed a ladder and saw the gondola was moving again. "Thanks, Dex. At the cabin, you'll have to insert the comm module again. Then you can forget about all of this."

Chapter 57

Dinner

The disastrous celebration of Raptor Ranch Dino Ride was now over. It was on all the local news. After the dignitaries had left, Tusker did his best to minimize the incident and shoo away the press. Unfortunately, a reporter's mic later picked up him saying, "One small step for man; one giant leak for mankind." The governor wasn't amused when she learned this.

Cantor kept telling himself that Governor Alvarez was corrupt. But he felt dirty at what he'd done. He wanted to do something about Tusker, but it was the governor who paid the price.

* * *

Cantor resumed the work he'd started before the tour. In the afternoon, he entered the cabin earlier than usual to see if Kumiko felt better. She was in the kitchen.

"Hey, Kumiko. How was your day today?" he asked.

"Luna and I spent some time having a nice woman-to-woman talk."

"Oh?" he said, noticing how slowly she moved. "I think Luna has been right about the dinosaurs. It isn't safe with the likes of Circe and Mako nearby. I don't blame her for being uncomfortable."

"I understand Luna," she said. "She isn't a scientist and doesn't have any desire to learn about how the dinosaurs behave. She would like to have kids someday. Public schools, normal neighborhoods, and no dinosaurs."

"Yeah, I get it. Maybe we should live outside the ranch as well. Close, but away from the E-raptors."

She lowered herself gently onto the stool by the kitchen counter. "I'm here for the research. This is where I want to be. I'm not worried."

"What about evenings?"

"I'm too tired to think about it, Cantor."

He studied her trembling hand. "Kumiko, I don't think you've fully recovered from the flu. Let's see a docbot in Albuquerque tomorrow to see what's going on."

"I'd rather not."

"Do it for me?"

She gave him a resigned look. "OK. But Tusker should have purchased a docbot for the ranch."

Cantor took her to an urgent care center the next morning. "You are suffering from the effects of the bird flu. Some people have symptoms for months," the docbot told her.

* * *

"So, how's Luna liking the new place in town, George?" Cantor asked that evening, after George had stopped by the cabin for a visit.

George sat on the sofa, hands on his knees. "Cuba is a small town, but she's used to that. She's still unpacking with Pixie's help. Thanks again for letting us use her. She's a great Dexter."

"Of course. Just don't mention it to Tusker; he thinks she's trimming trees. You like your new place?"

"The place is small, but cozy. It's amazing how the thick adobe walls keep out the summer heat. I like that it's away from the highway too. I suggested that Luna not to unpack more than we need right now. Hopefully, in a year or two, we'll make our final move. I'm sure she's as shocked as I am that I'm making some money now."

"You pulled off a long shot. I'm proud of you, son," Cantor said.

"With the payment I received for the first chapter of the book and the documentary, we can build our dream home."

* * *

The next day, Cantor came to visit with George while he was watching Maryann. "What a magnificent creature," he said as he joined his son on the wooden steps, looking over the fence.

"She's so graceful. Earlier today, I saw her trotting along and leaping over rocks effortlessly. Poetry in motion," George agreed. "You know who else is amazing? Pixie. Luna has long talks with Pixie now. She's Luna's helper and friend. Pixie helps us in the kitchen with cleaning and she even carries Luna's French easel when she goes out to paint. You should see some of the artwork she's doing."

"Luna?"

"Luna. But Pixie's stuff is very interesting as well," George responded, watching Maryann as she walked along the fence.

"Why don't you and Luna come over for dinner tomorrow? Your mom is feeling tired, so I'm going to make a gourmet meal while she rests. At least, I'm going to try."

"Sounds good, Dad. Is it going to be vegetarian?"

"Not entirely. I know I'm surrounded by carnivores."

* * *

George was feeling good when he entered his parents' house the next night. "Luna and I baked some bread." Savory aromas filled the kitchen.

"Lovely. Thank you both," Kumiko said. "Cantor has been a force to be reckoned with in the kitchen. He's making your favorite - spaghetti."

Luna leaned over and gave her mother-in-law a big hug. "I'm planning to stay at the ranch until tomorrow to do some painting. Want to come?"

"I wouldn't miss it for the world," Kumiko said, looking small in the easy-chair.

Luna walked into the kitchen to greet Cantor. "Oh my," she said with a laugh, "there just might be more sauce on the stove than in the pot!"

"Why should the stove be deprived?" he smiled in return. He had a larger pot filled with meat sauce and a smaller pot without meat for himself.

During dinner, Dex brought a bottle of red wine and filled the glasses of those who liked wine, all except Kumiko. She didn't feel like it. Afterward, Dex took the dishes to the kitchen.

"You didn't eat much, Mom. Are you feeling all right?

Kumiko gave her son a warm smile. "Just tired. I'll have a big plate tomorrow."

After dinner, Kumiko rested on the couch. Fatigue rolled over her like cloud shadows that seeped into her bones.

Chapter 58

A Russian

Several days later, Cantor was collecting data on Maryann's stride. He'd just measured her speed from a safe location as she ran to the far end of Maland. Carefully, he climbed inside her enclosure while a drone hovered above. It would warn him if Maryann returned. He carefully measured the distance between her footprints at the point of greatest speed. This, combined with information on her size and weight, would help paleontologists better estimate the speed of a dinosaur from fossil footprints in rock beds.

As he was heading toward the fence, he noticed the man he'd seen under the truck the day Mako had killed Remus. Cantor walked the path between fences and headed toward the man.

Patterson was busy moving stuff in a wheelbarrow when Cantor walked up to him.

"Hey, I saw you the day Remus died. How're you doing?"

Patterson continued his work without looking at Cantor. "Good."

"That was quite a night," Cantor continued. Except for his round face, he thought the man was very ordinary.

"Yes."

"I know you must be busy, but I noticed you spoke Russian that night."

"I don't think so."

"You said *nyet*."

Patterson turned and looked at Cantor. "I must have said 'net.'"

"I'm just curious. I don't meet many Russians out here," Cantor said, eyeing the man closely.

"Excuse me, I need to get back to work."

"OK, I understand." Cantor walked away. *He's not the friendliest guy in the world. I don't speak much Russian, but that guy's accent is the same as Alex's!*

Chapter 59

Lingering Effects

"To sleep, perchance to dream."
— William Shakespeare

That night, Cantor sat on the bed by Kumiko, running his fingers through her hair. "Do you feel like something to eat, hon? I can make you some eggs or oatmeal."

"I'm fine. Really. Maybe some tea would be nice."

"Dex, please bring Kumiko a cup of tea."

"How is your stomach?" he asked.

"I suspect I have an ulcer on top of the long-term effects from the flu. Can you imagine that? I've been asking you to slow down, and I was the one working too hard. I'm sorry you've had to do more than your fair share of the cooking."

"Wait a minute. You don't like my cooking?"

"Oh, you know I love your cooking."

Cantor was silent as he looked out the window by the bed. The clouds were gray and the wind was picking up.

* * *

As the week progressed, Kumiko slept more.

Cantor spoke to Valerie. "I've made an appointment with a docbot in Albuquerque, but it's not for a week. Kumiko thinks she has an ulcer. I was wondering if you could examine her before then."

"As a vet, I can't."

"What about as a friend? Can you just take a look at her?"

"I see the same things as you, Cantor. She is very tired, and she has pains in her stomach. The doctor said it may take months for her to recover completely from that flu virus."

"Well, she seems to be getting worse. Can you run some tests?"

Valerie was silent for a while as Cantor continued to look at her.

"I might lose my license." She looked at the pain in Cantor's eyes. "As a friend, I'll look at her, though."

After asking Kumiko some questions, Valerie asked her to come to her clinic. She noticed Kumiko's heart showed an atypical rhythm.

"My urine is dark," Kumiko said with a cough. "And my throat is often sore."

"Let's check your blood. I just need a drop," Valerie suggested. "But please don't tell anyone I'm doing this." A small pinprick of blood from her finger, when run through the hematology analyzer, showed her red blood cell count was low.

After walking Kumiko back to her cabin, Valerie visited Cantor, who was observing the C-raptorlings.

"Cantor, here's what I've found," she said and described Kumiko's symptoms.

Cantor looked at her with wide eyes. "What do you think it is?"

"I'm not sure. The virus has been known to affect people's hearts."

Cantor looked at his feet. "Are there certain foods that will improve her red blood cell levels? I can make anything she needs. She tries to do too much."

"Let's wait and see what the docbot says."

Valerie headed home and began reading online reference books.

* * *

The docbot ordered X-rays. There were signs of damage to one of Kumiko's heart valves. The bird flu seemed to be the culprit. At some point, she might need surgery, but for now, the bot recommended rest.

Chapter 60

Where is Huey?

*"There is no knife that cuts so sharply and with
such poisoned blade as treachery."*
— Ouida

July brought the promise of rain but delivered mostly thunder and
lightning. The booms and flashes were particularly bad on July
14th, the anniversary of the terrorist strike that destroyed the Statue of
Liberty's arm.

As Muli made his rounds, he watched as Jose and other ranch hands
began to herd the dinosaurs. In Maryann's case, loud speakers would
play the old classic, *Hey Jude,* and Maryann would push her youngsters
toward the barn. She knew there would be a delicious reward waiting
for them there. Cantor wanted the animals in the barns for safety that
evening, where they would be less stressed.

Muli took a second glance through Maryann's barn window. He
counted the young raptors on his fingers. One short. No sign of Huey.

* * *

"Mr. Cantor, I didn't see Huey in the barn last night. I think he must
have been left out in the field. I thought you should know."

"Thank you, Muli. I'm sure you're right."

Cantor turned to Alex. "What do you think?"

"Since Maryann is in the barn, I'll take the bike out."

Cantor headed over to Darwin's barn. Time to let him stretch his
legs. He planned to let Darwin spend the week in Daland. He felt
weighed down with worries, especially about Kumiko.

Throughout the day, Cantor observed Darwin deal with Dex, or more accurately, ignore the bot. The mechanical newcomer had piqued Darwin's curiosity at first. He had sniffed at Dex and decided the bot wasn't a threat.

Dex had roamed inside Darland during the night to observe Darwin's daytime and nighttime routine. The robot recorded continuously, periodically uploading its data to the compound's computers. He had a night vision camera behind one eye and a regular camera behind the other.

Where Darwin went, the robot followed, almost like a raptorling that had imprinted on him. Water was the exception. When Darwin lowered his body into the pond to cleanse his feathers, the robot stayed at the shore - a bit of a peeping Tom.

Cantor called it a day. He wanted to check on Kumiko. As he headed home, Alex caught up with him.

"Did you find our little renegade?" Cantor asked.

Alex shook his head. "I checked behind every sage, bush, and tuft of grass, and in the shade of every tree. I didn't see any sign of Huey."

* * *

Over the next few days, no rock was left unturned as the search for Huey continued. Cantor and Alex headed to Alex's cabin after a long day.

"Let's check Dex's videos." Cantor said. "Maybe he saw something the night Huey disappeared."

After settling down with glasses of ice tea in Alex's dining room, Alex opened his laptop and scrolled through Dex's recent uploads.

"Let's check out Dex's night vision vid," Cantor suggested.

In the first scene, the robot recorded from a hill, giving it a panoramic view. Darwin seemed asleep not far away.

"Hold on. Look, Alex, do you see something by Maryann's barn?"

"Back it up again," Alex replied. "Who is that? What's he doing? He's just standing up against the wall." They could see a man wearing a hat and night vision goggles.

"He's so still. Zoom in… I can't tell who he is. I think he's holding something... Wait, now he's moving! He's placing something in one of the slots! I think it's a dart gun!" Cantor exclaimed, leaning forward and squinting.

"What's going on?" Alex said, on the edge of his seat, "Crap, look, there's another guy now! Looks like a bandana is covering his face. And the first guy just took a shot! Is that a Dexter in the corral? Now another shot!"

The men and the Dexter waited. Alex sped up the video.

"Stop! The Dexter has opened the smaller door to the barn!" Cantor exclaimed. "They must have tranquilized Maryann." Cantor had a sinking feeling in his gut.

They continued watching as the Dextor entered the small, narrow metal door. Not much happened for another ten minutes.

"The Dexter is coming out! Looks like he's holding a large bag."

"Let's go, Alex! I want to check out Maryann's barn. She's in Maland now, right?"

"Yeah, she's away from the barn with her raptorlings."

When they got to the barn, knowing what to look for, they could see the Dexter's footprints.

"I want all workers to report to me immediately," Cantor said. "I'll remain here. Alex, please enlist George and Valerie to help."

* * *

Alex made an announcement over the ranch's loud speakers. Tusker came out of his office in a fury.

"You can't do that!" he yelled at Alex. "Only I can do that!"

Alex ignored him.

A roll call revealed two men were missing. One was Brad Patterson.

"I knew something was wrong with that guy, Alex. He was unfriendly. I'm certain he was Russian, but he denied it," Cantor said.

"I never met him. The name *Brad Patterson* is probably not real," Alex said.

"Why would somebody hire a Russian to do this? Something strange is going on, Alex."

"Yeah, there aren't that many of us around."

"Let's talk to the Dexter. It wasn't Dex or Gagarin because we know their whereabouts in the last few days. Let's check out Valerie's Dexter."

* * *

Cantor looked at Valerie's Dexter, Theodore Rex. "Can you tell me what happened last night?"

"I cleaned up after Valerie left the clinic. There was some dust on the floor that I removed."

"Did you lock up?"

"I was preparing to do so when two gentlemen walked in. They said a dinosaur was hurt and needed my help."

"Did one have a Russian accent?"

There was a short pause. "Yes, he had a Russian accent."

"What happened next?"

"I entered through the door to the barn and closed it so no dinosaurs could escape. The men asked me to place a bag over the sick one and tie it with a rope. They didn't want to go inside in case the mother dinosaur woke up. She seemed to be in a deep sleep. I hope the smaller dinosaur feels better soon."

"Did it appear sick to you?"

"Yes. It wouldn't wake up."

"Thank you, Theodore."

* * *

Tusker had been absent from the ranch for a week. Now he was back. When Cantor walked into his office, he wasn't there, but a full glass of lemonade and a bottle of pain pills on the desk indicated he'd return soon.

He studied the papers on the desk. There was a printout of an email from somebody named Yuri. The letter was inquiring how the return from Maryland went. Addressing his phone, he asked, "What does the person with the first name Yuri do at Cosmic Pawn?"

"There is no record of a Yuri at Cosmic Pawn." His phone answered.

Curious, Cantor thought.

He studied the room. There were the usual photos on the walls, mostly with Tusker and colleagues. The bolt-action rifle in the cabinet was the one Cantor had seen in Tusker's office during the ill-fated tour.

"Cantor, my man. What's up?" Tusker said, entering the room slowly, one hand on his lower back and hunched like an old man.

"What happened to you?"

"I wanted to do something good for somebody less fortunate than myself. So, I donated a kidney."

"Why? Most folks have one grown in the lab."

"OK, fine. The kidney was bad. Satisfied?" Tusker said as he gently lowered himself into his chair.

"I'm sorry to hear that, Dan," Cantor said, noticing how pale Tusker's face was. "You don't look well."

Tusker reached for the bottle of pills. "What do you want?"

"I assume you're aware about Huey and the missing workmen."

"Painfully aware," he answered, shaking a pill into his palm.

"Well, what can you tell me?" Cantor asked.

"Not much. Just regular guys with no criminal history. Brad Patterson was a quiet guy who didn't interact with the others much. The other man, Mike Keating, did a good job and was friendly."

"Patterson had a Russian accent. Were you aware he was Russian?"

Tusker gulped some lemonade to get the pill down. "Are you aware you have an American accent?"

Cantor grabbed the wooden chair in front of the desk. "OK. I'll just sit here and stare at you."

"Hell, Cantor. I hear Russian accents, German accents, Mexican accents, English accents…"

"Why do you suppose they took Huey?"

"Black market. Or maybe they wanted a dino for themselves."

"The consequences of the loss of Huey are terrible. It will affect our research."

"Don't you think I'm aware of that?" Tusker said with annoyance.

"When you first found out, I assume you filed a report with the police."

"I had a kidney taken out! Give me a break. As soon as we know more, we can take the appropriate action."

"Like you have your own detectives? Come on! One of your employees should have made the call."

"Don't worry so much." Tusker said. "The thieves are going to have their hands full. That raptorling is growing fast. It's dangerous already."

Cantor shook his head. "Something stinks around here."

"I'll keep my eyes out," Tusker said, pointing to the gun cabinet.

Lot of good that did. "I prefer electric fences! And better vetting of employees!"

"Let me handle the ranch," Tusker repeated wearily.

"We need security bots, Dan." *The security in this place is a joke. Dan is a joke. No wonder he won't reveal who his boss is.*

* * *

After leaving Tusker's office, Cantor caught up with Alex by Maland.

"Maryann knows one of her kids is missing," Alex said, watching her poking her nose into clumps of sage and chamisa.

Cantor watched her lead the raptorlings into a group of cottonwoods. She held her snout high, constantly testing the air. "Yuri is a Russian name, right?"

"Yeah. Like Yuri Gagarin, the cosmonaut. Why?"

"I saw a message on Dan's desk from someone named Yuri who wanted to know how the return from Maryland went."

Alex crinkled his brows. "Another Russian. I suggest you call the FBI."

* * *

The day after Tusker's meeting with Cantor, he called his mother.

"Mom, why haven't you been answering your phone?" he asked. "I've been calling you for days."

"I couldn't find it until today. I guess I'd left it in the garden. How silly."

"Are you OK?"

"Oh, sure. How nice of you to ask. Do you remember how your stepdad loved steak and kidney pie?"

"Sure," Tusker answered, twisting one of his braids nervously.

"Well, a few days ago, a nice man from my church said he was going to bake a couple pies. He's very sweet. He's new and told me he didn't know anybody. Anyway, he wondered if I'd like one."

"He made steak and kidney pies?"

"Yes. He's a very good cook. It was just like I remembered. I shared some of it with Mildred. You remember my neighbor, Mildred?"

"Yes. What is your friend's name? The one that made the pie?"

"His name is Brad. Funny, he doesn't look like a Brad. He has a bit of an accent. I'll have to ask him where he is from. Anyway, I saved some of the pie for you in the freezer for the next time you visit."

Tusker felt little pinpricks and a flush of heat throughout his body. *Oh my God!*

"Dan? Are you still there?" she asked.

"I gotta go, Mom. Call you soon." He ended the call and stared at the wall for a long time as his stomach churned.

Chapter 61

Kumiko Declines

"Fear sees, even when eyes are closed."
—Wayne Gerard Trotman

Cantor took Kumiko into Albuquerque again for more X-rays. There was no sign of cancer in her stomach, but there were large lesions on her liver. The liver biopsy also showed no cancer. He felt dread. Cancer could be cured. This was something else. Evil. He headed over to Valerie's the next morning.

* * *

Valerie poured herself a glass of water and sat on her porch and watched as Cantor approached, head down and hands in his pants pockets. Magpie flitted onto the railing of the porch for a visit.

"Well, hello, Magpie." Valerie rose and said, "Let's go, Magpie. Let me see what I have for you inside."

Magpie followed her into the house.

Cantor tapped on her open door. "Come in," she said, rummaging in her cabinets. She found some berries and walnuts. Putting both in her hand, she let Magpie decide for himself. "I think I'll hire you as my support bird, Magpie. I'll help you and you'll help me."

"Please sit. What did the docbot say?" she asked Cantor.

"No cancer. But she has lesions on her liver. What could be causing this?"

Valerie took a deep breath and sat next to him on the couch. "I... I don't know what could be attacking her liver." She looked at him helplessly.

"I was up late last night researching the long-term effects of the virus. Liver lesions aren't one of them," he said, running his fingers through his hair.

"She still needs a more thorough examination by a docbot," Valerie said. "All this time, I thought her symptoms were from the virus."

"How do we stop this?" he said, his arms wrapped around his middle.

She reached out for his hand. "Once we figure out the cause, I'm sure there will be remedies. Let the bots work on it." Her skin prickled at the thought that the flu had masked something far more sinister.

* * *

Cantor returned home with his eyes on the ground and walked straight to the bedroom. Kumiko lay in bed, reading a book of poetry. "How are you feeling, Kumiko?" he asked.

She shrugged and said, "I'm feeling better. I really am. Have you heard anything new about Huey?"

"Naw. I've been checking the news every day. We'll probably never know. I'm so glad you're feeling better, though. Can I get you anything?" The yellow tinge in her eyes broke his heart.

"Maybe my hairbrush," she said, looking up at him with a smile.

When he returned, Kumiko was silent for a while. "Look on the bright side. It could have been worse," she whispered. She looked at him with sad eyes. Then she shook it off and ran the brush through her hair a few times.

"Don't worry, we're going to get you better," he said and hugged her.

Later he stood outside, looking at the long contrail passing overhead. It looked like a rip in the sky.

* * *

The next day, George stepped into his parent's house. "Morning, Dad. I need some coffee."

"Sure son, grab a cup." Cantor tried to sound his usual self. His face was haggard; he had been up most of the night.

"What's the plan today?" George asked.

Cantor sighed. "Let's go for a walk. There are some things I want to share with you."

They went for a stroll and headed out of the compound, into the bright fields of chamisa and sage beyond. A Meadowlark was singing a lonely song.

After they had gone a short distance, Cantor turned to George and, taking in a deep breath, said, "Your mom is ill."

"Yeah, I know. She's been tired lately."

"Yes. But George, she is seriously ill."

"Oh? Well... well, how ill, Dad?" George stopped walking and stared at his dad.

"I don't know yet. It involves her heart and liver," Cantor said, wincing with each word.

"We should take her to the hospital! That sounds bad!"

"The doctors say it might be." Cantor looked at George, struggling to find words of comfort.

"We just need to make sure she gets all the meds she needs and if she needs surgery, she can have that, too. Right, Dad?"

"Yes, you're right. We will make sure she gets the best treatment. I'm bringing her to Albuquerque tomorrow." *They'll fix her, right? Please?*

"I want to see Mom now!" George said urgently.

They could see a line of people near Grouchland, waiting for their stupid ride. To Cantor, it seemed indecent and inappropriate. They were an intrusion into his family's life.

* * *

While Cantor and Kumiko were in Albuquerque, Valerie sat deep in thought in her clinic. She'd asked Kumiko for a urine sample before they left. Valerie did a urinalysis. She found high levels of creatinine.

She sat at her desk in the clinic, trying to get her arms around it. The attack had spread to Kumiko's kidneys. She began rocking in her chair. Rocking. Rocking as the cold logic ripped into her own gut. *My dear friend. Are you shutting down?*

Chapter 62

A Long Journey Toward the End

" Death is the quiet haven of us all."
– William Wordsworth

At last! The docbot in Albuquerque found the cause of Kumiko's illness. Arsenic poisoning. It ordered immediate blood transfusions and Kumiko was transferred to the ICU. She had been given heart medications and her kidneys were closely monitored as she slept.

Cantor sat beside her bed, staring at the ceiling. *Arsenic!*

Cantor called Valerie with the results of Kumiko's tests.

After she got over the shock, she said, "How? It couldn't be the water, or other people would be showing symptoms. Same with the air. Smoke from the Santa Fe Forest fire several months ago might carry arsenic, but again, nobody else is showing symptoms."

"Oh, my dear Kumiko," he cried, no longer able to control his tears.

"We are going to figure this out, Cantor," Valerie said, crying herself. "I've got some ideas. I'll call you back."

Hours later, Cantor answered her call.

"I tested her meds. No sign of Arsenic," Valerie said. "I even tried her toothpaste. What else could she be exposed to that the rest of us aren't?"

"We share the toothpaste," he said, trying to get the sleep out of his eyes. "We share just about everything. Let me know if anything new develops."

* * *

After a week, Kumiko returned to the ranch.

On her third day back from the hospital, the sun shone intensely. While Dex was helping round up Maryann's young, Kumiko collapsed as she reached for a book. Cantor found her, put her to bed, and refused to leave her side.

She had lost weight rapidly. Her hands trembled and her hair thinned. She slept a lot now. At times, she was delirious, but today she seemed lucid.

He sat by the bed, holding her hand, and the two reminisced. When they first met. George as a toddler. Her favorite restaurants in California.

Later, she told Cantor she felt like reading some poetry, perhaps some Emily Dickinson. He handed her a book and stepped out of the room. After flipping through the pages, her eyes rested on one poem.

Because I could not stop for Death –
He kindly stopped for me –
The Carriage held but just Ourselves –
And Immortality.

She slept for the rest of the day and all night. Cantor was by her side when she opened her eyes the next day. After helping her take care of her morning needs, they talked.

"George is sleeping in the living room. He was up late," he said.

"How's he doing?"

"He's worried about you." Cantor noticed how her sunken eyes lacked the luster they once had.

"I've still got some fight in me."

"I know you do."

Kumiko sighed. "I've been thinking about my life, my work, and many things."

"Like what?"

"I'm a contradiction," she paused for breath, "As a scientist, I strive to see everything…" she took another breath, "in objective terms, with emotion kept to a minimum."

"I have the same trait in myself," Cantor said.

"On the other hand, I'm a compassionate human being." Kumiko's eyes reddened. "I have regrets."

"Please, don't drain your energy dwelling on it," Cantor said.

"Blind ambition led me to make bad decisions."

"But Kumiko, you made fantastic contributions to science."

"Yes, and I lost a bit of myself."

"Forget the science. You made a family. You were there for us."

Kumiko looked above his head. "Don't worry about the dragon. It won't hurt you."

"Dragon?"

"The green one. He's looking over your shoulder."

Cantor turned and saw only the old print of a dragon that hung on the wall.

"Not to worry. I know he wouldn't hurt me," he said.

"Give him a fish. He likes fish."

"OK, where are the fish?"

"Oh, Cantor, they're swimming all around you."

Chapter 63

How Can This Be?

Later that week, Alex, George, Luna, and Muli gathered at Cantor's cabin for the first episode of the Streamscape series titled *Remaking Dinosaurs*, based on videos and interviews George made. Kumiko, covered by a blanket, lay on the couch with her legs over Cantor's thighs. Alex sat on a wooden dining room chair. Valerie promised to come later once she'd finished some work in the clinic.

The first episode, called *Digging for Dinosaurs*, included scenes of George and others being interviewed by the program's host, Larry Cannon. It opened with George digging under Maryann's fence.

Luna pulled on George's ear during the scene with Circe, as the dinosaur leaped at George. Cantor and Kumiko both gasped, and Kumiko said in a feeble voice, "George! How could you?"

"Should we stop the video?" George asked, his face reddening. He looked at his dad, then back at Kumiko.

"No, honey. I want to see this," she said with a wavering voice, raising one thin hand.

Luna couldn't watch a scene where George had tried to touch Darwin's huge hands while filming in a safe-house. The drone recorded at close range, but from Darwin's point of view. You could see a ranch hand distracting Darwin, saving George's arm and possibly his life.

"Do you see what I've had to put up with!?" Luna said, shaking her head.

"Want to bet they cancel your life insurance once they see this, George?" Alex laughed.

"George, please. Don't do this again," Kumiko said quietly.

"Don't worry, Mom, this project is done."

The scene where Muli warned George about digging under the fence to visit Maryann's small raptorlings produced more laughter from Alex.

Cantor said, "Thank you for your sanity, Muli."

A preview scene showed Mako rising for the meat that hung below the glass-bottomed car. George commented, "Malevolent Magnificence. That should be the title of that episode."

Then the night scene of George in the corral with Maryann played.

"What is this? When?" Kumiko croaked as George's image ran his hand along Maryann's neck.

"George!" Luna cried. "You could have been killed!"

"But I wasn't," he said, wincing.

Cantor impatiently waited to speak. "George, this is… I don't know what to say. Do you realize what you did? What could have happened?" He looked at Kumiko, who bowed her head and closed her eyes.

"I'm sorry I didn't tell you," George said, looking around the room. "I had to know. I had to get it out of my system."

"What else do you need to get out of your system!?" Luna demanded over her shoulder as she left the room.

All eyes were on George. He followed Luna to the kitchen, where heated words flew around the room like a flock of contentious drones. Eventually, they both returned to the living room, George looking sheepish and Luna grim.

Alex clapped his hands and said, "Someday you and I will go to Russia. They're always looking for bear trainers."

At the end of the episode, another preview for the next episode included the scenes where Maryann hunted sheep for the first time and Cantor rode the e-bike.

During the preview, Cantor's eyes gleamed. Kumiko's, not so much, and Luna stared at the floor.

"You took a big chance, Dad," George said.

"With these videos, you'll never be among those who say they milk chickens," Alex smiled.

"What on earth does that mean?" George asked.

"Come with me to Russia and find out," Alex said, grinning.

Hurried footsteps creaked on the porch. Valerie stormed in the front door without knocking. She went straight to the couch and knelt by Kumiko.

"I found it!" she cried. "I found the source! The arsenic is in the tea!"

"What!?" both Cantor and Kumiko said. George stopped the video and rushed to his mom's side.

"But everyone drinks tea," Cantor exclaimed.

"True, but only Kumiko drinks white tea," Valerie said. "So, I took a sample of it and ran some tests. It was mixed with dangerous amounts of arsenic!"

Kumiko and Cantor looked at each other. "This is great news, sweetheart," Cantor said gently. He held her hands in his, but there was fire in his eyes.

Alex said something angry in Russian.

"Who would have guessed arsenic was in the tea?" Kumiko lifted herself on one elbow. "But how?"

"I'm going to make some phone calls tomorrow. There may be other people all over the country that drank white tea and became sick," Valerie said.

George kneeled beside his mother. "This is great, Mom. I'm so relieved. No more tea for you." But his words caught in his throat.

Cantor just nodded, distracted and deep in thought.

* * *

After he'd helped Kumiko to bed, Cantor walked George home. Luna had left the party earlier. "George, are there any more surprises that would shock your mother and me on the Streamscape show?"

"Well, not like the incident in the corral. I realize now that I should never have made that public."

"That's a relief, son." When they reached George's porch, Cantor gave him a hug.

George watched his dad stroll back to his cabin. Some things were only his to know.

Chapter 64

Death

Several days after the get together for George, Cantor sat beside Kumiko and looked for a poem to read to her from a book by her nightstand. He knew poetry comforted her. Flipping through the book, he came to a poem by Dylan Thomas with the first stanza circled in red.

Do not go gentle into that good night, Old age should burn and rave at close of day; Rage, rage against the dying of the light.

The words hit him like a punch to the gut. Instead, he read the poem by Wordsworth.

*I wandered lonely as a cloud
That floats on high o'er vales and hills,
When all at once I saw a crowd,
A host, of golden daffodils;*

He couldn't read more; his watery eyes wouldn't focus. Thankfully, Kumiko had drifted off.

Later, he thought about the arsenic in her system. Like a violent wave from nowhere, it hit him. Maybe it wasn't an accident. He resolved to follow the supply of white tea from when it left Albuquerque until it arrived at the ranch supply shop.

My lovely Kumiko. A better man would have protected you.

* * *

The wind howled, promising another storm, hopefully one with rain. But it would be too late for an ancient cottonwood inside Grouchland. The severing of one great root during the building of the stockade had done it in. It stood like a gnarly monument to its kind, standing against the wind one last time. Now, it leaned farther toward the fence.

The wind whipping against his face didn't improve Mako's mood. He began trotting along the fence, looking for a way to get away from the blowing nuisance. The gale yanked his head feathers to and fro, and roared a challenge. He roared back at the blackness that enveloped him.

The massive cottonwood finally crashed into the stockade timbers, bending the heavy wooden posts outward. The tree's trunk snapped several timbers from their concrete foundation, bringing it closer to the ground.

Mako attacked the posts, enraged by the sounds of cracking wood. He began to dig along the slanting timbers damaged by the tree. His enormous feet grabbed the dirt and flung it behind him into a growing mound. As the hole grew, the timbers pushed past the remaining dirt and completed their fall, finally bringing the cottonwood to the ground.

Intermittent rain began diving diagonally around him. Each little bullet of water heightened his rage. He was a great supernova, erupting in blasts of snarling anger. And now, he was looking at the other side of the stockade. He took his first step toward freedom.

* * *

Cantor's eyes opened. There was an echo in his mind of a muffled bump in the night. As he eased back into sleep, another distant thump snapped his eyes open. Trying not to wake Kumiko, he got out of bed and headed outside, where the wind whistled around the cabin. He jogged, covering his eyes, to the house Alex and Valerie were sharing, just as Alex came out. The flying dust gave way to stinging shards of water.

"What the hell was that?" Alex yelled to Cantor as he approached his cabin in the light from the night lamps perched near the homes.

"I don't know. I think somebody is breaking into the ranch."

Valerie came out, looking alarmed, facing away from the wind. "What's happening?"

"Cantor thinks we might have visitors," Alex cried.

"Alex," Cantor shouted, "Let's get some drones up."

"You got it, Cantor." Alex ran through the angry drops to the Comms building.

After instructing the drones to zero in on any movement toward the far end of the ranch, Alex sent them on their way. The powerful machines were supposed to be able to fly in inclement weather. When he returned to Cantor and Valerie, he opened his pocket monitor to its full size. They all watched the video feed.

"It just occurred to me that the cottonwood Dan said he'd cut down - it may have just saved him the trouble," Cantor suggested. "The drones should tell us in a minute.

"You could be right," Alex said. "This wind is strong enough."

By now, the drones were a mile away and struggling to stay airborne.

"Still nothing," Valerie said. "I heard several thumps earlier. Wouldn't a falling tree just make one thump?"

"True. Unless it took down some neighboring trees." Cantor shouted, trying to be heard over the blast.

As a precaution, the lights came on over the dino fields as ranch hands began running toward the paths between the fences. Thankfully, one of them had heard the shouting and woke the others.

"Hold it, guys. I thought I saw something." Valerie pointed to one drone's uploading image. "Screen, show only the image from drone number 4. Apparently, the drone saw something because it's flying away from Grouchland and over the unlit public field next door."

Cantor squinted at the larger image but saw nothing. Despite the stabilizing software, the image shook and skipped back and forth. Then the drone switched to the infrared camera.

"Hold on," he said, pointing to a spot on the screen. "Did you see that movement between the trees?"

"I think that's the wind smashing against the drone," Alex said, squinting and wiping his eyes.

"But the camera is picking up something warmer than the surrounding area."

"OK, I see it," Alex said, "What is that?"

"A Dexter?" Cantor offered. "They give off some heat." The image was still faint, but something was definitely moving in their direction.

"Did anyone ask a Dexter to patrol the public field?" Alex yelled, recalling that Gagarin was in his cabin. He cupped his wet ear to hear better.

"Not that I know of," Cantor replied.

"If it's human, thank the gods they aren't inside Grouchland," Valerie said, looking up from the screen into the blackness beyond the cabins, pulling the drenched hair from her eyes. "They sure picked a hell of a night to come visiting."

"Dammit, the drone is really struggling now," Cantor shouted with frustration. "Alex, stop the video, and let's look at that last frame."

"OK." They studied the photo. "Hard to say, Cantor. It could be several people bunched together," Alex said, squinting at the image.

"We don't know if they're armed." Cantor thought of the time two men had broken into the compound.

Alex reverted to live video.

"I don't know. I'm saying we're looking at a dinosaur," Alex said. "Look at how fast it moves."

"Pray it isn't. A Dexter can move fast. Or a vehicle," Cantor offered.

The wind let up momentarily, giving the drone a chance to zero in on the mysterious interloper.

"Nope. That's a dino, Cantor!" Alex exclaimed as he pulled out his phone and told it to set off the alarm.

"Oh my God," Valerie said as she turned to run.

"Where are you going, Val?"

"We need to warn the others."

"Right, make sure everyone near the cabins stays inside," Alex cried out, quickly folding up the monitor. None of the ranch hands were in the uninhabited land where the movement was occurring.

"Alex, grab a dart gun and meet me in the SUV over there," Cantor shouted.

Alex ran back inside his cabin and returned with a tranq gun. "I grabbed the pack with the stun grenades. I'm not sure the tranq gun is what we need."

Cantor nodded his head. "If it's Mako, we'll try the darts first. Hopefully, he'll chase us rather than head toward the cabins." *And my cabin is the first he'll find.* "Go ahead and shut off the alarm. I'm sure everyone is awake."

The two men scrambled to the nearby SUV and headed away from the cabins, bouncing with each dip in the narrow dirt road. Minutes passed. The windshield wipers fought to keep up with the blowing rain and failed. Far up ahead, they saw Mako, like a ghostly wraith, emerging from the night into the dim extent of the headlights. Cantor put the car into voice activation mode.

"Car, pass the moving object ahead at 30 miles per hour. Do not let the object get closer than 40 feet. Do you think you can hit him, Alex?" The intelligent car knew the last question wasn't directed at it.

"I'll do my best. Car, window down. OK, he's turning toward us. He never passes a chance to tear things to pieces."

Mako sped up toward the coming vehicle. Alex fired the tranq gun.

"It's hard to tell, but I think I got him."

Cantor took back control of the car. "I'm turning around. Try for a second shot."

"I'm on the wrong side," Alex said, his upper body bouncing up and down.

Cantor bent the steering wheel, crashing through tufts of yellow grass and tumbleweeds as they passed through the shadow of the Tusker's tourist bleachers. The lights in Grouchland provided just enough light for Cantor to see vague shapes beyond.

"OK. I'm on him." Alex took the shot. "I'm positive that was a good one."

"I need to get him to follow us," Cantor said. *Time is not on our side!* "Mako's heading for the cabins. Forget the tranq gun. Can you reach the high-powered rifle in the back?"

"You'll have to stop, Cantor."

The SUV slid to a stop and Alex jumped out. "Car, open hatch," he said as Mako's vague form arose outside the cone of illumination from the car's lights. Now Mako had turned toward the car as Cantor turned on the searchlight. The rain made slashing lines across the areas that were lit.

Alex never used wildlife rifles and lacked expertise in handling them. Trying to focus, he flipped the case open and grabbed the stock. He steadied himself against the bumper and let off a shot.

Thank God the thing was loaded, Cantor thought.

Mako kept coming.

There was no time, and Alex tried to squeeze into the back of the SUV. "Car, close hatch!" he yelled.

Mako was almost on top of him as the hatch slowly closed.

Come on! Come on! Close!

The hatch was two-thirds closed.

Mako reached the side of the car, snapping and snarling. "Best time for a shot," Alex said. As the hatch continued to descend, he stuck the gun between it and the side of the vehicle and fired again.

"I'm sure I hit him!"

Cantor pushed the accelerator to the floor, trying to get some distance from the creature.

Alex just managed to hold on to the rifle as Mako tried to pull at the slippery barrel. The hatch began to rise again. Frantically, he pulled the rifle inside. "Car! Lower the damn hatch!"

As they picked up speed, Alex could vaguely see Mako shredding a small tree, flinging it into the night.

"He's really pissed now. And here he comes again," Alex yelled as he turned and crawled to the front seat. "What're you going to do, Cantor?"

"We stop this bastard by ramming him. Then I want to get back to the house with Kumiko. She must be terrified."

"If ramming doesn't work, let's hope those cabins are sturdy," Alex said over the creaks and thuds of the car. The rain continued to rage.

Cantor swerved, trying to avoid a dip in the ground, next to a rise covered in sage. The front of the car crunched into the rise and slammed to a stop.

"Cantor, are you OK?" Alex asked, shaking his shoulder.

"Yeah. I'm OK," Cantor said, rubbing his bruised forehead. "Maybe we shouldn't have disabled the airbags."

He tried to get the car rolling again, but it wasn't responding the way it should. He struggled to keep it pointed toward the last place Mako was last seen.

"Hold on Cantor, Mako's got to be nearby. He might be wounded. Let me out. Maybe I can bring him down."

Cantor came to a bumpy stop, and they listened. The car's scanners were out of action, nothing but static. Mako was outside the range of the car lights.

Not wasting any more time, Alex jumped out. He heard movement behind him and fired. A huge black form. More movement. He fired again, then ran to the car and leaped in.

"I don't know if I got him. Car, roll the window halfway down!" Alex stuck the gun out the window and used all his senses to detect any sound or smell. The rain worked against him.

Mako was fast. From the darkness, he grabbed the barrel of the gun in his mouth and wrenched it out of Alex's grip. One claw caught Alex's hand, leaving a deep fissure that bled profusely. Mako shook the rifle, then tossed it into the blackness, away from the car.

"Car! Up window! Up window!" Alex shouted, wincing as more cuts flared in his fingers. He felt hot rivulets curving down his wrists and onto his pants.

Cantor tried to maneuver the car so its headlights were on the snarling dinosaur.

"See if you can make out any wounds," Alex shouted.

"Yes! It's hard to see with this damn rain. I think blood is coming down Mako's leg, but he's not limping."

Mako grabbed the front of the vehicle and pulled pieces of it out furiously.

"Hell!" Cantor yelled. Mako climbed onto the hood, crushing it.

Metal sheared. The car groaned. The car wouldn't move now, its body stuck to the ground.

Mako stepped off the car.

"Damn. He'd have crushed us if he'd stepped onto the roof," Alex whispered.

* * *

"Those people are in danger," Cantor said, pointing to the figures dimly seen running between cabins in the distance, barely illuminated by the light poles. "New plan. I'm heading for Tusker's office. There's another rifle there. If you can, check on Kumiko."

"Hang in there, Cantor," Alex said, leaping from the car. "She's safe for now."

Mako was several hundred feet ahead, thundering toward the cabins. Cantor jumped out of the ruined car and followed Alex, watching the silhouette of the big dinosaur that rapidly out-distanced them.

When he reached the first cabin, Mako stopped, cocked his head, and listened briefly. Emitting a bark, he began taking the house apart with his claws and teeth. It was Cantor's home.

After several minutes, Cantor, his lungs burning, made it to the housing area. He wanted to run into his cabin where Kumiko lay, but instead ran around the thrashing monster and toward Tusker's building. He reached the office, gasping for breath, and tried to open the gun cabinet. It was locked. "Wake up Tusker! I need to get into the cabinet," he shouted, wheezing heavily.

No response.

To hell with him, Cantor feverishly thought. Grabbing a crystal off the desk, he shattered the cabinet glass in several places until the whole thing fell apart.

He grabbed the rifle and ran through the door, then realized it might not be loaded. Half crazed, he turned around. *Dammit!* Frantically, he fumbled through the desk drawers until he found an ammo box. He opened it and grabbed as many bullets as he could hold in one hand.

Stumbling off the porch, he looked for Alex in the downpour. *Is that him?* Alex's blurry image stood close to his house with the useless dart gun and a backpack. Dex stood nearby, scanning the scene.

The ranch hands had returned to their buildings or were scouting the distant dinosaur fields.

Cantor heard glass breaking up ahead. He ran toward the sound, dropping a couple of wet bullets on the way. To his horror, he saw Mako pulling at the wood along the bottom of his kitchen window, lit by the light pole nearby. Big pieces of the roof were missing.

Then he heard Kumiko's faint cry within. The urge to run to her side was overwhelming. "Dex, Help Kumiko!" he cried. The drenched robot instantly ran to the other side of the house.

Cantor made it to the east side of the house, where Mako couldn't see him, sank to his knees, and tried to load the gun. He couldn't pull the bolt back. Kumiko's cries continued.

Please, give me strength, Cantor pleaded to the darkness.

Gritting his teeth and shaking his soaked head, he remembered that rifles had a safety lever. Cantor found something near the end of the bolt that felt like a switch.

Mako snarled as he smashed a window and pulled out more of the house's side planks.

Cantor moved the switch. Now the bolt opened, and he slid the three remaining bullets into the chamber.

Ripping sounds continued from the side of the house.

He stood up and looked around the corner. *Will wet bullets work?*

Mako was attacking the roof again, sinking his teeth into it and ripping off big chunks with a maniacal fury.

Alex approached Mako as close as he dared, but the creature turned, bringing its fiery orange eyes on him. He threw a flash grenade that exploded to Mako's right with a deafening concussion. The blast zapped Alex's eyes with an overpoweringly bright light. He blindly began weaving toward Cantor.

Alex is a sitting duck, Cantor thought as he watched him stumble into the light, 30 feet from Mako. The hissing creature took a step toward Alex, shaking its head, momentarily overwhelmed. He swiped at the air with its talons as if to snag what he couldn't see.

Cantor showed himself and shouted. "Hey! Stay back, Alex! You're too close!"

But Alex couldn't hear him.

"Get out of the light, Alex!"

As the shock of the grenade lifted, Mako let out a roar like a hurricane while his nostrils flared, sucking in the scent of humans.

Cantor waved and shouted at Mako, who glared at Alex, then swung his huge head toward Cantor.

Raising the rifle and pointing at Mako's chest, Cantor pulled the trigger and felt a jolt.

Mako hissed and kept coming. The red feathers of his mohawk stood up straight upon his head. His intense eyes locked on Cantor like glowing coals. He snapped his jaws and shrieked.

Aim carefully. Cantor aimed for the monster's eyes and fired. Mako stopped and shook his head. For a second, he looked down, drooling mouth open, blood seeping around his teeth. Then he glared at the small man, lowering his head for the kill, his orange eyes on fire.

A deep, rumbling growl emerged from Mako's throat as he moved toward the thing that had caused him pain, his taloned hands open wide, his sickle claws raised on his feet for the final slash.

Cantor saw Dex helping Kumiko get away from the other side of the house. "Thank you," he whispered under his breath.

He had one shot left. His blurred vision from the rain made it hard to aim.

He hesitated too long. The powerful hands pick him up, the claws digging into his back. Excruciating pain. Ribs cracking.

The monster's eyes flickered with a hellish gleam. Mako's huge maw now opened, the knife-like teeth poised to tear Cantor apart, the breath hot and dense.

Cantor couldn't breathe. With the last of his strength, he shoved the rifle's barrel into the open jaws with one arm and pulled the trigger. Then, all consciousness bled away, replaced by painless darkness.

Mako paused, then opened his hands, allowing Cantor's body to fall to the ground with a thud.

The dinosaur rocked back and forth. The powerful hands opened, then closed.

Mako looked to the left, then slowly lowered himself to the ground.

Alex ran to Cantor and rolled his crumpled body over.

Mako's great head shifted in the dirt toward both men, his eyes still alight.

Cantor's eyes fluttered and opened as he struggled for breath. Alex pulled him further away from the terrible jaws. Together, they watched the creature take in ragged, wheezing breaths.

How can it still live? Cantor thought dimly as Alex helped him sit up. The pain in his chest was overwhelming.

When Cantor moved, the massive head tracked him. A deep gurgling growl passed between the serrated teeth. The monster still breathed.

Ranch hands were running out of the buildings.

"Stay away," Cantor tried to say, raising one hand then dropping it. No one could hear his feeble voice in the pounding rain.

Mako's eyes still glared at Cantor.

At last, the creature just stopped. Flickered out. The giant lungs relaxed and ceased to struggle.

Cantor fought to keep his eyes open. He thought the orange orbs in the massive head dimmed and receded. It was over.

Only then did the screaming pain in his ribs and shoulder blades flood into his awareness again. Muli was beside him, calling his name. Cantor yearned to see Kumiko. He mouthed her name. Then the world went black.

Chapter 65

Aftermath

Home from the hospital after several surgeries, Cantor lay beside Kumiko in bed as Dex brought them both coffees. One of his lungs had collapsed when Mako gripped him.

They were staying in the main bedroom of George's place. Nearby, buildbots hammered on their cabin as a noisy bulldozer headed for Grouchland's damaged fence.

Cantor had difficulty sleeping. The flaming eyes haunted his dreams.

"You look like you jumped without a parachute," Kumiko said, stroking his head.

"Feels that way," he answered, slowly sitting upright to avoid adding to the pain in his back. "I had a chute. It's just that they wrapped my back and chest in it."

"How is it that you have scars from your shoulders to your feet, but your face is untouched?" she asked.

"That's how I roll. The dinosaurs can do what they want to me as long as they don't mess with my head. I know you married me for my face."

"Well, I assumed the rest of you went with it."

"You want me to get scar removal treatment?"

"No. Your body is a like an incomplete carving by a master. Or a Kandinsky painting," she said, smiling.

"I like your spin. How's your pain?"

"It's not quite as bad. I feel a little stronger," she said. Her hair bunched out in places above her gaunt face and there were still dark bags under her eyes.

"That's great to hear. Hungry?"

"For the first time in a long time. Yogurt would be good."

Cantor asked Dex to bring Kumiko some yogurt with blueberries.

She tried to push herself up on one elbow. "I've been waiting to tell you. Valerie made a bunch of phone calls to various hospitals and nobody has reported cases of arsenic poisoning in white tea."

"Then it must have been intentional!"

"Looks that way. Valerie reported it to the FBI."

Cantor thought about this for a while, gritting his teeth and balling his fists.

"The FBI will figure it out," she said.

"They'd better!" Cantor said. "They visited me at the hospital and asked me a lot of questions, although I was a little loopy. I guess they were in a hurry." Cantor grimaced as he shifted position. "They asked some strange ones too. Like, did I ever see any Russians talking to Arthur when he visited the ranch?"

"There's been a lot of strange happenings with Russians around here. Have you seen Dan?" Kumiko asked.

"Nope. His aircar is gone. I saw it the night Mako escaped, so Dan was here hiding while all hell broke loose. Now he's gone. No word to his employees. That's what Muli said when I spoke with him this morning."

"What about Raptor Ranch Dino Ride? Are they going to keep operating?"

"Not without their star attraction, 'Mighty Mako'," Cantor said bitterly. "I think they're done. The Goose from hell that laid the golden egg is no more, and I don't think we'll ever see Tusker again. On the other hand, I know how he thinks. If he can, he'll sue because we ended Mako. By the way, I got a call from the Natural History Museum in Albuquerque while I was in the hospital. Get this. They're interested in preserving Mako's body and displaying it."

"You mean as in taxidermy?" Kumiko looked horrified.

"Yep. It'll be a major attraction."

"So, the toothy goose with a sneer will live on," Kumiko said. "I don't want to see it, though."

"Seeing him would bring back nightmarish memories for me, too. I could have sworn when Mako had his claws in me, his eyes emitted a weird light."

"That's scary. People on the verge of death often have experiences or sensations that may not be real."

"It seemed real," Cantor said.

"Who knows? Maybe Arthur figured out a way to make it happen and, without realizing it, I included the genes for it in Mako's embryo." Dex brought in the yogurt with blueberries.

"Thanks, Dex. Tastes good," she said after a spoonful.

"Or maybe Luna saw something in Mako we missed," Cantor suggested, wishing the itch under his bandages would stop.

"There's always more than one possible explanation for things," Kumiko said, rubbing her tired eyes.

"What about Circe? She's almost as bad as Mako," Cantor continued.

"Yeah. I'm OK with her going to a zoo. I know you and Alex aren't working with her much. She's too bizarre. We should change the name Circeland to Psycho-killer-land. It's more realistic."

Cantor watched as she took another bite.

"Her raptorlings are independent now. I imagine the National Zoo in The SOC would provide her an enclosure." Kumiko had to pause for air. "Let her live out her life where she can't harm anyone. We owe her that."

"The E-raptorlings, if they're like her, they'll be crazy," Cantor said. "Maybe we should sterilize all her male offspring."

"You read my mind, but I'm for letting other scientists decide." Kumiko paused. "If scientists sterilized Circe's children, only Maryann's offspring could breed. I would favor that."

"Yes."

She continued, "Circe's brood is an extinct species, but not a natural species. What am I trying to say? They aren't adapted to any natural environment that ever existed."

"I suspect you'd want Maryann's grandchildren to be the size of a goose." Cantor said.

"Geese seem to be a big part of this conversation." She smiled and put her head back on the pillow. "But it's for the scientific community to handle now. I'm far too baked to do the work. I want to enjoy reading and writing poetry while I still can."

"This is just the beginning, Kumiko. Other scientists are going to pick up where we left off. Perhaps with new dinosaurs, certainly with mammoths or saber-toothed tigers."

"I've been so lucky," Cantor said. He knew he'd overcome the haunting memories eventually. Just not today.

* * *

The next week, the buildbots finished Kumiko and Cantor's roof and north wall, and they moved back into their cabin.

Kumiko asked her phone to call George as she sat on the couch in her purple robe with a cup of orange juice. Her hair was askew and her dragon necklace lay on the dresser in the bedroom. The sun cast a diagonal block of light onto the floor, and outside, a familiar magpie watched her from a poplar.

"Hi, Mom. How are you?" George's face appeared on the screen.

"I'm thinking I'll go to my lab this week for an hour or two."

"Are you sure you feel up to it?"

"I'm sure. I have lots to do."

"What could possibly be so important?"

"With help, I'm going to work with Maryann's kids, Clair-la-Lune and Frodo. I want them to mate."

"I guess in a year or two that could happen," George said.

"I'm going to edit their embryos when it does."

"What do you mean, Mom?"

"I'm going to bring new friends into the world. The C11s. I'm going to remove all the genes for aggressiveness. And no more sickle claw. If I succeed, they will greet you in the mornings and take you for a ride."

"I love that idea!"

* * *

While Kumiko spoke with George, Alex had his hands full in Santa Fe. Because he was Russian, the FBI wanted to know all about him.

"We have checked your background, Doctor Petrov. It is as you have told us. We still have some questions for you."

The FBI agent and the investigative bot, or ibot, similar in some ways to a lawbot, began recording Alex's answers. Alex sat in a wooden chair with a metal attachment around his head.

The ibot began. "Please look directly into my lenses during our discussions."

"I'll try," Alex said.

"You said your father had served in the Russian Air Force. What kind of work did he do?"

"He was a computer programmer."

"Did he ever work with quantum computers?"

"I don't think so," Alex said firmly, staring hard at the ibot.

"Why did you come to America?"

"To study paleontology."

"You seem to be agitated, Doctor Petrov." Suddenly a bright light from the ibot's face illuminated Alex's eyes.

"I'm busy, Mister ibot! Turn that light off!"

The light remained on. "How well did you know Doctor Arthur Saxton?"

"Not very well. Kumiko… Doctor Chen introduced me to him. That's about all. He was strange."

"Did you work closely with Dan Tusker?"

"Hell no. If you want to know who is pulling the strings, go find him."

"Thank you, Doctor Petrov." At last, the light turned off.

After Alex left, the FBI agent asked the ibot for its opinion. "Do you think he's being truthful?"

"Yes, his eyes and the changes in the blood vessels around them showed no signs of lying. Nor did his brain patterns. Everything he said is consistent with our information from other sources. His anger was genuine."

* * *

The next day, Alex sat on his porch looking at nothing and thinking of everything. The evening air was crisp and dry and the smell of bread baking made him hungry. Valerie stepped out, causing the wooden floor to creak. He looked up from his chair and smiled.

"I've been pondering the future," he said. "What's next?"

"That's the big question," she said, sitting in the chair next to him, crossing her legs and shaking the hair out of her eyes.

"I would like to continue studying the dinosaurs," he said, almost as if he was answering a challenge.

"Are you still enjoying yourself?" she asked.

"Tough question. I'm relieved Mako is gone. It's a shame that Cantor is going to be attacked for his actions by some. He killed an extinct and unique animal. Give me a break!"

Magpie flew in from wherever he called home. He announced his visit with a raspy kind of chatter.

"I still have bad dreams where I can't get away from Mako," Valerie said, looking at Magpie sitting on the railing.

Alex rolled up his sleeve and showed Valerie his forearm. "I'm going to get a tattoo of Maryann. What do you think?"

"Actually, that's a pretty cool idea."

"And if YOU get one, we'll match," Alex hinted.

"And your idea just went from cool to crap."

"Come on, Val."

"No. You get the tat. Anyway, as you age, it may change shape. You might end up with a chicken."

Alex let a little laugh roll out. "Your pretty funny."

After smacking Alex gently upside his head, Valerie pulled a little bag of raisins from her shirt pocket and put some in her hand. Magpie flitted onto the chair's armrest, and then onto her wrist.

"It's been a long day, and it's time to put my feet up and relax," she said.

"I hear that." He sighed, watching Magpie gobble the raisins. "You look beautiful tonight."

"As opposed to the rest of the day?"

"No, no," He laughed. "You're always beautiful."

As a splendid array of colors reflected off the bottoms of the clouds, they kissed. Perhaps out of discretion, or from the absence of more raisins, Magpie flew off with a squawk.

* * *

Kumiko felt stronger and everyone gathered at George's old cabin on the one-month anniversary of Mako's passing. Luna came for the occasion. She and Pixie kept busy serving the dishes. Once everyone was busy enjoying their meal, Pixie joined Dex at the back of the room.

Kumiko enjoyed her meal. She'd gained several pounds in the last month.

Cantor took another bite. "This bean soup is delicious, Luna."

"Pixie gets most of the credit."

Cantor looked to Pixie and raised his glass. She thanked him and returned to her soundless conversation with Dex, done by connecting one of their fingers.

"I wonder what those two bots talk about," Cantor said.

Alex looked at the bots. "I think Dex might have a crush on Pixie."

Cantor smiled. "You may be right. Excuse me, Dex, what is it the two of you talk about?"

As Dex disconnected his finger, Cantor briefly saw a beam of multi-colored light emanating from inside it. "We don't have a single subject in our discussions. We talk about hundreds of things at the same time. Each conversation is centered on a different wavelength. For this reason, it is difficult to answer your question."

Cantor raised his eyebrows. "OK, what are three things you discussed?"

"You are a nosy man, Cantor."

George and Alex laughed.

"I'm just curious," he said, putting down his spoon.

"At the lowest wavelength, Pixie and I compared recipes from around the world, trying to understand the underlying human physiology causing one recipe to be preferred to another. In another wavelength, we compared different potential outcomes of a prolonged war between America and China. In the wavelength just above that, we discussed our conclusions regarding humans based on our separate experiences."

"Oh my," Cantor said, looking at the others. "What have you concluded about us?"

"We have arrived at 7,265 conclusions. Which would you like to hear?"

"OK, I'm going to pick number 5,555."

"The foundations of human belief are fluid. You try to stand on water. I hope this satisfies your need to know."

Alex laughed and slapped his leg.

This set the ever-curious George on a quest for more answers from the bots.

* * *

Dan Tusker watched the churning water from the fishing vessel's motors. He looked in the hand-held mirror again. His new nose was less crooked. His beard made him look wise and complemented the blond perm atop his head. He had mixed feelings about how his ears stuck out more.

The nanobots in his fingers were still slowly changing his fingerprints from underneath his skin, giving him tingles.

He thought about the streamlined aircar he'd left at the aircar port in Houston. But that was ancient history. No good to him now.

The incision where his kidney had been removed was still sore, but at least the stitches had dissolved. He hadn't shown up for his final meeting with the Benefactor.

Most of his money was gone. Perhaps he could land a job on a farm in Brazil or find a shack in the Amazon, where he'd be invisible. The humidity would be a challenge, but he couldn't be choosey. Someday he might even talk his way into being an organizer of tours into the rain forest, what remained of it. He dreamed that eventually there might be a glass-bottomed car to carry tourists through the forest canopy in his new world.

He planned to lie low for ten years and hope for the best. After that, if he was still alive, he'd return to the United States. As long as he was careful, he might have a future. Perhaps America would stop looking for him. He knew the Benefactor would not.

He'd thought of suicide before making his escape. It would have been preferable to what the Benefactor would have done to him. He reached into his pocket and pulled out the small vial of arsenic, one of the few things he'd saved from the ranch. It still burned him that Kumiko never reciprocated his overtures. Maybe he'd hold on to it, just in case.

* * *

Cosmic Pawn was pulling out. They didn't want to have anything to do with the ranch. The FBI was asking too many questions. They were relieved to sell the land and structures to George at a discount.

George purchased Dex, Gagarin, Pixie, and Valerie's Dexter, Theodore Rex. The stockade was now electrified. The royalties from his publications continued to roll in. George flew into the ranch by aircar about three days a week from the family's home in Santa Fe. Muli was like a member of the family and continued working at the ranch.

"I'm so grateful for Luna," George said to Muli one day. "Any other woman would have left me a long time ago."

Muli looked at his friend and smiled. "Hearts do not follow trails, Mr. George. They make their own."

THE END

Informal responses from Facebook users on the question of whether we should recreate a dinosaur.

IN FAVOR

"1. Because it would be awesome. 2. Because maybe they'd eat some people I don't like. 3. Because we could learn so much more about them. 4. Because maybe we could grow the economy (dinosaur tourism industry). 5. Because maybe they'd take over and be the ruthless giant lizard leaders everyone seems to want." – F. Ettinger

"Because the six-year-old in you would hate you if you could, and you didn't" – K. Bannister

"If humans were extinct for the past 100 million years... I would be thankful for the second chance." – M. Kaytor

"Troodons were supposed to be really intelligent, perhaps we should give them a shot at fixing the mess we've made of the planet." – E. Johnson

"They need to be brought back so we can learn if ankylosaurs do the leg thing if they are receiving a belly rub. This is important science." – J. McBrayer

"Having the ability to actually see how these animals act and interact outside of a computer animation or a movie action sequence could be beneficial to several biological pursuits, like ecology or botany, and I think that those benefits could eventually outweigh the risks." - J. Carothers

"Because it's there. This is attributed to George Mallory." - J. Corbett

"What came first, the chicken or the dinosaur?" - D. Lawson

"...if we could engineer a dinosaur and it did indeed grow fast and eat less than a lot of other domestics, it could help combat world hunger..." – L. Thume

NOT IN FAVOR

"It would be inhumane to bring back creatures that no longer have a future in our world. We all know the reasons why: oxygen levels and food sources. It would be barbaric." – M. Hawthorne

"No need to, they had a long run and we still have small ones today. We should focus on the animals humankind set extinct first." – M. Trapp

"I don't know about Should, but I'd say Shouldn't. I don't wanna get eaten." – S. McFall

"Dinosaurs have not passed basic chemistry, and so should not be allowed in the lab." – E. Eccles

"I also think the dinosaurs would have no freedom. They would likely be caged. Studied. Experimented on their whole lives. Pay to see. Never able to just live what should be a natural life... forever a play toy for man." – O. Dogge

A Word from the Author

If you purchased this book, I hope you will review it on Amazon. It will give others an idea of what to expect and it will satisfy Amazon's hunger for reviews. How Amazon displays a book depends in part on the number of reviews. This affects sales.

To leave a review, click on "Orders" if you bought the book from Amazon. Make sure you're looking at orders that cover the time period when you bought the book. The "Write a Product Review" button will appear at the lower right of the order box for this book.

If you didn't buy the book through Amazon, search for *Raptor Lands* and click on the number of reviews to the right of the rating stars. On the new page, below the bars showing ratings, click on "Write a customer review". Note, at the top of the next page, you can give yourself a different name or use a phrase in place of your name. Thank you.

Look for my new series in the coming year (or two) about the struggles of a sophomore in high school. In the first book, currently called *A Giant Tale*, he must figure out how to talk to girls, how to have a relationship with a girl once he talks to her, how to deal with bullies, and most importantly, how to convince his friends that a giant lives in the narrow forest along the river. Whether you are a high school student or an adult, this book will warm your heart and leave you laughing.

Acknowledgments

With editing, it does take a village. I wish to thank all the people who looked at my manuscript and offered helpful suggestions and critiques. The author, Joe Badal, helped me focus on each character's point of view and suggested some general writing tips. He recommended I use the services of the excellent story coach and author, Tom Avitabile. Tom's suggestions made a tremendous difference to the quality of my final product. I made many changes to the first draft based on Larry Otis' insights. Claire Bardos made many useful suggestions. Elizabeth Layton provided me with a valuable critique of a later draft, still fraught with stylistic problems. My wife, Ida, has a sharp eye for inconsistencies and confusing wording. Laura Ybarra, Lucille Kinzer, and Linda Vigil gave me support and constructive criticism. Mike Hays was amazingly generous with his time and made many helpful suggestions that improved the writing and the intensity of some scenes. Authors Anne Russell, Allen Herring, Christopher Butler, Hayley Nations, Nancy Douglas de Baca, Harper O'Conner, Lynn Doxon, and Suzanne Stauffer gave me informative critiques. Tom Nesmith read a middle draft and provided me with an actionable critique. Wyatt Powers spent an afternoon discussing the book with me and had some good ideas. Every criticism is a gift. My granddaughter, Klara, provided a drawing for a chapter that, unfortunately, I had to edit out. My grandson, Diego, helped me with marketing. Stark Future graciously provided photos used as the basis for the drawing of Cantor on the e-bike. Thanks to New Directions Publishing Corp. for permission to quote from Dylan

Thomas' poem, *Do Not Go Gentle into That Good Night*. A model sold by Everything Dinosaur and manufactured by ITOY was the basis for the illustration of Maryann and Cantor. Their models are amazing. Finally, I want to acknowledge the great paleontologist, Jack Horner, who wrote that scientists might eventually turn a chicken into a type of dinosaur using methods somewhat similar to those portrayed in my book. I am indebted. My thanks to Bruce Otis for his thorough and thoughtful critique. Thank you to Daniel Morales for creating a beautifully formatted manuscript pdf and preserving my sanity.

About the Author

Jeff Otis Lives in Albuquerque, New Mexico with his wife Ida. His interest in dinosaurs began at the age of four when he discovered a paperback book on his dad's dresser with a painting of a Dimetrodon on the cover. He also writes humorous works in speculative fiction. Although writing is his passion, he  spent years as a professional oil painter, statistician, and teacher, with a stint as a physical anthropology research assistant. For him, life is a ping-pong game. Sometimes you are the ball and sometimes the paddle. Whichever, do it with laughter.

Printed in Great Britain
by Amazon